TROUBLED TIMES AT HARPERS

ROSIE CLARKE

B
Boldwood

First published in Great Britain in 2025 by Boldwood Books Ltd.

Copyright © Rosie Clarke, 2025

Cover Design by Colin Thomas

Cover Images: Colin Thomas and iStock

The moral right of Rosie Clarke to be identified as the author of this work has been asserted in accordance with the Copyright, Designs and Patents Act 1988.

All rights reserved. No part of this book may be reproduced in any form or by any electronic or mechanical means, including information storage and retrieval systems, without written permission from the author, except for the use of brief quotations in a book review. This book is a work of fiction and, except in the case of historical fact, any resemblance to actual persons, living or dead, is purely coincidental.

Every effort has been made to obtain the necessary permissions with reference to copyright material, both illustrative and quoted. We apologise for any omissions in this respect and will be pleased to make the appropriate acknowledgements in any future edition.

A CIP catalogue record for this book is available from the British Library.

Paperback ISBN 978-1-78513-149-3

Large Print ISBN 978-1-78513-150-9

Hardback ISBN 978-1-78513-148-6

Ebook ISBN 978-1-78513-151-6

Kindle ISBN 978-1-78513-152-3

Audio CD ISBN 978-1-78513-143-1

MP3 CD ISBN 978-1-78513-144-8

Digital audio download ISBN 978-1-78513-147-9

This book is printed on certified sustainable paper. Boldwood Books is dedicated to putting sustainability at the heart of our business. For more information please visit https://www.boldwoodbooks.com/about-us/sustainability/

Boldwood Books Ltd, 23 Bowerdean Street, London, SW6 3TN

www.boldwoodbooks.com

1

LONDON, FEBRUARY 1929

'Lillie Langtry has died,' Fred Burrows remarked to his daughter-in-law, Beth. He sighed heavily and put down his newspaper, looking at her sadly. 'Sometimes it seems as though I'll soon be the last of my generation.'

Beth saw the deep lines of sorrow about his eyes, understanding that it wasn't truly the demise of a famous actress and courtesan that was troubling him. He'd been suffering deep grief since the loss of his wife, Vera. Vera had been Fred's second wife and they'd been happy together for a few years, but she'd developed a malignant tumour under her arm, which had been removed but grown again and her death the previous autumn had left Fred alone and sad.

'Lillie Langtry was older than you,' Beth said. 'You're still young enough to have a useful life, Dad. Why don't you look for a little job, something that requires your service for a few hours a week? It would give you an interest.'

'Am I getting under your feet, Beth?' he asked, but she laughed and shook her head.

'You could never do that. Surely you know how much the

boys love you – and Jack and I do, too. You think about the past too much...'

'Since Vera went?' Fred nodded and frowned. 'You need not be afraid to speak her name, Beth. I'm sad that she went too soon, but it isn't just that...' He shook his head. 'Don't you feel that an era is drawing to its end? My generation was different... more respectful somehow.'

The era of the roaring twenties had brought prosperity but also huge changes to the way people behaved and dressed, particularly the young women.

'I'm always hopeful that life can only get better,' Beth replied, smiling cheerfully. 'Yes, things have changed a lot since before the war – but there are lots of new openings for people who want to move with the times. You told me yourself that they've invented something called television and will be trying to broadcast it in more areas soon – and they've started commercial flights to all sorts of places. Where did you say the new destination was going to be? You told me only yesterday.'

'Next month, Imperial Airways are starting flights from London to Karachi,' Fred said and chuckled, his mood lightening. 'Whoever would want to go there...? Wherever it is!' He smiled at her. 'You always know how to make me feel better, Beth love. I don't know what I'd do without you to visit.'

'Why won't you do as Jack and I both want and move in with us?' Beth asked, looking at him earnestly. 'We've plenty of room and we do worry about you living alone, Dad.'

'Maybe I shall one day, when I need to,' he said and stood up. 'I'm going home now, love. I promised my neighbour I'd help him make a coop for his chickens. He says he will give me fresh eggs if the hens lay.'

'Come back later and eat with us, when the boys are back from school?' Beth asked with a smile and he nodded. 'I'm going to visit Sally this afternoon. We want to go through some new trade catalogues she's been sent.'

'You enjoy your job helping Sally Harper, don't you?' Fred sighed. 'I reckon I retired from Harpers department store too soon, but it seemed a good idea at the time.'

'I am sure she would have you back like a shot,' Beth told him. 'She says that the new stores manager isn't up to scratch these days, because some of the stock has been late getting into the departments. You might be able to help them get more organised.'

Fred hesitated. 'I couldn't do a full-time job.'

'No. Sally wouldn't expect that,' Beth replied. 'Do you want me to ask her if you could work a few hours a week?'

Fred thought and then nodded his acceptance. 'Don't push for it, Beth love, but if she needs a bit of help, I'd be glad to come in four mornings a week.' He smiled. 'That wouldn't interfere with my picking the boys up and taking them somewhere after school.'

'I'll see what she thinks,' Beth replied and kissed his cheek. 'It would still give you plenty of time to help your neighbours and take Jack and Timmy to their football and cricket.' Fred took them to football practice in the winter and cricket in the summer, because their father, Jack senior, was working in the restaurant he and Ben Harper jointly owned and ran – life in the hospitality business consisted of long hours and late nights.

After a bit of bother a few years back, when Jack and Ben had nearly split their partnership in the restaurant, they were good friends again and the business was thriving and they were talking of opening another in the West End of London. The only reason they hadn't done so was because Ben had been on a long visit to America to see his aunt, who owned shares in a large store in New York, and was unfortunately very ill. After many years of talking about it, Ben and Sally had gone for their first overseas holiday, taking their son and daughter with them. Sally and their children, Jenny and Peter, had returned three weeks later. Ben had stayed on at his aunt's request to help her sort out a few problems, and then to do some buying for the store he owned in London, but he was expected back soon.

'I'll see you later then,' Fred said and went out, leaving Beth to tidy her kitchen and wash a few cups and saucers. She was thoughtful as she went upstairs to change her dress. It was the first time she had visited Sally since her return from America a few days previously. She'd been helping to oversee Harpers store while Sally was away.

There was an overall manager named Mr Stockbridge at Harpers in Oxford Street. Unlike Fred, he was well beyond retirement age but showed no sign of wanting to give up his job. Kitty Wilson had stepped into Sally's shoes at Harpers while she was away. Reading her correspondence and overseeing any queries to do with the buying on the departments that Sally normally ran. Beth had assisted her and kept a general eye on things, but Harpers could rely on their staff and supervisors and everything had gone smoothly – just as Ben had persuaded Sally it would before they left.

Beth had been surprised at how quickly Kitty had learned to do Sally's job these past few years. They normally worked in conjunction, but Kitty was quite capable of making decisions regarding the stock herself and of late Sally had been leaving it more and more to her.

'It is my intention that Kitty will take over my job one day – unless she decides to get married and leaves to have a family.' Sally had sighed when they'd spoken about Kitty and the work at the store before she'd left for her trip to America. 'I do love my job, Beth, but there are times when I feel I don't wish to go in. I know I shouldn't be lazy—'

'You—? Lazy?' Beth had laughed heartily, because Sally was always working. If it wasn't the shop business that occupied her, it would be one of her many charities that needed help. Or simply something the children wanted, like attending school meetings, watching her son, Peter, play football, or making costumes for the Christmas concert that Jenny had starred in the previous year. Jenny, Ben and Sally's eldest child, was growing up into a lovely girl, her childish tantrums a thing of the past – at least they didn't happen so often now – and she was proving to have a beautiful singing voice. 'I don't think Kitty will be getting married just yet,' Beth had reminded Sally of the man Kitty had loved and lost. 'She loved Larry and when he was killed in that accident on the docks, I believe she made up her mind never to get married.'

'Yes, she told me as much,' Sally had agreed, looking sad for a moment. 'Surely that will change one day? She can't want to live alone forever.'

'As you know, she lives with Mariah Norton, Larry's sister. I believe Mariah has a little shop selling antiques – or bits and pieces, really. I suppose you could call it a junk shop, though they do have a few nice things. Kitty does the paperwork for her, I know.'

'Yes – but that isn't like living with a man you love, is it?' Sally had questioned.

The conversation had been left there, but Beth had wondered. As far as she could see Kitty was content to work at Harpers and be Sally Harper's assistant. She loved her job and nothing was too much trouble for her.

Sally had sounded odd on the phone when she'd asked Beth to visit her at home that afternoon. Beth suspected she had some news but could not imagine what it might be. Perhaps it had something to do with the Harpers' visit to New York and Ben's aunt...

* * *

'So, you see, Ben is in a bit of a quandary,' Sally said later that afternoon, as they sat with a pot of tea and the delicious little cakes Mrs Hills – Sally's devoted housekeeper – had made. 'His aunt told him that she wanted Ben to take over the store in New York when she passes.'

'But doesn't Ben's aunt have a son?' Beth asked, puzzled. 'I seem to remember something about the shares when Harpers in London was first opened... Ben's cousin had some that he eventually sold to him?'

'Yes, but Ben's aunt and her son don't get on well,' Sally explained, frowning now. 'Hugh isn't interested in the business, just the money he gets from his dividends. Ben's aunt has always taken an interest and tried to keep things right behind the scenes, but Hugh just lives like a playboy, spending money, gambling – oh, you can imagine. I felt sorry for her and Ben does too.'

'Ben can't be in two places at the same time,' Beth objected. 'He can't really keep an eye on things from London – can he? Besides, they must have managers and supervisors. Why is he needed?'

'Aunt Aggie is leaving her shares in the New York store to Ben,' Sally said. 'You remember it was her who let Ben buy his uncle's store in London for himself. He was left some of the shares, but it was his aunt who made it easy for him to have her shares and she persuaded Hugh to sell his to Ben – so Ben feels he owes her. The store in New York is much larger than ours, so her shares are worth a lot of money...'

Beth stared at her, an icy tingle at her nape. 'You won't go and live there?'

'I can't say no for definite yet,' Sally replied with a little sigh. 'I don't want to leave London. This is my home and I'm happy here – but it depends on what Ben wants to do. He is American, though he always says he feels more British these days. I know he believes he is duty-bound to help Aunt Aggie as much as he can.'

'But what about Harpers in London? You couldn't just leave it?'

'No, we couldn't,' Sally replied but didn't sound certain. 'Unless... I mean it does run very well. We have good managers and staff – and there's Kitty and you—'

'No, Sally.' Sally looked at Beth enquiringly. 'Kitty is very young still. One day she might be able to manage alone, but not yet. I help you with the buying, but I couldn't run the place – even with all your managers and supervisors. I couldn't be responsible.'

'That is what I told Ben before I left,' Sally said and sighed again. 'He says we don't have to be hands-on the whole time now and I sort of agree – but I'm not sure we could just go off to America to live and expect the business to carry on the same. Yes, we can employ buyers to do our jobs, but we might not like the stock they purchase. I am meticulous in my research for new stock – and Ben has sourced a lot of the overseas stock for us.'

'Without you and Ben the heart would go out of Harpers,' Beth insisted. 'Yes, I expect you could find good people to take over your job, Sally – and Kitty can do a lot – but you and Ben make the big decisions, don't you?'

'Yes, as things stand...' Sally looked at her hesitantly. 'Ben considered putting Harpers on to the stock market years ago, but I didn't approve then. He says now is the time to do it. We would just be shareholders then and a board would make the decisions. We could come back a few times a year to attend the board meetings...'

'Oh, Sally – you wouldn't,' Beth said, feeling as though the bottom had dropped from her world. 'What about the children – did they enjoy their stay?'

'Well, it was all new and exciting, but Peter missed his friends. They would make new ones easily enough, I suppose – but...' She shook her head. 'It would be such an upheaval.'

'What about the restaurant?' Beth asked, frowning.

'Jack runs that, so it wouldn't be affected,' Sally reassured her. 'Ben was thinking we might open one in America. Jack could be a partner, but Ben would oversee it...'

'You are making my head buzz,' Beth protested, feeling that she was caught up in a whirlwind. 'It just sounds so— so not you, Sally. Not the girl I know so well. You're a Londoner and belong here.'

'To be honest, it isn't me.' Sally exhaled and ran her fingers through her short dark hair that curled naturally about her face. She had been a very pretty girl and the years had only brought new maturity, making her beautiful rather than pretty. 'I've argued the same things you have, Beth, but Ben is torn. I know the New York store is bigger and it would be a challenge to put it back on track. I think the only solution is for Ben to stay there for a while and run it while I do the same here.'

Beth felt a rush of relief. For a while she'd thought Sally was all fired up to move to America and she feared the loss of her company and friendship.

'If you do that – what about your marriage, your relationship?' she asked, looking at her friend intently. 'Would you be happy for Ben to live in America and you here?'

'He would be the one on his own. The children will stay here...' Sally frowned. 'Ben says it would only be for a year, two at most. The American store was floated on the stock market a few years ago, so his aunt and cousin only own 65 per cent of the shares. Ben will get 35 per cent, if his aunt leaves them to him, as she says...'

'In that case, why does he need to be there?'

'Because Aunt Aggie thinks that something is going on that she doesn't know about. She says profits went down sharply this past year and she wants Ben to investigate. He says that once he gets things straight again, he will just leave it to the managers and go over for board meetings.'

Beth nodded. 'Yes, I see that Ben's aunt might be worried and upset – but surely his cousin could step up now and root out the cause of the problem?'

'Apparently, Aunt Aggie thinks Hugh may *be* part of the problem. Ben doesn't see how he could be, but he sort of promised his aunt he would look into it...'

'So he has made up his mind to stay?' Beth thought Sally didn't look particularly happy about things but she just shrugged.

'He hopes it will be a simple job to sort out whatever has gone wrong – and then he'll get good people in to look after things in America and come home. It may mean several trips a year to oversee things, but travel is getting easier now there are more commercial airports and he can go part of the way by air.'

'Yes, I suppose so,' Beth agreed. 'I'm sorry, Sally – but if it were me, I'd be wishing my aunt had left her shares to someone else.'

'Yes. I feel the same way – but Ben is grateful to her for the help she gave him when he set up Harpers in London. I don't feel I can stop him doing what he feels duty-bound to do, Beth. It will be hard for us – but we managed during the war. He was often away. It will be the same now, I imagine...'

Beth nodded. Her heart ached for Sally, who she could see was doubtful and anxious about the immediate future, but there was not much she could say. Instead, she steered the conversation away from Ben, gradually bringing it round to Harpers and the possibility of her father-in-law returning to the store part-time.

'Oh, that's lovely,' Sally said, cheering up at the suggestion. 'Yes, I can use him in the stores. My stores manager just isn't up to it. Ben says I should sack him, but I think that is harsh. I might suggest that I've decided he needs another assistant and leave it to Fred to sort out...'

Beth nodded. 'Dad will soon find the problems and sort them. He ran Harpers stores like clockwork when he was manager.'

'I have no doubt Fred will put things right in a trice,' Sally said. 'I only hope Ben finds it as easy in America.'

2

Kitty Wilson looked up from the catalogue she was perusing when Sally Harper's new secretary brought in the coffee and biscuits. 'Thank you, Ruby,' she said and smiled at her. 'Did you finish typing up those sale figures? Mrs Harper is coming in later this morning and she will expect to see them on her desk.'

'Not quite,' Ruby Rush replied, looking a little flustered. 'I've got another three pages, I think… it's more difficult than I thought to get all the departments' bits and pieces together.'

'Well, you'd best get on then,' Kitty said and frowned as Ruby went back to her desk in the outer office. Ruby wasn't as quick or efficient as the last girl, Rosemary, had been, but she'd left to have a baby and wasn't expected to return as she and her husband wanted a big family. Sally Harper had been disappointed to lose a very efficient secretary but glad that her longstanding friend had at last conceived the child she so desperately wanted.

Kitty was sorry to see Rosemary leave, too, because they had got on well and the young woman had helped her a lot when she was first settling into the job of being Sally Harper's assistant.

It was a job Kitty loved, because it was so varied and exciting. Kitty kept a strict eye on all the departments that Sally ran. There was the bag, hat, glove, and jewellery department that had been Sally's first responsibility, but over the years she had added on more and more, which was why she'd taken Kitty on to train her up to help her. There was also the dress department, lingerie, shoes, cosmetics and perfumes, and a children's department. All the other departments were technically under Mr Harper's jurisdiction, but Kitty knew that Sally advised him on much of the stock; it was normally a joint decision when merchandise was ordered for the store.

Then there was Mr Stockbridge, the overall manager, who opened up each day and made sure the staff turned up for work; also supervisors in each department, as well as the shop girls and a few men who worked in the men's clothing and the furniture departments. The stores had a manager, Jim Manders, overlooking the 'goods in', as well as four lads under him, and there was Ernie who worked the lift, taking customers and staff from floor to floor. Ernie had been badly injured during the war, which had left him with facial scars, but he was always cheerful and obliging. The larger body of staff was women: Harpers girls as they were known. Sally had collected a loyal band of young women who were devoted to their jobs and to her.

Kitty wondered how Sally Harper seemed to know what was going on in all the departments, even if she didn't come in every day. Of course, Mrs Burrows reported to her. Beth Burrows came in three times a week and walked the store; her keen eyes often picked up small things that the supervisors and managers had not noticed. She reported to Sally, as Kitty did. Mr Harper normally came into the office most days, but he seemed content to take executive decisions and leave the day-to-day business of the store to his staff, and he'd been away in America the past few weeks. Occasionally, when he was in London, he would visit the various departments and consult with the supervisors regarding their needs, but Kitty believed that it was Sally Harper who was Harpers' beating heart. It was Sally who had kept it going during the war and it was Sally who knew the name of every employee. Mr Harper greeted the supervisors by name but he didn't know all the shop girls' names.

Kitty was, of course, biased towards Sally. Sally had taken her from the shop floor and given her a chance to rise in Harpers. At first, she'd had a special job of helping customers to co-ordinate their outfits, matching shoes to bags, and hats to dresses and coats, but then, gradually, she'd begun to help Sally with the stock more and more. Kitty had sharp eyes and a good memory. She regularly visited every department and looked through the stock, making a mental note of what was selling and those items that lingered and might need to be included in a sale at reduced prices.

In fact, there was very little in Sally's departments that lingered. In the dress department, there was the occasional damage when lipstick was smeared on a garment, making it spoiled goods. The gentlemen's department had few sale items, but that, Kitty believed, was because men seemed always to purchase the same safe shirts and suits they always wore. Whereas ladies liked to follow fashions – and the dresses had been getting shorter these past few years, at least for the young flapper girls who enjoyed the high life. Kitty herself wore dresses that reached mid-calf, as most of the shop girls did. Sally Harper wore a similar length herself, apart from an occasional evening dress if she was going to a smart cocktail party.

Kitty knew that her employers enjoyed a busy social life when not at work. Sally Harper had become friends with Lady Diane Cooper and was often invited to join her at her home, where she had met other rich and influential people. Kitty herself led a very quiet life in comparison. Her day revolved around her work and, in the evenings, she went home to a tasty meal cooked for her by Mariah, the sister of her beloved Larry, who was very dear to her. They kept house together, sharing the chores, and it was seldom that either of them went out in the evenings.

Occasionally, Mariah would go to the theatre or cinema with a friend of hers. Arnie had been courting her for years, but she said she only wanted friendship. Kitty was always asked to accompany them but rarely agreed. She preferred to sit at home and sew or read a magazine or sometimes a novel she'd borrowed from the library.

'You should go out and have fun,' Mariah had said to her time and again. 'Larry wouldn't want you to go on grieving for him, Kitty. He loved you and would want you to be happy.'

'I know and I am happy in my way,' Kitty had told her. 'I have the best job in the world, Mariah. I love what I do – and when I get home, I just like to relax and talk to you. Besides, you only go out now and then.'

'I'm content here, but I'm older.' Mariah would shake her head and look sad, but Kitty only smiled.

She knew she would never forget the kind, gentle man she'd fallen in love with when her world had turned upside down. Her mother had abandoned her to find a new home after she'd refused to marry a man she'd disliked and her mother had favoured. Larry had come to her rescue, giving her a home with his family and she'd learned to love him. His death, followed by that of his father, had devastated both Kitty and Mariah.

* * *

Kitty shook her head to clear it of unhappy memories, and applied herself to her work. She had been compiling a list of items that had sold out in the glass and silverware department. It wasn't truly Sally's department to oversee, but Kitty had noticed that they were getting low on certain items and she'd researched replacements, discovering some new styles that she thought her employers might like.

Her list was written in clear handwriting. Normally, she would have passed it to Sally's secretary to type up, but she knew Ruby was struggling, so she used the small typewriter they kept in the office to do it herself. She had just finished when she heard Sally's voice in the outer office and then she entered, smiling.

'Kitty, how are you? I know you've coped marvellously while I was away, because Beth told me so.' She bestowed a dazzling smile on Kitty. 'Oh, it is good to be back. I loved New York, but it was so busy! I never seemed to stop rushing here and there. Ben wanted to show me everything. He visited his aunt twice a day, but the rest of the time we spent exploring.'

'How is the poor lady?' Kitty asked as Sally divested herself of coat, bag, and various parcels. 'I know you were very worried.'

'Not well at all,' Sally replied, looking sadly at her. 'Ben thinks she doesn't have long. It makes one wish we had been able to see her more often – she is all the family he has over there. Apart from his cousin, but I'm afraid they don't like each other.'

'I am sorry to hear it,' Kitty replied. 'I know you hoped she might recover.'

'I hate losing people,' Sally told her and sighed. 'Well, I suppose we'd better do some work. What are the sales figures like for last month?'

'Ruby is just finishing them, but from my first appraisal I

would say down on the previous month. Not by much but—'
She broke off as Ruby entered apologetically with a sheaf of typed papers.

'Sorry I'm a bit late with them,' Ruby said and blushed. 'I'll be quicker next time.'

'Yes, you will get more efficient as you learn our ways,' Sally said pleasantly, though it was taking Ruby a while to get proficient. 'Do you think we can have coffee now, please? It is cold out... and you can have your own break then.' She nodded as she looked at the paperwork and whispered to Kitty. 'Neat but a little slow perhaps?'

'Rosemary was so efficient.'

'Yes. We shall miss her, but hopefully Ruby will speed up.' Sally sat at her desk, her head bent over the papers. She read them through quickly and then nodded. 'You are right, Kitty. There is a slight drop, particularly in three departments: the men's clothing, furniture, and glass and silver.'

'I think the glass and silverware is understocked,' Kitty told her. 'I noticed that we don't have much choice in wine glasses – and all those Art Deco silver teapots have gone.'

'Ah, then that might account for that one,' Sally said. 'If the stock isn't plentiful, it won't sell. Our customers like choice, as do I.' She smiled. 'We must find something nice to replace them.' She laughed as Kitty handed her the lists she'd typed. 'Ah, I see you've been busy. I will look at your suggestions while we have coffee.'

Ruby brought in the tray and departed. Kitty poured the coffee the way she knew her employer liked it and then her own. Sally was deep in the list, cross-referencing it with the catalogues Kitty had used.

'Yes, I like everything you've highlighted, and we'll order them all. Are you certain we can't get the teapot everyone liked?'

'I rang them and was told they've stopped making that design.'

'Then we must try to source someone who does,' Sally said and sipped her coffee. 'This is lovely, just the way I like it. The coffee in New York was too strong for me. They laughed when I said I wanted it weaker and said put more cream in – but I like it my way.'

'I did find this teapot,' Kitty said and showed her one that was almost the same as those they'd sold out of. 'But it is more expensive… I wasn't sure if it would sell.'

Sally looked and nodded. 'Yes, expensive. I will ring and see if I can negotiate a better price. I have used this firm before; their merchandise is good but costly.'

'Yes, that was my opinion too.'

Sally finished her coffee and looked at her. 'So, what have you been up to while I was away – other than work?'

'Nothing very much,' Kitty replied. 'I made myself a new dress for Sundays…'

'Well, how would you like to come to a little party at my house?' Sally said, surprising her. 'It isn't high society, Kitty. I'm inviting some friends like Beth – and Rosemary, perhaps my friend Maggie, if she can get up to town, and several ladies who serve on the committees of various charities I work with. I'd like you to come, Kitty, because I have a favour to ask – I wondered if you might like to take on some of my work for them. It would be in your own time and I'm afraid it isn't paid. I simply will not have time to continue with all of it and I wondered if you might be interested? It would mean giving up an hour or two of your weekends – or even an evening, but there are social events, tea parties and other things going on you might enjoy. Of course, if you would rather not, please say no. It is rather a lot to ask, I know…'

'Charity work?' Kitty looked at her, surprised and uncertain. 'I'm not sure. I have time to spare – but what would I have to do?'

'Just attend on my behalf,' Sally said. 'It is usually to decide how to raise money for the good causes we support. We still have our homes for the men who were so badly harmed during the war that they can never return to their families. There is also the hospital I visit and support with funding. I've got a list of donors that I invite to various functions for fundraising. And then there is the orphanage I am one of the patrons. I visit them with toys and clothes for the young children. So I need to raise funds for that as well and I sit in on their board meetings occasionally.'

'How on earth do you manage all that?' Kitty looked at her in awe. 'You must have a wonderful memory.'

'Well, I do, but it can get overloaded and I think with the extra work at Harpers...' Sally sighed. 'I haven't told you yet, Kitty, but Ben will be away a lot more for the next couple of years. It means we'll have to oversee his work as well as our own.'

Kitty smiled. 'I shall be glad to help in whatever way I can – though I am not sure your committees will accept me in your stead.'

'Oh, I am sure they will when I explain you have the authority to make promises on my behalf. They just like my name on their letterheads, Kitty. I often just nod and agree with whatever they want to do – but sometimes I do have good ideas.'

'Then, of course, I'll come to your party and I will do whatever you wish. Mariah says I should get out more – but I don't wish to go dancing or meet young men. The only time I go is when she offers to help at the church social or perhaps occasionally to the theatre.'

'Mariah is quite right,' Sally replied. 'You should have more fun, Kitty. I am afraid that what I'm asking of you is probably rather boring, but at least there are some pleasant fundraising events during the year.' She nodded. 'Now, what is next? Oh yes, Fred Burrows is going to come in part-time; he used to manage the stores but retired a while ago. I am hoping he can get things back to the way they used to be.' She wrinkled her brow. 'Are there any more changes you think we need here at Harpers?'

'The men's department is doing their normal steady trade, or almost,' Kitty said. 'But I'm not sure what we could do to brighten it up.'

'Oh, it has always been one of the slower departments,' Sally said. 'However, I saw a very smart line in silk ties and cravats when I was in New York and I have managed to source them. Hopefully, that might pick it up a bit when they arrive.'

'Oh that sounds like fun,' Kitty said, smiling.

Sally glanced through the stock lists Kitty had made. 'Yes, reorder all these. I think I will take a tour of the store before lunch and... Oh, yes, I bought this small gift for you, Kitty.' She handed her a little box. 'Please go for your lunch if I am late back. I will see you before I leave.'

Kitty looked at the little box as her employer went out, leaving the scent of expensive perfume behind her. Sally Harper was like a whirlwind. The idea of charity work had surprised her at first, but when she thought about it, she realised it might be interesting.

Kitty opened the box and discovered a small bottle of very expensive French perfume inside. She unscrewed the stopper and sniffed. It was gorgeous. Smiling, she put it to one side and picked up the phone, beginning the task of reordering all the stock Sally had approved.

3

Ruby was worried as she hurried through the gloomy streets near her home in Poplar. It was well past six thirty, because she had stopped late to finish typing the lists Miss Wilson had given her. Miss Wilson had told her to call her Kitty, but Ruby didn't like to, because it seemed disrespectful and Ruby needed her job at Harpers so badly. She knew that she was struggling and out of her depth, but she was determined to keep going, if they didn't decide to dismiss her.

Ruby had only just begun her typing classes when she applied for the job as Mrs Harper's personal secretary. She'd told them that she hadn't yet passed her exam at night classes, but for some reason Mrs Harper had given her the job anyway. Ruby adored Mrs Harper. She wanted to be just like her one day, smart and clever, and sure of herself and her place in the world, but she knew it was unlikely to happen.

It was after Ruby read Mrs Harper's story in an old copy of *Tatler* that she'd found on a market stall that she had decided to become a secretary. Sally Harper had been an orphan and a cockney girl just like Ruby; she'd started at Harpers' store as a shop girl but she'd married the boss. Ruby wished she could be so lucky, but she knew she was fortunate to have been given a job that paid so well. She couldn't imagine why, unless Mrs Harper had seen the burning ambition inside her. Ruby had learned from some of the other Harpers' staff that Kitty Wilson had been a shop girl, too; now she was Mrs Harper's personal assistant. Miracles did happen at Harpers!

'You're late!' The harsh voice of her landlady greeted Ruby as she entered the small terraced house where she currently lodged. 'Your meal is in the oven, but it will be spoiled now. I cook for a quarter past six and if you're late it's your fault.'

'I'm sorry, Mrs Flowers,' Ruby apologised hastily. She didn't like her landlady, whose mean eyes and harsh tones belied her pretty name. However, her house was clean, the food was good and the rent for her room affordable now that Ruby had a good job. 'I had to stop late at work and then the bus took ages.'

'Indeed.' Mrs Flowers sniffed in disgust. 'Well, I hope they pay you overtime then.'

'I don't think they will. I was behind, so I had to catch up.'

'That's what comes from getting above yourself,' Mrs Flowers declared. 'A girl like you from the orphanage wanting to be a personal secretary. I never heard the like.'

Ruby made no reply, simply taking her plate from the oven in the range and sitting down at the kitchen table to eat it. It was steak and kidney pie with cabbage and carrots and had dried at the edges, but inside the gravy was still thick and tasty.

'This is so nice, Mrs Flowers,' Ruby said between mouthfuls. 'Thank you for keeping it warm for me.'

'I nearly gave it to the cat,' Mrs Flowers said and banged down a cup of strong tea in front of Ruby, but her tone had softened. 'You want to learn to speak up for yourself, girl. If you work overtime, they should pay you extra.'

'Oh, I dare not,' Ruby replied meekly. 'I don't want to lose my job. I need to be able to type faster.'

'Are you going to your classes again this evening?'

'Not this evening, tomorrow,' Ruby said, knowing what was coming. 'Would you like me to do anything for you, Mrs Flowers?'

'Well, there's some mending and my eyes are not good enough these days – if you're volunteering.'

'I'll be glad to do it,' Ruby said and had the satisfaction of seeing her landlady smile.

Mrs Flowers poured herself a cup of tea and plonked down in her chair. 'It's that rascal in my front bedroom,' she confided. 'I don't know what he gets up to, but he's torn my sheets again – and he asked me to sew buttons on his shirts. As if I hadn't enough to do without running after him all the time.'

'Mr Saunders can be a bit strange, though he is always polite to me if we meet in the hall. He lets me use the bathroom first in the mornings because I have to get to work early and he doesn't,' Ruby said. 'I think he has nightmares sometimes. I heard him cry out twice the other night and I'm sure he came downstairs.'

'Probably looking for a drink, but I don't keep alcohol in my kitchen.' Mrs Flowers sniffed. 'I haven't seen him drunk, but I am sure he consumes whisky. I can smell it on him.'

Ruby thought so, too, but Mr Saunders held his drink well, for he was never rude. He just nodded when he saw Ruby and disappeared back into his room. 'Do you know his history?' she asked, curious now. Ruby hadn't truly taken much notice of the other lodger, except to see that he was thin and pale with a drawn face that always looked tired, perhaps in his late thirties, though he might be younger. Men who had been to war often looked older than their years.

'I suppose it was the war,' Mrs Flowers conceded. 'He was a

captain in the army, I think, though he calls himself plain "Mr" – and he won't talk about the past. I wouldn't have taken him, but a friend of mine asked me to. He had been lodging with her since 1920, but she had to give up her house and go to live with her daughter, because she was too old to carry on.'

Ruby nodded. 'I don't remember much of the war. I was too young – but I do remember that the street I lived in went up in flames and it was after that I was sent to the orphanage.'

'Were your parents killed then?' Mrs Flowers looked interested.

'I think my mother was. I don't recall having a father. We lived with Gran and her house was bombed. She died and I think my mother, too. I can only recall waking up and seeing everything burning – and then someone took me away. I stayed in the orphanage until I was sixteen and then I had to find work and somewhere to live.'

'Where did you live before you came here?'

'In Bermondsey. In a room found for me by Matron. I worked in a canteen until I decided to learn to type. I'm going to learn shorthand too when I can afford the lessons.'

'You girls!' Mrs Flowers shook her head. 'In my day, we worked in service or in a factory and thought ourselves lucky to have a job. You young things have your heads full of nonsense – flapper girls!' She gave a sniff of disgust.

'I'm not a flapper girl,' Ruby said and laughed. 'Just a hard-working normal girl looking to better herself, Mrs Flowers.'

'Well, look for a husband then,' her landlady said with a scowl. 'That was the way we got on when I was young. You want someone with a bit of money, his own little business...' She smirked in satisfaction. 'Mr Flowers had a small shop when I married him. After he died, I sold it and bought this house with half the money. It gave me a little nest egg and I've only needed to take lodgers when I wished. If I don't take to someone, I send them packing.'

'I hope you like me then,' Ruby said and held her breath.

'You are not a bad girl,' Mrs Flowers conceded. 'You might have your head in the clouds, but you're obliging and clean.'

Ruby hid her smile. It was hardly high praise but showed that doing the little jobs Mrs Flowers hated had paid off. She had a home here for as long as she kept on the right side of her landlady, and for the time being that suited Ruby very well.

* * *

Later that evening, when Ruby had finished the mending, Mrs Flowers told her to take Mr Saunders' shirts to his room and hand them to him at the door.

'I'm not tellin' you to go in. I don't hold with young girls in single gentlemen's rooms. Just take them, knock, and hand them to him when he answers.'

'Yes, Mrs Flowers.' Ruby picked up the shirts, which she had ironed after mending them, and went upstairs. Mr Saunders had the front room looking out over the street below. It was the largest bedroom of the three, but noisier than Ruby's, which overlooked a small back yard.

She knocked and waited for a moment. There was no answer, so she knocked again, louder this time. 'Mr Saunders? It's Ruby with your shirts.'

'Go away!' Ruby heard what sounded like a strangled sob.

She hesitated and then disobeyed her instructions by turning the handle and entering. What she saw shocked her. Mr Saunders was squatting on the floor with his naked back turned towards her and his head bowed, wearing only his trousers.

Ruby saw the deep ridged scars on his flesh and an icy tingle ran down her spine. What had caused such injury?

'I'll leave these on your bed,' Ruby said and moved towards it. Before she knew what was happening, he had jumped to his feet and pinned her to the bed, his hands around her throat. Terrified, Ruby made a cry that was meant to be a scream but was cut off by the hands around her neck. 'It's Ruby—' she managed and, in an instant, something flicked in his eyes. Then his hands dropped away and he was helping her to sit up. 'Why did you try to kill me?' she demanded, her fear gone as swiftly as it had come; he was the man she had come to like, despite his sometimes strange looks.

'I thought you were someone else…' He dropped to his knees before her. 'Punish me. Beat me. I am sorry.' Suddenly, a sob burst from him and she saw his shoulders were shaking.

Ruby's pity stirred. This man must have endured terrible things to make him so vulnerable. She extended a hand towards him, not daring to touch him in case he attacked her again. 'Don't cry, Mr Saunders. You only hurt me a little. I am all right, truly I am.'

'I should be dead,' he muttered between gulps and tears. 'They all died, my comrades, but they kept me alive… to torture me for their amusement. Every night at this hour they came…' He raised his head suddenly and looked at her. 'Please go. I am ashamed.'

'Were you captured in the war?' Ruby asked, her feet refusing to move. 'Was it the Germans who tortured you?' She saw the slight shake of his head.

'Russians… they killed anyone caught up in their surge of revenge. They had suffered terribly themselves but can be a cruel people. We were actually prisoners of the Germans in an old castle, but then the Russians came and we were left to their mercy. At first, they left us to starve and then—' His voice broke and he could not continue.

'It must have been terrible...' Something inside Ruby stirred. She had known suffering herself in the orphanage and the pain of having no one to love her, but this man must have endured hell and her heart went out to him.

'Hell could be no worse,' he said and raised his head to look into her eyes. He smiled feebly. 'You should go. I am not safe to be near when I have these attacks. Didn't Mrs Flowers tell you?'

'She said not to come in. I'm sorry I upset you, sir. I never intended it.'

'Of course you did not,' he replied and suddenly he was a different man. He stood up and put on one of the shirts she had mended and she saw a hint of the pride that he must once have had. 'I've seen you helping Mrs Flowers out often. You are a lovely girl, Miss Ruby. It was good of you to mend my shirts. I'm afraid I am careless sometimes – when the black mood descends...'

'I think I understand,' Ruby said and found that she could move at last.

'You could never understand. No one could unless they were there, nor would I wish you to, my dear child. Keep your sweet innocence, Ruby; it is a precious thing,' he said and for a moment the way his eyes seemed to dwell on her face made her breathless. 'Goodnight, Miss Ruby. You should go now.'

He was back to the normal reserved man she had met in the hall. 'Goodnight, sir,' she said and went out, closing the door behind her. For a moment, she stood with her back against it, breathing deeply. What was it about him that had touched her so deeply? She didn't know the man and he certainly didn't encourage friendship – and yet she'd felt something.

Shaking her head, she told herself not to be foolish. It was her loneliness that was making her long for intimate contact – with anyone really. She heard a sound like a cry of despair from within his room and hesitated, wanting to return and comfort him, but something told her he would not welcome her sympathy.

As she went to her own room, Ruby reflected that he was right. No one who had not been subjected to torture could understand what it did to a man's soul. Her heart was touched and she felt tears on her cheeks. Ruby had read a little of what happened to some men during the war, but she would go to the library and find more reading matter tomorrow. She wanted to know what could make someone become the pitiful wreck that had no resemblance to the proud man Captain Saunders had clearly once been.

4

'As if you haven't already got enough to do,' Mariah said, shaking her head when Kitty told her that Sally Harper had asked her if she would take on some of her charity work. 'You should be out having fun at the weekends, my love, not sitting on a committee with a load of old fuddy-duddies. She's got a cheek asking you!'

Kitty shook her head but smiled, because she knew Mariah's concern came from the abiding love that had grown between them. Mariah had taken her into her home and her heart when Kitty's mother had abandoned her, and since the death of her brother and father, Mariah tended to cluck over her only chick.

'I think some of it will be fun,' she said, sipping the hot strong tea that Mariah had poured for her. 'I've been invited to a tea party at Mrs Harper's on Sunday and there will be fundraising events. Last year, I know Mrs Harper arranged a fancy-dress party in aid of her children's charity. I did help with some costumes, if you recall?'

Mariah nodded. 'Well, eat your supper, Kitty. It's bacon pudding this evening. I fancied something warming with all this miserable weather...'

'It was really foggy when I came home,' Kitty said. 'You could hardly see where you were going. That's why I was a bit later, because the bus was so slow I got off and walked the last mile or so. The poor driver said he couldn't remember there being such a pea-souper.'

'Yes, I know. I looked out for you a few times, because I worried, but then I thought it must be the weather.' Mariah served up a plate of steaming suet and bacon pudding with mashed potatoes, cabbage and carrots.

'That smells really good and I'm so hungry,' Kitty said as Mariah sat down and they began to eat. 'Did you have many customers today – or did the weather put them off? I'm not sure I would go out if I didn't need to get to work.'

'I had just one this morning,' Mariah said. 'He bought the Flight Bar and Flight dinner service, a Chinese bronze bowl, two silver coffee pots, a Minton tea service – oh, and a mother-of-pearl inlaid chess set, too.'

'Gracious, he was a good customer,' Kitty said, pausing over her meal to look at Mariah in surprise. 'He must have spent a lot of money with you?'

'More than a hundred pounds, even with the discount I gave him.' Mariah chuckled. 'Dad's treasures sell well to the right customers.'

Mariah's father, Alf Norton, had amassed a huge number of interesting items over the years he'd been at his junk yard. When they'd moved from there to the house on the corner of Dressmaker's Alley, they had brought much of it with them and Mariah had turned one large room of their house into her little curiosity shop. Alf's treasures were not all perfect, for he'd loved beautiful things for themselves, keeping good pieces even if they had a chip or a dent. Kitty had learned to love them too and many of Alf's precious but damaged pieces were in their home, but he'd had far more than they needed and so Mariah opened her shop when she felt like it and sometimes sold a few bits. It didn't normally earn them much, but it paid for things like food and coal.

'He has been in before,' Mariah went on, pushing away her empty plate. 'I think he is a dealer and has a shop somewhere up the West End. He has a good eye and only buys the best. I didn't put that dinner service out until last week, but no one else looked at it. He knew what it was, though most folk would think it a bit plain.'

'If he is a dealer himself, he will sell them again for more money,' Kitty said. 'Do you think we are selling stuff too cheaply?'

'I don't know,' Mariah admitted. 'Dad knew what everything was worth, but I never took much interest – and you didn't have time for him to teach you enough before he died.' She shrugged her shoulders. 'Perhaps it doesn't matter. I bought that chess set from someone and I made a profit of five pounds on it. That's a lot more than I could earn in a week if I went out to work. If Mr Harvey makes a profit on it, good luck to him.'

'Yes,' Kitty agreed after a moment's thought. 'I expect you are right. We have all we need anyway. And I earn good wages now – far more than I could ever have dreamed of when I first joined Harpers.'

Mariah looked at her. 'You don't need to work at Harpers unless you want to, Kitty. Dad left us a nice nest egg and you have what was Larry's. We are both lucky.'

'Yes, we are,' Kitty agreed. 'I know Kettle's Yard was left to both of us, Mariah, but I always think that the money it fetched should be yours. Alf hardly knew me...'

'He loved you from the first and so did Larry,' Mariah declared. 'You've been a sister to me, Kitty. We share what we have and always will – but I know you love your job, so I'll say no more.'

'It is exciting and fun to work with Sally Harper,' Kitty said, smiling. 'When she comes into the office, it's like a whirlwind. She is always so full of plans and so decisive. I enjoy being around her.'

'Well, as long as she doesn't take advantage of you,' Mariah said. 'She's a nice lady and she helped us when we needed her – I don't forget that, Kitty. I just want you to be happy.' After Larry and Alf died, they had been threatened by Kitty's adoptive mother, Mrs Wilson, and Mr Miller – the man who had tried to force Kitty to be his wife. They'd planned to have Kitty incarcerated in an institution for the mentally ill so that they could steal her share of Kettle's Yard, because Mr Miller wanted to own all the property there and develop the land for his own financial gain and Kettle's Yard was an important part of his plans. However, Beth Burrows had got wind of it and gone to Sally Harper. Together they had routed the evil pair and Kitty would always be grateful.

'I am happier living with you than I was most of my life,' Kitty told her. 'I loved the man I thought of as my father – but Mrs Wilson was never a mother to me. I never understood why she disliked me so much until our friend, Bella, told us that I wasn't her child and that Mr Wilson had forced her to accept me.'

'That woman is nothing to us now,' Mariah said, then, deciding to change the subject: 'So, what are you wearing to this party Mrs Harper is giving, Kitty? You'll want something smart if it's going to be posh.'

'I don't think it will be. Mrs Burrows will be there and Rosemary – she used to be Mrs Harper's secretary but left to have a family. I shall just wear my Sunday afternoon dress.'

Mariah nodded. 'I suppose that will do for a tea party, but I think you should treat yourself to a pretty dress from Harpers. You get a discount on your clothes, don't you?'

'Yes, I do, but some of the clothes are very expensive.' Kitty looked thoughtful. 'There is a beautiful dress that just came in – it is from Miss Susie of Dressmaker's Alley, just down the road from us. Pale blue silk with chiffon sleeves and a matching scarf that trails down the back – there is a very low V-neck at the back. I'm not sure I would dare to wear it, but it is lovely.'

'You should try it on,' Mariah said. 'It will be your birthday soon, Kitty. I'll give you something towards it, if you like it.'

'You spoil me,' Kitty laughed but looked at her with affection. 'I suppose I could treat myself. I've made most of my clothes until now and the dresses I wear for work are plain but smart. It would be nice to have something pretty – though I'm not sure when I'll wear it.'

'Get it just in case you get invited to an evening event,' Mariah encouraged. 'And now I'm going to wash the dishes and then listen to the wireless you got me for my birthday.'

'You sit down, Mariah,' Kitty insisted. 'You cooked our meal; I will wash the dishes.'

Mariah protested but then laughed and agreed. She went through into their little sitting room to the comfort of the fire and Kitty soon heard the soft music coming from her wireless. Mariah loved listening to it and they spent most winter evenings by the fire listening to a concert or a play. Kitty often sewed and Mariah did a bit of mending, but mostly they just listened, laughed, and talked, content to be together in their comfortable home.

Kitty hummed a little tune to herself as she cleaned their dishes, dried them and set them out on the dresser, which was Mariah's pride and joy, with all kinds of porcelain set out on it.

Despite Mariah's warning that Sally Harper's request would swallow much of her free time, Kitty felt pleased to have been asked. As much as she loved their quiet evenings together, she sometimes wished for more variety. Kitty had no desire to go courting. Larry's sudden death had been too cruel. She'd given him her heart and wasn't sure if she would ever love again. For the moment, her life was dedicated to making Harpers continue to run smoothly – but it might be interesting to help with Sally Harper's charity work too.

Her chores finished, Kitty went up to her own room to fetch her sewing. She was making a nightgown for Mariah and her thoughts turned towards her friend. Who was this man who had spent so much money with them – was he a good customer or was he taking advantage of their lack of knowledge? Mariah and Kitty had learned to appreciate good things from a past age through Alf's extensive knowledge. He had taught Kitty a lot about how to recognise genuine antiques and what was good, but prices had never been mentioned, because Alf collected from a genuine love of beautiful things and seldom sold those special pieces he brought into the house. He'd earned a good living from scrap metals and rags, but whenever something beautiful was offered to him, he'd carried it into his home and stored it, either in the house or in boxes. The parlour had been stacked with them for they'd never used it, living mainly in their kitchen.

Kitty shook her head. Perhaps it didn't matter. As Mariah said, they had all they needed and more. Yet she didn't like the thought that someone might take advantage of the woman she loved as a sister.

5

'You would hate it if Mrs Harper went to live in America, wouldn't you?' Fred looked at Beth in concern. 'I mean, it wouldn't be permanent. I am sure she would come back as often as she could – but you'd miss her.'

'We've been friends such a long time,' Beth said and sighed. 'Maggie only gets up to London now and then. She and Colin spend most of their time in the country with the children these days. We write and phone now and then, but it isn't the same.' Maggie had been one of the first shop girls at Harpers, applying on the same day as Sally and Beth. They'd formed a friendship which remained strong throughout the years. Maggie had been engaged to Tim, Fred's younger son, who had been killed during the Great War, but had married a badly injured soldier when she'd recovered from her deep grief for late fiancé. 'Sally doesn't want to; I am sure she doesn't – but if Ben gets too involved over there, she may have to make the choice between him and staying here with her family.'

'It isn't a good arrangement – him over there for months on

end and her here alone in London. I know she has her friends, the children, and her mother, but all the same...'

'She says it will be like it was in the war when he was away a lot.' Beth sighed. 'I think she is upset but trying to hide it.'

'What does Jack say?' Fred asked. 'How does he feel about his partnership with Ben now? It is hardly fair on him – I thought they had plans for another restaurant?'

'They did...' Beth frowned. 'Sally said that Ben thinks they could open another in New York; he would oversee it, though they would employ managers to run it, of course. Jack isn't certain he wants that. He says he has no plans to visit America and would prefer his assets here.'

'Ah, I thought as much,' Fred nodded. His son had a good business head and would know that he was better off with something he could oversee himself rather than something in a country he might never visit. 'I wonder he doesn't ask Ben to sell him his share of the restaurant...'

'He almost did when they quarrelled a couple of years ago,' Beth reminded him. 'Only Jack wanted to sell then and leave London because he thought the children and I were in danger.' There had been some bother with gangsters visiting the restaurant, who had threatened her and the children, but in actual fact Beth had been protected by a more powerful gang. Her friendship with Jerry Woods, who was a barrow boy but also the brother of one of the most powerful gangsters in London, had meant that she was watched over and protected without being aware of it at the time. 'I wasn't in danger because Jerry's friends protected me.'

Fred nodded. 'Have you seen Jerry lately – or Bella?'

Bella was Jerry's mother and Beth had helped her when she needed medical attention. Beth still visited her occasionally, though she was much better now that her eldest son, Tel, had bought one of the new houses in what had been Kettle's Yard for her. It wasn't damp and there were no bugs creeping out of the walls at night, which had contributed to the improvement of her health.

'Yes, I visited last week. I still take her to the clinic when she needs to go, though her leg is much better, thank goodness. We have a lot to be thankful for, because without Jerry and Tel something nasty could have happened to me or the boys.' Beth smiled. 'Since Jack bought me my own little car, I don't use the Underground so much so I hardly ever see Jerry. Bella told me he is selling his barrow and opening a little fruit and veg shop. Just round the corner from her, I think she said.'

'Going up in the world, is he?' Fred smiled and nodded. 'Do you reckon he is one of them – that gang that warned off the men who threatened you?'

'Jerry?' Beth looked thoughtful. 'I don't think he is involved with criminal activity, but you know he has connections. Tel is one of those in the shadows who control a lot of stuff. I think Jerry keeps an eye or an ear on things for Tel. He meets lots of folk when he's selling his fruit and veg on the streets.' She shrugged. 'To be honest, I don't want to know. They helped me and they helped Kitty Wilson – because if Tel hadn't warned us, she might have been spirited away to an asylum and never heard of again.'

Fred grunted. 'Not all bad then – though I don't hold with the rackets they run – gambling and, well, things we can't approve of.'

'I know what you mean, Dad. Bella doesn't like what Tel does either. For years she refused to touch his money. She still won't let him give her money, but she does like her house. Jerry persuaded her to move into it when her old rented property was knocked down.'

'She's a game old girl,' Fred said with a chuckle. 'I'm glad you still visit her, Beth.' He stood up and stretched. 'I'd best get home. I'm helping my neighbour three doors down with his windows. The frames have rotted, so we're taking them out and putting new ones in.'

Beth smiled, because Fred always had a project with one of his neighbours. 'Next week you'll be back at Harpers, Dad. Four mornings a week. I shan't see you for coffee every day. I'll miss it.'

'You'll be off to work yourself in a bit,' Fred reminded her. 'Hasn't Sally suggested that she would like you to go in every morning apart from Saturday, just for a couple of hours?'

'I've said I will try,' Beth replied. 'I have time to see the boys off before I go in – but there's other things to consider. I have shopping and other people to visit.'

'Yes, well, you must do what suits you,' Fred said and smiled. He kissed her cheek and took his leave.

Beth washed up and then put her coat on. The fog had cleared at last, though it was still grey and dull as she went out. She planned to do a big shop later that day, so that she would be ready to start her new routine on Monday, though she wasn't sure she could manage every morning, as she'd already told Sally when they'd discussed it just after she returned from America.

As she locked her front door and looked about her, Beth saw her neighbour arrive in his new car; it was a Bentley and very smart and shiny. He waved to her as she got into the small, second-hand Ford that Jack had bought for her. Beth smiled and nodded in the mirror. The family had moved in a few weeks earlier and she hadn't seen anything of the wife or child since moving day when she'd noticed them arriving as she went into her own house. She wondered if it was time to pay a friendly visit to welcome them to the neighbourhood. Beth had given them time to settle in. Perhaps she would invite the lady of the house to have coffee with her one morning... though she wouldn't have much time in the mornings. And tea time was always a mad house when the boys came home from school.

Perhaps she would just call and ask her new neighbour round for a cup of tea in the early afternoon. And Beth would visit Bella, too, in case she didn't have time for a while once she started doing more hours at Harpers.

* * *

Bella was sitting in her kitchen knitting when Beth went in. She'd knocked and been invited to enter. The elderly woman put her knitting down and smiled as Beth placed a paper bag on the table.

'And what have you brought me this time?' Bella asked, looking pleased as she peeped inside and saw the iced buns. 'You're a good woman, Beth Burrows. Pop the kettle on and we'll have a cup of tea.'

Beth moved the kettle onto the hotplate. The range had been cleaned recently and shone as it radiated warmth. 'So what have you been up to lately then?' she asked as she fetched the cups for them.

Bella cackled. 'Livin' the high life, o' course,' she mocked. 'Been down the pub and got drunk, then up the Pally and had a knees-up. What do yer think I do?'

'I know you don't go far, but you could go out now and then if you chose. Jerry would take you to a concert or something...?'

Bella snorted her disgust. 'Don't want to see no bleedin' concert. I liked the Music Hall when I was younger – that was a good night out, but I ain't bothered these days. I sit and listen to me records – Jerry got me a gramophone.' She smiled and nodded. 'He knows what sort of music I like – the good old songs. Harry Lauder and Marie Lloyd. Got me a wireless, too, some of them American singers ain't bad. I'm all right 'ere.'

'Yes, I know. Have you seen Kitty recently?'

'She comes now and then on a Sunday morning,' Bella said. 'I do miss her. She used to come most days when she lived at the junk yard.'

'I expect she is busy these days,' Beth said and poured their tea, adding several spoons of sugar to Bella's. 'Tuck into those buns, Bella. I know you like them.'

'I do,' Bella admitted and sank her teeth into the sweet cake. 'Tel knows it – he brought me some last week; knows I can't resist 'em. I tell 'im to clear orf, but he ignores me. I couldn't throw 'im out, 'cos he brought his son to see me.'

'Is he married then? I didn't know.'

'Not that I know of. Tel don't tell me his business and I don't ask. He says the boy is his and I believe him. The lad is the splittin' image of him.'

'That is nice for you to have a grandson.'

Bella snorted. 'Not if he grows up like his father! I don't 'old with what Tel does, even though I don't ask for details. I know it ain't right. Jerry likes his brother or I would have done with him years ago.'

Bella loved her son but her morals were strong and Beth knew it pained her that her eldest boy was mixed up with criminals; indeed, if Jerry was right, he was the big boss these days. The last time Beth had spoken with him, he'd told her his brother was now in control of much of the criminal underworld in London.

'Tel's better than a lot, Mrs Burrows,' Jerry had told her. 'There will be no drugs while he's in charge – and no murders of innocent folk neither on his patch. Ma says what he does is wrong and she's right – but he ain't evil. It's just all he knows. He had to look after us when me dad died and I was a kid – and he got in with folk. Now he can't get out, even if he wanted.'

'It isn't for me to judge,' Beth had replied. 'I am grateful for what he did for us and I'll say no more.'

'You've got Jerry still, Bella,' Beth said now to change the subject. 'Has he got a girlfriend?'

'Mebbe. I ain't seen her yet, but if he's serious, I'll be glad of it for his sake. As long as 'e treats her right and puts a ring on her finger, I'll be happy.'

'Will you live with them?' Beth asked, because at the moment, Jerry lived at home and took care of his mother.

'That's up to them,' Bella said. 'I'll not be moving again. I've told Jerry the next time I leave my house, it will be in a box – so they can live 'ere or go where they choose. I'm not budgin'.'

'No, why should you?' Beth agreed, though she wondered how Bella would manage without her son.

They talked for a while and then Beth took her leave, promising to come again when she could. It was nearly time to start preparing tea for her children so she would have to put off visiting her new neighbours for a while longer. Beth reflected that she was mostly busy. She wasn't sure that she could manage more than the three mornings she already spent at Harpers. It would be a challenge and she wanted to help Sally, because she had so much more to do, but Beth enjoyed her life the way it was now. She had made several friends in the area and liked helping out with church events, as well as at Jack and Tim's school when they had something on. Sally was going to find the management of Harpers a huge task without Ben to help her. She knew that Kitty would do all she could to lend a hand, but did she have enough time to give to Harpers and her friend herself... well, they would have to talk about it at Sally's tea party on Sunday.

6

Ruby finished the page she was typing and looked at it. She was pleased that she'd actually managed to get all her work done, then she saw two typing errors and her heart sank. Erasing those mistyped letters and replacing them did not work well. You could always see where the white chalky stuff was and the new letter often smudged or was not quite in line – and Mrs Harper didn't like messy work. There was no option, she would have to type it again, slower, making sure there were no errors.

Sighing, she removed the page from the typewriter and began again at a steadier pace so that when she'd finished it was perfect. Glancing at her cheap wristwatch, her present to herself on her eighteenth birthday, Ruby saw that it was already twenty minutes into her lunch hour. She'd wanted to go shopping in her break so that she didn't have to when she left work, but there wasn't time now. She took the kettle in her office to the small cloakroom and filled it with water at the basin and then returned, setting it on the gas ring she used to boil water for tea and coffee. Spooning tea leaves into a pot, she waited until the kettle boiled, then turned off the gas ring and made her tea.

Ruby brought sandwiches to work with her each day. She purchased them from a small café across the road from Harpers. The lady who ran it had them freshly made for Ruby every day and they were cheaper than the canteen at Harpers, even with her discount. Ruby sometimes ate in Betty's Café, but more often did not have time so she'd asked if she could have a packed lunch and Betty had obliged her. Today they were egg and cress and very tasty. She also had a small piece of lemon tart wrapped in greaseproof paper.

After she'd eaten, Ruby went to the cloakroom and washed her hands. When she returned to her office, she was startled to see a man standing by her desk. He was reading the document she had finished typing earlier and she stared at him indignantly.

'That's private, that is,' she said. 'Who are you – and what are you doing in my office?'

The man turned to look at her and grinned. 'And you'll be Ruby, me darlin'? I've called on the off-chance that Sally will be in the office this afternoon – and I beg your pardon for reading your letter. I think you type very well—'

'Don't you think you can bamboozle me,' Ruby flashed at him. 'Mrs Harper has gone to lunch with an important client, but she'll be back soon. I will ask her if she has time to see you...' She glared at him. 'What did you say your name was?'

'I'm Michael O'Sullivan,' he said and his eyes twinkled at her. 'Mick to my friends – are you a friend, Miss Ruby? Or a deadly enemy?'

'I don't know you,' Ruby began. 'I think you should leave and —' Even as she said the words, the door opened and Mrs Harper entered carrying several parcels.

'Mick!' Mrs Harper gave a little scream of delight and dumped her parcels on Ruby's desk, flinging herself at the man.

He laughed and opened his arms and they hugged each other, exclaiming and kissing cheeks. 'When did you arrive? Why didn't you let me know you were coming?' She looked up at him. 'How is Andrea?'

'I know I should have told you.' In an instant, the smile left his face. 'Forgive me, but I couldn't write to you, Sally,' he said and there was a break in his voice. 'She was fine at Christmas, as I told you in my letter – then she became suddenly ill and died last month. It was an embolism, so the doctor said. I was stunned and her son is broken-hearted. I thought I should tell you in person...'

'Oh, Mick, I am so very sorry,' Sally said and took his hands in hers. 'Come into my office and we will talk.' She glanced at Ruby. 'Please make us some tea and bring it in, Ruby – but knock before you enter.' She took Mr O' Sullivan's arm and drew him into her office, closing the door firmly behind her.

* * *

Ruby fetched water and boiled the kettle, feeling confused. She'd never seen Mrs Harper greet someone that way and realised they must be old friends. She felt a fool for her attitude towards him and wondered if he would complain of her to her employer. However, when she entered after knocking, they seemed engrossed in their conversation and Mrs Harper just smiled and asked her to set down the tray. Mr O'Sullivan was smiling again and he gave Ruby a friendly nod as she left.

Back in her office, Ruby got on with typing up some stock lists Mrs Harper had asked for and was still at it when Kitty arrived. 'Is Mrs Harper in?' she asked. 'I've been longer than I expected, but I found a new jewellery workshop and I want to show her some samples of their work.'

'She has a friend in there at the moment – a Mr O'Sullivan...'

'Oh, yes. I've heard her speak of him,' Kitty said. 'Is there any tea going, Ruby? I'm parched.'

'I think the water is still hot – would a cup of cocoa do?' Ruby asked. 'Mrs Harper has the teapot, but I've got a tin of cocoa here.'

'Yes, lovely. Mariah and I often have it in the evenings...' Kitty perched on the edge of her desk and picked up the letter Ruby had typed earlier. 'This is very neat, Ruby. Your work is getting better all the time.'

Ruby flushed with pleasure as she brought the mug of hot cocoa to Kitty. 'Thank you, Miss Wilson. I do try very hard to get it right.'

'I know you do, Ruby.' Kitty smiled at her. 'Are you happy here with us?'

'Oh yes. I love my job,' Ruby said enthusiastically. 'I should hate to lose it.'

'I don't think you will as long as you do your best,' Kitty said. 'Mrs Harper is very loyal to her employees and she expects good work and loyalty in return.'

'I know. Everyone wants to work here. The girls I used to work with in a canteen think I am lucky to have my job at Harpers.'

Kitty nodded. 'I don't know much about what you did before you came to Harpers. Would you like to tell me...?'

'Oh, me? There isn't much to tell. I was in an orphanage and it wasn't good but—' Ruby hesitated and then took a deep breath. 'I would like to ask you something... it is about a man who lodges at the same house as me...'

* * *

'It must have been a terrible shock for you, Mick,' Sally said, looking at him in sympathy. 'Andrea always seemed so well.'

'She would never let anyone know if she had anything wrong, even a headache – but the doctors told me that it was a blood clot in her head and it caused a kind of stroke. I was away on business the previous day and when I got home, she was in bed so I fetched the doctor to her, but she died soon after he got there. All she would admit to was a headache...'

'I am so sorry, Mick. Ben's sister had something similar and that was very sudden too. At least she didn't lay and suffer too long.'

'No, that is something. I remember when Jenni died...' Mick sighed. 'It was the suddenness. When someone dies with no warning – well, you don't get a chance to say goodbye.' Sally placed a consoling hand on his arm, her eyes conveying her sadness. Mick placed his hand over hers. 'We've been through some things, the pair of us, Sally. I know you were fond of Jenni...'

'Yes. Ben was devastated...' A look of pain passed across her face and Mick squeezed her hand. She smiled and shook her head. 'He is in America with his aunt. She is slowly dying...'

'I'm sorry to hear that, Sally.'

'Yes – and the worst part is that he may have to stay out there for months, perhaps for a year or two. The business there has problems and his aunt asked him to look into things for her.'

'I think a few businesses may have problems in the near future,' Mick said with a shake of his head. 'We've all grown used to prosperity, but I believe that may change in the next few years. I was in America last year and, even then, I noticed things. I feel this slowdown in trade has been coming for a while.'

'Do you?' Sally looked at him, arrested by his tone. 'Ben thinks it is all set to boom once he gets a few things straightened, and of course he will have his aunt's shares in time, but I've noticed a small decline in Harpers' profits these last couple of years. It dipped a bit in 1926, but then picked up again, but I've thought…' She shook her head. 'Ben thinks I am too cautious.'

'No, you're not,' Mick said. 'I've got my finger in a lot of pies, Sally, and I've noticed the same as you – things are slowing. It was bound to happen. The twenties have boomed and we've all been drunk on the glory of coming through a terrible war, carried on by a wave of enthusiasm for life. No bad thing in itself, but it won't go on forever. I'm selling the less profitable parts of my business off. I feel I'd prefer to be back in London. Ireland has too many memories of Andrea. I'll put my money somewhere safe for the moment… wait until I'm ready to invest again.'

'I wish Ben would do that, too,' Sally replied. 'He is always investing in something or other and we have overdrafts at the bank. Our assets far outweigh what we owe and we could settle our debt if we sold something, but Ben just keeps expanding. He is very keen on the New York store and hopes he might buy his cousin's shares in the business one day…'

'Ben has always had an eye to the main chance,' Mick replied. 'It is a good thing when times are booming – but he'd find it hard if everything collapsed.'

'It won't, will it?' Sally looked alarmed.

'No, I shouldn't think so,' Mick replied, 'but I think trade may be a lot slower than it is now before we know it.'

'If I had my way, Ben would sell his shares in America once he has sorted the business out and invest over here.' She sighed. 'He listens to me sometimes, but he is very excited about the potential there at the moment.'

'Perhaps he is right to be,' Mick said. 'I might be getting too cautious in my old age.'

Sally smiled. 'You're not old, Mick – not much older than me – and you always had an eye to the main chance too. I remember when you just had one pub to manage.'

Mick looked at her fondly. 'They were good times...' His eyes twinkled as he looked at her. 'Why didn't you marry me, me darlin'? I think we would have been good together...'

Sally laughed. 'There was a time when I thought I might,' she said. 'Then I fell in love with Ben – and you loved Maggie, didn't you?'

'Aye, I loved the lass,' Mick replied with a sad smile. 'But I never stopped loving you...' She threw him a challenging look and he nodded. 'Andrea was a good wife and companion, but we were neither of us in love – you must have known that?'

'No, I didn't,' Sally said. 'I thought you were fond of her.'

'Yes, fond,' Mick agreed. 'You know well enough that isn't the way I felt about you or Maggie...' He nodded as she met his eyes. 'I'll always love you, Sally Harper – and if Ben hasn't the sense to look after what he has, mebbe I should knock some sense into his head.'

'Oh, Mick,' Sally gave a little sob of emotion. 'I am so glad you'll be around. I have missed you. I'm going to need my good friends with Ben away for months on end.'

'Then it's a good thing I'm here to look after you, me darlin',' Mick said. He stood up. 'I have an appointment – but we'll go to lunch soon. Marlene still looks after that pub for me. We'll go there and it will be like old times.'

'Yes,' Sally said and stood up to kiss his cheek. 'They were good days, Mick. Before the war and all the pain it brought. I'm really happy to see you again – and so sorry for your loss.'

* * *

Sally watched as Mick went out. She sat at her desk and closed her eyes for a moment. Talking of old times had brought back memories, both good and bad, blotting out for a while her distress that Ben had to be in New York. She had quarrelled with Ben over his decision to remain in America, and, although they had made it up before she boarded the liner bringing her home to England, it still rankled in her heart. Yes, she understood that he was upset over his aunt's illness and had felt compelled to make that promise, but it wasn't fair on her or the children. During the war, they'd been small and hadn't noticed their father was often away, but now they expected and needed Ben at home – especially Jenny, who tended to cling to her father.

Sally had tried to see things his way, to understand his excitement in owning a large chunk of such a prestigious store in New York – but *her* heart was here in London and the store they had run together.

She couldn't help feeling that Ben had put his aunt's wishes before their lives and happiness, let alone the success of the store Sally had worked so hard to preserve all these years. Perhaps she was being selfish, but Peter hadn't liked being in New York. After his first thrill of seeing the sights and visiting famous places, he'd asked her when they were going home; he missed his school friends and his granny. Jenny was more content because her father had taken her on several trips. However, she asked constantly when her father was coming home, as did Peter.

So it wasn't just Sally. They all liked being at home best.

7

They had been working in silence most of the afternoon, checking sales figures and stock lists, each at their own desks. Kitty saw that it was almost five thirty and time for them to leave for the day.

'Is something wrong, Sally?' she asked. 'Have I done anything I shouldn't – or was it your visitor who upset you?'

Sally seemed to startle out of her reverie. 'Wrong? No, you've done nothing wrong and Mick is my very best friend from years ago. It is just... I have things on my mind.' She smiled. 'I should go home now. Mrs Hills will be wanting to have some free time and the children will have finished their homework and I like to spend some time with them. I shall see you on Sunday afternoon.'

'You won't be in tomorrow?'

'No. I have appointments most of the day,' Sally said. 'There are things that need to be sorted out for Harpers and I want to see a clothing manufacturer about our men's department. It is looking very dull. In New York, the clothing was more modern.

Ben always insisted traditional sold best, but I'd like to make a few changes.'

'Before you go,' Kitty said as Sally stood up to pull on her coat with its large, creamy fur collar. 'You have some interest in a home for men who were damaged in the war, don't you?'

Sally paused in the act of buttoning her coat. 'Yes, I do – why?'

'Someone told me about a man – a soldier who was tortured as a prisoner of war. She thinks he is suffering mentally, plagued by nightmares and terrible memories. Is there anything the doctors can do for men like that?'

'Sometimes. It depends how deep the trauma is. If it is still causing problems after all this time, it must be bad. The most we can do in the worst cases is to offer peace and quiet in one of our homes. Often, just sitting and talking to the person helps.'

'There is no cure then?'

'I think not, in the worst cases. I know that some poor devils have been driven to take their own lives. It seems as if they live in a black world of their own and it takes a long time and patience to help them. As I said, some cannot be helped.'

'That is a shame,' Kitty said. 'We don't really know what our men went through, do we?'

'No, we can only imagine,' Sally said, looking sad. 'If this person needs help, tell them to go here and ask for Matron.' Sally wrote down an address and gave it to Kitty. 'I must go now.'

Kitty thanked her and watched as Sally left in a hurry. She finished the list she had been checking and then placed all the papers in her desk, locking the drawer before she reached for her coat.

* * *

Ruby was just putting her coat on when she went through to the outer office.

'Mrs Harper gave me this address, Ruby. She isn't sure if your friend can be helped but said he should ask here if he needs somewhere to rest and be cared for.'

'He isn't exactly a friend. I just feel sorry for him,' Ruby replied, though in her heart she felt that Captain Saunders was important to her, important enough that she wanted to discover all she could to help him. Perhaps it was because for a moment or two he'd seemed to need her help, and that was something she hadn't experienced previously. She took the paper and slipped it into her pocket.

They walked to the lift together and went down to the ground floor. The shop girls were covering their displays for the night and all the customers had gone. Mr Stockbridge was there, saying goodnight as the girls left one by one.

'Goodnight, Mr Stockbridge,' Kitty said.

'Goodnight, sir.' Ruby gave him a half smile as he nodded and watched them leave.

'I catch my bus across the road,' Kitty said and smiled at Ruby.

'I'm going on the Underground,' Ruby replied and they parted.

Kitty was thoughtful as she joined the small queue. She was clutching a large paper carrier bag containing the dress she'd liked. Kitty had tried it on in her lunch break and loved it, but her thoughts had wandered. She wondered who the man was that Ruby was concerned for and how she'd met him, then she put it out of her mind. She couldn't wait to show Mariah the new dress she'd brought after some persuasion from her friend.

* * *

'It's lovely,' Mariah said when Kitty tried the dress on later that evening. 'And you look beautiful. It suits you well – goes with your hair.' Kitty's hair had tints of red, especially in the sunshine. The pale-turquoise blue set off those highlights and made her look more sophisticated than her normal grey and black clothes did. 'Yes, I approve. Now all you need is the chance to wear it.'

'I hesitated, because I may never wear it or hardly at all, but then I thought why not? I work hard, we both do – and that is why I bought this for you, Mariah.' Kitty handed her a small parcel.

'For me?' Mariah looked surprised. 'It isn't my birthday…'

'No, but I love you and I wanted to get it for you.'

Mariah opened the parcel and discovered a soft, pale-blush silk blouse with a frilled stand-up collar and cuffs. She turned pink with pleasure as she held it to her cheeks. 'It's beautiful, Kitty, thank you. I love it.'

'It will go with your Sunday costume.' Kitty smiled as Mariah nodded. She had a skirt that was softly pleated with a fitted jacket in a dove grey and the silk blouse would go well with it. 'You can wear it when you next go to the theatre with your friend.'

'Yes, and that's next week if he has his way,' Mariah replied darkly, but she was smiling and humming to herself as she went upstairs to her room to hang it up.

'Mrs Harper was very thoughtful today,' Kitty told Mariah when she returned to the kitchen. 'I think she is worried or upset over something, but she doesn't tell me and I can't ask.'

'Some folk keep their worries to themselves,' Mariah said, nodding.

'Yes, I know. What sort of a day have you had?'

'I opened the shop for a few hours – and that man came

back. Mr Harvey. The one I told you spent a lot of money with me.'

'Did he buy anything?' Kitty looked at her.

'A set of glassware.' Mariah paused, then, 'He asked about you, Kitty. He wanted to know if you ever worked in the shop...'

'Asked about me?' Kitty startled. 'How does he know me? Did you speak of me to him?'

'Yes, once or twice,' Mariah replied. 'He says he knows about your parents.'

'You mean Mr and Mrs Wilson?' Kitty frowned.

Mariah shook her head. 'No – your birth mother and father.'

'Really? How? I mean, I was just a baby when Mr Wilson took me home to his wife and I thought they were my parents for years... How could this man know my real parents?' Kitty shivered as a coldness touched her nape. 'No one ever came forward and claimed to know my parents before. Are you sure that he is genuine? He couldn't be trying to find out about me for Mr Miller and my mother?'

Kitty felt a stab of fear. Had Beth and Sally Harper not intervened at the crucial moment, she might have been shut away for the rest of her life with no hope of escape, but Bella had heard about it from her son Tel and come to warn them.

'They wouldn't dare try to take you now,' Mariah said fiercely. 'Mrs Harper would know who to blame – and we have friends, Kitty. I didn't know your real mother or father – but perhaps they had siblings, a brother maybe. He would be your uncle...'

'Why does he want to know me now?' Kitty shook her head. 'I don't think I want to know him, Mariah. It makes me uncomfortable that a stranger should ask after me.'

'Well, I shan't tell him anything more, though I did tell him you had an important job at Harpers.' Mariah looked regretful.

'He seems a gentleman and always has money in his wallet. He spent another fifty pounds with me today – and I know there wasn't much profit in it for him, because it was just lots of ordinary bits and pieces.'

'I think that makes him more suspicious,' Kitty said thoughtfully. 'I thought he was buying a lot because we were selling it cheaply, but if he just bought anything, to make you trust him... What does he want?' Kitty was suddenly a bit frightened, because why should this stranger take an interest in her?

'I hadn't thought of that,' Mariah replied nodding. 'Well, we shall have to be wary for a while. Next time he comes I shall ask him what he wants and if I think he is lying, I'll send him packing with a flea in his ear.'

'Perhaps it would be wiser to say nothing and just be careful,' Kitty said. 'I can't see what Mrs Wilson and Mr Miller would have to gain now, for they cannot inherit my nest egg. My will is made and they are not blood relations – unless it is simply for revenge.'

'They would not be so wicked.' Mariah shook her head but looked horrified. 'I would kill him before I let him harm you.'

Her fierce looks made Kitty laugh, dispelling the fear. 'I dare say your Mr Harvey is just being friendly,' she said. 'But I shall be wary of strangers just the same...'

Alone in her bedroom later that night, Kitty sat staring into her dressing mirror, her thoughts going round and round. Why would a stranger be interested in her – a girl he had never met?

* * *

Kitty found herself looking over her shoulder as she made her way to work the next day, and more so on her way home.

However, nothing untoward happened and no one followed her or attempted to approach her.

On Sunday afternoon, she arrived at Sally Harper's house for tea, wearing her best dress that she'd kept for special occasions. Now she had her new one, she could wear this one more often and keep the Harpers' dress for best. She had wondered if she might find it uncomfortable at her employer's home with people she hardly knew, but Beth Burrows was there and so was Sally's former secretary, as well as six other ladies. All of whom seemed to be friendly and helpful people intent on their good causes.

Everyone was sorry that Sally would not always have time to attend all the meetings and functions that they oversaw during the year, but welcomed Kitty and Rosemary in her place. Rosemary was with child, so her time would also be limited, though she promised to do any typing that they needed if Sally provided her with a typewriter. This was agreed and everyone settled down to discuss what was going on in the world.

The previous month, the Bank of England had set up the Lancashire Cotton Corporation to protect the industry, which had fallen into decline. One of their charities had been set up to help the families in the mill towns and it was decided that this would continue for a while despite the bank's interest.

It was a pleasant afternoon as the ladies chatted about their hopes and fears and it was agreed that a fete should be held later in the year, in aid of a children's home they sponsored.

'We hold several fundraising events each year,' Beth explained to Kitty. 'However, there are so many needy causes that we have to rotate those we donate to.'

Kitty was asked to help make posters and distribute them to the stores and shops on Oxford Street and in the surrounding district, other ladies would do the same in their localities. Most businesses were pleased to help a good cause and would willingly display a nice poster, either in their window or inside the store.

'I was wondering whether we should have a flag day for the care home,' a lady name Mrs Hilary Beeton suggested. 'The last one raised three hundred pounds – most of it in pennies.' She laughed. 'It took such a long time to count them, but it paid for new bedding and a new toilet and bathroom.'

'Yes, that was quite successful,' Sally said. 'The fancy-dress ball that Lady Diane put on for us did much better – we raised almost a thousand pounds.'

'Yes, that was marvellous, but we can't expect her to do that every year.'

'No, I agree. We must think of something else.'

'What about a parade at Easter?' Kitty suggested. 'We could ask small businesses if they would dress up and decorate their lorries and delivery vans and drive through the West End. We could have children marching and a band – make it partly religious and partly for fun. Volunteers could collect donations on the way, in buckets perhaps.'

'It is a bit tight on time for Easter,' Mrs Beeton objected. 'Otherwise, it is a splendid idea. If we did it in the summer, the weather may be better and there is time enough for people to make costumes and think up themes to decorate their vehicles.'

'Yes, that is splendid,' Sally said. 'Can I leave it to you both to work on that? If you need any advice with getting permissions from the authorities, please come to me. I know a lot of people.'

'I think that is something worthwhile,' Mrs Beeton said, smiling at Kitty. 'You are a clever young woman to think of it.'

Kitty blushed as everyone looked at her approvingly.

The conversation flowed as they ate tiny sandwiches and drank tea from delicate porcelain cups and the afternoon flew past.

* * *

It was dusk when Kitty left Sally Harper's home and went out into the gloom of a chilly February evening.

'Can I give you a lift?' Mrs Beeton asked.

'I live on the corner of Dressmaker's Alley – do you know the way?'

'No, I am afraid I don't, but I could ask...'

Kitty smiled and shook her head. 'I will go most of the journey on the Underground from here and then walk. Thank you for the offer, it was very kind.'

'We shall meet next Sunday,' Mrs Beeton reminded her. 'You are coming to my house. I will send my chauffeur to pick you up. He can find his way anywhere. Unfortunately, he is away today, visiting his sister. Next week he will come for you at two.'

Kitty thanked her and they parted. Thankfully, it was a clear night and she had an easy journey. She left the Underground station and walked along Commercial Road, her mind busy with all that she had discussed that afternoon. Everyone had seemed excited by her ideas, especially the parade, which had turned into a pageant with a theme. It was only some minutes later, as she approached the corner of Dressmaker's Alley, that she had an odd feeling that she was being followed. She turned her head to look over her shoulder and thought she caught sight of a man, but he pulled back into a doorway and she could not be certain that he had actually followed her. She shivered, suddenly feeling cold.

Could it be the mysterious Mr Harvey? If he was following her, what did he want? Kitty had been left some money, which had made a big difference to her life, but it was not a huge fortune. Would someone go to such lengths just for that? Yet how could a stranger hope to benefit? It was all very unsettling.

Surely it could not be the woman she had once thought her mother behind this mystery?

Kitty's steps quickened and she saw that Mariah was at their door looking out for her. She glanced behind her once more, but there was no one to be seen. Perhaps she had just imagined it?

8

Ruby woke suddenly. For a few seconds, she lay wondering what had broken her sleep, then she heard a noise. It sounded as if someone was trying to open her door! Sitting up, she lit the lamp by her bed and stared at the door. The handle rattled and she jumped out of bed, running to the door.

'Who is it?' she asked. 'Mrs Flowers, is that you?' Ruby heard something like a strangled sob. 'Captain Saunders, are you there?' His voice was muffled but Ruby heard his cry for help.

She opened the door and he stumbled into her room. She stepped back in alarm but then realised that she had no cause to fear him as he collapsed in a heap on her floor. He was shivering and shaking and Ruby realised that he was in great distress. She knelt down beside him and put her arms about him, holding him as his body shook and he sobbed, his head on her shoulder.

Ruby didn't know what she ought to do, but she was a kind girl and her sympathy was stirred by this man who had suffered so much. She'd always liked him, despite the way Mrs Flowers grumbled about him, but since she'd discovered his secret, her feelings towards him had become protective, even tender. Her hand hovered tentatively and then she let it fall softly on his head, stroking it gently and murmuring words of comfort.

'It's just a dream,' she said. 'They can't hurt you now. It's all over. I promise you, you are safe now, sir.'

He wept for a few minutes and then suddenly went stiff. He drew back from her and she saw the effort in his face as he brought himself under control. Then he pushed her away from him, firmly but without hurting her, and got to his feet, giving his hand to Ruby to pull her to her feet.

'Forgive me,' he said and his tone was reserved, his eyes unable to meet hers. 'It was unforgivable of me to force that on you, Miss Ruby – but I ask that you will try.' He turned to walk away, but she caught his arm and he looked back at her.

'There is nothing to forgive, sir,' she said. 'I don't mind. I want to help you...' She hesitated then, 'I was told of a place where men who have bad dreams can get help...'

A shuttered expression came over his face. 'I will thank you not to discuss my business with others...'

'I only want to help,' Ruby said, but she saw a flash of anger in his eyes before he walked away. 'I'm sorry. Please don't hate me...' Her heart ached for him and she longed to comfort him. 'I am here if you need me...'

He mumbled something but did not look back and she locked the door after him. She went back to bed, but found she couldn't sleep and took up a book that she had borrowed from the library. It was a novel by Ethel M. Dell and she found it a bit too romantic, but she persevered for a while until she grew sleepy. Ruby realised that she had hurt Captain Sauders' pride and decided that she would write him a note of apology and slip it under his door. She hadn't meant to offend him, but something had made her brave enough to ask Miss Wilson if she knew of anywhere that helped such men and Mrs Harper had known.

It wasn't any of her business, of course, but Ruby couldn't help worrying about Captain Saunders, though she hardly knew him. She thought that he must have family. Perhaps they didn't realise how much he was suffering? If only he would trust her, perhaps she could help him.

* * *

Ruby asked Mrs Flowers the next morning if Captain Saunders had relatives, but her landlady was unhelpful. 'I don't ask my lodgers that kind of question,' she said primly. 'If they wish to tell me that is nice, but Captain Saunders keeps himself to himself. I would not even have known he was an army man if his previous landlady hadn't told me.' She frowned at Ruby. 'I don't see that it is your business to ask either, Ruby. I hope you've not got foolish ideas, my girl. I'll have none of that in my house.'

'I wouldn't dream of it,' Ruby said indignantly. 'I'm just concerned that...' She recalled Captain Saunders' anger because she had spoken of him to others and hesitated. 'Well, he doesn't look well – does he? I thought his family might want to know.'

'I was told his family refused to take him in because he acts strange sometimes – not that it bothers me. I sleep like a log and he doesn't disturb me.'

Ruby nodded and turned to leave. There was nothing to be gained by telling Mrs Flowers and if she knew what he was like in one of his odd fits, she might put him out. Ruby didn't want to be responsible for Captain Saunders becoming homeless. He might turn into a vagrant, like those she sometimes saw under the arches by the River Thames, brewing their tea in old tin cans and shivering over a tiny fire.

* * *

At work later that day, Ruby was still wondering what she could do to help Captain Saunders. For the moment, she had just a few letters and orders to type and file. She made coffee for Miss Wilson and took it in to her, hesitating before asking, 'Is Mrs Harper coming in today?'

Miss Wilson glanced up from some paperwork she was reading. 'No, I don't believe so, Ruby. She was going to see a clothing manufacturer this morning, then she had a lunch appointment, and then some meetings with lawyers and bankers. Perhaps tomorrow.' Miss Wilson looked at her. 'Is it anything I can help with, Ruby?'

Ruby shook her head. 'I don't think so, Miss Wilson…' She turned to leave.

'No, stay and have coffee with me,' Miss Wilson said, making her pause. 'Please, Ruby. We don't often have time to talk, but we're not busy today. I can see you are worried about something.'

Ruby hesitated and then sat in the chair Miss Wilson indicated.

'Do you like milk and sugar?'

'Yes, please,' Ruby said. 'I don't like strong coffee.'

'I'll put plenty of milk in then,' Miss Wilson said. She poured coffee for both of them and handed Ruby her cup. 'Now – are you certain I can't do anything? Sometimes it helps just to talk—'

'Captain Saunders, the man I told you about, was angry because I spoke of him to someone else, but…' Ruby took a deep breath and then told Miss Wilson what had occurred the previous night. 'I didn't want him to be hurt, I just wanted to help him... I like him, even if he is a bit strange at times.' She blushed, revealing more of her feelings than she knew. For some reason Captain Saunders had found his way into her head – and, perhaps, into her heart. No one had ever needed her like that before and she had felt a curious happiness as she'd stroked his head and comforted him. Ruby had never known love so she didn't know what it felt like, but she knew he had become important to her.

'I see, no wonder you are anxious,' Miss Wilson said and nodded. 'I think it is kind of you to be concerned for this man, Ruby. Yet I worry that he came to your room at night... you must be careful. It does not sound as if he would harm you but...'

'Oh, he isn't like that. I've met that sort,' Ruby said. 'Captain Saunders isn't like them. Not at all.' She smiled wistfully. 'If you saw him, Miss Wilson, I think you would pity him, too. It breaks my heart to see a fine man like him weep so terribly.'

'Yes, I can see that,' Miss Wilson murmured, looking at her with sympathy.

'I think he needs to see a doctor – a special doctor that can help folk like him. His spirit has been broken, but he still has pride. The memories haunt him. He needs love and care I think.'

'You are very thoughtful, Ruby. Most people would turn their heads aside and not want to know.' Kitty regarded her with a thoughtful smile.

'I know what it is like to be lonely and afraid,' Ruby said, and for a moment there was remembered pain and grief in her eyes. 'But I shouldn't bother you with this...'

'On the contrary. I will speak to Mrs Harper and hear what she thinks – but I believe that he would have to agree before he could be admitted to the home she helped to found.'

Ruby nodded. 'I was afraid that might be the case, because I am sure he wouldn't agree. I just hoped there might be something...' She sighed. 'I'm not clever enough to know what to do, Miss Wilson.'

'I don't think you need to be clever,' Miss Wilson replied. 'If he came to you in his distress, it must mean that he trusts you. Yes, he withdrew afterwards, but it is his pride that made him. Perhaps all that is required is a few kind words when needed.' She smiled at Ruby. 'You know that you can call me Kitty, don't you? And I am always here if you need to talk.'

'Thank you. Miss... Kitty,' Ruby said and blushed, because it still felt wrong to call Miss Wilson by her Christian name. They'd been very strict about that in the orphanage. The wardens did not encourage intimacy with the unfortunate children in their care.

'You'd best get back to your desk, unless you've finished those letters?' Kitty picked up some papers. 'These need typing. They are repeat orders for the glass and silverware department, so it is very straightforward.'

Ruby thanked her and took them, returning to her office. She sat down and began to type. It didn't seem as if there was much she could do to help Captain Saunders, so perhaps she should just put him out of her mind – and yet she knew she would not.

* * *

Ruby ran the last few yards from her bus to the row of terrace houses where she lodged. It had suddenly started to pour with rain and she ducked her head as it drove into her face and eyes.

'Here, let me shelter you,' Ruby looked up at the man who had spoken. She hadn't seen Captain Saunders coming from the opposite direction, but he was holding an umbrella and now he moved it so that it protected her and not him. Ruby moved closer to him so he was partially protected and he smiled. 'You are determined to look after me, aren't you?' he said in a tone she had not heard from him before. Her lonely heart responded instantly and it was all she could do not to throw her arms around him and hug him. Yet she knew she must not – for she was just a girl from the orphanage and he was a gentleman. He would never look at a girl like her.

'Oh— Yes,' Ruby squeaked. 'I didn't mean to offend you, sir.'

'Your note made that quite clear,' he said, still smiling, and now Ruby's heart was fluttering because surely that look in his eyes meant he liked her, too? 'I regret if I was rude to you last night. I am not myself when it is really bad. I apologise for having disturbed you.'

'I didn't mind,' Ruby replied, standing still, and looking up at him in the rain outside Mrs Flowers' house. 'Really and truly I didn't. If ever you need me, I will always help...' There, she'd said it to his face. She blushed and looked down as she saw amusement in his eyes. 'Or I will try...'

'And that is more than most,' he said, his gaze intent on her face now. 'I have been to one of those places, just after the war ended, Ruby. They tried but they couldn't help me. I was better for a while, but then it all came back. I may be all right now for weeks or months.' He shrugged. 'However, it means a lot to me that you cared enough to ask. Thank you for doing so – and please forgive me for my rudeness.'

'Oh, I have. I understood or thought...' Ruby looked up at him, unaware of how innocent and lovely she looked. 'I just wish I could help you, sir.'

'You already have,' he replied and his smile seemed to caress her. 'Now, I think we should go in before we both drown, don't you?' He was chuckling now, a sound that was like music in her ears.

Ruby laughed and went in as he paused to shake the rain from his umbrella and close it before entering the house. He was putting it in the stand in the hall when Mrs Flowers came to see who it was. Ruby was halfway up the stairs and her landlady didn't notice her.

'There's a letter come for you, sir. Looks official,' she said and handed it to him. 'Supper will be ready shortly. Do you wish it in your room, as usual?'

'Yes, thank you, Mrs Flowers,' he replied and took the letter. He then reached into his jacket's inner pocket and took out his wallet, handing her three crisp pound notes. 'I will pay you in advance for the next month. I may be going away for a while and I hoped you would keep my room for me.'

'Certainly, sir. I'll keep it as long as you pay the rent on time.'

'Thank you.' He nodded and moved towards the stairs. Ruby ran up ahead of him and along the landing to her own room. She wasn't sure why she'd paused to listen. It was none of her business and yet she felt oddly sad that he was going away. He hadn't told her and she'd thought… she'd really thought he might like her a lot. Of course that was just her imagination, because she so needed a special friend, one she might truly love – and who might love her in return.

* * *

Ruby slept soundly that night and no one disturbed her. She ate the piece of toast offered to her for breakfast and drank her tea, before leaving for work. There was no sign of Captain Saunders.

Mrs Harper was already at her desk in the office when Ruby

got in. She glanced at her wristwatch, fearful that she was late, but then Miss Wilson entered, so she knew she wasn't.

'Mrs Harper is in already,' Ruby told her.

'I know. She works harder than most people,' Miss Wilson replied with a smile and a glance at the door. 'Even when she doesn't come into the office, she is often working. There is a lot more to do with Mr Harper away.'

Ruby nodded. 'When is he—?' Her question went unanswered as Mrs Harper opened the door to her office.

'Ah, Kitty, Ruby – you are both in. Good. Ruby, can you make us some coffee before you start, please? I have several letters I want you to type up. And, Kitty, can you please visit all the departments this morning and look at the volume of stock each one has. I thought some of our counters looked a bit dull – not quite up to the standard our customers expect. I don't have time, because I have a business meeting and a lunch to attend. So I must rely on you...'

Ruby went to fill the kettle and put it on her little gas ring to make their coffee as the door closed behind them. Even if she'd wanted to ask Mrs Harper for advice she wouldn't have dared when she was so very busy. After their meeting in the rain, Ruby felt that she might have made too much of Captain Saunders' distress the evening he'd come to her room. He'd spoken and behaved in a way that was completely normal – and now he might be going away somewhere. Ruby decided that she must stop worrying about a man who was really no concern of hers.

She took the coffee in a little later and was thanked, but Miss Wilson and Mrs Harper were deep in conversation and she crept out again, taking Mrs Harper's handwritten letters and notes to type up for her.

* * *

Ruby worked all morning to get the letters done and Miss Wilson signed them and told her to post them in her lunch hour. She did as she was requested and then went window shopping. Ruby was saving hard for a smart pair of shoes, but all the ones she saw were so expensive. All her life, she'd worn second-hand clothing and shoes. At the orphanage, she'd been given hand-me-downs from girls older than her, and she was determined that when she finally bought her shoes, she would have a new pair. She wasn't sure if she had quite enough in her purse for the pair she truly wanted, but she took it out to check, because they had a reduced ticket on them and were now three pounds and five shillings. She had just enough, but alas, her rent for the month was not yet paid and so she couldn't afford her shoes.

Ruby sighed, putting the purse back into her pocket as she turned away, deciding to return to her office rather than linger in the busy street when she couldn't afford to buy much. As she turned towards Harpers, a man came barging into her and she felt his hand in her pocket, realising instantly that he had stolen her purse.

'Stop!' Ruby cried desperately, because all her money was in that purse. 'Stop thief!' She began to run after him, but he dodged easily in and out of the people thronging the busy street. 'Oh, please, don't take it – it's all my money...' Ruby cried, tears springing to her eyes. He was far ahead of her and she knew she would never catch him. She stood watching him about to disappear amongst the crowd, tears running down her cheeks, because how would she pay Mrs Flowers now?

Hearing shouts and loud voices, Ruby looked and saw that two men were struggling. It took her a moment or two to realise that one of them was the thief, but as she watched, she saw the other man land a heavy blow and the thief went down hard. His attacker bent over him and wrenched something from him, looking back at her, he raised his arm and shouted something. A small crowd had gathered now and Ruby saw a policeman talking to the man who had halted the thief's flight and then he was handcuffing the man who had stolen her purse and the other man was walking towards Ruby.

Now she could see that he was young and had pale blonde hair. He was smiling and his blue eyes twinkled as he came up to her.

'I believe this belongs to you, miss?' he said and handed her the purse with a little flourish. His accent was not English, but he spoke it perfectly. Ruby wondered at where he was from, but thought it would be rude to ask him.

'Thank you so much,' she said, feeling flustered and overwhelmed. 'You were so brave.'

'It was nothing,' he said and grinned. 'I heard and saw a lady in distress and I acted.'

'It was both brave and kind,' Ruby said. 'I was foolish enough to bring all my money with me today, because I wanted to buy some shoes...' She blushed again, because why would he want to know that?

'Then I am glad to have been of service,' he replied and bowed once more. 'My name is Rupert Marsh – and I am looking for a department store... Harpers.' He took a small piece of paper from his pocket and checked it. 'Yes, Harpers.'

Ruby laughed. 'I work there. I'm going there now, so I can show you – it is only a little way further along the street.'

He glanced at his watch. 'I would ask you to have a cup of your English tea with me, but I have only a little time to purchase what I need before a very important appointment...' He smiled at her. 'I am going to buy a present for a lady I hope will be my wife.'

'Oh, then you must go to the department on the second floor

– hats, bags, scarves and jewellery,' Ruby told him. 'They have some lovely things there but... they are expensive.'

'That is good. The lady I hope to marry likes expensive things...'

Ruby laughed. He seemed so nice, his smile friendly and he was obviously a decent, honest man. She was so grateful to him for rescuing her purse.

'Ah, I see it now,' he said and held out his hand. Ruby took it and he shook it gently. 'Do you work in this department of which you have told me?'

'No, I am in the office, but I like to visit and look at all the beautiful things there.'

He nodded and they parted.

Ruby had time for a drink and a sandwich before she returned to the office so she went across the road to Betty's Café and parted with one shilling and sixpence for a cheese roll and a pot of tea. It helped her calm down after the unpleasant incident, but she was a resilient girl; she'd needed to be in the orphanage.

As she crossed the road after her meal, she saw Mr Marsh leave Harpers and hail a taxi. He was carrying some of the distinctive black and gold bags. He did not see her.

Some women were very lucky, Ruby thought as she made her way back to the office and took off her jacket. She had never met anyone who was interested in her, never been kissed by a man, and never known love. It wasn't likely that she ever would, though she hoped one day she would meet someone who would love her.

* * *

When Ruby got in that evening, Mrs Flowers was waiting for her rent. Ruby handed it over to her, thankful that she hadn't had to ask for more time to pay. She wasn't sure that Mrs Flowers would have let her stay if she couldn't pay on time.

'Well, he's gone, him upstairs,' her landlady said as Ruby went into the kitchen for her supper. She always ate with Mrs Flowers, though she could have asked to take it to her room as Captain Saunders had. 'Went off with his bags. He said to keep his room, but it wouldn't surprise me if we didn't see him again.'

'What makes you think that?' Ruby asked, disappointed. How could he go without saying goodbye? She shook her head, knowing she'd made too much of a brief interlude. He was just being friendly because she'd helped him. She was stupid! Why would a gentleman like Captain Saunders be interested in her?

'He took a lot of stuff – more than he needed for a holiday,' Mrs Flowers sniffed. 'Went off in a big car, too. Chauffeur got out and opened the back door for him.'

'Perhaps he hired the car,' Ruby suggested to be met with another sniff.

'I reckon he's been hiding something,' Mrs Flowers said, eyes narrowed in suspicion. 'I was led to believe he had nowhere to go, asked to take pity on a man who was down on his luck – but the suit he was wearing cost more than you and I would see in a month of Sundays, Ruby. Handmade shoes, leather gloves and a gold watch...'

'Well, he is a gentleman,' Ruby said. 'They have things like that...'

'Somethin' isn't right.' Mrs Flowers grumbled. 'Don't ask me what, for I don't know – but he isn't what I thought him...'

'Well, perhaps that is a good thing,' Ruby said. 'He might be going to visit his family. He might decide to stay with them.'

'Then I've got to find another lodger.'

Mrs Flowers was clearly put out. She liked to know everything, even though she pretended she wasn't interested in her tenants' lives. She'd thought her lodger a poor, friendless man and now it seemed different she was annoyed over it.

Ruby hid her smile. She was sorry Captain Saunders had gone off without saying goodbye to her, but glad that he was perhaps going to visit his family. They might know how to help him. If they were well off, they could surely afford to take him to the best doctors, and that was what he needed, Ruby thought.

9

Kitty was almost home that evening when a man stepped out in front of her, blocking her path. He was smartly dressed in a nice suit and overcoat and wore a silk hat and good leather gloves and shoes. As she hesitated, uncertain of which way to move to avoid him, he tipped his hat to her.

'Miss Kitty Wilson?' he enquired in a pleasant tone.

'Yes...' Her pulses quickened. He appeared and spoke like a gentleman, but she didn't know him. 'Excuse me, I wish to pass.'

'May I ask for a moment of your time, Miss Wilson?' He looked at her and smiled. 'Please. I mean you no harm.'

'Are you Mr Harvey? Have you been buying things from Mariah and asking questions about me?' Kitty's eyes narrowed in suspicion.

'Yes, I'm afraid I have.' He sounded apologetic. 'I know you may think it suspicious – but I was employed by a client and he wanted me to make sure what kind of a woman you were...' He took a card from his pocket and handed it to her. Kitty looked down and saw that it was a solicitor's business card. 'May I perhaps come in – or would you prefer we went elsewhere for a cup of tea?'

'I don't know you, Mr Harvey – and you've lied to Mariah.'

'No, I assure you, only a white lie. The shop I buy for exists, but it belongs to my mother. I find stock for her sometimes and she has been very pleased with what I purchased from your friend.'

'I suppose you had better come in,' Kitty said. She led the way into the house and through to the kitchen, where Mariah was busy at the stove, a cloud of steam issuing from saucepans and giving off a wonderful aroma.

She turned with a smile that disappeared when she saw who was with her. 'We are closed, Mr Harvey.'

'I came to see Miss Wilson,' he said and again he sounded apologetic. 'I have misled you a little, Miss Norton, but... well, if I may explain.'

'Please do. We are waiting...' Mariah said, looking like thunder.

'I work for a firm of lawyers – and we undertake to search for people,' he said. 'Recently, we were approached by a man – a gentleman...' He looked at them but saw they were still suspicious. 'He is an old man, Miss Wilson. Quite well off, I understand, but not a nabob or anything like that, though he has been abroad for the last twenty-five years – before you were born, Miss Wilson.'

'What has that to do with us?' Mariah demanded.

Kitty held up her hand. 'Please sit down, sir. Would you like a cup of tea, Mr Harvey? Let him tell his story, Mariah.'

Mariah poured them all tea but still looked angry. 'He deceived me.'

'Perhaps there was a reason,' Kitty suggested and Mr Harvey looked at her gratefully.

'My client came to London searching for his brother and his family. He had had no contact with them for many years and now feels that he would like to speak to them before... well, that bit is for him to tell you.' He paused, but neither Kitty nor Mariah spoke, so he went on, 'He discovered that his brother had died in an accident on the docks and then he was told that the Wilsons adopted his brother's child – a girl – when her mother died giving birth. He traced Mrs Wilson and...' Mr Harvey cleared his throat uncomfortably. 'He was told that you were a bad girl... that you had lived with a man without marriage and... some rather nasty things...'

'How dare that woman blacken Kitty's name!' Mariah cried in outrage. 'She lived with my family and there was no wrongdoing. She would have married my brother had he not been killed saving another man's life.'

'Yes, well, my client did not know any of that – so he came to us and asked us to discover the truth, where you were, and if you were well and living decently. He is a man of strict morals, you see.'

'Yes, I do see,' Kitty said, lifting her chin. 'And so you were set to spy on me and report to your client – before he decided if he wished to know me.' There was both hurt and anger in her voice. 'So now that you have discovered that I am blameless, what do you want?'

'You are angry,' Mr Harvey said. 'I did advise my client to make a direct approach, but he wanted to be sure...'

'Well, now you may tell him that he has wasted his time,' Kitty said. 'I take it that you are here to tell me that he wishes to meet me?' He nodded and she gave him a flashing look that spoke of her anger. 'He may wish to meet me, sir – but I have no wish to meet him.'

'You are upset,' Mr Harvey said. 'I may have handled this

badly – but he was so insistent that you must be of good character...'

'I hope he will be satisfied, but I think we shall bid you goodnight, sir.'

'You will not reconsider? I may be exceeding my duty – but I believe he means to offer you a home and much of what he owns when he dies. He has no other family.'

'I am sorry for him,' Kitty replied with dignity. 'I thank you for your trouble, sir, and I decline his kind invitation. Please leave now.'

'Kitty, think,' Mariah said. 'It might be that you would come into a significant sum of money.'

'If my uncle had been here when I needed him – if he had ever tried to trace me when I was a child, then I should welcome the chance to meet him,' Kitty said, pride in her eyes. 'However, Larry was there when my life fell apart. He did not question but took me into his family. Because of Larry and your father, Mariah, I have enough money for my needs.' She turned back to the lawyer. 'Thank you, sir, for giving a good opinion of me to my uncle – but my answer is still the same.'

Mr Harvey stood up. 'I shall give him your answer, Miss Wilson. I am sorry if I have offended you by my clumsy efforts.' He nodded to them both, took his hat from the table where he had placed it and went out. They heard the door close behind him.

Mariah looked at Kitty. 'You are hurt, my love. It was wrong of him to deceive us, but it was his duty to do as his client instructed.'

'Mr Harvey is forgiven,' Kitty said. 'This man who claims to be my uncle I cannot forgive – he did nothing when I was at the mercy of an uncaring woman I believed my mother. Why does he suddenly wish to see me now?'

'When folk reach a certain age, they sometimes feel the need for family when they never have previously,' Mariah suggested. 'And he did not know you were born or what had happened to your parents.'

'Yes, I accept that – and if he had been open, come to me, and told me who he was, I should have been glad, but to pay someone to spy on me to make sure I was not a bad girl— That is not the behaviour of a gentleman, Mariah.'

'No, it is not, but I blame that woman for spewing filthy lies about you,' Mariah said fiercely. 'It was she who gave him doubt. It is she you should blame for the insult, Kitty.'

'Perhaps,' Kitty said and the anger drained out of her. 'I have been worried about what Mr Harvey was after – I feared he might harm one or both of us. When I learned the truth, I just felt so angry.'

'And hurt,' Mariah said. 'I understand, my love. Forget about him now. As you said, we have more than enough for our needs.'

Kitty smiled at her. 'He offers me a home, but I have one here with you and it is all I want.'

'One day you may fall in love,' Mariah told her.

'If I do, then he will have to be prepared to live with us here or offer you a home, for I shall not desert you.'

Mariah laughed. 'If that's all that is worrying you! Arnie would wed me like a shot so I'll not be lonely.'

Kitty looked at her. 'Would you wed him if it were not for me?'

'Mebbe,' Mariah admitted, because she was always honest. 'Mebbe I will one day. He is used to waiting – and I still don't get on with his mother.' She gave a snort of laughter. 'When the old battleaxe hangs up her clogs, then I'll think again, but she's still going strong at seventy-five, so Arnie says...'

Kitty laughed her sudden anxiety gone. 'We both have lots to look forward to, Mariah. You to marrying Arnie, whenever that might be – and me to a good life and career at Harpers.'

'Well, you can always live with us. Arnie likes you. He would take us both like a shot.'

Kitty smiled and then they were both laughing. 'At least that mystery is cleared up. I think you may have lost your best customer, Mariah – though his mother owns that shop he told you about and he was buying for her.'

Mariah shrugged. 'A few pounds now and then are all I need to keep the house goin', and Dad's treasures will last us a few years yet.'

'How I wish he and Larry were still with us,' Kitty said and for a moment tears were in her eyes.

'Aye, so do I,' Mariah agreed. 'But tears won't bring them back. We have to be thankful for what we have, my love.'

'Yes, we do,' Kitty agreed and crossed the room to hug her. 'I do thank God for you every day of my life…'

'Go on with you, daft girl,' Mariah said but lifted her apron to wipe her face. 'Now, while I serve our supper, tell me, what sort of a day did you have before our guest arrived?'

10

Sally chose to wear a navy dress and matching coat with a velvet collar to meet Mick that lunchtime. February's fogs and chilly weather had given way to a brighter day and in the weak March sunshine, it was milder than of late. She left the house and walked to the Underground station, pausing to buy a newspaper when she saw the tragic headlines. An underground fire at Coombs Wood Colliery, near Halesowen in the Black Country, had caused the death of eight miners. It was a terrible tragedy for an industry that had not long begun to recover from the damaging strike in 1926. Sally's heart went out to the women who had lost their husbands and the fatherless children. There was little anyone could do for them other than to raise some money.

Sighing, Sally waited for her train to arrive, boarded it and settled down to read more of her paper as she made her way into town. She had agreed to meet Mick at the Savoy Hotel at one o'clock but had two other appointments before then. One with a jeweller in Hatton Garden and another with her lawyer just off Bond Street. She was looking forward to the first appointment and being shown some new stock for Harpers but not so much to the second meeting.

Hatton Garden was always busy, the narrow streets surrounding it thronged with all kinds of people, and the cheerful sound of cockney voices calling to one another lifted Sally's spirits. She was at home here in these streets and though she'd enjoyed her visit to New York, she knew she would not wish to live there, but Ben's latest letter had told her that he was becoming more and more immersed in his life there. Sally wasn't sure what she would do if he decided he wanted them to make their home in America. She had always thought London would be their home, and although Ben had spoken of his birth country, he had never seemed to wish to return there.

She paused to gaze in the windows of a shop with rows and rows of diamond and precious stone rings. Harpers did not sell this kind of jewellery at present and she sometimes wondered if they should try more expensive items. Yet she had done very well with the silver she'd chosen in the past. Occasionally, she had bought a range of gold or gold and silver mixed; Harpers' stock was aimed at the middle class rather than the very rich and perhaps she should stick to that, she thought as she reached the workshop she had patronised for many years.

Sally rang the bell and was admitted, smiling at the familiar faces as a chair was fetched for her and tea was offered. She was a valued customer here and they were anxious to show her three new ranges they had created.

* * *

Sally was feeling pleased with herself when she left the workshop, she had placed a substantial order for some wonderful bangles and rather bold necklaces made in silver with enamelling and semi-precious stones, all within her preferred price range, Sally was feeling pleased with herself. Seeing a passing taxi for hire, she hailed it rather than return to the Underground and sank back into the comfortable back seat that smelled of leather and polish. The driver was a cheerful cockney and kept his cab immaculately, chattering away in a friendly manner so that it was a pleasure to drive with him.

Arriving at the solicitor's, Sally sighed. Ben had written instructions to his lawyers, which she had presented to them three weeks earlier, but they had procrastinated, insisting on contacting him because they wanted to make him aware of the huge step he was taking in handing over the reins to her. It was impossible to explain that she had always had more than a small input to the business. Everything of a legal nature had been signed by Ben in the past and now that was to change so that Sally could make any decisions she found necessary on her own. She hoped that they had now accepted he really intended to hand over control of Harpers to her, at least until he had finished his investigations into his aunt's store in New York.

She was shown into the very smart reception and invited to sit until Mr Bently could see her. Sally found a copy of a leading fashion magazine and flicked through its pages while she waited. The glossy pages were filled with pictures of women in elegant dresses and she saw that two pages had been devoted to women wearing smart trousers with soft silk blouses. It was still considered unseemly by many for a woman to wear trousers, but Sally had some cream ones herself; they had wide legs and draped on her much like a long skirt. She wore them occasionally, but preferred her calf-length dresses.

'Mrs Harper, please do come in...'

Sally rose and replaced the magazine on the neat pile before following the young woman into the lawyer's office. Asked whether she would take coffee, she agreed and the secretary left.

'Ah, Mrs Harper.' Mr Bently rose and came round from behind his desk to take her hand. He placed his right hand over hers and pressed it gently in a fatherly way. 'I am so sorry to have kept you waiting – and I am pleased to tell you that we have now heard from Mr Harper on the points we raised and have his permission to go ahead.'

Sally was invited to sit in the comfortable elbow chair opposite him as he retired behind his desk and sat down, shuffling some papers.

'We have drawn this up for you to sign...' He pointed to two dotted lines which required her signature.

She took the document but rather than sign immediately, she sat back and read through it.

'I do not think this is exactly what my husband and I discussed,' Sally said with a little frown. 'Ben wanted me to have complete control – and this says that if I wish to make a major change to either the property or the way it is run at present, I must apply to him.'

'The small change was suggested by us,' Mr Bently replied, careful in his choice of words now. 'The day-to-day running is all in your hands, Mrs Harper – but if you felt you needed to purchase another building, say – or sell off a part of your holdings – you would need to consult Mr Harper and we would need his written consent.'

'I am not likely to do either,' Sally replied. 'And what about this...? Where it says that if I wished to appoint someone to take my place within the business, I must first consult my husband? Also, if I wish to appoint a new manager, I must consult my husband...' There were a few other petty clauses which would tie her hands and make it almost impossible for her to make any decisions. A flash of annoyance was in her eyes as she looked at the lawyer. 'This is not what Ben and I agreed. I do not have complete control and I can't see that this is viable.' She saw his expression falter, a hint of uncertainty in his face, and knew that these suggestions had come from him. 'No, Mr Bently. I shall not sign this. You will remove these clauses restricting my freedom to make decisions and then I shall sign. I am very certain that Ben did not initiate them, because they make it impossible for me to keep the business running smoothly. So you will go back to Mr Harper and then try again.'

'But... these are very minor changes,' the lawyer protested. 'I suggested far more.' He frowned. 'I know that you have experience in some areas, Mrs Harper, but a woman does not always think as clearly as a man – and these positions of authority ought to be scrupulously examined.'

'Which I am perfectly capable of doing,' Sally said. She got to her feet and pulled on her gloves. 'I am a busy woman, Mr Bently. I suggest you change the document back to what was originally agreed and not waste my time nor my husband's. I shall return when you have something suitable ready for me.'

Sally left the office without a backward glance. She was fuming inside – how dare he think that she would try to sell off part of Harper's without Ben's knowledge! She would never dream of such a thing. His attitude from the beginning had clearly shown her that he did not consider a woman capable of running a business like Harpers.

Women did not always think as clearly as men! It was such a bigoted idea and so unfair.

* * *

Sally was so angry at the lawyer's condescending manner that she could hardly contain it as she hailed a taxi and was driven to the Savoy Hotel. She waited in the lounge, where a piano was being played softly in the background. Normally, she would have appreciated her surroundings and the elegance of the Art Deco and Art Nouveau décor, but today her pleasure was spoiled by her earlier meeting.

'Ah, there you are, Sally darlin',' Mick's voice hailed her and Sally looked up, forcing a smile. Mick hesitated and then sat down. 'Is that black look because I'm late – or is something else troubling you?'

Sally gave a rueful laugh. 'Oh, Mick. You aren't late. I was early, but I am very angry—'

'Tell me,' he said, watching her as she launched into her encounter with the pompous lawyer. Mick listened and nodded and then burst into laughter. 'I'd give a monkey to have seen his face when you walked out, Sally Harper. The man is a fool if he thinks you need to run back to Ben all the time. All these years, you've done more to make Harpers the success it is than Ben ever did.'

Sally smiled reluctantly at first and then, as his twinkling eyes continued to hold hers, she laughed. 'He did look as if all the wind had gone from his sails,' she said. 'But to claim that women do not always think as clearly as men – as if I would appoint a man as manager who did not have all the right credentials. I would check them too... Ben would more likely take a man on trust than I would.'

'Well, perhaps the lawyer thinks some women might not – again, he doesn't know you the way I do. I'd back you against any man I know, just as I would Marlene,' Mick assured her and then laughed. 'The reason I asked to meet here and not at my pub as we'd agreed, is that Marlene has closed it for a week. She says it needs redecorating right through – and who am I to question her? She's kept it running for years and it's doing better than ever.'

'I like it here, anyway,' Sally said, relaxing. She understood his change of subject and thanked him for it. 'Ben prefers the Ritz, but I like this because it has a peace and charm of its own.'

Mick smiled at her. 'Shall we see if our table is ready – or would you enjoy a drink first?'

'Oh, let's have a drink,' Sally said. 'I need to unwind.'

Mick summoned the waiter and gave his instructions. 'Champagne it is then, me darlin'.'

'I didn't tell you to be extravagant...' she scolded, but he just grinned.

'I'm thinking of setting up another restaurant,' he told her. 'I thought I might go for French cuisine this time. What is your opinion? Would a posh French restaurant take in London?'

'Are you really liquidising all your other assets?' Sally asked, looking at him curiously. He nodded. 'Why would you do that, Mick? It has puzzled me.'

'Not sure I know the answer,' Mick replied. 'It's just a gut feeling. I've sold a lot of shares – not those I hold in Harpers. I wouldn't do that to you, Sally. No, I had investments in a lot of big companies, but I decided I wanted something different – and I've no intention of returning to Ireland, so I'll be buying a house here. Andrea's son is training to be an Army officer and won't be around much – and he will come to me when he feels like it.'

'Is he difficult?' Sally asked, hearing something in his voice. 'I know at times Andrea found him so.'

'The lad is fine with me, always has been – but he wants to be an officer like his father and so I agreed that he should join the cadets. Andrea was reluctant at first, but I persuaded her that she should let him do as he wished.'

'Yes, I think that is wise,' Sally agreed. 'Jenny wants to learn the piano. She sings well and I think she has some idea of being a performer on the stage when she is older. Ben won't hear of it, of course, but – well, I don't know. I've told her she can have her lessons.'

'She is a pretty girl. Andrea remarked on it when we saw you the other Christmas. If she has talent, too, she might do well in such a profession. What of your boy Peter?'

Sally's smile lit her face. 'Peter is a darling – everything any mother could wish for. His manners are so good and he is so caring – of me and his sister. He thinks he would like to be a pilot at the moment, but that changes as often as the wind. It was a train driver for ages, but then we took an internal flight in America and he loved it – so for now he wants to fly a plane himself.'

'He sounds like a good lad,' Mick said, smiling as he saw that her ill mood had fallen away. 'So, what are your plans for Harpers when you get your hands on it, Sally?'

She laughed. 'Who says I have any?'

'If I know you, there are a hundred things buzzing in that beautiful head of yours.' He looked at her consideringly. 'Your hair is longer. It suits you.'

'I had it styled in New York – Thelma Todd – the film actress's style, so they told me. I quite like it.' She touched the smooth pageboy haircut and then smiled. 'I do have a few small changes in mind – but nothing major... yet.'

'Ah,' Mick said and then the waiter arrived with their champagne and the cork was popped. He lifted his glass to her. 'To you, Sally. To Harpers – and the future, whatever it brings. May it all be good.'

'Thank you, my dearest friend,' Sally said and sipped her champagne, laughing as the bubbles tickled her nose. 'I didn't expect this today, but it is a lovely thing to do, Mick. I feel so much better.'

'Champagne will do that,' Mick said. 'So, tell me, why are there still shadows in your eyes?'

Sally hesitated, then, 'Ben... I'm worried about him, Mick. Perhaps it is just me, but I feel he has changed. I am not sure why. Whether it is excitement at having a large share of the American store or something else...' A little shiver went down her spine. 'I've always felt that our marriage was solid. We've had ups and downs, like everyone else, but they were never big quarrels – until the last one. I think he is still angry with me. His letters since then have just been business.' She gave a little gulp of distress. 'I fear our marriage might crack under the strain of being apart for months on end.'

'Ben wouldn't be such a fool. He'd never risk losing you, Sally. He adores you.'

'Yes, perhaps.' Sally lowered her eyes. 'It was good for a long time, but even before we left for New York there was a change... I can't explain, and I wouldn't tell anyone else.'

'You know I shan't speak a word of what you tell me,' Mick said and reached across to squeeze her hand. 'I'm sure you're wrong, Sally. I dare say he's just worried about something and doesn't want to upset you.'

'Yes, perhaps you are right,' Sally agreed. 'Let's take our drinks and go through now, shall we?'

'Yes, I'm ready.' Mick smiled at her. 'I don't think Ben is stupid enough to have an affair, Sally. Whatever is up with the man, I'd swear he'll change the instant he's home.'

'You're a good friend,' Sally said, picking up her bag. Mick had summoned the waiter to take their champagne into the Grill Room. 'At least I know I can always rely on you.'

* * *

After lunch, Sally parted with Mick with promises of meeting soon. 'Ben says he will be home in about a month. You must come to dinner with us,' she said and there was more in her eyes than just a casual invitation; she was thinking she might need his help in making Ben see how much they might lose if he was set on living in New York.

Mick kissed her cheek and gave her hand a gentle squeeze. 'I'd love to,' he replied easily. 'It will be interesting to hear what Ben has to say about the vibes in America – we all follow what they do, so if business is booming it helps investment here and can also lead to a downturn if things go badly there.'

Sally was thoughtful as she took yet another taxi to Harpers. Mick had something going on in his head. He wasn't ready to talk about it, but she knew him to be a wise businessman, and if he gave her advice, she would take it.

She took the lift up to her office and found both Ruby and Kitty hard at work.

Kitty looked up and smiled at her entrance. 'I finished that report on the stock levels you wanted,' she said. 'I'm not sure what made you ask, but there is a definite trend. The more expensive items are hanging on the rails – or shelves – but the cheaper ranges are still selling through.'

'That is what I suspected,' Sally said with a thoughtful nod. 'We must watch and see if the trend continues, Kitty. I don't think we need to change our ordering too much for the moment – though I believe I'll cut down on some of those very expensive evening gowns. They aren't moving much right now.'

'No, and some of them are gorgeous,' Kitty said. 'I would love to own just one of the Miss Diane range, but they are too costly for most young women.'

'It is such a shame, because last year we did well with them,' Sally replied. 'I shall have to speak to Miss Susie and ask her if they are going to produce a less expensive range this year. We have to move with the times.'

'I read somewhere that the economy is slowing down,' Kitty said, looking concerned. 'I don't really understand all that stuff, but do you think it means we are in for hard times?'

'We've been through a period of unprecedented change and prosperity,' Sally told her. 'The Roaring Twenties, the newspaper called it. It couldn't go on forever, Kitty. I think we have good times and not so good, but I can't see that we're in for a depression – at least I do hope not. As a nation, we struggled to get through the war and it all seemed so wonderful afterwards.' Sally shook her head. 'No, I refuse to believe it will all come tumbling down just like that. We shall simply follow the trends here at Harpers. I will read these lists and make my decision, but I believe that a slight adjustment is all that is needed for now.'

She thanked Kitty for all her hard work, said goodbye, smiled and had a few words with Ruby, and then went home, choosing the Underground this time. Yet as she settled back to relax on her journey, a little nerve flicked at Sally's temple. Mick had begun to liquidise most of his assets and he was one of the most astute businessmen she had met. Most of them were still investing in shares, still spending money and seemed confident that the boom would continue.

Sally wished that Ben was home, mainly because she and the children needed him, but also so that she could discuss her gut feelings with him. As yet, she knew Harpers was still doing well enough. The profits had been slightly down the previous year, but nothing to worry about. They were still in profit. The past few years, since the war ended, had been good ones and Ben had invested substantial amounts in various shares. She wondered if she ought to suggest he sell them, liquidise his outside assets, in case Harpers needed support in the coming years.

It would be foolish to change her normal pattern of buying too much, though she would cut back on the very extravagant eveningwear she stocked. However, if she could build up a sum of money in the bank that would tide them over if trade became very sluggish. Sally wasn't sure what cash reserves Ben had personally, because she had never enquired. She had a small nest egg of her own and there was always a float of several thousand pounds in the bank for their stock, but any surplus had been handled by Ben. Harpers belonged to him, even though he'd gifted Sally some shares. Her concern was the running of things day-to-day and she had an income from her shares plus a wage and whatever Ben gave her. He was always generous, so she had never needed to ask for anything.

Surely there was no need for caution? Yet the tingling continued until she reached home to be greeted by her children with hugs and a noisy clamouring as they told her about what they'd been up to at school. For the next hour or so, Sally's thoughts were only for her children. They had a delicious high tea together of home-cooked fish and chips, prepared by Mrs Hills, followed by fresh fruit salad and cream.

Sally played board games with them for a while afterwards, checked that they had both done their homework and then tucked them up in bed. Jenny objected to being seen into bed and kissed goodnight, saying she was too grown up to need a bedtime story, but Peter hugged her and asked her to read him stories of King Arthur and his knights.

Sally enjoyed the bedtime ritual and read him the tale of the Green Knight, before leaving him to snuggle up and go to sleep. Mrs Hills had gone when she went downstairs. She was taking a friend of hers to the cinema and had left as soon as supper was served.

The house felt big and lonely to Sally as she went into the kitchen and washed the dishes. Mrs Hills had promised to do them on her return, but Sally welcomed the practical task. When she retired to her sitting room and sat down, she felt a return of her loneliness. During the war, she'd become accustomed to Ben's absence, but since then they had shared their evenings, either with talk of the business or simply enjoying music together. They went out two or three evenings a week, to join friends or visit the theatre, and enjoyed a pleasant social life, entertaining most weeks. Sally would still have friends to tea or dinner, but it wasn't the same.

If Ben decided to stay in New York, Sally knew she would have a decision to make. Either she must give up her life here and join him, or accept many more nights like this when she felt alone.

'Nonsense!' Sally gave herself a little shake. She was being silly. Ben wouldn't tear their marriage apart. He wouldn't risk losing her. She just wished that his aunt hadn't asked him to look into her business and, if she was honest, Sally would have preferred it if his aunt's shares had not been left to Ben. Yes, they were worth a great deal of money – but how could Ben live here and keep a firm grip on the store over there? Sally wasn't sure it was possible. It would mean his staying there for long periods or making the decision to live there – and that would turn her world upside down. Had already done so.

Sally reached for the lists Kitty had prepared for her. She would go through them thoroughly, make the difficult decisions to retrench a little on the more expensive items. Just for a while. It might be a blip and things would start moving again.

11

It was now nearly the end of March and the nights were still chilly. Ruby had travelled home by bus and as she walked the last few yards home, she shivered, pulling her collar up around her neck. She would be glad when it was summer.

Entering the house, she heard voices in the kitchen and caught the sound of a man's voice. Captain Saunders was back! She had an irrational feeling of pleasure and was smiling as she went into the kitchen, but her landlady's words as she entered banished her smile.

'Well, I wish you'd told me this a few weeks ago. I might have let my room by now, Captain Saunders.'

'I wasn't sure what I would do,' he replied calmly. 'I shall of course give you a month's notice and pay for my room until the end of that period.'

'Come into some money, have you?' Mrs Flowers sniffed, glaring at Ruby. 'He's leaving.'

Captain Saunders glanced at Ruby and smiled, then turned back to his landlady, the smile gone. 'As a matter of fact, I shall shortly inherit my father's estate. He is unwell and has begged me to return home and, in the circumstances, I felt I ought – not that it is your concern, Mrs Flowers.'

'Like that is it?' Mrs Flowers glowered at him.

'If you mean I am returning *because* I shall inherit the estate, you far mistake the matter, madam,' he said, his eyes flinty. 'I stayed away because I did not wish to distress my family by—' Captain Saunders shook his head. 'No, I shall not explain myself to you.' He took some money out and placed it on the table. 'I shall collect my things and return your key.'

Nodding his head, he left the kitchen. Ruby hesitated and then ran after him. 'Captain Saunders—'

He stopped, turned, and looked at her, an oddly wistful look on his face.

'I just wanted to say… I am sorry I shan't see you again, but I am glad you are going home to your family, sir.'

'Ruby, my comforter,' he said and took two steps towards her and then held out his hands. She hesitated before placing hers in his. He lifted first one and then the other to kiss them. 'Your kindness gave me the strength to do it. I can never thank you enough, for without you I do not believe I should have found the courage to visit my home again. I shall never forget you, Miss Ruby.'

'Nor I you,' Ruby said, fighting the urge to cry. She was happy for him, but she knew she had hoped he would return and they might be friends, or perhaps more. Oh yes, if she was honest she wanted much more.

'If I were younger, and things were different,' he sighed, looking regretful. 'Then I might have dared to dream, but it cannot be. Please take good care of yourself, Miss Ruby, and have a wonderful life.'

Ruby's throat was tight with emotion, her heart aching. He was not so very much older than her and she would not have minded his moods. She longed to tell him so but knew she could not. He was a gentleman of means and she was a girl from the orphanage.

'I shall miss you,' she managed to say, the lump in her throat making it hard to find the words. 'I wish you a good life, too, sir, and...' Taking her courage in her hands, 'If you visit London and have time, I work at Harpers in Oxford Street and... and I would love to see you...'

He hesitated for a moment, seeming torn. 'Thank you, my dear. Perhaps we may meet again, though not for many months. My father has a slow progressive illness and I must devote myself to him.'

'Yes, of course you must.' Ruby gulped and smiled, unaware that her feelings were in her face. 'I must not delay you, sir. It was lovely to know you.' Her throat was tight and she could barely hold back the tears.

'The pleasure was mine, Miss Ruby,' he said and then turned and walked slowly up the stairs. She watched him all the way to the top, but he did not turn his head, so she reluctantly went back to the kitchen.

'Well!' Mrs Flowers said looking indignant. 'Why you want to run after the likes of him, I don't know. A gentleman like that wouldn't look at a girl like you – not if he wasn't weak up here.' She tapped the side of her head.

Anger flared in Ruby. She wanted to refute it, to tell Mrs Flowers that he was a brave man who had suffered when in the service of his country, but she held her tongue. Captain Saunders would soon be beyond the spite of the woman's tongue, but Ruby had to go on living in her house, so she said nothing as Mrs Flowers banged a plate of sausages with onion mash in front of her on the kitchen table. There was no sign of the money he'd paid in lieu of notice, which Mrs Flowers had been quick enough to pocket.

Ruby ate her meal in silence, though it was hard to swallow it. She was hungry and she paid for an evening meal so she forced it down. The food itself was always tasty, which was the main reason she stayed.

When she had finished, she pushed her plate away. 'If you will excuse me, Mrs Flowers, I must wash my hair,' she said and left the kitchen.

'Make sure you tidy up my bathroom when you've done,' Mrs Flowers called after her.

Ruby let the words flow over her head. She went to her room, sat on the bed and let the tears flow. It was silly to cry over something that could never have been more than a passing friendship and after a while, she told herself not to be silly. After all, she didn't know him well – but he'd always been pleasant, like when he'd told her to use the bathroom first so she wasn't late for work.

She went to the bathroom, filled the bath and soaked in it until the water was chilly. Her wet hair wrapped in a towel, she rinsed the bath down and then went to her own room. As she went in, she caught the smell of something – Captain Saunders' cologne, she thought, and then she saw a little box on her bed. She went to open it and found a pretty little pendant that she thought might be real pearls with a small diamond at the heart, its chain fine and shining gold. There was a note where the box had been. Swooping on the small piece of paper, she scanned the words.

This once belonged to my mother. The only other woman I have loved. I wanted you to have it, my dearest Ruby.

Ruby dropped the box and the note on her bed and rushed along the hall to his room, but the door was open and she realised he had gone while she was bathing.

Returning to her room, Ruby's spirits were low. She had never loved anyone, but she thought that the tiny feelings that had begun to grow in her heart towards Captain Saunders might have been love. It hurt that she might never see him again. From his note, it seemed that he'd cared for her too.

Surely, if he did, he would come back and find her, when he was no longer tied to his father's sickbed. Despite all the reasons why it was foolish to hope – the age difference, the gap between the classes, and all the other things, like his nightmares – Ruby felt a flicker of hope.

She saw pictures of him bringing her flowers and telling her he'd always loved her from the first moment they'd met on the stairs, or when their hands had touched on the bathroom door handle… how he'd held back because he had those bad memories that made him act violently and…

Ruby shook her head. She was daydreaming again. Matron had punished her for that when she was a small child, caning her hand until she'd cried. She really must accept that her life wasn't likely to change unless she made it, and she was lucky to have her job at Harpers.

Captain Saunders had left her a farewell gift, because she'd helped him, nothing more, and she would only store up grief for herself if she let him dominate her thoughts.

* * *

Mrs Flowers went out of her way to be friendly the next morning. 'I'm going to advertise for a lady this time,' she told her. 'A nice young woman like you, Ruby dear. Someone your age who will be a friend to you – with proper manners like yours.'

'That would be lovely, Mrs Flowers,' Ruby replied. Clearly, her landlady was feeling chastened, perhaps wondering how easy it would be to fill her rooms if Ruby were to leave.

'I don't suppose you know anyone suitable requiring a room?' Mrs Flowers asked. 'If she works at Harpers, she will be a decent young woman like yourself.'

'I will ask around,' Ruby agreed and finished her breakfast. Two nicely poached eggs on toast with a pot of tea.

Ruby was thoughtful as she caught the bus to Oxford Street. She would pop down to the other floors when she had her lunch break and see if anyone knew of a young woman needing a room.

* * *

The hat and bag department were busy when Ruby entered. She loved this department and longed to try on some of the gorgeous hats, but they were too expensive for her, and although the supervisor, Miss Shirley Smith, was pleasant to speak to, she might frown on Ruby trying on hats she could not afford.

She waited until the girl at the scarves and gloves counter was free and then asked her if she knew of anyone who needed a room, but the girl shook her head. A few minutes later, Ruby asked the girl at the bag counter, and then the older woman at the hat counter. All of them said they were settled but would ask around for her. As she was about to leave, Miss Smith came from behind the jewellery counters and called to her.

'Ruby,' she said and Ruby turned to her. 'Did I hear you say there was a room at your lodging house?'

'Yes, Miss Smith,' Ruby said. 'A gentleman was occupying it, but Mrs Flowers would like a lady with good references to take it next time. I said I would ask for her.'

'Is it a nice room? And what is her cooking like?' Miss Smith asked, clearly interested.

'It is a nice clean house and I enjoy her cooking. She can be a little sharp and she wants her rent on time, but it is the best I've found.'

'Then I will come back with you this evening and speak to her,' Miss Smith told her with a smile. 'If you don't mind, Miss Rush?'

'No, of course not,' Ruby replied and felt pleased. Miss Smith would be an easy person to meet in the hall in the mornings.

'Oh, good, that is so nice. Thank you for giving us the chance, Miss Rush.'

Ruby nodded and left the department. She walked towards the lifts. There was just time for her to have a coffee and a bun before she returned to walk. As she went to enter the lifts, a man came out and they nearly bumped into one another. Ruby stepped to one side and he did the same, then they looked at each other and laughed.

'I think we have met before,' he said and Ruby nodded, remembering his accent as much as his face.

'You caught the thief who stole my purse...' She smiled. 'You were going to buy a present for your fiancée, I recall.' To her surprise, the smile left his eyes. 'I'm sorry. I ought not to have said...'

'Not your fault, she turned me down,' he said, his frown clearing. 'It seems she had her eye on someone richer. I have a good job, but he owns his business and a lot more besides...' There was a note of bitterness in his voice.

'And you bought her lots of nice things...' Ruby blushed as he looked at her. 'I saw you leaving with several of our bags.'

He shrugged. 'I gave them to my mother and sister. Oh, well, live and learn.'

'I am sorry all the same...' Ruby faltered as he looked at her. His eyes dwelled on her face for a moment.

'Did you get the shoes you wanted?' he asked.

'I shall when I get paid this week,' Ruby told him. 'I have been saving for ages. They are smart black suede courts and I do so love them.'

Her enthusiasm brought a smile to his face, the shadows gone. 'I don't suppose you'd like to wear them to come to tea at my house on Sunday? My mother is giving a tea party and she is nagging me to bring a young lady... No strings attached, of course.' He laughed. 'Of course you've only met me once. You might remember my name is Rupert Marsh. I work in a publishing house. I am an editor – and my uncle's dogsbody. I get to do all the jobs no one else wants, like telling hopeful authors their books are rubbish.' He laughed as Ruby smiled. 'And your name?'

'Miss Ruby Rush – and I work in the office here.' She hesitated, then, 'Yes, I should like to come – if your mother would find me acceptable, Mr Marsh.'

'Whyever wouldn't she?' he asked. 'Shall I come to your home or...?'

'Could we meet outside Harpers?' she asked. 'My landlady is so... well, nosy.'

He laughed again. 'My mother, too, but I should be so happy to meet you here, Miss Rush – and perhaps you would allow me to call you Ruby when you meet my family.'

Ruby blushed and nodded, told him she must return to work and they parted. In the lift on the way up to her office, she wondered at herself for agreeing to meet a man she didn't know. She was grateful for his help in returning her purse to her, and going to tea with his mother was respectable – even the matron at the orphanage would have agreed to that, she thought. Besides, he'd looked so hurt when he'd told her that the girl he loved had preferred a richer man.

Mr Marsh wasn't Captain Saunders, and though he seemed nice, Ruby had no particular feelings for him, but it was a way to make friends. He had a sister and perhaps she would ask Ruby to be her friend. She did feel so lonely at times, especially in the evenings, when she had nothing to do but sit in her room on her own.

12

Kitty was tired as she made her way home that evening. She had been working hard in the office and then she'd been asked to help an elderly customer in the dress department. She'd recognised the customer at once because, possibly two years or so earlier, she had served her with clothes for her two granddaughters when they were going on a trip overseas and had secured a large order for Harpers. This time, Lady Rowbottom required a new spring and summer wardrobe for herself, which required a lot of effort on Kitty's part.

'I shall need three morning gowns, three afternoon gowns and two evening gowns, perhaps six hats, gloves, shoes, scarves – you know what I need, young woman.' Her manner was as autocratic as ever and she was difficult to please.

Kitty had spent two hours with her, matching hats and shoes to the various dresses she chose. The bill came to a sizeable amount when she'd finally found garments to her liking. Lady Rowbottom then demanded a discount. Kitty now had the authority to offer a 10 per cent discount, which seemed to please her customer and she'd agreed to purchase the outfits.

'You may have them delivered to my address – and send me the account, as usual.'

'Yes, my lady,' Kitty had replied. 'I will have them boxed and delivered by tomorrow afternoon.'

Lady Rowbottom had inclined her head and left. Kitty then asked the various departments to box up the chosen goods and they were entered on the list for delivery the next day.

She'd returned to her office to discover that Mr Stockbridge had been to see her. 'He asked if you would go to his office,' Ruby had told her and Kitty acquiesced.

Kitty had then spent almost an hour with Mr Stockbridge discussing a problem that he had discovered in accounts. 'We have now at least twenty unpaid accounts,' he'd told her. 'I am not sure whether we should revise our policy. Some of the unpaid accounts are customers who have always settled immediately in the past.'

'Oh dear, that is unfortunate,' Kitty had said. 'I have just allowed one of our regular customers to purchase six hundred pounds worth of expensive clothes, hats and shoes. She asked for them to be delivered and to pay by account as normal.'

'May I enquire the name of the customer?'

'Lady Rowbottom,' Kitty had replied and he'd checked a list.

'She has always paid on time, perhaps a few days over but no more.'

'Then, should I allow the delivery to go ahead?' Kitty had asked.

She'd been given the go-ahead, but asked to copy his list and deliver it to all departments. The supervisors would be instructed not to offer accounts and to check the list before allowing goods to be taken away or delivered. If the customer had still not paid, credit would be refused.

Kitty had been thoughtful as she'd taken the list and

returned to the office. To her knowledge there had never been a black list at Harpers before. It might be difficult for the supervisors to refuse credit when customers had always been granted it previously and she'd been unsure whether it was the right approach. She'd thought that perhaps she would wait until Mrs Harper came in and ask her for advice before distributing the list to all departments. The amounts outstanding were not huge but could obviously prove a problem if allowed to grow. Mr Stockbridge had seen it and his reaction was a fair one, but Kitty still had felt that it might not be what Mrs Harper would like and so she'd asked Ruby to type the lists but had decided she would wait before handing them out.

* * *

As Kitty went into her home, she heard voices: Mariah's, and another – a man's voice. Something prickled at the nape of her neck and she paused before entering. A man was sitting at the table, drinking a cup of tea. Kitty frowned as she saw it was the lawyer who had visited them before.

'Good evening, Mr Harvey,' she said as she took off her coat and hung it up on a hook behind the door. 'I could do with a cup of tea, Mariah. It has been a busy day.'

'You look tired, my love,' Mariah said, then, uncertainly, 'I would have sent him packing, Kitty, but I think you should at least listen to Mr Harvey.'

'Very well, if you say so.' Kitty sat down at the table and sipped her tea. 'I haven't changed my mind and I don't want my uncle's money.'

'He understands that,' Mr Harvey said. 'He has made other arrangements but...' He paused, then with a sigh, 'I am afraid my news may distress you, but you see my client is very ill and does not expect to live long. He feels guilty for not having known of his brother's death or your existence and he wants to see you so that he can die in peace.'

Kitty stared at him, a chill again at her nape. 'How do I know you are telling me the truth?' she asked.

'You have to trust me,' he said, 'and I know that is difficult – but if you would visit him, a car could be sent for both you and Miss Norton. You would both be welcome. Your uncle says that Sunday would be convenient, should you agree.'

'Mariah, what do you think? Would you come with me?'

'You know I will,' Mariah replied. 'I don't think Mr Harvey is trying to trap you – he isn't like that woman or Mr Miller.'

'I was going to help with preparing for the pageant on Sunday morning, but I suppose we could go in the afternoon…' Kitty sighed, wishing that she need not agree.

'I think if your uncle is dying you should see him,' Mariah said. 'If the poor man needs forgiveness before he can rest easily—'

'Very well…' Kitty gave in. 'You can send the car for two thirty, sir. Is it far?'

'Your uncle is staying at the Savoy Hotel for a few days,' Mr Harvey replied. 'He has been to see a consultant in Harley Street – and he is arranging to be looked after by a special nurse, because he has no family to care for him.'

'I am sorry he is ill,' Kitty said. 'I was very angry that he paid you to spy on me but…' She shook her head. 'I can forgive. I was given a decent home and treated fairly while Mr Wilson lived. It was only after—' She broke off, then laughed. 'I do not believe I even know my uncle's name.'

'He is Sir Peter Hamilton.'

Kitty gasped. 'How can that be? My father was an ordinary dock worker – how can I possibly be related to a baronet?'

Mr Harvey smiled. 'Your uncle was given the baronetcy for services to the crown. He is a very brave man, Miss Wilson – and your father came from a decent family. I don't know what you've been told...'

'I know nothing of my birth parents,' Kitty said.

'It is quite a story,' Mr Harvey said. 'It ought really to be your uncle's place to tell you, but I think it would explain a lot.' He hesitated and then went on, 'Your father was meant to go into your grandfather's business. Your uncle went into the diplomatic service...' Mr Harvey took a deep breath. 'Your grandfather was an honest but proud man. When your father fell in love with a woman he considered of low breeding, he refused his consent to the marriage and ordered your father never to see her again. You were already on the way, which shocked and angered your grandfather, and so your father defied him and married her. He was banished from his family and resorted to working on the docks when he could not find other work.'

Kitty stared at him in shock. 'Is that why no one ever enquired about what had happened to me?'

'Your grandfather had turned his face from the son he believed had disgraced his name – but perhaps he did not know whether you had survived or where your parents had gone. Your uncle was not aware that he had a niece until he hired my firm to search for his brother.'

'I see.' The tears trickled down Kitty's face then and she could not stop them. 'I have wondered and— My poor mother.'

'I believe they struggled to support themselves until your father found work. He was to have been the manager of a fine factory, but he had never had to apply for work. He discovered that it was hard to find the kind of work he'd been trained for without references – and so he turned to manual labour.'

Mariah handed Kitty a large white handkerchief and she

wiped the salty ears from her cheeks. 'It must have been so hard for him – and then to die in an accident in a place where he ought never to have been.'

'I imagine it was his ignorance of his surroundings that may have led to his death,' Mr Harvey said. 'I could not discover much about the accident – too many years had passed and only a few recalled it. It was pure chance that someone told me about you.'

Kitty felt as if her head was in a whirl. To discover so much about herself, the truth of her existence, and the double tragedy it had caused. Her mother had died giving birth to her on the day her father was killed in an accident on the docks, leading to her adoption by Mr Wilson. Since her mother was already carrying her when they eloped, they could only have had a few months of married life before tragedy struck.

'Yes, I do understand now,' she said. 'I would still have been happier had my uncle sought me out himself rather than have you spy on me – but I will see him on Sunday.'

* * *

'Well,' Mariah said after Mr Harvey had thanked them and taken his leave. 'Fancy that, Kitty. Your uncle a baronet and your grandfather a wealthy man. It is a pity that he was too proud to look for his son and forgive him.'

'It can't matter now,' Kitty replied, stretching her shoulders tiredly as Mariah took their supper from the oven where it had been kept warm. 'In a way, I am glad he didn't – because I might never have known Larry or you.'

'That's true,' Mariah said. 'Yet you would have had a different life – been brought up as a young lady, I dare say.'

Kitty laughed. 'I don't think that would have suited me,

Mariah. I enjoy going to work and I like my life – now that I have you.'

Mariah smiled but looked thoughtful. 'Quality will out,' she said, but Kitty's thoughts were miles away.

'My poor mother...' she said softly, half to herself. 'I wonder how she felt about it all, the fact that she had caused the man she loved to leave his home and live in poverty with her. I hope they were content despite the hardship they endured.' Kitty was thoughtful for a moment. 'I have always wondered where she is buried...'

'Mr Harvey might be able to discover it if you ask him.'

Kitty looked at her. 'I should like to visit and lay flowers on her grave,' she said. 'I don't think she had anyone to care for her except my father. She must have been remorseful...'

'Why do you think that?' Mariah asked. 'She must have loved your father and he her.'

'Yes, but she had ruined his life, torn him from his home and family.'

'It was a long time ago,' Mariah comforted. 'It might be best to think of them as happy to be together, no matter what.'

'Yes, perhaps you are right,' Kitty said. 'I shall ask Mr Harvey if he could trace where she is buried, though.'

'As you wish, my love. Now, eat your supper.'

Kitty smiled at her and did as she was bid. Mariah had made a delicious steak and kidney pudding with mashed potatoes, carrots, and onions. It was warming and filling and Kitty was soon telling her friend about her day at work, forgetting for the moment the hurt Mr Harvey's revelations had caused her.

13

Ruby dressed in her smartest dress and jacket to meet her new friend. She was nervous as she caught the bus to Oxford Street, wondering if he would be there. Perhaps he had regretted the impulse to ask her. Several times she'd almost decided not to go, because, after all, she knew nothing about him, but he had saved her purse and so she thought must be trustworthy, and so she had come.

She got off the bus and walked towards the prestigious store, pausing to look in at the windows, which were a riot of colour this week. Mr Marco, Harpers' clever window dresser, had set a scene that resembled a harlequin and others dancing as a piper played. The scene was painted on a backdrop and the merchandise displayed ranged from a pair of silver dancing shoes to the most beautiful dress Ruby had ever seen – all silver spangles that somehow picked up all the other colours and radiated them across the whole display. She was so engrossed in all the detail that when a hand touched her shoulder, she jumped and looked round.

Mr Rupert Marsh was standing there wearing a smart suit

and a white shirt with a starched collar and a grey tie. He smiled at her and Ruby's nerves stopped fluttering, because he looked nervous, too.

'I've been telling myself you wouldn't come,' he said. 'You must think me very forward, Miss Rush, but I don't normally ask out girls I've never met – except that we did meet when I caught that thief and I thought— But I'm talking too much. Thank you for coming.'

'I wasn't sure if I ought, for all the same reasons,' she told him and laughed. 'We haven't been introduced properly but...' Ruby gave a nervous giggle. 'If everyone waited to be introduced, how would we ever make friends? I don't have a family...'

'No family?' He had turned and offered her his arm as they began to stroll down Oxford Street.

'I was brought up in an orphanage in London until I was sixteen,' Ruby told him. 'Then I had to find work and support myself. I never knew my parents...'

'That is rotten for you,' Rupert said. He gave her arm a gentle squeeze. 'I have a mother, father, sister, and several uncles and aunts.' He made a sound of depreciation that she couldn't quite understand. 'Rather too much family at times. They take too much interest in my affairs – or lack of them. My family want me to marry and settle down. They think that I am too frivolous and keep bad company.'

'Do you?' Ruby asked and he wrinkled his brow.

'Occasionally, I suppose, but nothing that a young man isn't entitled to experience. I enjoy going to nightclubs and I like to gamble, but I've been lucky so far – lucky in cards, unlucky in love. Isn't that what they say?'

'I don't know,' Ruby admitted. 'I've never been to a nightclub. I've never been anywhere much. I just go to work in the morning and back to my lodgings at night. I suppose that is why I said yes to meeting you. I'd like to make some friends...'

'Well, you will meet people at my mother's house,' Rupert told her. 'She is a collector of people and their stories. Other people collect stamps or precious china, but Mother collects people. There will be all sorts there this afternoon, maybe an actress, an artist or a circus performer. You just never know who she will have met. She gets talking to the oddest folk and then asks them to tea.'

Ruby laughed, because that sounded lovely to her. 'Much the same as you did me,' she suggested and he shook his head.

'No, because I could see you were a respectable girl. You work in Harpers and no one could look at you and accuse you of being decadent.'

'Just dull,' Ruby replied and he shouted with laughter. She looked at him curiously. 'You have a slight accent. Are your family English?'

'Oh yes. I do have a French grandmother and I spent a lot of time with her as a boy, because I needed a warmer climate. I was quite poorly as a child. *Grandmére* looked after me, but, as I grew up, I acquired a taste for the good life along with my accent; she held many gay evenings at her home, which was a beautiful chateau. *Grandmére's* second husband was a wealthy man, you see, whereas my grandfather was a man of modest means.'

'I'm afraid I must seem very ordinary after all the clever and sophisticated ladies you've met.' Ruby looked at him curiously.

'Not at all,' he said. 'I think my family might like it if you were. They believe I've been led astray. In short, my mother was delighted when Janine turned me down.'

'Janine? Is that the name of the girl you asked to marry you?'

Rupert nodded. 'Yes, except that she isn't a girl. Janine is... well, she is a divorcee and often in the social columns for being seen leaving a famous nightclub with some millionaire. My mother was terrified that she would say yes, but of course I ought to have known better. I don't have a house in Monte Carlo or a yacht.'

'If she loved you, that wouldn't matter,' Ruby told him. 'If she didn't, you would have been unhappy married to her.'

'You sound just like my mother,' he said, amused. 'I know you are both right, but she was so beautiful and... alluring is probably the word I should use. I was bewitched by her. At least that is what my dearest Mama thinks.'

'Was she very sophisticated and elegant?' Ruby asked and sighed when he nodded. 'Like some of the customers who ask to see Kitty... She helps them to put their outfits together. Kitty says that they are very smart and witty, but when it comes to parting with their money, they are often very careful.'

'That's because they live as if they are rich, but they aren't,' Rupert said with a hollow laugh. 'It's why my mother feared for me – because I was being drawn into a circle I could not afford. My friends spend their lives flitting between all the most expensive hotels in the world – Paris, Milan, Madrid, New York... Switzerland and on each other's yachts. When you only have good looks as currency, you can soon find yourself deep in debt, just from trying to hang on to their coat-tails...'

'Did you?' Kitty blushed as his gaze narrowed. 'Oh, I shouldn't have asked. I'm sorry.'

'The answer is yes. I was lucky and my uncle bailed me out. I had to promise to give up the life and behave properly...' Rupert looked down at her as she met his gaze, her eyes anxious. 'Yes, that's why I asked you, Ruby. You are a sweet, normal girl and I want them to think you're my girlfriend.'

* * *

That night, as Ruby lay in bed, sleep evading her, a smile on her lips, she wondered at the world she now found herself in. After Rupert's revelation, she knew many girls would have turned and walked away, but she hadn't. They'd walked to the bus stop and Rupert had paid their fares. His mother's house was in a beautiful part of south London, old and slightly shabby, the paint peeling on the door and window frames, but inside it was like a fairyland to a girl who had never known a real home.

The furniture was old, perhaps antique, but its patina was dull and worn with years of merely being dusted and not polished to within an inch of its life like that in Mrs Flowers' house. The old silver bowl on the hutch in the hall was beautiful but dull and filled with odds and ends; the large porcelain vase was crammed with all kinds of walking sticks, some with handles of gold or silver. Everywhere you looked, there were pictures, ornaments, small tables crammed with things; silver cigarette boxes placed side by side with abandoned gloves, and a long hatpin, as if someone had taken it out and forgotten it. Cabinets in the huge living room were filled with objects that might have been precious, though amongst them were cheap fairings and seaside trinkets. The sofas were deep and comfortable but worn, the carpets threadbare in places, but on the walls hung wonderful paintings and huge mirrors in gilt frames.

Rupert had given her a rueful look. 'Weird, I know, but Mother is like that – she collects things as easily as people.'

Mrs Marsh – or Flora, as she begged Ruby to call her – had been dressed in something long and flowing. Her clothes paid no heed to fashion but looked to be made of silk and flattered her less than svelte figure. Her hair was long but waved naturally, framing a pretty face wreathed in smiles. As soon as she saw Ruby, she came to her, hands outstretched. 'My dearest girl,' she'd gushed. 'I have positively longed to meet you since Rupert told me you had met by chance. I knew at once that it was Fate. You have been sent to save my poor boy from himself.' She embraced Ruby warmly. 'He is a good, kind boy, you know, but he was led astray. Now I am sure all will be well again.'

Taking Ruby by the hand, she'd led her into the garden room at the back of the house, where a host of people were gathered, drinking tea or wine, and partaking of tiny sandwiches and fruit tartlets. Flora had introduced her to aunts, uncles, Rupert's sister, Marianne, who looked very like her mother but wore a calf-length cardigan suit that was probably a copy of a Chanel original, then so many other people that Ruby knew she would never remember their names. There was Nicholas Grant, an artist, who eyed Ruby with interest but found her too dull to be useful in his work and thereafter ignored her; also an assortment of theatrical folk, a politician, a doctor of science, a historian, and someone who called himself a farmer but who was in fact the owner of a large country estate.

Ruby might have thought herself lost amongst so varied a company, but Rupert's Uncle Matthew was a kindly soul and took her under his wing so that when her hostess drifted off to greet another guest she was not abandoned.

Marianne had brought her a dish of sweet cakes and some tea and told her how much she enjoyed shopping at Harpers.

'I love the clothes,' she had said to Ruby as she nibbled a tiny sandwich, 'but I can't afford some of the evening gowns. They are gorgeous, but my allowance would be swallowed by one gown.'

'Yes, the ones by Miss Diane gowns are very expensive,' Ruby had replied with a sigh. 'I would love to just try one on, but I dare not in case I spoil it.'

'I have tried them, but I fear I cannot buy one – at least until

I marry a rich man...' She had tinkled with laughter and her uncle shook his head at her.

'Marianne likes to tease,' he'd said. 'She is courting a man – he is in the Army and he certainly could not give her that sort of dress. I have offered to buy her one she really likes, but she says no.'

'Dearest Uncle Matthew, I would marry you instantly if you were not my uncle, but yes, I am only teasing. And you have already done more than enough for us...' She had glanced at Rupert, who was talking to the politician, and then at Ruby. 'I dare say my brother told you that he ran into debt through unwise spending – and Uncle Matthew paid it for him.'

'He told me a little of it,' Ruby had said cautiously. 'It is really not my business...'

'Quite right, m'dear,' Uncle Matthew had agreed. 'A young man is entitled to a bit of fun – better now than later.'

'Men! They always stick together,' Marianne had said and looked around her. 'I should like to get to know you, Ruby. Do you have a half-day off?'

'Yes, I do, on Saturday,' Ruby had said. 'I work in the office, not the store. Sometimes, if they need help, I do help out behind the counters on my free afternoon but not often.'

'What do you do?' Marianne asked.

'On my afternoon off? I might go shopping, if I can afford to buy anything – or sometimes I walk in the park or have a cup of tea and a cake at a tea shop.'

'Then perhaps we could meet,' Marianne had suggested. 'I like to window shop even if I can't buy – and I like to have tea and meet friends. You could meet some of my friends and they may invite us both to theirs on Sunday for tea...'

'I'm not sure. I live in lodgings and I can't ask anyone back...' Ruby had faltered uncomfortably.

'Oh, poor you,' Marianne had looked at her in sympathy. 'Sometimes I find Mama's friends so boring, but on Saturdays I can sometimes invite my own friends – and you can be a part of that. We should be friends, Ruby.'

'Thank you, I should like that – but you do know that Rupert and I... we are just friends.'

'Oh yes. He told me everything. He always does.' Marianne had smiled. 'Poor Mama does so desperately want him to settle down. Perhaps you will like him enough to become more than friends one day, Ruby...'

Ruby had blushed and not known how to answer her. Now, as she lay in bed, her thoughts going round and round in circles, she smiled. Her life had changed so quickly that it was like a dream. She had liked Rupert's family, who were all friendly and kind, and some of the other guests had spoken with her briefly – but Marianne had reached out to make friends and pull her into her circle. It was the first time Ruby had made friends outside work, because at the orphanage friendship had not been encouraged. It was punished, made to seem wrong if two girls spent too much time together. So a small smile and a whispered word of comfort was all that most had offered – though one small girl had wanted to be Ruby's friend. For a short while, they had supported each other, crying in each other's arms when life seemed too hard. Then, one day, Sissy had been called to Matron's office and was never seen again. Ruby was told she had gone to a distant member of her family, but she'd never been sure if that was true. Now, it looked as if she might have made some new friends.

Rupert had thanked her on the way home.

'Mama really liked you, Ruby. She will stop badgering me to find a girl now.' He'd looked at her uncertainly. 'I usually go once a month – do you think you could bear to go again?'

'I enjoyed myself,' Ruby had told him. 'I liked your family – and Marianne has invited me to tea with her.'

'Shall you go?'

'Yes, we have arranged it for next Saturday.' Rupert had nodded. 'Thank you for taking me. I enjoyed it.'

'Thank you,' he'd said. 'Perhaps we could go somewhere another Sunday. Have tea, just the two of us – a walk in the park. Or would you rather go dancing on Saturday night?'

Ruby had stared at him, holding her breath. 'Do you mean it?' she had asked at last when she could speak again. 'I've never been to a dance. I don't know how...'

That had seemed to amuse him. 'Then I shall teach you,' he'd said. 'It won't be this week. I have something arranged. I'm going out of town for the weekend – but don't tell my family. The following Saturday. I will come to Harpers and leave a message for you with... the lift boy.' He'd nodded to himself. 'Ernie is a nice fellow. He will see you get my message.'

Ruby had agreed to Rupert's suggestion, though a little warning voice in her head told her she must not rely on Rupert too much. He was bold and gallant, his rescue of her purse had told her that much; he was also nice-looking and had a lovely family – but she had a feeling that he was still seeing his wild friends. He was probably using her to hide his activities from his mother.

Well, that was all right, Ruby decided. She would allow it, but she would use him, too, as a stepping stone to a new world – the world that his sister had promised to introduce to her.

Turning on her side, Ruby smiled. Rupert had not touched her heart. She liked him well enough, but she liked his sister and his uncle more. For the time being, she would continue to oblige him. Ruby was still ambitious to make something of her life, but there was no harm in having a little fun on the way, was there?

14

Kitty reached for Mariah's hand as they got into the expensive car, which had been sent for them that Sunday afternoon, sensing that her friend was feeling out of her depth, as did she. Both of them were wearing a new dress, which had been bought from Harpers using Kitty's discount since there had not been time to make them. Mariah had on the smart black coat she'd bought for her father's funeral and not worn since and Kitty had one she'd bought in Harpers' sale that January. It was a mid-grey and looked well with her cherry-red hat and silver-grey dress. Mariah's hat was black, but as she said, no one was going to be looking at her; she was there simply to give Kitty courage for this first meeting with her uncle. However, Kitty wasn't sure whether she was giving or receiving courage as they arrived at the prestigious hotel and were shown in by a man in a smart uniform.

Kitty gave them her name and was told that her uncle was waiting for her in his suite; a young porter was sent to show them up and he knocked on the door, which opened almost immediately.

A middle-aged woman, wearing the uniform of a nurse,

opened it and smiled, asking them to enter. 'Sir Peter is expecting you,' she said in a refined voice. 'Please do come in. May I take your coats?'

It was exceptionally warm in the room into which they were led and so they agreed, allowing her to take away their coats. The sitting area was luxuriously furnished and there was a huge display of expensive flowers standing on a table near the window, also a bowl of fruit and dishes of sweets. To one side was a tea trolley set with cups and saucers and various platters of food, but missing its teapot. The food was hidden beneath silver covers, but it all looked very nice and welcoming. However, Kitty's attention was almost instantly drawn to another door, where the nurse stood with a man in a wheelchair. The nurse pushed him into the room, taking him to where two comfortable armchairs had been set.

'I will see about making the tea, sir,' she said, addressing her patient. Then, turning to Kitty, she said, 'Please sit down. Sir Peter finds it tiring to talk, so please listen to him for a while. I will be back shortly.'

Kitty inclined her head and sat down in the chair nearest to the man she'd been told was her uncle. At first glance, he just looked old and tired, but then she saw that despite the lines and the silvered hair, he was still a handsome man. His eyebrows were dark, as his hair must once have been, his mouth firm and his chin determined. She thought that this was a man who had enjoyed having his own way for most of his life.

Even as she studied him, it was clear that he was doing the same. After a few moments, he nodded, as if satisfied. 'You look very like your grandmother,' he announced in a voice that rasped, his breath harsh and difficult. 'I wasn't sure until this moment, but I am now. You are John's daughter.'

'Was that my father's name?' Kitty asked and he nodded. 'I

did not know until two years ago that the Wilsons were not my parents. I believed she was my mother and I knew she resented me, but I never understood why.'

'Yours was an unfortunate story,' Sir Peter agreed. 'The man who took you in out of kindness was mistaken. Had my mother known of your existence, she would have made better arrangements for you.'

'He acted in good faith, believing I had no living relatives. He was a decent man and I loved him as my father.'

'That is good. I am sorry you suffered in other ways.'

'I was lucky to find good friends – but Mr Harvey has told you my story.'

'Yes – a sad one, I think.' He cleared his throat and then reached for a glass of water on a small table beside him. 'Would you like to be our hostess, Kitty? I believe you may find something nice under those covers.' He indicated the tea tray.

Kitty acquiesced, going to remove the covers. What she saw was a feast for the eyes: tiny sandwiches that were no more than one bite, little cakes and tarts, marzipan comfits and crystallised fruits, as well as a bowl of fresh strawberries.

'Where did you get these at this time of year?' she asked in wonder.

A smile touched his lips, banishing the signs of illness briefly. 'When you are rich enough, there is always a way,' he said. 'I had them sent over from my home in the South of Spain. We have many delicious fruits and vegetables all year round that you only see for a short time in this country…' A laugh escaped him as her eyes widened. 'I had them flown in – and yes, I do have my own plane. Just a small one that I flew myself until this foolish body of mine let me down.'

Kitty offered him one of the silver salvers on which were an array of sandwiches, but he shook his head.

'The food is for you; both of you,' he nodded to Mariah. 'Though I will have a cup of tea when it arrives.'

Kitty took the sandwiches to Mariah, who gave a little snort as she saw them. 'Not big enough to taste,' she muttered.

Looking at her uncle, Kitty saw a gleam of appreciation in his eyes. 'I agree,' he said. 'I liked my food heartier when I could do it justice – Miss Simpson thought you would appreciate a fancy tea.'

'Well, I certainly do,' Kitty said and helped herself to several of the salmon and cucumber ones, giving Mariah half-a-dozen, because she knew she wouldn't help herself to more than one. 'It was kind of you, sir, and I shall enjoy them. If I eat enough, it will save us cooking this evening.'

Sir Peter's gaze narrowed. 'Your grandmother would not have approved of your going to work, even though I have been told it is a prestigious job. And I know things have changed since the war.'

He broke off then as Miss Simpson brought in the tea. She poured one for him, then Kitty and Mariah, and then left them again with a little look at Kitty as if to warn her not to tire him.

'Take no notice of her,' Sir Peter grunted as she went out. 'I'm not going to die just yet – though it was a near thing.' He looked at Kitty. 'I had hoped you might come to live with us and protect me from her.'

'I am sorry I can't do that,' Kitty said. 'I have a home with Mariah and a job I love.' She hesitated. 'It might be possible to visit occasionally, but I don't think I could come to Spain...'

'I dare say the journey would be too much for me now,' he said with a sigh. 'I came home when my father died, to sort out his estate, and I imagine that will take me as long as I've got – though I wonder if it is worth the effort. You want nothing from me I am informed...' He raised his brows.

Kitty's cheeks were warm. 'I don't know you, sir. I would not feel comfortable with inheriting money from someone I don't know. Surely you must have someone – a friend if not a relative?'

'There are friends,' he admitted. 'And worthy causes...'

'That is good,' she said. 'I am glad you have friends, sir.'

He inclined his head. 'Will you not call me Uncle Peter?'

'If we meet again, I will try,' Kitty said. 'It doesn't feel right just yet.'

'You're very like my mother,' Sir Peter said, his voice a harsh rasp. He picked up his cup with shaking hands and drank the fragrant liquid. Afterwards, he sat for a moment with eyes closed, hands clasped on his chair as if the effort had almost been too much.

'Should we leave you, sir?' Kitty asked softly.

His eyes opened again. 'Please, finish your tea.' A sigh left his lips. 'I came to London to see my lawyers and in the hope of seeing you. I leave for the country the day after tomorrow. I will write to you and invite you to stay at my home – this Harpers gives you a holiday, I suppose?'

'Yes. I can have a week in the summer and another near Christmas, if I choose to take them, and Mariah doesn't need to open her little shop all the time.'

'Then I will invite you both to stay this summer,' he said and smiled at her. 'I have hoped for this for so long, my dear. I was fond of John as a lad and I had no idea that he was in trouble. My father never mentioned it in his occasional letters – my mother might have, but she died soon after I left home. I was not able to return for her funeral.' He hesitated, then, 'Your father ought to have been buried in the family crypt. As it is, we have not yet discovered where either of your parents were buried, but the search is continuing.'

'I wanted to ask about that...' Kitty said her throat tight. 'You will let me know if they are discovered?'

'Yes, of course,' he replied, looking at her in a way that could only be described as fond. She blinked hard as the tears threatened, because her life might have been so very different had her father not been killed – and yet she was lucky, because she had met Larry.

'Thank you,' she said and saw that he was looking pale. He was clearly very unwell, though she had not been told what was wrong with him, but he was very thin and she thought it might be the wasting sickness that was called cancer. 'Are you in pain, Uncle?'

He opened his eyes, which had been half closed. 'No, I have medicine to control it, Kitty. However, that makes me sleepy, I fear.' His eyes met hers. 'The doctor has told me to expect no more than a year at most.'

'I am very sorry you are so ill,' Kitty told him sincerely.

'No matter – save that I should have liked more time to know you, my dear.'

Kitty felt a tear on her cheek but ignored it. 'You are very tired. I think perhaps we should go...?'

'Maybe that is best,' he agreed as his eyelids flickered and closed. 'I hope we shall meet again?' He tried to rally himself but sat back in his chair, exhausted by the effort.

'I hope so,' Kitty replied and stood up.

As if by telepathy, Miss Simpson arrived with their coats. 'Thank you for coming,' she said in a low voice. 'He will sleep for a while now.'

'Goodbye, Uncle Peter,' Kitty said, touched by the way his eyes sought hers across the room and something made her say, 'If I can come, I will.'

Then she was outside the door and it was closed behind

them with a little snap. 'She couldn't get rid of us soon enough,' Mariah remarked with a sniff. 'Got an eye to his fortune, I dare say.'

'Oh, Mariah,' Kitty said and laughed. 'She is just looking after him. Besides, she is entitled to something, I suppose, and I don't want his money. I do feel sorry for him, though – as I would for anyone who was so obviously unwell.'

'Have you forgiven him for what he did?' Mariah asked. 'Having you followed and investigated?'

'I think so. I could have been a bad girl, as Mrs Wilson told him.' Kitty shrugged. 'It doesn't matter now. I have seen him and spoken to him. He isn't an ogre.' She gave a little laugh. 'We can go home now – and make ourselves a proper tea.'

'Cheese on toast, I fancy,' Mariah said. 'Those little cakes weren't half bad, though.' She patted her handbag. 'I popped a few in a brown paper bag I happened to have – some strawberries, too. We can enjoy them with a pot of tea later.'

'Oh, Mariah, I do love you,' Kitty said and squeezed her arm. Laughter bubbled up inside her. 'I am just so lucky to have you.'

'Aye, well the shoe's on the other foot as far as I'm concerned,' she said. 'Best day of my life when Larry brought you home.'

15

Beth popped in to see her father-in-law at Harpers stores before she went home at lunchtime one spring morning. Time passed so quickly once the fogs of winter had passed. The beginning of April seemed to bring sunshine and showers and everywhere was fresh and bright.

Fred was busy in the stores, a pencil tucked behind his ear, wearing his old khaki overalls. He had been checking through a load of tea chests, discovering, as he told Beth, some goods that had been delivered six months earlier but had not yet reached the shelves on the shop floor. He looked as happy as a sand boy when Beth saw him and his face lit up when she spoke to him.

'Enjoying yourself, Dad?' she asked and then he told her about discovering the stock that had been signed in but never checked or unpacked.

'That would never have happened when you were stores manager,' Beth said with a frown at the present manager, who was actually engaged in taking in some parcels and making notes.

'Jim is a nice enough bloke,' Fred told her. 'I think he's just a bit out of his depth. He told me he's never managed a department for a big store like this. He was a stores manager before but for a much smaller hardware store.'

Beth nodded. 'Sally has been complaining about her stock level not being what she'd hoped,' she said. 'The sooner you can get that merchandise on the shop floor, the better, Dad.'

'It's just as well it wasn't for the fashion department,' Fred said with a grin. 'Glass and silverware don't date in quite the same way.'

'I intend to do a bit of shopping before I go home – anything you need, Dad? I can get it and you can collect it when you come for your tea.'

'I wouldn't mind a bit of bacon for my breakfast and I'll need bread and milk,' Fred said. 'If you've got a lot of shopping to do, Beth, I can buy them from my corner shop as I walk home; they stay open all hours.'

'I only need a few bits, so I'll get them for you,' Beth said and smiled. 'I'll leave you to your work now.'

She left him to it and went out into the pleasant warmth of the early afternoon. Her shopping took her about an hour, because she decided to look for new trousers for Timmy, who was growing fast, then she drove home, thinking how pleasant it was to have her own little car. When Beth had landed her first job at Harpers all those years ago, she had never expected to own a car or live in a four-bedroomed house. Even during the early years of her marriage, money had not been plentiful, but since Jack had become a partner in the restaurant, things had improved so much.

She parked her car in the quiet residential street she called home and got out, unloading her parcels from the boot. When the voice spoke from behind her, she jumped and nearly banged her head as she jerked out to look at the man who had spoken.

'Are you all right?' he asked. 'I never meant to startle you. I was just wondering if you needed any help taking those parcels into your house.'

Beth blinked as she realised it was her new neighbour. He was smiling at her and she saw that he was rather attractive, with grey eyes, dark hair, silvering at the temples.

'Oh, thank you,' she said. 'I do have quite a lot. I did some shopping for my father-in-law – that bag there...' Beth indicated it with a nod and he reached into the boot and took it out for her, closing the door.

'Don't forget to lock your car. It seems a nice neighbourhood, which is why we chose it, but you never know.'

'Yes, I shall,' Beth said and locked the car before picking up her bags. She opened her front door, hesitating, then, 'Please come in – the kitchen is just through here.' He followed her in, placing the bag he carried on the table and looking about him.

'This is nice. Have you been here long?'

'Four and a bit years,' Beth said. 'We've made a few changes gradually, but I've got most of it how I want it now.' She offered her hand. 'I am Beth Burrows. My husband, Jack, has spoken to you, I think?'

'Yes, we met briefly,' he replied. 'We've still got a lot to do to our house. I'm Terry Forrester. My wife is a bit shy, but I am hoping she will make friends here. Perhaps you'd come round for tea one day – or perhaps to dinner, you and your husband?'

'Well, I am sure we'd love to, but it is a question of time. I have been meaning to pop round and introduce myself – but I've been working longer hours recently. I help out at Harpers – the store in Oxford Street.' Beth broke off, realising she was talking too much. Something was bothering her about him, but she wasn't sure what. 'I could come round for a cup of tea sometime about three in the afternoon – or your wife could come to me.

I'll try to pop round tomorrow, because I'm not working. It will probably be in the morning, though.'

'Lovely, I'll tell her,' he said and smiled. 'It was nice meeting you, Beth.'

* * *

After Beth had seen Terry out and shut the door, Beth returned to the kitchen. It was a little forward of him to call her by her first name. In time she would have suggested it – but there was something in his manner that made her think he'd spoken and acted as if he knew her. He couldn't know her because she'd only seen him driving to and from his house. He'd lifted his hand on occasion and she'd waved back. Jack had spoken to him a couple of times and thought he seemed a decent sort.

Beth unpacked her goods and tidied them away. She put the kettle on and set out a tray, then made a pot of tea and took it into the sitting room that overlooked her walled garden. It was lovely and private. She hadn't thought anyone could get in over the wall, but Jerry had managed it when he'd been shot a couple of years back. The young barrow boy had come to her for help...

She exclaimed, almost choking on her tea as it clicked in her head. Jerry Woods. His brother, Tel, was someone important in the criminal world. Terry Forrester. Of course! No wonder she'd thought there was something familiar. She had only seen Tel – the man who had sent his bully boys to scare off the gangsters who had threatened Beth – once, briefly, as he'd left Bella's house. He looked different now. His suit was expensive, as was the car he drove. His hair was shorter and the silver at his temples made him look older. She wondered if that was a natural change or if he'd deliberately altered the way he looked, just as he'd changed his name.

Why would he do that? Perhaps he wanted a different identity and a fresh start to his life?

It was best not to let anyone know that she'd guessed his secret. If Jack knew that their new neighbour was a gangland boss, he would probably want to move away. He certainly wouldn't agree to have dinner with him. Beth wasn't sure how she felt about things. She hoped that Terry wouldn't bring his bully boys into their residential area, but she was certain he didn't intend that.

Beth was torn. She ought to keep her distance and yet she'd made a promise. As she finished her tea and decided to get on with preparing their evening meal, she decided to take things easily. She would call on his wife, just as she'd intended, but she wouldn't make a habit of it. Until she was sure Mr Forrester did not mean to cause trouble for her or her family and friends, she would be very careful. Yet she didn't want to offend them and there was a chance that she had jumped to the wrong conclusions, though her instincts were usually right.

* * *

Beth didn't speak of her suspicions to anyone. When she popped round the next morning, once the boys had gone to a football match at their school playing field with Fred, she was greeted by a very pretty young woman.

'Please, will you come in,' she invited. 'Te— My husband, Terry, said that you might call today. We haven't met many of our neighbours yet. My name is Elizabeth. I prefer to be called Betty, but Terry says that Elizabeth sounds better.'

'We have the same birth name then,' Beth told her. 'I was christened as Elizabeth but I have always been called Beth.' She heard a little cry and then a little boy of less than two years came toddling into the room. His face was stained with tears and his little sailor suit was dirty where he had spilled something on it.

'Oh, Telly darling,' Elizabeth said and scooped him up in her arms. 'I wanted you to look clean and tidy for once...' A look of tenderness was in her face as she wiped the marks from his cheeks. She glanced at Beth shyly and smiled. 'I can never keep him clean five minutes.'

'I think boys are like that,' Beth said. 'Mine were forever into something at that age. Even now they sometimes come home with scuffed shoes and torn shirts. I have no idea how they get that way – Jack is thirteen and Tim is nearly eleven; my father-in-law says their father and uncle were just the same.' Beth hesitated, then, 'My husband, Jack, runs a restaurant in Oxford Street – and Tim, my brother-in-law, died in the war. He was a pilot.'

'That is so sad,' Elizabeth said. 'I can't remember much of the war. I was too young...'

Beth nodded. She couldn't have been much more than eighteen or nineteen but had lovely big dark eyes and an air of fragility— No, not quite that, perhaps uncertainty. A kind of fear was in those dark eyes that reminded Beth of a stray kitten she'd once befriended, which had been tormented by local lads. Something told her that Elizabeth – or Betty, as she'd been used to being called before her husband made her change it – had suffered in the past.

'It was a horrible time,' Beth told her. 'I have a friend who was a nurse. She saw some terrible things during the war. So many young men died...'

'Yes, I've been told some sad stories,' Elizabeth replied. 'I am sorry you lost a member of your family.'

'It affected my husband a lot,' Beth said. She watched as Elizabeth set the little boy down and he went to sit on the mat and play with his toys. 'Did you lose anyone in the war?'

'I don't have a family – only Terry and little Telly...' she replied with a sad smile, then she looked up. 'They are all I want.'

'I feel much the same, though I am fond of my father-in-law. My aunt brought me up, but she died some years back.'

Elizabeth nodded. 'Would you like some tea? I'm not sure if that is what I should offer – perhaps it should be coffee? I'm not certain how to make coffee. Terry makes it for himself, but I like tea best.'

'A cup of tea would be lovely,' Beth said. She had intended to make it a quick call but found that she liked this young woman, who was so out of her depth in this neighbourhood. Some of the women and families here would make mincemeat of her.

Her efforts to set a nice tray were a little uncertain, but the tea was brewed just right. Beth drank it and smiled and asked her what she liked doing when she had free time.

'I don't really go out without Tel— Terry, except for shopping,' she said. 'Sometimes he gets someone to look after the little one and takes me somewhere quiet to eat or to the cinema. I like the pictures better than the theatre.'

'Yes, I like the talking pictures much better than the silent ones,' Beth agreed. 'We don't get out that much either, because of my husband's work, but I meet friends and have tea with them. Sometimes, we go to the ballet. I love that, but Jack can't stand it so Sally takes me.'

'Is that Sally Harper?' Elizabeth asked and smiled when Beth nodded. 'I've heard about her and I like to shop there. There is a nice lady called Kitty Wilson who helps me pick proper clothes...'

'Yes, Kitty is good at that,' Beth agreed. 'She knows what hats and shoes will go with various outfits so she can help people choose things without having to walk halfway across London to find what they need.'

'Harpers has such lovely things. Terry gives me money and I buy something nice to wear when we go out.'

'That dress you are wearing is very pretty,' Beth told her. 'I don't think it came from Harpers, did it?'

'No. I made it,' Elizabeth said. 'I see pictures in magazines and then I try to copy them. They aren't as smart as the things I buy in Harpers – but I think they are nice for at home.'

'Yes, that dress certainly is,' Beth said. 'Did you work as a seamstress before you married?'

Elizabeth's cheeks went pink as she shook her head. 'No – but I sometimes helped other girls I knew to make their clothes when— well, before I married Terry.'

Beth saw she was embarrassed and changed the subject. She hadn't volunteered any information about her job or indeed her previous life. Her world clearly centred around her husband and child. They talked about their homes and the price of food and then Beth got up to leave.

'I must go. I have lots to do this morning. It was lovely to meet you, Elizabeth. I hope you will come round for a cup of tea one afternoon. I am normally home at around three – but the children aren't long after and they always want their tea.'

'Thank you. I should like to,' Elizabeth replied and smiled. 'It was nice of you to come, Beth. I don't have any friends here yet.'

'Then *we* shall be friends,' Beth said and bent down to touch the child's head. He giggled and looked up at her.

Beth was escorted to the door and she promised to visit again when she could. Back home, she found herself wondering about Elizabeth's past. She felt there was some mystery, some secret hurt that the young woman held inside. However, she would not pry. Everyone was entitled to their secrets. She was certain now that Terry Forrester was in actual fact Tel Woods and an influential member of the criminal underworld. Beth wondered whether she'd been right to promise further meetings. Jack would not like her being friends with the wife of a criminal, but she liked Elizabeth and felt sorry for her.

The phone rang and she went to answer it. Sally had called to invite them all for Sunday lunch and in the laughter and chatter of the next few moments, Beth forgot her misgivings. Right or wrong, she intended to go on visiting her new friend, at least until Jack forbade her or— well, it was best not to think of anything that might or could go wrong.

16

'It's lovely seeing you happy again,' Beth said to Sally when she helped clear the used dishes to the kitchen after they'd eaten a special meal to welcome Ben home. 'You are enjoying Ben being home again.' It was evident in the way Sally's eyes sparkled.

'Yes, I am,' Sally agreed. 'He will be home for a month or so to sort some things out and spend time with us, but then he thinks he has to return to New York for a while.'

'His aunt passed away,' Beth reflected with a frown. 'Is there a lot to do over there?'

'The lawyers are working on the various changes that need to be made. Ben will have a big say in future policy when he returns, as the largest shareholder – but that isn't the problem.' Beth raised her brows and Sally lowered her voice to a whisper. 'Ben thinks the profits are being milked in some way. He hasn't had time to discover how it is being done yet, but when he goes back, he means to investigate it properly.'

'How could anyone do that?' Beth asked, genuinely puzzled. 'It must be more than petty pilfering. I mean, a certain amount goes on in most businesses, I imagine...'

'Yes, there is always some loss you can't account for,' Sally agreed. 'It might be spoiled stock, thefts by customers, or even staff, but usually it isn't enough to affect the profit ratio.' She sighed. 'This is quite a large drop, so Ben says. It upset his aunt in her last months, so he feels obliged to get to the bottom of it.'

'Yes, I understand that,' Beth said. 'Yet it isn't very good for you or the children if he spends too much time over there.'

'That is the problem. They were all over him when he got home and it will upset them when he leaves again. They didn't want to go to bed when he got back, but he read them a story and they settled in the end. And Mum has taken them shopping this morning. I think they want to buy a gift for their daddy's birthday next month.'

'We're lucky. Fred is always ready to look after the boys for us and they adore him, so we get out without too much fuss.' Beth smiled fondly. 'Jack can be a handful, but Timmy is such a good boy.'

'Jenny is difficult at times, but Peter is such a caring child.' Sally sighed, then, 'Ben has to put his plans on hold for expanding the restaurant or opening a new one here.' Sally looked apologetic. 'He is talking to Jack about it now. If Jack wants to do something on his own, perhaps he should go ahead without Ben?'

'Jack will decide,' Beth replied. 'I don't get involved in his business, Sally.'

Sally nodded and then smiled and changed the subject. 'Fred found some stock that had been overlooked,' she said. 'I was puzzled when I learned that the silver and glassware counters were looking a bit sparse, because I knew we'd ordered on time. I checked and the order had been ticked as having been received.'

'Fred says that Jim isn't used to dealing with the quantity of goods that Harpers needs,' Beth told her. 'And that he was a bit out of his depth...'

'Yes, so I understand. I didn't interview Jim Manders myself, but he seemed quite competent when Ben took him on. I would hate to have to let him go, as Fred told me he had been ill for a while before he took this job and has a wife and two small children.'

'Oh, that makes it difficult,' Beth sympathised. 'Yet you can't have stock getting lost in the stores.'

Sally laughed. 'Fred assures me it won't happen again. I feel very lucky that he decided to return for a few days a week.'

'He retired too early. When Vera died, he felt the house was empty and he didn't have enough to do. I'm glad he is being useful, because he's happy again.'

'There are times when I feel I'd like to just sit back and let Harpers take care of itself,' Sally admitted. 'Yet I know that if it suddenly wasn't there, I would miss it terribly. I would rather be too busy than have nothing to do.'

'I can't imagine you with nothing to do,' laughed Beth. 'It wouldn't happen. You would find something else to fill your time.'

'Yes, I probably would,' Sally agreed.

They returned to the sitting room to find Jack and Ben talking and laughing, so whatever business had been discussed it had been amicable.

* * *

The rest of the afternoon was spent in pleasant chat amongst old friends and it was nearly seven when they left, promising to entertain Sally and Ben at their home before Ben returned to

America. It was not until they were getting ready for bed later that evening that Jack told Beth what had been discussed.

'Ben thinks it would be unfair to open another place over here while he's stuck in America,' he said. 'I told him I wasn't interested in taking a share of anything over there and he understood that I wouldn't feel comfortable with it. The restaurant is doing well, so we've decided to leave things as they are for the moment.' Jack wrinkled his brow. 'Ben thinks he might go ahead on his own over there, but that's up to him. We're suited the way we are, Beth. I don't want to invest my savings in something I could have no say in.'

'Ben is always looking to invest,' Beth revealed her own thoughts. 'Sally used to worry in the early years that he would stretch himself too far and I know things were difficult at times. I think you're wise, Jack. Sally says she thinks trade is slowing a bit, though not enough to bother her as yet, but...'

'Yes, I know. I read the *Financial Times* and they've been saying for a while that the boom years are over.' Jack sighed and drew Beth into his arms. 'I'm probably too cautious to ever be a millionaire, love, but I'm happy the way we are.'

'I don't need you to be a millionaire,' Beth said and lifted her face for his kiss. 'We have far more than my family ever did and I feel lucky to have you and the children – and Dad.'

'Yes,' he agreed. 'We are lucky. If Ben decides to concentrate his assets over there, I might be able to buy his shares in the restaurant. That would suit me just fine.'

'Did he say that?' Beth was surprised.

'No – but I sensed it was on the cards. I believe his heart is there now. He hasn't said as much to Sally yet, because she doesn't want the move.' Jack shook his head. 'I can't see how he can give enough attention to his business here if he is over there half the time...'

'Because Sally runs Harpers and always has since the war,' Beth said promptly. 'I know Ben is supposed to be in overall charge, but... well, he makes mistakes and Sally has to put them right.'

Jack raised his brows. 'You didn't hear that from Sally?'

'No. She would never say, but I know. Kitty tells me things. The departments Ben runs are never as profitable as those Sally is in charge of – and she's been working hard to put a lot of things straight since Ben handed over the reins to her.'

Jack looked thoughtful. 'Ben is impulsive. He always has been – look at the way he put us all at risk with that American government agent working undercover at the restaurant.'

'I thought you'd put that out of your mind?' Beth looked at him anxiously. He'd been so angry when he'd discovered what Ben had done putting her and the children to at risk. They'd fallen out over it and she wasn't sure Jack had ever really forgiven Ben.

'I've put it to one side,' Jack told her. 'I haven't forgotten that my wife and children were threatened over something he hadn't even told me about...'

'Oh, Jack. I was all right. Jerry's friends kept an eye on me.'

'Criminals the lot of them!' Jack said harshly. 'I was grateful that they helped get rid of that gangster who tried to blackmail us – but a leopard doesn't change its spots, Beth.'

Beth nodded, feeling guilty. If Jack suspected that she'd had tea with the wife of one of the criminals he despised, he would be very angry with her. Yet how could she turn her back on a friendless young woman, especially as she knew that Jerry's brother had made sure she and her children were protected?

17

'I wondered if you would like to help with the preparations for the pageant we're planning,' Kitty asked Ruby when she took a tray of coffee into the office that following Monday morning. 'We've got Harpers' float decided on. Mr Marco came up with a wonderful idea for us...'

'He does the windows for Harpers,' Ruby said, nodding. 'If I see him, he always says hello. What was his idea?'

'It is a tribute to the Suffragettes, for all the work they've done to help bring about change, and also to the men who suffered terrible injuries in the war – so they are going to have Suffragette nurses and men in uniform, wearing stained bandages and so on. Mr Marco says we should remind people of what both our women and men did in the war. He thinks that it helps to keep the memory fresh, because we should never forget their suffering – and both the soldiers and the Suffragettes suffered in their own ways.'

'I think that is a wonderful idea,' Ruby said, smiling at her. 'People don't realise what some of the men went through – and how badly it affected their lives. If a man comes home, they just think he is lucky to be alive but—' Ruby broke off and blushed as Kitty looked at her. 'I would be happy to help with the float.'

'I am working on it this Sunday afternoon,' Kitty said. 'We'll go together. We meet at someone's house and we're making the uniforms for the nurses and the men.'

'Oh, that sounds nice,' Ruby looked pleased. 'I would enjoy helping with Harpers' float. Are a lot of people taking part in the pageant and when is it to be held?'

'In July because the weather should be better then,' Kitty told her. 'A lot of the big shops in Oxford Street and some other places are taking part. It is all for charity, you see. We shall collect money for various good causes – and there will be bands playing and people dressed up walking with the procession. I think they are putting on a tea for children in the park with swings and roundabouts, and all sorts of things.'

'It sounds lovely,' Ruby said. 'Was it Mrs Harper's idea?'

'It was mine for a start, but then other people took over and it has spiralled far beyond anything I might have imagined,' Kitty said laughing. 'It is rather fun being involved. I wasn't sure at first, but I have enjoyed myself.'

'That is nice,' Ruby said. 'I shall enjoy it, too.' She looked pleased. 'Shirley is moving into the spare room at my lodgings next week, too. She has suggested that we might go to the cinema together sometimes...' Kitty raised her brows. 'Oh, Miss Smith is a supervisor, but she asked me to call her Shirley when we're not working. I found her the room, you see.'

'That sounds lovely, Ruby.' Kitty smiled at her. 'I'm glad you've begun to make friends. I know it is difficult when you start work at a new place. I am lucky because I have Mariah and we do most things together. Until I moved in with her, I had few friends and just went home at night to help...'

'I don't help my landlady now, unless she asks, because she

doesn't like her lodgers messing around in her kitchen, or that's what she says. After I've eaten, I just sit in my room and read or have a bath and wash my hair. It will be nice having someone to go out with in the evening sometimes.'

'You don't have a boyfriend?' Kitty asked.

Ruby hesitated, then, 'I have a man friend – but he is just a friend. We met recently and I went for tea at his home. We were going to go to a dance, but he had to go somewhere else. He says he'll take me another time.'

'Well, at least you are making friends,' Kitty said.

Ruby nodded and left Kitty to get on with her work.

* * *

Ruby spent most of the day working after that. Because they had a lot of lists to type up, she didn't bother with taking her lunch break but just had a cup of tea and a bun she'd bought on her way to work. Mrs Flowers gave her a good meal each evening and she had an egg or toast for her breakfast each morning so she wasn't very hungry at midday, and the money she saved by not eating lunch had helped her purchase her new shoes, some lovely black suede ones with heels. Now she was saving for a pretty dress. She'd looked through Harpers' rails and seen a pale green silky afternoon dress, which would be just right when she was invited out to meet Marianne's friends, or if Rupert took her to tea at his mother's again. The dress was a bit too expensive for her, even if she saved on food and tried walking to work in the mornings.

It was a big decision to make for a girl like Ruby. She only had what she earned and her rent had to be paid on time. It might be a good idea to buy the material and a pattern and try to make a similar dress instead, but even though Ruby could sew, she wasn't sure whether she could cut it out properly. One dress she'd made for herself had never hung properly and she couldn't go out with Marianne and her friends in a shoddy dress. So for the moment she was saving every penny she could get.

It was a pleasant evening when she left, a hint of warmth in the air, as if spring had really come. Ruby emerged into the street, deciding that she would walk home, but she had only gone a few steps when she felt a touch on her shoulder. She turned quickly to find herself looking at Rupert.

'Oh, hello,' she said, surprised to see him. 'We're closed now – have you been in the store?'

'No. I came in the hope of seeing you, Ruby,' Rupert smiled. 'Marianne asked me to tell you she won't be able to meet you on the day you agreed, but she says same place same time the following week if that is all right?'

'Yes, I am sure it is,' Ruby said but felt a bit let down.

Rupert must have sensed her feelings because he said, 'Her fiancé is home for leave, so that's why – but she will meet you the week after.'

'Oh, that is good for her,' Ruby replied. 'I'm pleased, because she doesn't see him much.'

'That's the problem when you choose a man who gives his life to his country,' Rupert said. 'The Army comes first and if she weds him, she'll have to follow the drum, never have a settled home.'

Ruby thought about it and then said, 'I don't think I should mind that if I loved someone. I should just want to be with them.'

'That is what Marianne says,' Rupert remarked and gave her a long considering look. 'How would you like to go somewhere with me this weekend, Ruby?'

'Oh...' She was surprised as she'd thought he'd forgotten his offer to take her dancing. 'Well, I should like that, but on Sunday afternoon I am helping Kitty to prepare for the pageant.'

'What is that all about?' Rupert asked and she explained that various businesses were dressing floats and parading on a certain day in July and collecting money for charity.

'Oh, another good cause,' Rupert's interest faded. 'Mother has so many, I lose count, but a pageant is different. Who came up with the idea – you?'

'No,' Ruby laughed. 'I wouldn't have the faintest idea how to start. It was Kitty. She works with Mrs Harper in the office and she asked if I would like to help. I didn't have much to do at weekends, so I said yes.'

'Well, this party is on Saturday evening. I've been invited to a friend's house and instructed to bring a girlfriend.' He shrugged. 'Can you pretend for another evening, Ruby?'

'If you want me to,' she said. 'But I don't have an evening dress.'

'A cocktail dress will do?' he said and saw the slight shake of her head. 'I'll ask Marianne to lend you one. I'll bring it tomorrow at about this time – that will give you time to make any alterations you need.'

'Will Marianne mind me borrowing her dress?' Ruby was uncertain.

'She has plenty,' he replied. 'I am sure she won't object.'

'In that case – yes, I'd like to come,' Ruby said, feeling pleased.

'I'll wait for you here tomorrow at closing time,' he promised. 'I have to go now – thanks for being a good sport, Ruby.'

Ruby nodded and hurried to her bus stop; if she walked home, Mrs Flowers would complain that her meal had spoiled again. She was thoughtful as she took a seat on the bus and paid her fare. From the first, she had suspected that Rupert was using her so she didn't mind that he'd made it so obvious. She would play along for a while, because it was getting her out.

Marianne had cancelled their appointment but made a new one. It crossed Ruby's mind that her new friends might not be too different in their ways, though she'd thought the sister more genuine than the brother. Perhaps she was being a bit unfair, because if she had a chance to meet the man she loved after a long absence, she would cancel everything else, just as Marianne had.

Ruby's thoughts went to Captain Saunders then. There was a little ache around her heart. She'd hoped he might write to her, though she'd suspected when she'd found his gift that it was not his intention to meet again. For a few moments, that thought was like a knife thrust in her breast, but then she pushed it away. She would be foolish to let herself dream of a love that could never be. Ruby wasn't sure why the man who had been so badly afflicted by the torture he'd received as a prisoner of war should have had such an effect on her. Yet she'd known that as she'd comforted him, she'd felt a warmth and a need to protect and to love. Something she'd never known before. Ruby had lived inside a sterile bubble in the orphanage, never really making friends and never trusting the wardens. Kindness was something she'd hardly experienced until she started to work at Harpers.

Perhaps the thawing of the ice around her heart had begun there, but it had melted as she held a sobbing man in her arms. She knew that she wanted to be with him, to be there for him whenever the fear and pain kept him from sleeping. She supposed it wasn't the kind of romantic love that you read about in books or watched on the big screen at the cinema. Yet it was more than she'd ever felt towards anyone else, and, for a short time, she'd thought that she might mean something to him – but he'd gone away and her mind told her he would not return, even though her heart wouldn't accept that.

So, although Rupert meant nothing to her, she would play the part of his girlfriend while it suited her. After all, she didn't have much else to do with her free time.

18

'Ben, you promised you wouldn't leave before the end of May,' Sally cried, hurt and distress in her voice as she listened to his change of plans. He'd only been home a week and now he was talking of leaving again.

'They are calling a board meeting,' Ben told her. 'That means I need to be there, Sally. I have promises of support to elect me as the next chairman and it is important that I am there. Otherwise, my task of sorting things out will be even harder. I am certain my cousin has had the date brought forward because he doesn't want me to have the casting vote. I imagine it is his plan to put his own name forward...'

Sally looked at him, her eyes blurred with tears she was fighting. 'Do you think he knows you suspect him of bleeding the profits?'

'Quite possibly. My aunt thought it likely, though she didn't want to believe it of her own son, but she didn't trust him – and I'm afraid I don't either. I think he wants the majority share of the business and he's hoping that by forcing the profits down he can get his hands on enough shares – then I believe the profits would soar again.'

'That is surely illegal?'

'Oh, most definitely,' Ben said and looked at her. He reached out, taking both her hands in his. 'Forgive me, Sally. I understand that it is difficult for you being stuck here – and for the moment I can't think of a way out.'

'You could just sell your cousin your shares and come home,' Sally suggested. 'We have a good business here in London, Ben. Why not be satisfied with that – as you were until your aunt left you her shares?'

'It isn't that I don't care about Harpers – just that it irks me that one man can hold the rest of the shareholders to ransom. My aunt felt it deeply, worried that she'd let her shareholders down because of her declining health – and I gave her my word I would sort it, Sally.' His mouth tightened. 'Please, support me in this. It is important to me.'

Sally was silent, though she wanted to protest with all her heart. Ben was wrong. Something was telling her that he would find it more difficult than he believed to stop whatever fraud was going on. And her instincts were screaming that he must just let the whole thing go, but she saw the answer in his eyes. Ben had changed. She wasn't sure when it had begun or if it was reversible, but the loving man she'd known seemed to have disappeared behind a wall of implacability. Whatever she said, however much she argued, he would go.

'Well, if it is more important than your business here, your wife and your children, you must go,' she said quietly.

'Now that's bloody ridiculous!' Ben snapped. 'Don't make this a challenge, Sally. It's business, pure and simple. My aunt's shares are worth a lot of money. Don't make it an us or the American business situation.'

'I'm not making it anything, Ben,' Sally told him, holding back fresh tears. She refused to beg. 'It's your choice – but the children will be upset, and I'm not happy. I can hold the fort here. Harpers is the least of my troubles – but what is the point of it all if we don't have you?'

'For goodness' sake, Sally. I'll be back, hopefully by August, and then it will only be a matter of a few visits a year. Once I expose my cousin for what he is, I can hand over to one of the others, and leave them to get on with it.'

'Can you, Ben, really?' Sally looked into his eyes and saw what she knew to be the truth. He was fascinated by the thought of a multimillion-dollar business and being the main shareholder. Perhaps it was the cut and thrust of big business that excited him; she wasn't sure, but she knew that for the moment he was only interested in getting back for that board meeting.

'There is an alternative,' he said and now he was accusing her. 'We could sell Harpers and live over there – or just sell most of our shares and let someone else manage it.'

'You know I prefer to live here in London.' Sally knew that she was being stubborn, but all her instincts were against the move.

'Then it's your choice,' Ben said. He lifted his brows sardonically. 'What happened to the adventurous young girl I married, Sally? She would have leapt at the chance for a new adventure.'

'Several years of hard work, two children, and a dog, plus my mother and friends,' Sally replied, looking fearlessly into his eyes. 'Yes, I would have gone with you when we first married, but now my roots are here. I thought yours were too. During the war, you said you felt more British than American.'

'Life moves on,' Ben said. 'Don't you see the exciting possibilities, Sally? Harpers is doing well, but I can't see it ever reaching the size of the store in New York. My aunt told me that she had other shares, too, in projects that are expanding. She invested small amounts over the years and has quite a substantial holding in a munitions factory and other outlets. I looked into them and they could be real money-spinners in a few years—'

'Money, money, money!' Sally cried in disgust. 'What about love and enjoying life? Surely, we had enough without all these shares of your aunt's? We had a good life, Ben. We were happy – or I was and I believed you were too.'

'We are still happy or could be,' he said. 'I've always wanted to expand and move on. You know that, Sally. We could be dollar millionaires if I get this nonsense sorted and look at the lifestyle we could have then. A beautiful house in Florida, an apartment in New York, maybe even a yacht and—'

'Stop!' Sally cried and she was angry now. 'I don't want that, Ben. I see all that stuff as false and shiny like tinsel on the Christmas tree. I want real friends, real life, the pleasure of knowing you've kept a business going through hard times and that it is doing well – but I don't want all that other stuff... like something from the movies. Harpers is a family business. I want to see it continue that way, something we can pass on to our children. Why can't you be happy with that and realise how lucky we are to have our family and friends around us?'

Ben swung away from her. He poured himself a large whisky and drank it straight down. Sally didn't protest, even though she knew he was drinking too much. He seemed as if he was on fire, unable to relax, always wanting more. It was as if some alien disease had entered his body, making him restless, dissatisfied with his life.

'Is that your final word, Sally?' he asked.

'It is how I feel,' she said. 'Please, Ben. Sort it out for your aunt's sake, but then sell your holdings and come back to us – for all our sakes.'

'I'm not sure that there is much to come back for,' Ben said and slammed his glass down before marching out of the room. She heard him run upstairs and hesitated, torn between following and making up their quarrel and holding to her principles. Ben knew that she was settled and happy here in London. For so many years, she hadn't even known she had a mother. Now her mother lived close by and they saw each other most days. How would Sally's mother feel if they went to America to live? The children loved their granny – and they were English. She didn't want them to be brought up as Americans, to learn to expect a lavish lifestyle. They had a comfortable life, why ask for more? Besides, something was screaming in her head, telling her Ben mustn't do this.

She heard him come downstairs and went through to the hall. He had a suitcase with him. 'You're leaving already?'

'I may as well go to a hotel for the night and then get the first flight out. I can fly to Ireland and then take a ship from there. It will be quicker than waiting for a passage from here,' Ben said. 'I'm sorry, Sally. At the moment, I am angry – but we will talk again, when we've both had time to calm down.'

'Ben... please don't go. I have a terrible feeling about all this. It's not just me being selfish. I know this is wrong.'

'Your instincts again, I suppose,' Ben said with a wry smile. 'I'll be in touch, Sally.' He went out without kissing her goodbye.

* * *

Sally stood where she was when Ben had left, feeling frozen. How could Ben put their lives at risk like this? How could he just walk away without trying to sort out this mess? She turned away, sat on the sofa, and let the tears come; then, as she heard her mother's voice and the children's in the hall, she ran quickly up the stairs to wash her face in cold water. The children would be upset enough as it was that their father had gone without saying goodbye; she didn't want them to guess that he might not come back.

Now, where had that thought come from? Sally shook her head as she bathed her eyes until they stopped feeling gritty. She patted her face dry and applied make-up, even though her eyes were still red she looked better. Her children mustn't realise her heart was breaking.

'Where's daddy?' Jenny asked when she walked into the sitting room.

'Daddy had to leave,' Sally told her. 'He has urgent business in America and so he had to go – he said to tell you and Peter that he was sorry and loves you very much, but he had no choice.'

'He promised to take me to ballet class tomorrow,' Jenny said, pouting. 'I bet you made him go. All you think about is your job… never about me…!' She burst into noisy tears.

'Dad promised to come to my cricket match next week,' Peter said, looking at her intently. 'Did he forget, Mum?'

'No, darling. He was really sorry he had to break his promises,' Sally told him. 'I shall come and watch you and I will take Jenny to her ballet class.'

Peter nodded. He walked towards her; his young face thoughtful. 'You're sad,' he said and put his arms around her. 'I love you, Mum. I wish Dad didn't go away so much.'

'I wish that, too,' Sally said and hugged him. She looked at her mother and saw the anxiety in her face. 'It's all right, love. I am sure Daddy will write to you and send you things – and he'll come home when he can.'

'Promise?' Peter said, looking up at her earnestly.

'I promise I will always love you,' Sally told him. 'But I can't promise for your daddy. He has said he will come, so I believe him – that's all I can tell you.'

'Of course he will,' Sally's mother said. She held her hand out to him. 'Let's go and see if Mrs Hills has left us any cake, shall we?' Her eyes met Sally's and spoke the words she would not say until later when they were alone.

* * *

'You quarrelled with Ben before he left and didn't make it up?' Sally looked into her mother's face. 'You shouldn't have let him go like that, love. Always make up a quarrel – even if you believe he is wrong.'

'He wants us to float most of our shares in Harpers on the exchange and go to live in New York, because it excites him, Mum. It seems as if it has taken hold of his mind and won't let go. He was talking about being a dollar millionaire and some fantastic lifestyle – I don't want all that. I like my life the way it is now. We have more than enough for ourselves and we have so many friends here – and you...'

'You mustn't let me hold you back,' her mother said and reached for her hand. 'I should miss you and the children – but if it's what Ben needs to make him happy, perhaps you should consider it.'

'So I just give up everything for his idea of the high life?'

'No, you go because he is your husband and you love him. You could make a life there. It doesn't have to be so much different to the one you have now. You could find work – at the store there or somewhere else. You are bright, Sally, and could get on anywhere. I know it wouldn't be easy, but it might save your marriage.'

Sally stared at her. 'You think I was wrong to tell him it

wasn't what I wanted? You think I should just let it all go – all I've built up – and follow Ben. He wouldn't want me to work. He would say it wasn't necessary...' Sally shook her head, still too upset to accept that her mother could be right. 'Is it too much to ask that he does what I want – thinks of his children?'

'I'm not saying you're wrong,' her mother said softly. 'I can see you're unhappy, Sally. But I think you might lose Ben if you refuse to do what he clearly wants to do with his life. You have to make a choice – Ben or what you have here. Think, my love – what would the rest of it mean to you without him?'

'I don't know,' Sally replied. 'At the moment, I feel bruised, as if I've been beaten all over – and yet... something in my gut tells me this is wrong, for Ben and for us. I can't explain it. Even if I was prepared to change my life so much for him... it's wrong.'

Sally's mother shook her head sadly. 'I don't agree with what Ben is doing, my love. I think it is selfish and unfair for him to suddenly expect you to give it all up and go with him, but it happens. Men do expect their wives to go where they want to go – and it often causes unhappiness. All I am saying is, be sure of what you want most, Sally. The life you have here – or Ben. It may come to that so be sure you know what is most important to you.'

Sally tensed and then nodded, letting the frustration melt away. 'He said he was angry but we'd talk. I think he still loves me – so perhaps he will see that it isn't fair on any of us to simply wrench us away from all we know.'

'Ben is impulsive and can be hasty in his actions,' her mother said. 'When he calms down and really thinks about it, he may see the sense in what you say – but be prepared, because he can also be stubborn, as stubborn as you, my love. One of you will have to give – or...' Sally's mother shook her head. 'You don't need me to tell you. You know just where you're headed if Ben asks for a divorce.'

'He would sell his shares in Harpers and I'd have to sell mine to keep my home, I suppose,' Sally said. 'I suppose he would be fair and give me money for the children, but...'

'Yes, Ben would do the right thing, but even if you had this house and found yourself a good job, you would be lonely. I know what it feels like to be alone for years, Sally. So think carefully, dearest. Don't cut off your nose to spite your face.'

Sally laughed, but inside she was weeping. She knew her mother's advice was sound and a part of her wanted to ring Ben at the first opportunity and tell him she would do whatever he wanted, but her feeling that it was all wrong just wouldn't go away. It wasn't just stubborn pride, even though she knew she could be too much that way, but something deep and unfathomable that she couldn't explain.

* * *

As she lay in bed that night, Sally's mind was restless. Had she been wrong? Had she put her marriage in jeopardy by refusing to listen to Ben's ideas? Was there anything so terrible in becoming the wife of a millionaire?

No, no, and no.

And yet, the nape of Sally's neck prickled and she sat up in bed with a start. Ben mustn't go back to America. He mustn't go on with his investigations – it was too dangerous. Ben's life was in danger!

Where had that thought come from? Sally had no idea, but it was there in her mind, churning away in her gut. He was getting into something he didn't understand, believing he could sort out whatever was happening to his aunt's holdings. His cousin must be ruthless if he was prepared to ruin a business simply to take it over… but Sally's instincts were telling her there was much more to what was going on than she could guess. Ben was about to stir a hornets' nest and a hornet's sting could be life-threatening.

She jumped out of bed, pulled on her dressing robe and ran downstairs. Which hotel would Ben be likely to stay at for the night? Probably near the airport since he intended to fly the first stage of his journey back to America rather than go on a ship. Yet he liked his comfort and familiarity. He would likely go to Claridge's. Ben had used the hotel a few times during the war.

Looking through their phone book feverishly, Sally found the number she was looking for. She lifted the receiver and asked for the number in her book. The operator put her through, but it was early in the morning and a while before anyone answered. Then a sleepy voice asked her if he could help.

'Could you put me through to Mr Harper's room please?' she asked. 'Mr Ben Harper.'

'Just one moment, madam. I will look for you…' After a pause, the voice returned. 'I am sorry we don't have anyone staying by the name of Ben Harper.'

'Are you quite sure?'

'Certainly, Madam.'

'Thank you.' Sally replaced the receiver and sat down. She had stopped shaking now, begun to think clearly. She was behaving foolishly. It was just a silly night-time fear, brought on by her distress. Ben would think she was making it up.

Sally shook her head. Even if she rang every hotel in London, she was sure Ben would just dismiss her fears and now she was properly awake, she thought it was foolish too. Ben would be fine. She was letting her imagination run away with her.

'Are you all right, Mrs Harper?' Mrs Hills stood in the doorway of the sitting room, looking at her. 'I heard you get up – are you ill?'

'No, I just couldn't sleep...' Sally said and smiled. 'Forgive me if I disturbed you.'

'I wasn't asleep,' her housekeeper said with a smile. 'Now you go back to bed and I'll bring you a nice hot drink with a drop of brandy. That will get you off.'

Sally thanked her and went back to bed, feeling a bit silly and knowing she had probably woken Mrs Hills. It was funny how everything seemed so much worse in the dark hours. Her quarrel with Ben had shaken her, because although they had quarrelled over the years it had never ended the way this one had and she knew it would return again and again to haunt her. Surely, Ben would come to his senses after he'd calmed down and realise that a business, no matter how large and important, was not as necessary to him as his family. Despite their recent quarrels, Sally still loved him and couldn't believe that he'd stopped loving her and his children. No, he'd just lost his temper and said things he didn't mean. He would apologise to her in his own time and they would sort things out between them. Once all Sally's ideas for Harpers were in place, perhaps she could go with him for a month or two now and then. A compromise; their home to remain in England but another home in America for part of the year.

Her spirits lifted as she started to plan how she could manage that and she was smiling when Mrs Hills brought in her drink and wished her goodnight. Yes, with a little give and take perhaps it could be made to work, though she would be much happier if Ben would just sell his shares and come home for good.

19

Ruby heard Mrs Flowers calling to her as she got ready to go out that Saturday evening. She went downstairs wearing the beautiful dress Marianne had loaned her. It fitted her well and because they were almost the same height, she hadn't had to alter the length. It just covered her knees and Ruby felt a little bit conscious, because she normally wore her dresses at about mid-calf, but she knew that young women were wearing their dresses much shorter, especially a smart cocktail dress like this one. It was midnight-blue and had diamanté-encrusted straps and a squared neckline. She was wearing a pair of navy-blue suede shoes that she'd spent all her savings on and, as she looked into the mirror, she hardly knew herself.

The dress seemed to have brought out chestnut highlights in her hair and her eyes looked more green than hazel. She didn't have any nice jewellery to wear with it, except the pendant Captain Saunders had given her, and somehow it didn't seem right to wear that when she was going out with another man – but perhaps a dress as gorgeous as this one didn't need it, Ruby thought as she patted her hair, which she'd curled in rags since she got home and now hung in soft waves about her face.

A sharp knock at her door brought Ruby back to herself as she heard Mrs Flowers' impatient voice. 'I've been calling you. I don't need to keep traipsing up here after you, girl.'

Ruby opened her door and looked at her landlady, who frowned as she saw her. 'Going somewhere special?' she asked disapprovingly.

'Yes, I've been asked out to a party,' Ruby replied, smiling despite the look on Mrs Flowers' face.

Her landlady sniffed. 'Gadding out all over now. I thought you were a nice, settled sort of girl...'

'I don't often get invited out,' Ruby said. 'It's nice to make friends, don't you think?'

'Never had any that didn't want something,' Mrs Flowers retorted. 'Anyway, this was delivered for you by special courier.'

She handed Ruby a small package. Ruby took it, thanked her and retreated into her room without opening it. Mrs Flowers was clearly dying to know what was inside and who it was from, but Ruby had no intention of showing her.

Sitting on her bed, Ruby broke the seal on the package and opened the layers of brown paper. Inside was a large flat box and a letter. Ruby opened the box first and saw a pair of earrings that sparkled in the light from her lamp. She took them out reverently. Looking at them, she realised that they matched the pendant Captain Saunders had left for her as a parting gift. Her heart beat rapidly as she placed them back in their box and opened the letter.

To her surprise, it was not from Captain Saunders but a solicitor. The name on the heading was not a London one but from somewhere in Cornwall. Her breath caught in her throat as she began to read.

Dear Miss Rush,

I write to tell you that my client, Captain Robert Saunders, has recently passed away. He left these earrings to you and I am pleased to tell you there is a small amount of money. Captain Saunders left a sum in trust for you, from which I am to administer a three-monthly income. The income will be sixty pounds each quarter. I suggest that it will benefit you to open a bank account so that this money may be paid in each quarter.

I hope that you are happy to accept this bequest and will write to me and let me know you have received the earrings and whether you wish me to send you a cheque each quarter or have the money transferred to your account.

Yours sincerely,
Philip Rowley
Rowley, Jones and Rowley, Solicitors at law

Ruby gasped, the tears starting to trickle down her cheeks. She dropped the letter on the floor as she bent her head, her body racked by the burst of grief that overcame her. Captain Saunders was dead and all her dreams of one day being together had crashed. How foolish she had been to hope that he would return and tell her how much he loved her. In her dreams, he confessed that he had tried to stay away but his need of her was too great.

He must have been ill, she supposed, for the man who had wept in her arms had been physically strong. What had happened to him that had caused his death? She could scarcely believe he was gone and yet this letter was proof. Ruby covered her face with her hands, then flopped back on the bed and curled up, knees to chest as she sobbed and sobbed. It was a long time before she could think clearly or stop crying.

Perhaps she was just a foolish girl or had let a small kindness go to her head, but her heart and mind had focused on the man she knew had suffered so much and she'd allowed herself to love and to dream. Now he was dead and he'd left what seemed to Ruby a lot of money.

She sat up and shook her head, trying to clear it of the muzzy feeling that had come over her. What could have happened to him? Why hadn't the solicitor told her more?

Wiping her face, Ruby decided that she would write and ask them how he'd died, because she needed to know. Her heart was aching too much to think about what Captain Saunders' bequest could mean for her, but she knew she had lost something far more precious.

* * *

It was only when Ruby heard the church clock strike eight that she realised she had forgotten all about meeting Rupert. He would have given up on her long before this and gone to his party alone. It didn't matter. Ruby couldn't have enjoyed herself knowing that the man she'd loved, however hopelessly, had died.

She took off Marianne's dress, which had become crumpled as she curled up on the bed, and hung it up. She would return it to her when she saw her – if Rupert's sister still wanted to meet her after she'd stood Rupert up. He would be very angry, of course, but perhaps his sister might be more understanding. Ruby didn't much care at that moment.

She put on her old bathrobe and went along the passage to wash her face. Her eyes felt gritty and she was drained of all emotion other than regret for what might have been.

After washing, Ruby returned to her bedroom and sat down.

She picked up the beautiful earrings and put them away carefully with her pendant. They would always be her most treasured possessions, but she wasn't sure she could ever bring herself to wear them.

Picking up the solicitor's letter, Ruby read it through again. On Monday, she would ask Kitty if she could use some typing paper to write her letter to Mr Rowley. She would also need a reference so that she could open a bank account, because she had never had one and didn't know where to start. Sixty pounds a quarter was far more than she could earn and Ruby felt a bit daunted by it. It would make life so much more comfortable for her, but she mustn't waste it. If she saved for a while, perhaps she could set herself up in a little business – or buy a house of her own one day. Her head whirled with all the possibilities. To a girl who had always had to fight and work for everything she wanted it was an absolute fortune. She couldn't imagine what she had done to deserve such a bequest.

Perhaps he had loved her, too. The thought struck Ruby like a blinding force. She would rather have married him, Ruby thought, but the knowledge that he had tried to make sure she would be secure for her lifetime warmed her and her grief was lifted for a while.

Ruby blinked as fresh tears filled her eyes. One day she would go to stand by his grave, take flowers and tell him how much she had come to love him. Ruby wasn't sure if there was a heaven. Yet if there was, surely Robert Saunders would be there, at peace at last. That thought brought a little smile to her face. She would think of him as being in heaven with the angels.

'Oh, Robert,' she said softly. 'I do wish I could have told you that I loved you, just once.'

Regret pierced her, but the tears had stopped now. Ruby

knew that she must live with her regret, but Robert would be there in her heart for the rest of her life.

* * *

The next afternoon, Ruby met Kitty as arranged and they went together to the house where the sewing circle was meeting. She was greeted kindly and welcomed into their midst. Another pair of hands was always welcome and Ruby soon lost any nerves she'd had at the start.

Most of the chatter was of the pageant, which was exciting. Some of the women would be playing the part of the nurses and either their sons or husbands would be the wounded soldiers. Harpers' float would honour both the Suffragettes and the war heroes.

'Mariah said you would be welcome to come back with me for tea afterwards,' Kitty told her. 'She is looking forward to meeting you.'

'Oh, thank you,' Ruby said. 'Mrs Flowers only serves a cold luncheon on Sunday as she refuses to cook on the Lord's Day. So it won't matter what time I get back – as long as it is before ten. She locks her door then and won't open it after that...'

'She sounds a bit of an ogre,' Kitty said and laughed. 'The last bus to get you home is just after eight thirty, so you will be back in plenty of time for her curfew.'

Ruby laughed. 'Yes, she can be a moaner, but I think her bark is worse than her bite. She keeps everything spotless and her cooking is nice, so I am happy to stay there despite her dire warnings.'

'Good...' Kitty looked at her thoughtfully. 'You look as if you're upset over something, Ruby. I wasn't sure whether to ask – but are you all right?'

Ruby hesitated, then inclined her head. 'Someone I was fond of died recently. I had a letter about it yesterday evening.'

'Oh, I am sorry,' Kitty replied. 'I know that can make you feel terrible for a long time.'

'I was going to ask if I could use some office paper to write to the solicitor who told me. He... he says I've been left a little money, in the form of an income. I have to open a bank account and I shall need a reference.'

'I am sure Harpers can do that for you,' Kitty told her. 'I needed to do the same thing and Mrs Harper showed me how. I can show you, if you like.'

'That is so kind of you,' Ruby said and smiled. 'I want to ask them how he died, too. They just said he'd passed away. One day I want to stand by his grave and tell him... things.'

'Yes, I understand,' Kitty murmured. 'I do that, too, Ruby. It sometimes helps me a little.' She hesitated, then, 'It does get easier in time.'

Ruby looked at her. 'You were to be married when your Larry died, weren't you?'

'Yes, but it didn't happen...' Kitty sighed and shook her head. 'I am grateful that I have Mariah. At least I don't have to live with an ogre of a landlady.'

Ruby nodded. 'In time, if I save, I might be able to own a house... I'm not sure if I'd want that. It might be more lonely still. Mrs Flowers is grumpy, but she is there to talk to – and Shirley lodges there too now...'

'Yes, that is better for you. Do you travel to work together?'

'Sometimes,' Ruby said. 'If it is a fine day, I walk to work, though perhaps I don't need to do that in future.'

'How much income will you have – if that isn't an impertinent question?'

'I don't mind telling you. I can hardly believe it, but I will have sixty pounds a quarter.'

Kitty looked impressed. 'That is a considerable sum, Ruby. How long for?'

'Oh, I don't know. I suppose I should ask,' Ruby said. 'It might only be for a year or so. I don't think he was rich... but I don't know...' she breathed deeply. 'We only knew each other a little while.'

'It was the same for Larry and I,' Kitty told her. 'I had seen him around for a long time, but when he took me to his home to live with his family, I wasn't in love with him; at least I wasn't aware of it – but then, when I really knew him, I understood that he was the only man I could ever love.'

'Surely you might meet someone else?'

'No, I don't think I shall,' she replied. 'Larry was special and...' Kitty shook her head. 'Mariah says I should keep an open mind. She wants me to be happy – but I am. I love my job and I have her and a few friends. It is all I need.'

'I've always wanted to be loved,' Ruby told her, a little break in her voice. 'I believe I was loved but...' Ruby blinked away her tears. 'I shan't cry again. It doesn't help.'

'No,' Kitty agreed. 'Crying never helps me either, just wears me out and makes my face blotchy.'

They smiled at each other.

'You do have a friend,' Kitty told her. 'We have much in common, Ruby, and I am sure Mariah will like you. You will love her. Everyone does.'

Ruby nodded, her heart lifting. She was glad she had agreed to help with the sewing for the pageant. Robert was gone so there was no use in crying for him. She would make as many friends as she could – and one day she might find love again.

20

At work that Monday morning, Kitty helped Ruby with her letter to the solicitor and told her about the bank she used. She also gave her a letter from Harpers to type out and signed it on behalf of Mrs Harper, which she was allowed to do with internal matters.

'Mrs Harper would certainly have signed had she been in, but she has meetings most of this week,' Kitty told Ruby. 'Have you got any savings to open the account with?'

Ruby shook her head. 'I'll wait until I get my first payment from Mr Rowley and then I can open the account. I did have five pounds saved, but I bought a pair of shoes. I have just a pound left to last me until I get paid again.'

'Well, it might be best to wait until you get the first remuneration,' Kitty said. 'Be sure to ask how long they will go on, Ruby. You can't make plans until you know.'

'Oh, I will,' Ruby said. 'I shall type the letter up in my lunch hour and then I'll post it on my way home.'

Kitty nodded and went back to her office, leaving Ruby to get on with her work. At lunchtime, she made herself a cup of tea and ate the bun she'd brought with her, then she wrote a letter, taking care to ask all the things she needed to know.

She put it in her bag to post as she went home. There was a red postbox not far from Harpers and when she left work, she walked to it and popped in her letter. Ruby had used one of the stamps from Harpers' stock but put the money for it in the cash box. As she turned to make for her bus stop, she almost bumped into a man, and glancing up she saw Rupert. He was looking very angry.

'Where were you on Saturday night?' he demanded. 'I waited at least half an hour!'

'Oh, Rupert, I am so sorry,' Ruby cried. 'I didn't mean to stand you up, but I had some bad news and I was very upset. I lay on my bed and cried for an hour and it was too late to come then. Besides, my face was all red and I couldn't have enjoyed a party.'

'So I had to go on my own,' he said a snarl in his voice. 'When were you intending to return my sister's dress then?'

'I thought when we next meet...' Ruby said tentatively.

'*If* she wants to when I tell her you let me down. I thought I could trust you, Ruby...'

'I have apologised,' she said, but now she was cross. 'I really couldn't help it – and if you wish to meet me here tomorrow evening, I will return the dress. If not, I will take it to your mother's house at the weekend.'

'No! I don't want her to know about that party,' Rupert said and his tone was less harsh than before. 'You can give it to my sister when you see her. I shan't tell her that you upset me.'

'I am sorry if it ruined your plans,' Ruby said. 'I dare say you went to the party on your own?'

'I did, but that wasn't the point. They all wanted to know

where my fiancée was...' He broke off as her eyes widened. 'I let my family and friends think that we were getting engaged.'

'Why?' Ruby asked. 'You aren't in love with me, Rupert. I know that – so why tell people lies?'

'It suits me.' He suddenly laughed. 'My uncle threatened to cut me out of his will if I didn't settle down and get married. He liked you a lot and said I was a fool if I let you slip through my fingers – so I told everyone I was going to ask you to marry me.'

'You shouldn't do things like that,' Ruby said sharply. 'I didn't mind pretending to be your girlfriend at your mother's tea party, but a promise to marry is a different thing...'

'Why? You don't have a boyfriend. You told me so – and we can always have a quarrel and break it off before the wedding.'

'With me being the one to break it off, I suppose,' Ruby replied. 'Do you think that is fair to your family? It could cause a lot of distress – not to mention the plans they will make for us.'

'Well, we could go through with it if you like,' he said with a shrug. 'You know I want my freedom and I wouldn't interfere with you. You could even go on working at Harpers if you wanted.'

'The answer is no,' Ruby replied. 'I don't mind being thought a casual girlfriend if that keeps your family happy for a while – but I won't wear your ring and pretend to be in love with you.'

'You're not then? Not even a little bit?'

'You haven't given me any reason to be,' Ruby said, looking him in the eyes. 'I knew you were just using me, but I didn't have much to do, so I went along with it.'

'So what has changed?' he asked with a shrug.

'I don't want your family to be hurt – they are nice people, Rupert. I won't lie about a thing like that...'

'Oh, all right. I'll tell them you aren't ready to commit yet – but you will still come for tea the week after next?'

Ruby hesitated, then inclined her head. 'I said I'd help you and I shall – but no more lies, Rupert. I won't be a part of that. I am just a friend.'

'Understood,' he said and shrugged, then grinned. 'I don't think it would be such a terrible idea if we did marry. I know I'm a bit of a selfish pig. Marianne says I've been spoiled – but you would gain a family and I'd have them off my back, because you don't love me so you wouldn't mind if I carried on in my own way.' There was a look of mischief in his eyes and he'd slipped back into his easy charm.

Ruby knew it wouldn't be difficult to go along with him. She would have what she'd always longed for, a family – but not a loving husband, and that was what she truly wanted. Someone who would love her.

'Please, don't be silly,' she said. 'I will return Marianne's dress to her when we meet – and I'll be your friend and visit your mother with you, but no lies, Rupert.'

'All right.' He capitulated and nodded, a look of dawning respect in his eyes. 'My uncle was right about you, Ruby. You are too good for me. I am a rogue. I shall never be anything else. I know that... but I do like you and we can be just friends.' He grinned. 'To make up for it, I'll take you to the cinema on Saturday night. Will you come?'

Ruby laughed and then nodded. He did have such charm when he tried. 'Yes, I will come. You can call for me at this address.' She took a little notebook from her bag and wrote her address. 'Just remember, we are friends and no more.'

'Fine. It's a bargain,' he said and tucked the scrap of paper into his pocket. 'I'll pick you up at six and we'll have time to have a cup of tea before we catch the last showing.'

* * *

Ruby wondered if she should just have walked away as she rode home on the bus. Her instincts told her that Rupert could only be trouble in the end, but it hardly mattered. A man who hadn't touched her heart couldn't harm her. It might end in a quarrel one day but that would hurt him rather than her she thought. She liked his sister and his family.

A little smile touched her mouth as she thought of Rupert's uncle. He must really have liked her to threaten his nephew with being cut out of his will if he let her down.

Ruby's smile vanished as that thought made her recall her own legacy. She would be well off for as long as the payments lasted, but, oh, she would so much rather have had her Robert Saunders – her captain. Tears prickled again, but she fought them off. You couldn't bring back the dead.

She hoped the solicitor would reply soon. She would like to journey to wherever Robert was buried and pay her respects. Ruby had never dared to tell him the secrets of her heart while he lived, but she would do so as she stood by his grave and wept.

Lifting her head, she fought off her tears. Life went on and she had promised Shirley that she would give her a home perm that evening. Ruby was quite good at doing hair. She had pinned up the hair of some of the girls in the orphanage in the year or so before she left and curled her own regularly. It would be fun and she was sure she could make her friend's hair look nicer than it did just now.

21

The following Saturday, Beth was making a cake when her doorbell rang. She dusted flour from her hands and went to answer it, surprised to see her new neighbour standing outside. She smiled and invited her in, taking her through to the kitchen.

'I am in the middle of making a sponge cake,' she told Elizabeth. 'I'll put the kettle on and we'll have a cup of tea. I was just about to pop this in the oven.'

'Oh, I've come at a bad time,' Elizabeth said. 'I didn't mean to disturb you – should I go?'

'No, of course not,' Beth replied. 'It's lovely to see you, please sit down.' She looked at Elizabeth and realised that she was upset, her eyes red rimmed. 'Is there something wrong?' she asked and slid her cake tin into the oven.

'I didn't know where else to go,' she admitted. 'I can't stop long, because I've left my son sleeping – only—' Elizabeth drew a sobbing breath. 'I don't know what to do, Beth. Tel hasn't been home for three days...' In her distress, she had forgotten to use her husband's new name.

Beth frowned. When she thought about it, she hadn't seen

his car around for a few days. 'You mean he just went off and you don't know where he is?' she asked.

'He went to work same as usual,' Elizabeth said. 'He kissed me. We hadn't quarrelled and he said he might be a bit late home – but I expected him that evening.' She looked at Beth, her face strained. 'I think something has happened to him.'

'If he is missing...' Beth was thoughtful. If her husband was the man Beth thought, then going to the police wasn't an option. 'Have you tried ringing the hospitals?'

Elizabeth shook her head. 'Tel said I wasn't to do that if he suddenly went missing. He wouldn't like it if I went to the police or started ringing people.' She brushed a hand over her eyes. 'He is... a very private man, you see.'

Beth did see. She felt sympathy for the other woman but wondered what she could do to help her. 'What about Jerry?' she asked after some reflection. 'Have you thought about asking him?'

Elizabeth looked startled. 'You— mean—?'

'Jerry Woods, yes,' Beth said. 'I know Jerry and his mother well. I visit Bella sometimes.'

'Oh...' Elizabeth looked awkward. 'Tel wondered if you had guessed. Have you told anyone?'

'I wasn't certain, so, no, I haven't,' Beth replied gently. 'It isn't my business why your husband has changed his name, Elizabeth. I shan't talk about it – and I shall continue to be your friend, but I dare not ask you both to dinner, because my husband would be angry if he knew who and what your husband is.'

The other woman hung her head, then it all came out of her. 'Tel wanted us to have a better life. We had a small house on the corner just off Dressmaker's Alley and I was happy there – but Tel wanted to keep his business away from his family, so he moved us here and we use a different name. He bought an expensive car and thought we would make friends, but we haven't. You are the only one who has called – and I'm too nervous to call on any of them. They all look down their noses at me...'

'I am sorry you've been unhappy,' Beth said. 'It was a while before I made friends here. Of course you find it difficult, Elizabeth. With a small child and no family nearby.'

'I don't have any family, or none I wish to see,' Elizabeth confessed. 'I don't see much of Tel's family either. He takes the boy to see his mother sometimes, but I rarely go – he says his mother has a rough tongue and he doesn't want me being hurt.'

'Bella has a rough tongue but a heart of gold,' Beth told her. 'I think you need to contact Jerry – he usually knows what is going on.'

'Tel might be angry with me...' Elizabeth bit her lip.

'Would you like me to contact Jerry and ask if he knows where his brother is?' Beth saw the relief in the younger woman's face. 'Yes, I will do that for you, Elizabeth. I was going to visit Bella this afternoon.'

'Oh, thank you,' Elizabeth said, then, hesitating, 'Could you call me Betty or Betty Lou? Elizabeth doesn't feel like me. Tel likes it, but he doesn't need to know.'

'If you wish, Betty,' Beth replied and smiled. 'Now, I'll make that tea...?'

'I'd better go,' Betty said. 'I mustn't leave the little one alone long. If he wakes up and I'm not there, he might be frightened. Thank you for your help, Beth. I just didn't know what to do.'

Beth nodded and saw her to the door. 'Don't be afraid to call, Betty – and bring your little boy with you when you visit.'

She was thanked once more and Betty ran round to her own

house, letting herself in, almost as if she was afraid to be seen out of doors.

Beth frowned as she went back to the kitchen and took her cake from the oven. The smell of baking made her hungry and she decided she would have that cup of tea and something to eat, then she would pay Bella a little visit. She would leave her small car at home and take the Underground. If Jerry was on his old pitch, she could speak to him privately. If not, she would have to ask Bella to pass on a message, but for the moment she wouldn't tell Bella why she wanted to get in touch with Jerry.

* * *

Beth took some cakes and a bar of Fry's chocolate for Bella. She spent time talking to the elderly woman and asked her if Jerry would pay her a visit.

'What do yer want to see 'im for?' Bella asked.

'I want some nice fruit for a special occasion,' Beth replied easily, having decided on her excuse before she came. 'Jerry always gets me nice quality things, but I don't see him on his pitch these days.'

'I thought I told you he was selling it and his barrow,' Bella said, her eyes bright with curiosity. 'He's got a shop now, down the old Kent Road. Still goes to the wholesale markets every morning to buy fresh, but says it's warmer than standin' on the streets in the bitter cold. Don't know where he got the money from and he don't tell me.' She sniffed. 'Knows I'd clout his ears if it came from his brother.'

'Oh, Bella. You know that Tel only wants to help his family. You don't approve of what he does, but you must try to ignore that if you can.'

'Don't hold with things he does for that boss of his,' Bella sniffed.

'Got in with a bad crowd after his dad died. I know he has a good heart, but you can't tell me you approve of what he's mixed up in.'

'I don't know what he actually does,' Beth said with a grimace. 'I dare say I would dislike it as much as you if I did – but I ignore what I can't change.'

Bella gave a cackle of laughter. 'You should've been a bleedin' diplomat, Beth Burrows. Why don't you tell me what you really want to ask Jerry? Is it somethin' his brother's done?'

Beth hesitated, then, 'Jerry will tell you if he thinks you should know, Bella.'

'Ha! That's all you know – tell me, or I shan't pass on your message.'

Beth sighed, knowing the old lady was quite capable of carrying out her threat. 'Betty Lou is worried. Tel hasn't been home for three days.'

'Her!' Bella looked disapproving. 'Mebbe he's gone orf and left her – he knows what I think, taking up with a girl like that...' Bella sniffed hard.

'And left his son? You know how proud he is of his boy, Bella.'

Bella stared at her, then shook her head. 'It's what I've always feared – why I didn't want him in with that crowd – I've always thought that one day they would do fer 'im...' There was a glimmer of tears in her eyes, then she looked up at Beth. 'Who will take care of the boy and 'er if he's gorn?'

'I dare say Betty Lou could manage,' Beth replied. 'But you mustn't give up on him, Bella. Perhaps he is— just— well, keeping his head down for a while?'

'In trouble with the cops?' Bella glanced up, eyes narrowed. 'You might be right – though they haven't been near me.'

'Perhaps he— well, who knows?' Beth said. 'I would rather

not have told you, Bella. Now you will worry over him and upset yourself, probably for nothing.'

'You did right, girl. I won't be lied to or kept in the dark.'

'Well, if anyone knows where he is, Jerry will.' Beth checked her watch. 'I have to go. Fred has the boys, but I want to take them shopping. Tim needs some new shoes and Jack wants some plimsolls. I will let you know if I hear anything – but please ask Jerry to call on me with some fruit.'

'I shall – and I shan't tell him why you want him. If he hasn't told me, he doesn't want me to know. You can come and tell me when you find out what's goin' on...'

Beth laughed. 'You're a clever woman, Bella. I'll come as soon as I can – and if I find out anything I promise to tell you.'

Bella nodded and grinned, grasping Beth's hands as she took her leave and squeezing hard. 'You're a good woman. Thank you, Beth. You've made a difference to my life. You tell that girl, if anything happens to Tel, she is to bring the boy to us. We'll look after her and him.'

'Bless you, Bella.' Beth bent and kissed her cheek, tears stinging her eyes. Bella's leg was much better than it had been, but her feet still pained her and nothing the doctors did seemed to clear up the trouble. Although the treatment had stopped the breakdown of her skin into blisters and sores, the pain never left her.

'You've become a friend, Bella,' Beth told her. 'I care about you – and your family, though I don't know Tel enough to know what he might do – but I like Jerry and your grandson is a little darling.'

'You tell her she must come to me,' Bella said suddenly fierce. 'If he's dead and she's on her own, we'll look after her – no matter what she was...'

'It's what she is now – what your son saw in her – that matters,' Beth said. 'I'll visit soon.'

* * *

On her way home, Beth wondered if Bella was right. If you played with fire, you got burned, so the old saying went, and Tel Woods had certainly been living dangerously for some years. Beth didn't know anything about the criminal underworld, over which he had apparently ruled, but she did know there were people around who wouldn't think twice of killing someone like him, if they thought they could get away with it.

There was no sign of Jerry as she left the Underground. Once upon a time, she'd bought all her fruit from his barrow, because she always knew it would be fresh, but recently she'd had to buy elsewhere because she didn't want to travel just to buy fruit. She wondered if he could deliver some each week. She would speak to him when he visited and see if that was possible, but first she needed to ask him if he knew where his brother had gone.

Letting herself into her house, Beth went into the kitchen to put the kettle on to boil. She went upstairs to leave a couple of parcels on her bed. She'd seen a nice dress she liked on her way home and popped in to buy it. Hearing a slight noise downstairs, she called out, 'Jack, is that you? Fred...?'

There was no answer.

Beth frowned as she went back to the kitchen and then stifled a scream as she saw the man standing by her kettle. 'It was boiling over,' he said as he turned to look at her. She saw that he had a plaster on the side of his face, which was badly bruised.

'How did you get in?' Beth asked, though she was not afraid. 'You look as if you're in trouble.'

'Jerry said you were a remarkable woman,' Tel said but didn't smile. 'Most would've screamed their heads off if they'd seen me – and you really should make sure you lock your downstairs windows, Mrs Burrows. A thief could do this place and be gone before you got back from wherever you've been.'

'To your mother's to ask if Jerry could visit me,' Beth told him, almost certain she had turned the catch on her windows. 'Betty Lou is worried out of her mind over you.'

'Which is why I came to you, rather than let her see me like this,' he responded with a half-smile. 'I thought she might turn to you since you're the only one she knows…' Tel hesitated, then, 'May I ask you to do something for me? For Betty and the boy really…'

'Providing it isn't against the law,' Beth replied and heard him chuckle before he moaned.

'It hurts to smile,' he said ruefully. 'I am just asking you to reassure her – and to help her get to me when I send for her. I can't be seen here or anywhere in London. I came in the back way like this because I don't want you to suffer a visit from some nasty people. I think they may know where Betty is and the boy, but I've tried to protect them – I still have some loyal men.'

'What do you want me to do?' Beth asked, because she couldn't refuse to help Betty and the child and she was already committed whether she liked it or not.

'Thank you.' He smiled now despite the obvious pain. 'I will send word and then I want you to bring them to me – it will be outside of London. Not too far, but I can't risk a meet in London in case we're seen.'

'I can do that,' Beth said. 'I have my car. What about her clothes – and yours?'

'She will have to leave most of it,' he replied. 'Tell her to pack a couple of bags and throw them into your back garden. If anyone sees her leaving without bags, then they won't know she is coming to me.'

'Yes, that would be best,' Beth said, wondering at her own calm in plotting a desperate escape. 'Perhaps you could arrange for the house to be cleared – by one of your men – and put everything into store? It might be a while, but eventually you may be able to reclaim them.'

He looked at her appreciatively. 'It is what I intend, but the stuff doesn't matter much. I have money and Betty Lou didn't care for the posh house anyway. She'd do better in something more modest.' He gave a sharp laugh. 'I trained to be a carpenter once. I might set up a little business – somewhere my enemies will never find me.'

'I think Betty would appreciate that,' Beth said and smiled. 'I was picturing you dead in the river. For her sake, I am glad you aren't.'

'Thank you for being her friend. One day I will do something for you.'

Beth nodded, then as she heard voices, 'That is my father-in-law and the boys. You'd better go...'

'I'll go the way I came,' Tel said and opened the back door into the walled garden. 'I'll send word – and don't forget, be more careful with your windows...'

He was gone just before Tim burst in. He looked red-cheeked and healthy. 'Is there any cake, Mum?' he demanded. 'I swam three lengths of the pool. Jack only did one. I'm hungry...'

'Yes, I made a coffee and walnut sponge this morning,' Beth said, picking up the jacket her son had thrown over the back of a chair. She smiled as Fred walked in, with her son, Jack, following. 'Hello, Dad. Did you all have a good time?'

'It was lovely,' Fred replied. 'The lads enjoyed themselves.' He looked around him. 'Is Jack here?'

'No. I don't expect him until about nine. He has been at the restaurant all day, but this is his early night, so he will be home by then.'

'Oh – just thought I smelled cigarette smoke. Must be going daft in my old age.' Fred laughed at himself. 'You don't smoke, do you?'

'No, I don't.' Beth frowned. Had Tel been smoking in her kitchen? Her eyes lighted on an ashtray. There were two stubs in it. 'Look, that's what you can smell. I must have overlooked it when I cleaned up this morning.' She picked up the ashtray and emptied it into the range fire. 'I was in a bit of a hurry when I left.' She hoped Fred hadn't noticed the cigarette ends, which were not the brand her husband used, but some kind of flat cigarette that she thought might be a Turkish variety; they were certainly foreign.

Fred didn't say anything, but she caught an odd expression, as if he knew she had lied to him, but then he was smiling at her. 'Jack spent most of his time diving. He is getting really clever at it. You should come with us one day, Beth. Swimming is good for you.'

'Yes, I will,' she said. 'I went to visit Bella this afternoon. I'm hoping Jerry will bring me a box of fruit regularly. His is always so fresh – and the apples I bought on the market last week were nowhere near as good...'

'Ah, I see,' Fred said and nodded. 'Well, you're a good girl, Beth, and whatever you choose to do, you do it for a reason.'

Beth turned away to make their tea. Fred had heard or seen something, but he loved her and trusted her. She felt terribly guilty, because if her husband knew that she'd promised to help Tel Woods, he would be angry.

22

Ruby dressed smartly for her meeting with Marianne. She'd folded the dress Marianne had loaned her carefully and tied it up in brown paper with string so that it would be easy to carry. The past two weeks had gone quickly for Ruby. She'd been out twice with Rupert: once to the cinema, which she had enjoyed very much, and the second time to a party at one of his friend's house. She hadn't enjoyed that much, even though she'd worn the beautiful dress his sister had loaned her. She'd looked much as the other young women did, but she wasn't one of their set and they knew it. She'd seen them mocking her and Rupert, but he didn't seem to notice. He'd spent most of his time trying to get a very beautiful woman, older than him and obviously rich, to talk to him. However, she had greeted him with a kiss blown from her fingers and then ignored him.

If his object in taking Ruby along as his girlfriend had been to arouse jealousy in the woman he was clearly besotted with, it didn't work. Ruby had felt sorry for him, because she thought he looked like a scolded puppy and when he finally gave up and told her it was time to go, he sulked all the way to her home, before bidding her goodnight. He hadn't made any further plans for seeing her, though she knew he could suddenly turn up outside Harpers when she was least expecting it.

Dismissing her thoughts, Ruby left her lodgings and caught a bus up to the West End. Marianne had arranged to meet at a café that Ruby had been to once before. It was a quiet little tea shop and Marianne said it was where she often met friends.

It was a quarter past two when Ruby arrived. She went in but couldn't see Marianne, so she found a table and sat down. When the waitress approached, she told her that she was waiting for a friend but would have a pot of tea for now. It was served promptly and Ruby poured and drank one cup. She glanced at her watch. Marianne was late. Would she come at all?

Ruby poured herself another drink. She would finish the pot and wait another fifteen minutes and then, if Marianne didn't come, she would go window shopping. It was her favourite pastime if she came to the West End, but she couldn't afford to buy anything, although she knew that sixty pounds was to be placed in her account in May.

The solicitor had told her that it would continue for her lifetime. If she lived for a normal lifespan that amounted to thousands of pounds. Ruby still hadn't come to terms with her legacy, especially as the lawyer had not answered her questions about the way Robert Saunders had died. Why was that? Ruby felt uneasy and knew she must write once more, because why wouldn't they tell her?

She glanced at her watch as she put down her cup. It was nearly a quarter to three. Deciding that she had waited long enough, Ruby stood up, but as she did so the tea shop bell sounded and Marianne rushed in, looking across at Ruby. She came straight to her.

'You are still here! I am so glad – and sorry to have kept you waiting.' She moved towards Ruby and kissed her cheek. 'You look very well and that colour suits you. Is it a new coat?'

Ruby admitted it was. She'd spent a whole week's wage on it, but had felt she could afford it now that she had her legacy to look forward to. The coat had a tiny mark on one sleeve and it had been on Harpers' reduced rail. With her staff concession, Ruby had just managed to afford it.

'I wasn't sure about the colour,' she admitted to Marianne as they sat down. 'I've normally had grey or brown – but this is such a lovely French blue and I liked it when I tried it on.'

'It suits you so much better than grey,' Marianne told her. She was wearing a smart black coat with a velvet collar and cuffs and a bright red hat. 'I am so pleased to see you, Ruby. I was sorry to cancel last time, and I know I shall see you tomorrow at Mother's house – but I wanted a little time alone with you.' She smiled, her lovely face alight with happiness as she took off her leather gloves. Ruby saw the pretty three-stone diamond and emerald ring on the third finger of her left hand. Marianne nodded. 'Yes, I have my ring now. Mother has finally accepted that no one but Jonathan will do for me.' She smiled. 'I want you to be my bridesmaid, or one of them, Ruby.'

'Are you sure?' Ruby asked, feeling pleased but surprised. 'I mean – yes, I would love to, but don't you have other friends you would rather ask?'

'Yes, I have three others,' Marianne agreed. 'I want you to meet them – shall we go now? We can have tea with them at Rachel's home…'

'Yes, I am ready. I've paid for my pot of tea,' Ruby said and stood up as a waitress approached. She gave the girl an apologetic look, because she'd taken a table for a long time just for a drink.

Once outside, Marianne hailed a taxi and they were soon on

their way. Marianne explained that her friend lived in Southwark and two others would be there that afternoon. 'Sarah and Janet are friends I grew up with,' she told Ruby. 'Rachel is Jonathan's younger sister...'

Ruby smiled and listened as Marianne chattered excitedly. She was a little nervous, wondering whether Marianne's friends would snub her as she'd been snubbed at Rupert's friend's party. However, when they finally arrived at the smart terraced house, she was warmly welcomed and soon found herself chatting and laughing with the other girls. Rachel, Marianne's fiancé's sister was particularly friendly and Ruby liked her a lot. She discovered that Rachel worked as a secretary in Swan and Edgar, a large department store and very similar to Harpers, which meant they had a lot in common. In fact, all of the other girls did some kind of job, although Sarah and Janet's work was unpaid for a charity, because their fathers gave them a small allowance but refused to let them do paid work. To Ruby's surprise, they both envied her, her life and her independence.

'What I would give to be able to please myself where I went without having to explain it all to Mummy,' Sarah sighed. 'You are so lucky, Ruby. You can do whatever you like.' Janet nodded and agreed.

Ruby had never considered herself lucky before. She thought of girls like Janet and Sarah, and Marianne, as the lucky ones, but now she began to see that, yes, she was very fortunate. She had a good job which she enjoyed more and more and she was making a circle of friends – and then there was her legacy, which was quite wonderful, far beyond her wildest dreams. She could still hardly believe it, and yet her heart yearned for the man she'd known such a brief time.

Ruby learned a great deal from Marianne's friends that day, including how to have fun with other young girls. All of them had their measurements taken for the dresses that would be needed and with much giggling and laughter, styles, materials and colours were discussed; in the end, they all decided the bridesmaids' dresses should be a pale peach silk which would blend well with the ivory satin Marianne would be wearing and suit them all.

The time flew by and it seemed too soon when she and Marianne departed with Sarah. Janet was staying on at Rachel's a short time, until her father's car came to fetch her, but Ruby, Sarah and Marianne shared a taxi to the railway station, where they all said goodbye and caught separate trains.

* * *

It was past seven when Ruby entered her lodgings and Mrs Flowers gave her a sour look. 'Been gadding out again,' she said and sniffed. 'This came for you by hand this afternoon.' She handed Ruby a letter and she recognised the handwriting on the envelope. It was from her lawyers. Oh, how grand that sounded. She had her own lawyers, something she knew would astound Marianne's friends.

'I shan't need anything to eat this evening,' Ruby told Mrs Flowers with a new confidence. 'I shall be out to tea again tomorrow, I think.'

'You'll be getting too big for your boots – some folk don't know how lucky they are.'

Ruby nodded but didn't reply. Mrs Flowers no longer had the power to reach her. It would be a simple thing for a girl with her legacy to find new lodgings, but for the moment it suited her where she was. A few weeks ago, she would have been trembling with fear at the thought she might be turned out into the street! Captain Saunders had given her so much more than money. Her eyes misted. How she wished he was alive and could see what he had done for her – but perhaps he was watching her from heaven. That thought made her smile and she found it comforting.

She took her letter to her room and turned it over suspiciously, nodding to herself as she saw it had been steamed open and stuck down again. It was hardly noticeable apart from a small tear one side and she might not have spotted it had her landlady not made that remark. It was an intrusion into her private life and Ruby was angry, but if she quarrelled with her landlady she would have to move and she wasn't yet ready to do so.

Opening the envelope, Ruby read the few lines written there. It confirmed her initial payment was on the first of the month. At the bottom of the page, Ruby saw a small, typed postscript.

> It is to your credit that you wish to visit the grave, Miss Rush, however, it would be difficult to obtain permission for you to do so. Captain Saunders was interred in a family crypt and I would need to obtain permission from them for you to go in. I must advise you not to pursue this as I know that Captain Saunders would not wish it.

Ruby stared at that last paragraph, feeling puzzled. It was true that she had only known Captain Saunders a short time – but why would his family deny her the release of spending a little time by his grave? She hadn't thought he would be buried in a family crypt. Only aristocrats had family crypts, as far as she'd ever heard. Why then had he chosen to live in a small boarding house like Mrs Flowers'? It could only be that he'd wanted to hide away from his own world. Scarred by his terrible affliction, he had felt compelled to disappear where his friends and family could not find him – and only a solicitor's letter telling of his father's impending death had forced him from his refuge.

Ruby felt the sadness of Robert's situation and his death. If only they'd had a little more time together, she thought. She was sure that she could have made him happier. Love healed, didn't it? His care for her had already healed her so much, though now she had her regret and grief that they could never be man and wife or even friends. Just to know him, to be able to talk to him, to help him and share his life. It was all she would ask.

Sighing, Ruby put her letter away with the others from the solicitor. She kept them in an old leather case that she could lock. A little smile touched her mouth. Her landlady must have been ridden with curiosity over the letters that had suddenly started arriving for her. Ruby didn't think she'd ever opened one of her letters before, but she'd only had one from Harpers when she was first employed there.

Well, now she knew that Ruby had been left some money, though this letter hadn't told her how much. No doubt she was curious and wondering whether Ruby would leave to find accommodation closer to her work. Ruby had decided that she would stay here for the time being, unless Mrs Flowers made life too uncomfortable. She had Shirley's companionship some evenings now; they had been to the pictures once and planned to go dancing one weekend with some other girls.

Ruby's life was certainly changing for the better. She would have tea with Marianne's mother the next afternoon. The following weekend, Ruby was helping the sewing circle again and returning with Kitty for tea at her home. Mariah was lovely. Ruby had taken to her immediately. There was such a warm atmosphere in their little home that she'd been reluctant to leave.

Yes, Ruby thought, her life was changing fast and next week she would have sixty pounds in her bank account. It was so much money for a girl who had been reared in an orphanage and never owned anything. She had thought it through and decided she would allow herself to spend a few pounds each month, but she would let most of it stay in the bank to earn something called interest.

Perhaps in time she could buy her own home and even have a friend to live with her and share the expenses. It was something Ruby needed to think about. Having money was exciting but decisions came with it. What she really wanted was to be with someone who loved her...

Ruby shook her head and got out her dress for the following day. She must just make the most of her life, enjoy all she could. Kitty said that she would never love another man – but at least she'd had someone who wanted to wed her, even if it had never happened. Ruby wished with all her heart that Captain Saunders – or Robert as she now called him in her head – hadn't died. She would so much rather have had him as her friend. Or, if she'd been really lucky, as her husband.

23

'So that's what they've been doing!' Ben Harper stared in disbelief at the piece of paper that he'd discovered discarded in a trash can he'd accidentally knocked over. It was an invoice for twenty thousand dollars, for diamond and precious stone jewellery and expensive cocktail watches. Something had made him check it against the stock book for the jewellery department. Not one piece had been recorded and when he looked in the counters themselves, nothing matched the invoice.

He frowned over the evidence. The delivery had taken place only a week ago. He would have to request a search was made for it – and then heads would roll if it couldn't be found. Just how many consignments of expensive merchandise had gone astray? His mind boggled to think it was still going on under his nose and he was determined to discover who was behind this fraud on a massive scale. No wonder the profits had diminished if this amount of theft had gone unnoticed – and yet it surely couldn't have? Someone in authority had turned a blind eye – and Ben was pretty certain he knew who to blame.

It wasn't going to be pleasant, confronting his cousin with

the evidence, but he couldn't ignore this. Ben couldn't imagine what possessed a man like Hugh to do such a thing. How could he have cheated his own mother – and the shareholders?

As Ben left his office, nodding to Jaco, the elderly janitor as they passed in the hallway, he wondered if he would ever have got to the truth if someone hadn't carelessly discarded the invoice, and if he hadn't accidentally knocked over the trash can. He frowned as he wondered why the invoice was there in his office. Who had put it there and why hadn't the trash been emptied? Or had it been placed there on purpose? Did someone want him to know what was going on? Maybe, he should have a word with the janitor. Nodding to himself, he walked out into the busy street, the noise of the traffic louder after the stillness of the empty store. People like Jaco saw and heard things that might be dangerous for them to repeat – but perhaps he knew something. Ben would ask another day.

As he began to cross the road, he was honked at several times. Some of the cab drivers were impatient and rude, yet he enjoyed the cut and thrust of New York. He walked swiftly, knowing that he must confront his cousin. Theft on such a grand scale must be stopped. He wished he knew someone he could trust with his suspicions, someone he could talk to – but he didn't know anyone well enough to show them what he'd discovered...

Suddenly, Ben had a longing to be back in London with the simpler life he'd enjoyed. He felt a pang of guilt as he recalled his harsh words to Sally, muttering to himself, 'Bloody fool!' as he approached the prestigious building where his cousin resided. He squared his shoulders as he went in. It had to be done but it wasn't going to be pleasant.

* * *

The letter from Ben arrived at the end of May. Sally took a deep breath before opening it, her heart racing as she wondered what it might say. Had her husband written to tell her that their marriage was over because she didn't want to move to New York?

She used her silver paperknife to open the envelope, swiftly read the first few lines and expelled her caught breath in a sigh of relief. It seemed that Ben had had time to reflect on his hasty words and had apologised, she thought sincerely.

Tears stung her eyes, but then she caught her breath once more as she read the last few paragraphs.

Things here are much worse than I realised, Sally. My cousin is deeply involved in something I fear is beyond me. I know that he takes cocaine and believe that he may be controlled by a powerful criminal element that wants to invest its ill-gotten gains in a thriving business. Apparently, some of these criminal bosses want to move into ownership of legitimate businesses, and my aunt's store is one they have targeted.

I am not certain yet, but I believe my cousin has large gambling debts to these men and that in fact they own his shares, though his name is the figurehead for a company set up to include the shares. After I confronted my cousin with my evidence, I was approached to sell my shares by someone highly suspicious. I was offered favours, involving young girls, that I found disgusting. Some pressure was brought to bear, but I refused. I believe you were right, Sally. It would be foolish to invest our lives in something that may be beyond saving. I dare say the store will thrive once more if these people get what they want.

I have discovered how they are milking the profits. Stock that has been paid for has never been delivered, or has been appropriated by someone in authority at the store, some of it extremely valuable. Because of the size of the stocks held it wasn't noticed until I ordered a spot check and took them by surprise. It was discovered that expensive watches, jewellery and valuable silverware was not in the stock rooms only a few days after a delivery had been made, nor was it on the floor. How long or how much of this has gone on, I cannot say, but certainly for some months.

There was some write-off last year, but as you know there is always a certain amount of lost or damaged stock. The store's manager swears he checked it in himself, but is lying. I have not yet dismissed him, because I need to have him before the Board for questioning. However, he must have been involved and may well decide to leave without notice. This being the case, I am determined to lay the facts before the regulatory board and the law enforcement authorities as shareholders have been defrauded. I will then sell my shares on the open market. I cannot exclude the possibility that they will be purchased by these unsavoury persons, but I feel I shall have done my duty by my aunt and the other shareholders by exposing this fraud.

Threats against my life have been made, but I do not see what they have to gain by my death. At least, not until they discover what I've done with the evidence I've gathered. My one fear is that it may not be enough. These people are enormously wealthy and can employ clever lawyers who may well pour scorn on my evidence. However, I have kept my word and got to the bottom of it. Once I hand it over, it is up to others to go forward.

So, my dearest Sally, I expect to return home within two months and I ask you to forgive my behaviour before I left. I had dreams of making a huge fortune, but what I have discov-

ered has sickened me and I know that the life I have with you and the children is of far more value.

Believe that I love you all.

Ben

A trickle of fear ran down Sally's spine as she finished reading his letter. Her eyes filled with tears, because despite his ambition and his big dreams, Ben had come to his senses and realised what was good and true in life. However, her instincts had been right the night Ben had walked out on her. His life was in danger. She felt it to her very core – but Ben wasn't taking the threats seriously. He believed they were just threats, but men like those he described were ruthless and if he got in their way, they would not hesitate to swat him like an annoying gnat.

What should she do? Could she contact Ben and persuade him to return home at once? He was determined to expose the fraud he'd discovered. When the end-of-year accounts were published, the shareholders would sell shares for a price far below their true worth. In fact, she knew from what Ben had told her before he left that the shares had already lost a third of their value, due to rumours that the business was failing. It was fraud and theft and the people behind it stood to gain much, because they would take over a profitable business for far less than its true worth, and the money invested could not be traced back to their criminal activities.

Sally decided she would send Ben a telegraph asking him to come home. She would use the words: *Just come home. Need and love you, Sally.*

If only he wasn't all that way off. It was impossible for her to get to him swiftly enough to stop him doing as he intended. If Ben placed evidence before the right authorities those behind this illegal takeover might be stopped – and the kind of men he was dealing with would strike back and strike hard. Her throat felt tight with fear, because she knew how stubborn her husband could be. He had admitted he was wrong to put the dream of huge wealth before her and the children, but he would never give into threats, no matter how she pleaded with him.

'Oh, Ben,' Sally said, her eyes wet with tears. 'Please come home safely to me.' She needed him here with her and the children. Sally knew that by her refusal to go to America with him she had put her happiness in jeopardy, but, had she gone, she and the children would also have been at risk – indeed, they might have been used against Ben. Had she and her children been kidnapped, Ben must have given way to their demands.

Sally shivered and involuntarily looked towards the windows. Were they all locked and the doors secured? If those men knew where to find her... But she was letting her imagination run away with her. However, she would be very careful for a while.

Dashing her tears away, Sally reached for her jacket and bag. She would send her telegram and then go into the office. Mick was meeting her that afternoon for tea. Sally would confide some of her fears to him. He might give her some much-needed advice.

* * *

'I think you've done all you can,' Mick said and touched her hand as they sat opposite one another in the small tea shop later that day. 'Sure, if you sent that to me, I'd be on the next ship home.' His smile caressed her, then he looked serious. 'Ben knows what he's dealing with, Sally. I've come across the sort of people he's up against. Not the same but similar... they come in all shapes and forms, but many of the really wealthy ones are seeking to take over big business, because there has been a crackdown against them. If the law enforcement can't tie the boss into the rackets he controls, they go for his tax accounts, anything they can get to put him away for a while. It just means that his family – and by that, I mean his lieutenants as well as sons and wives – they just continue to run it without him until he is released.'

Sally gave a little shudder. 'It is all horrid. These people are evil.'

'What they do is evil and morally wrong, but some of them are pleasant enough,' Mick said. 'I dare say you meet them on the street or at parties you go to and you don't know – they don't have "criminal" branded on their foreheads.'

'I know…' Sally shook her head. 'A couple of years ago we had reason to be thankful to a London gang boss…' Mick raised his brows. 'It was something to do with the restaurant, but I shan't go into details – but this man – Tel Woods, I think his name was, he sorted it in his own way. So I suppose some of them are OK according to their values – but these men have threatened Ben.' She looked at Mick. 'I'm frightened. I had this feeling that his life was in danger but… I thought it was just me being silly.'

'Of course you worry about Ben,' Mick said. 'I would like to tell you I could fix it, Sally – but even if I could get a message to him, he wouldn't listen. You know Ben can't be pushed. He is too stubborn. If he is determined to expose these people, he will.'

'I know. That is what frightens me.'

'I could go out myself,' Mick told her.

'No, don't waste your effort,' Sally said. 'He would just be angry that I had told you.' She smiled. 'He is still jealous of you, Mick.'

'We've always been friends, Sally, but just friends. He must surely know that you love him and the children too much to throw it away for a fling – not that it would be on my part. You know I've always loved you,' Mick said. 'Whatever you need, Sally. I shall always be here for you. I know that doesn't help with your fears for Ben, but if you need me...'

'I know,' Sally said, smiling mistily at him. 'You are such a good friend, Mick. Why didn't I marry you?'

'Because that Yankee came and stole you from me,' he said with a glint of mischief in his eyes. 'I'd like to say everything will be fine, Sally, but I shan't lie to you. I think Ben should cut and run. Lay his evidence if he must, but then get out fast... I have friends, Sally – they are from an Irish organisation and they sometimes break our laws. I try not to be involved with them, but they have a wide network over in America. I can get word out that Ben is to be protected. It will be a few days, but these gangsters won't murder him unless they know what he is planning. His shares would then come to you and they wouldn't benefit, unless they could persuade you to sell...'

'Are you talking about the IRA?' Sally asked, frowning.

'You don't need to know who my friends are – and don't go thinking I approve of what they do,' he said. 'I worked with some of them years ago and because of that I am owed a few favours. I will make contact but...' Mick shrugged. 'It doesn't mean this gang can't get to him if they really want to. You too and the children. So I shall ask for you to be shadowed wherever you go – and the children. Make sure someone takes them to school and meets them.'

Sally drew a sobbing breath. 'Why did his aunt leave him those wretched shares?' she asked. 'If she'd left them to her son, Ben wouldn't have been involved in any of this.'

* * *

Sally lay in bed thinking for a long time that night before she could sleep. She'd always known that Mick had powerful friends; long ago when he'd helped Ben sort out a building problem, he'd called in some favours. The builders Ben had employed had walked off the job after demanding an extortionate amount to finish the work. Mick had found builders to take over – men who weren't afraid of the violence that was offered them by the fraudulent gang.

The newspapers sometimes carried reports of the bombing of public places that was put down to an organisation called the IRA. Was Mick in touch with them? Sally suspected it but tried not to dwell on the possibility. He was very well informed on things that went on behind the scenes, but she knew that he was right. In big business there was often corruption and fraud, tax evasion and all kinds of illegal stuff. Just because he knew people didn't mean he was like them. Mick was just Mick. He might scoff at rules and regulations, but he had his own high principles and that included looking after his friends.

Well, there was nothing she could do about it either way. Anyway, if there was an organisation that might protect Ben from some nasty people who were threatening him, she didn't much care who they were.

A cold chill went down her spine as she recalled Mick's words, 'If these people really want to get to him, they will...'

Oh God, no! Please, please don't let anything happen to Ben. I love him. I need him.

Sally closed her eyes, tears trickling down her cheeks. If Ben went ahead and exposed these men and what they were trying to do, would he ever be safe again? Even if he got home, there was no guarantee he wouldn't be targeted right here in London.

'Ben,' Sally murmured. 'What have you got yourself into, my love?'

24

Kitty was feeling a little tired as she let herself into the house and heard voices from the kitchen. A visitor – and she knew who it must be. She felt a chill at her nape, something telling her that her uncle must have taken a turn for the worse. Mr Harvey was here and she could only think of one reason why he should come – because he wanted her to visit Sir Peter at his home.

'Mr Harvey – no, please don't get up,' Kitty said as she entered the kitchen. He was sitting at the table, a cup of tea and cake in front of him. 'What can I do for you?'

'Sir Peter asked me to call and invite you to visit him one last time.'

Kitty nodded. It was as she'd expected. 'I do have some holiday due, but Mrs Harper is so busy at the moment that I don't like to ask for time off.'

'I know it must be difficult for you – but perhaps a Saturday to Monday would be acceptable? A car will fetch you both and bring you back. It is almost certainly your last chance to see him alive, Miss Wilson.'

'I think you should, dearest,' Mariah said. 'It would be unkind to refuse and I think you might regret it.'

Kitty sighed, because Mariah was right. 'Very well, I will speak to Mrs Harper tomorrow. Make the arrangements and I shall visit him.'

'Thank you.' Mr Harvey's face lit up. Kitty realised he was nice-looking and still a young man. She hadn't paid too much attention to him before now, because he'd annoyed her by spying on her, but his obvious pleasure because she'd agreed made her realise that he did care about Sir Peter. 'He will be happy to see you again, I know.'

Kitty smiled in return. 'I only wish that we had been able to meet years ago,' she said. 'It was foolish of me to resent the investigations you made on his behalf. I was upset and angry, but in the circumstances it was understandable.'

'I am so glad,' Mr Harvey replied and offered his hand. He looked at Mariah and nodded. 'Thank you for your hospitality, Mariah. It has been a pleasure talking to you – both.'

Kitty walked with him to the door and then returned. Mariah had poured her a cup of tea.

'Supper will be ready soon,' she said. 'I've made a chicken pie this evening.'

'Lovely. You're such a good cook, Mariah.' Kitty looked at her. 'How long has Mr Harvey been addressing you as Mariah? Is he being impertinent or did you allow him?'

'I like the man,' Mariah told her and laughed. 'For goodness' sake, Kitty. Can't you see the poor man has fallen head over heels for you?'

'Nonsense!' Kitty exclaimed in astonishment. 'He doesn't know me – and I haven't been very nice to him.'

'Well, I've got eyes to see,' Mariah said. 'I wonder what excuse he'll find to visit next time.'

'What do you mean?'

'He could have sent you a letter or a telegram. He didn't need to come himself – even a clerk could've delivered your uncle's letter.' Mariah pointed to an envelope on the table.

Kitty frowned. 'He's nice enough, Mariah, and I've forgiven him for what he did – but he's nothing to me.'

'You can't stop him from hoping, though, can you?'

Kitty just shook her head. She had no interest in romance or marriage. Her heart was with Larry Norton and always would be.

* * *

'Of course you must visit your uncle,' Sally said when Kitty told her the next day. 'Take longer if you wish, Kitty. You are due some holiday.'

'I know how busy we are and I don't want to let you down,' Kitty said. 'But it will probably be my last chance to see him. I can't claim to love him, because we only met recently – but I think he is a good man and it would be unkind not to visit after he went to the trouble of having me found.'

'As I understand it, he is your only relative?'

'Yes – and one I never knew existed.' Kitty explained briefly how angry she'd been at first but now felt merely sorry they had not known each other years before.

'Yes...' Sally nodded. 'Something similar happened to me when my mother followed me for a while before telling me who she was.' She smiled. 'I was angry but then so happy to have met her, but then I was ill...' Sally shook her head at the memory. She had been carrying a child and her illness had almost killed her. 'When do you wish to go?'

'I would like to leave on Friday and return on Tuesday.'

'Are you sure that is long enough, Kitty?'

'Yes, I think so,' Kitty replied. 'My uncle is well cared for and I can't really do anything for him, other than to just sit with him for a while.'

'Then you have my blessing,' Sally told her smiling. 'If you should feel it necessary to stay longer, just let me know. It is true that I need your help more and more, Kitty, but you must have your own life, too.'

Kitty blushed and thanked her. It still felt like a dream that Sally Harper had taken her from the sales force and made Kitty her personal assistant. She knew that she was very fortunate, because she loved her work. There was so much variety, such a lot happening all the time that she felt stimulated and excited, determined to do her very best for her employer.

'You've been so good to me,' she said impulsively. 'I'm not sure that I ever thanked you.'

'Many times,' Sally replied with a laugh. 'Now, tell me, what did you think of the latest batch of summer hats? Did we order enough?'

'I'm not sure we did,' Kitty said. 'Those latest creations are very popular. I spoke to Ruby this morning and she says that Shirley sold ten of the straw yesterday; five navy, two black, two red and a pale blue. Shirley thinks we need to order extra.'

'Then we must certainly order more,' Sally said. She glanced at her watch. 'Will you do that for me, please? I have an appointment at a new bag manufacturer's in an hour. I am a little tired of our normal stock. I think we need to freshen it with some new ideas.' Sally smiled as she reached for her jacket and then placed a jaunty red hat on her head, before picking up her gloves and bag. 'I'm having lunch with some friends, but I shall be back this afternoon and we'll go through the stock lists for the men's clothing department, the shoe department and the glass and silverware.'

'I'll have them ready for you,' Kitty promised. She nodded as Sally left and then picked up the telephone receiver and gave a number to the operator, who put her through to the lady she needed.

'This is Kitty Wilson from Harpers,' she said. 'How are you, Sarah?' She nodded as the response came, 'Good. I am very well, thank you. I need to reorder those straw hats you created for us. You have some new styles too?' Kitty listened to the description. 'I think we will take three in each colour, as well as six of the navy, three red – and the white straw. Yes, the white sold out yesterday. I think we'd better have six of that one.'

They chatted some more before Kitty replaced the receiver and then reached for her notepad to jot down what she'd ordered so she could tell Sally when she returned. It was time for her to take her break, but she would ask Ruby to bring her some coffee and eat her sandwiches at her desk. The lists Sally wished to go through were ready, but Kitty wanted to go over them herself first so that she could make things easier for her employer. She would also ask the heads of department to inform her of anything they had sold a lot of since the last results were typed up. Sometimes, there would be a run on things – like those latest straw hats and it made sense to reorder quickly if something was selling fast.

* * *

When Kitty left work that evening, she stopped to buy some bits and pieces that Mariah needed on her way home. She was smiling as she entered her home and placed her parcels on the hall table, then caught the sound of voices, frowning as she heard Mr Harvey answering Mariah. Her heart caught. Had something happened suddenly to Sir Peter?

'Ah, there you are, love,' Mariah said as she entered the kitchen. 'Mr Harvey just called to tell you that Sir Peter has also asked him to go down to Hampshire this weekend and to make sure that we would be happy to travel with him.' There was a little gleam of mischief in Mariah's eyes. 'I was sure you wouldn't mind...'

'No, of course not,' Kitty answered and smiled. 'I've spoken to Mrs Harper and she is happy for me to have the time off.'

His face lit up and Kitty's heart caught. She'd thought Mariah was imagining things, but now she wasn't so sure. 'That is very good of you,' he said. 'I could go down by train, of course, but Sir Peter's car is large and comfortable and there's no waiting about on platforms to change trains.'

'Well, it makes sense for us to go together,' Kitty replied. 'Is it a long journey, Mr Harvey?'

'Nearly two hours,' he replied. 'Perhaps longer if there is heavy traffic out of London. I shall provide a hamper, Miss Wilson. Just some drinks and a few bits and pieces should you feel hungry.'

'How thoughtful,' Kitty replied. At that moment, she thought he resembled an eager puppy and her mouth trembled as she looked at Mariah, holding her laughter back.

Mr Harvey talked for a few minutes longer and then left. Kitty's eyes met Mariah's and then, as soon as the front door closed behind him, she giggled.

'Now, *was* I talking nonsense?' Mariah asked. 'It's as plain as can be – he is besotted.' She laughed and Kitty shook her head.

'No, we mustn't laugh,' she said, suppressing her mirth. 'It is sad, because I don't feel the same. I can see he is a nice person but—'

'Don't close your mind to the possibility of love,' Mariah said. 'I know you loved Larry, but he wouldn't want you to mourn him forever. He would want you to be happy. I know you are content just now – but one day you might regret all you've lost, dearest. Just give yourself a chance – I don't say you will love Mr Harvey, but be open to the idea that you might once you get to know him.'

Kitty smiled at her. 'I love you,' she said. 'For the moment that is enough – but I know you are right, Mariah. I shan't cut off my nose to spite my face.'

25

Beth heard her letterbox rattle that morning. The post was later than usual, she thought as she went through to the hall, bent down, and picked up the one envelope. Opening it as she returned to the kitchen, she felt a start of unease as she started to read, realising it was from Tel Woods. She looked back at the envelope and saw there wasn't a stamp or postmark; it had been delivered by hand. Returning to the few lines he'd written, Beth saw that he'd asked her to bring Betty to him the next day. It was a Saturday and the boys would be home from school. Jack would be at work, so she would need to ask Fred to have the boys all day.

Betty had thrown her bags over the fence a while ago and Beth had them packed in the boot of her car. She'd had qualms about this ever since she'd agreed and not just because she was deceiving her husband. Supposing she was being watched by Tel Woods' enemies? What would happen if they were followed? Her mouth felt dry as she allowed herself to think about what she'd vowed to do. She wished she had refused him and yet... Betty needed help. The men who were still loyal to him couldn't help because they must be marked men, probably in hiding for their lives. She would just have to plan things very carefully.

Beth couldn't start to imagine what was behind all this – the change of name and then the assault on Tel Woods and his urgent visit to her. She'd known that he was close to being the Big Boss, had in fact taken over the organisation, according to his brother Jerry, but something must have gone badly wrong for him. Beth didn't know what and didn't want to – but she had to keep her promise. She wished that she could just put the letter on the fire and forget it, but her conscience wouldn't let her. It wasn't only Betty and the child, it was Bella, too. Despite all her protestations, Beth knew that the old lady she'd come to think of as a friend loved her eldest son. Bella would take it badly if anything happened to her son and his family.

So, she'd promised and she must keep her word, Beth thought, her nerves jumping. If someone was watching Tel's house, they might try to follow, but she just had to hope that whoever it was didn't have a car. Normally, they wouldn't need it to follow Betty, because she rarely went further than the local shops. Beth nodded to herself. She had an idea that might just work. She took a deep breath and then went round to tell Betty when to be ready and what to do.

* * *

The next morning, after Fred had taken the boys off for the day, Beth got her car out and drove away from the house. She'd arranged to meet Betty outside the shop they both frequented. Rather than take her from the house, she'd thought it might look more natural if she just picked her up from outside the shop, as if just giving her a lift home, but instead they would drive out of London, to the new life that Tel had planned for his wife and child.

Fred hadn't objected when Beth told him she needed him to look after the boys. He'd looked at her a bit oddly when she'd said she was meeting a friend and would be gone for some hours, but he hadn't asked questions. She knew that he trusted her and she felt guilty, because Fred wouldn't approve of what she was doing any more than her husband would. Both of them would be afraid she was getting into something dangerous that she didn't understand, and they would be right.

Beth's heart raced as she saw Betty waiting for her, but she simply drew to a halt, opened the door and Betty got in with her child. She had just her shopping basket with her, as arranged. It was filled with food she'd bought in case the child got hungry on the way.

Beth glanced in the driving mirror as she drove away. She thought she caught sight of a man starting to run, but wasn't sure it had anything to do with the fact that she'd picked up Betty.

'Do you think you were followed this morning?' she asked as she drove away, checking to see if a car was following. She saw two lorries and a baker's van, but that was local and turned off after a few minutes.

'I don't know,' Betty replied. 'I didn't see anyone – but they know how to follow without being noticed.' Her eyes were wide as she looked at Beth. 'It is so good of you to do this. I hope it won't make trouble for you.'

'Why should it?' Beth said but knew it could. Her stomach was tying itself in knots. If whoever was after Tel came knocking, she could be in for a difficult time – but she wouldn't think about that... 'I don't know what Tel has done and I don't want to

– but I think it must have been pretty bad. I hope whoever it is doesn't catch up with him.'

'It wasn't Tel,' Betty said. Beth glanced at her and saw how pale she looked. 'They tried to move in on his territory and he... Well, I shouldn't tell you, but he had to do it. He killed someone or thought he had... but the person survived and he sent someone to kill Tel. He only got away because someone helped him.' She gave a little choking cry. 'They'll kill us if they get to us, Beth. All of us. I pray they don't ever find us...'

'My God!' Beth was horrified. What had she got mixed up in? She hadn't dreamed it could be that evil – murder! A shudder went down her spine. She prayed she hadn't endangered her family because of what she had done.

* * *

It was three o'clock in the afternoon when Beth returned home. She had dropped Betty at the arranged meeting place and watched as Tel emerged, snatched up her bags, bundled them all into a battered old van and drove off. He'd saluted her, but Betty had thanked her.

'I shall never forget what you've done for us,' she'd said moments before she jumped out of the car to be reunited with her husband. 'Tel won't forget it either, Beth. One day he will repay you.'

'You owe me nothing. I just pray that you can settle to a new life and be happy, as you deserve.'

'Oh, I shall. Tel has promised me he has finished with his old life. He has enough money put by to set up his own little business and keep us. All I want is for him to be safe and us to be together.'

'Well, just be happy...'

Betty had kissed her, jumped out of the car and was gone in the blink of any eye.

Beth had been thoughtful on her way home. Her part in Betty's escape was over and no one need ever know about it. She hoped Tel's enemies wouldn't come asking awkward questions. As far as Beth was concerned it was over. She would probably never hear from them again and that would be the best thing for all concerned.

She had taken off her coat and hat when Fred arrived with the boys. She smiled at him. 'I was just about to make a cup of tea,' she said. 'Would you care for one?'

'Yes, please, love,' Fred said. His eyes sought hers. 'Everything all right, Beth?'

'Why don't you boys go upstairs and wash your hands?' she asked and the children ran off obediently.

Fred's expression was serious but trusting. 'Are you and Jack OK?'

'Yes.' Beth laughed. 'I haven't been having an affair. I just helped a friend in need. Jack wouldn't approve of the friend, but I felt obliged to help. I can't tell you – and Jack wouldn't be happy if he knew – but it is all over. Please believe me, Fred.'

'I do,' he replied with his easy smile. 'I'd trust you with my life, Beth. I won't ask anything more. I don't need to know.'

'It's over now,' Beth repeated, crossing her fingers behind her back. She could only pray that the men who had been watching Betty's every move wouldn't come calling.

26

That Friday afternoon, Kitty was able to leave early and prepare for her visit to her uncle. She packed a small bag and Mariah did the same. They were ready and waiting when the large Rolls-Royce car came to pick them up. Mr Harvey got out, as did Sir Peter's chauffeur. He stowed their cases in the boot beside the hamper Mr Harvey had packed for them, and Mr Harvey opened the rear doors for Kitty and Mariah to get in.

'There is a rug provided if you feel cold,' he said. 'We can stop halfway and have the refreshments from the hamper – and if either of you feel the need of a comfort break, please tell me. We are here to assist you – aren't we, Rawlings?'

Rawlings acknowledged it, getting back into the driver's seat as Mr Harvey took his place in the front beside him. 'Yes, sir. Sir Peter asked that you have every comfort, ladies. Please ask if you need anything at all.'

Kitty assured them that they would and the chauffeur started the car and moved off. Mariah looked slightly nervous for a moment as she was unused to travelling by car, but then she relaxed and sat back on the comfortable seat.

'Well, this is nice,' she said to Kitty. 'I'm sure it will be no hardship to travel in this car, my love.'

'No, it is very comfortable,' Kitty said, smiling. 'We are lucky that Sir Peter sent it for us.'

'He considers himself lucky that you've agreed to visit,' Mr Harvey said, looking round at them. 'He was very favourably impressed when he met you, Miss Wilson.'

'Of course he was,' Mariah replied. 'She is a lovely girl – always thinks of others.'

'Indeed, I know that to be true,' he replied.

Kitty blushed and shook her head at Mariah. 'I brought some magazines if you want to look at them?'

'I'd rather look out of the window,' Mariah said. 'This is a rare treat and I don't want to waste a minute of it. I don't often get to see green fields and open countryside.'

Kitty laughed, amused at her friend's pleasure in the outing. 'It is a treat, isn't it?' she said. 'What would your dad have thought if he could see us now?'

'Oh, Dad would take it in his stride,' Mariah said confidently. 'He'd think we deserved it – always liked nice things, my dad.'

'Yes, he did, and he taught me to appreciate them, too,' Kitty said, her smile half-sad and half-pleased. She missed Alf and Larry so much, but the memories were sweet. Larry might have been impressed by Sir Peter's car, but Alf would have said it was just about good enough for his girls.

* * *

They stopped twice on their way down to Sir Peter's home. Once so that Mariah could go to the bathroom in a nice hotel with grounds they could park in and the second time in a pleasant village with a green, where they ate some sandwiches and tiny cakes and drank tea from a flask. After that, the scenery was nearly all countryside and Kitty enjoyed watching all the new sights as much as Mariah. They passed churches and big houses, as well as open fields and lots of trees. Sheep and cattle grazed peacefully in the fields as they drove through more rural areas, and then Mr Harvey announced that they were nearly there.

For more than ten minutes, they passed through an avenue of trees and then what looked like a country park and then the chauffeur pulled up outside a modest country manor house. Mr Harvey confided that the avenue of trees was the start of Sir Peter's grounds.

'It isn't a huge estate, like some you will find in this part of the country,' he said. 'Perhaps fifty or sixty acres of parkland and a wood – but the house is old and I think you will enjoy your stay.'

He got out and opened Kitty's door. Rawlings did the same for Mariah and then he fetched their suitcases, saluting smartly.

'I hope you had a pleasant journey, ma'am?'

'Yes, very nice, thank you,' Mariah replied and looked at Kitty, her eyes brimming with mischief.

Mr Harvey led them to the front door, which was opened by a woman in a dark dress with a white collar. Her eyes were bright and searching and her hair was grey, but she greeted them politely, clearly bubbling over with curiosity.

'Miss Kitty and Miss Mariah,' she said. 'I hope you had a good journey. Sir Peter is waiting for you. He would like to see you before lunch. Miss Kitty, Miss Mariah, Lily will take you up to your rooms. I have given you adjoining ones so that you can communicate with each other easily. In a house like this it is easy to feel a bit lost and I thought it would be more comfortable.' She turned her bright birdlike eyes on Kitty. 'I'll take you straight up to him, miss. He is in his rooms. He never leaves them now, but luncheon will be served downstairs in the morning room. We use that when there are only a few guests rather than the big dining room – if that is all right for you?'

Mariah was taken off by a young maid in a black dress and white cap, Rawlings following on with the cases. At the top of the rather grand staircase, Kitty was led in another direction. Her first impression was that everything was old and a little shabby. Not at all what she'd expected of a large country house, but as she progressed towards Sir Peter's rooms, she saw that the carpets were very good, though not new, she thought they were Persian in design, and the walls had silk paper, which had faded into a very pale duck-egg blue. It must all have been glorious once upon a time. A family who owned such a house and parkland must have been well respected, perhaps wealthy once. It was no wonder that Kitty's mother – a girl from a poor family – had not been considered good enough for a son of this family. She began to understand how a father might cut his son off for disobeying him. One son had gone to make his fortune in the diplomatic service and the other was expected to run the factory and bring it back to prosperity. In running off, he had disappointed his father and perhaps contributed to their failing fortunes.

'This is Sir Peter's suite,' the housekeeper said. 'Forgive me, miss – I should have said, I am Mrs Rawlings.' She was the wife of the chauffeur.

'Ah, I see.' Kitty smiled at her, pausing before knocking. 'Have you been with the family long?'

'Yes, miss. I started as a kitchen maid and worked my way up. The old man was a tartar, but his wife – she was lovely. You'd have liked her, miss.'

'Yes, I am sure I would,' Kitty said and smiled at her. 'You must tell me all about her – and my family when we have time.'

Mrs Rawlings blushed with pleasure. 'I'd enjoy that, miss – perhaps after you've seen Sir Peter and had your lunch...?'

Kitty nodded, then knocked at the door. It was opened by the nurse she'd seen in London. The nurse inclined her head, gave Kitty an icy smile and invited her in.

Kitty walked past her, her eyes seeking Sir Peter. He was propped up in a chair with lots of pillows and a blanket over his knees. He gave a glad cry as he saw her, holding out his hands in greeting.

'My dear girl,' he said, eyes alight with pleasure. 'Thank you for coming. I know you have forgiven me now and I can go to my Maker with an easy heart.'

Kitty's eyes stung with tears, though she would not let them fall. He was so clearly dying, his hands shaking in hers, his skin shrunken against the bones of his face, his eyes sunken back in their sockets. Yet despite the signs of deterioration, his spirit shone from those yellowed eyes with a fierce determination. Seeing his bravery and genuine affection for her, Kitty's heart melted with love and she felt an ache in her breast at the knowledge that this would be the last time she would see him.

Oh, how she wished that he had coming looking for her years ago! She would have loved to know him, to grow up as his beloved niece in this old house – but she knew that life was not always fair or just.

Sir Peter sat back with a sigh and she saw the effort it had cost him to take her hands. 'You must rest, dearest,' she said softly. 'I am here and I shall sit quietly here for a while. Is there anything you need me to do?'

'You must go down and have your lunch,' the nurse said, clucking and fussing round, tucking in Sir Peter's blanket. 'He needs to return to bed. He would get up to greet you, but he isn't fit.'

'She is right,' he agreed with a wry look at the nurse. 'You must have your meal. Come back later, when I am in bed and read to me. I should like that.'

Kitty nodded in assent. She did not like the nurse's possessive attitude, but Sir Peter clearly needed to be back in bed and there was no point in making a fuss; it would only distress him.

* * *

The next day was spent partly walking about the grounds, which were extensive and beautiful, gracious trees sweeping down to caress the smooth lawns, and the flower beds that looked as if they had been someone's pride and joy, the roses just coming into bloom; their perfume was a joy to the senses. The rest of Kitty's time was spent either just sitting by Sir Peter's bed, reading to him until he fell asleep or talking when he felt able. He told her things about her father, but had not known her mother, describing the larks the brothers had got up to boys, climbing trees and roaming the countryside. It gave Kitty a sense of family in a way she'd never had before and brought tears to her eyes several times. Regret that she had never known her family was strong, but she reflected that she was lucky to have met her uncle if only for a short time.

When it was time for her to leave, he pressed a small box into her hands. 'Please keep this in memory of me. It is the gold watch my father gave me when I left to join the diplomatic service and belonged to my grandfather before him. My mother's jewellery was all sold to keep things going after the factory declined, but I have kept the watch and I want you to have it.'

Kitty's face was wet with the tears she could not hold back as she accepted it from him. 'I shall treasure it always and my memory of you,' she told him, gulping back her emotion. 'Thank you, dearest uncle. Thank you for finding me and giving me some memories of my father that I could never have had otherwise.'

'I am sorry I didn't know your mother, but I now know where she is buried and your father. He wanted to be buried near her rather than here. Harvey will give you the details...' Sir Peter managed to grip her hands. 'Dry your eyes and be happy. I want you to be happy, dearest girl. Please live for me and keep me alive in your memory.'

'I shall,' she promised and he told her to leave. She did so, turning back at the door to blow him a kiss. 'I have come to care for you a great deal, Uncle Peter.'

Downstairs, Mariah was waiting with their cases as the car was brought round. Mr Harvey was staying on for a couple of days. He came to say his farewells.

'I had hoped we might see a little more of each other,' he said regretfully. 'But it did not happen. When you were not with Sir Peter, he needed me...'

Kitty nodded and smiled, because she had turned aside on her walks on more than one occasion so that they would not meet in the seclusion of the woods. To meet at breakfast or lunch was fine, but she had not wished for intimacy with Mr Harvey. He was a nice man, but Kitty wished to avoid giving him pain.

'We must go, sir,' she replied as Rawlings came to tell them the car was ready. 'Thank you for your kindness. It was much appreciated.'

Mariah gave her a speaking look and thanked him warmly herself. He had spent time with her, showing her the house and gardens, and she'd spent some happy hours in the kitchens with the cook discussing the proper meals to send up for an invalid.

* * *

'Well, how do you feel now, my love?' Mariah asked Kitty when they were sitting in the luxury of the comfortable car. 'You know where your father came from – and your mother was a parlour-maid there before they ran away – did you know that?'

'Who told you that?' Kitty looked at her in surprise. 'My uncle didn't know her.'

'She came to the house after he left,' Mariah replied. 'The housekeeper knew her – told me she was a lovely girl. She thinks you look much like her, but your hair is darker – you take after your father with that...'

'Oh, I wish she had told me,' Kitty exclaimed, but then reflected that there had been little chance for her to have the long chat with Mrs Rawlings that she'd wished to; she had either been in her uncle's room, partaking of a meal, or walking in the fresh air. It seemed that Mariah had learned much more. 'I have so many questions.'

'She thought you might be embarrassed if she told you about your mother, Kitty.' Mariah smiled and handed her a small box. 'When your mother ran off with your father, she left these behind. Mrs Rawlings kept them and she gave them to me for you. She didn't know your mother well. She was the assistant cook in those days and worked from dawn to dusk, but she says she was a helpful girl, Mary, and always ready to help.'

'Her name was Mary?' Kitty stared at Mariah in wonder. 'Oh, Mariah, that means so much to me – just to know that she was lovely and to know her name.' She opened the box and gasped. Inside was a handkerchief. Plain white but for the initial 'M' – and a small brooch. Picking it up, she saw it was obviously brass, but the blue and white stones were foiled, which made them sparkle. It was fashioned in the name Mary and had clearly been much worn, a favourite trinket left behind in the rush to go before the lovers were discovered in the act and prevented from escaping.

Kitty burst into tears. It was all too much for her. Her dying uncle had told her of her father and now Mariah had given her these items the housekeeper had saved for years. She would put them with her uncle's gift of the gold watch in a safe place, and treasure them for the rest of her life.

'Oh, Mariah,' she said when she could at last control her tears. 'I am so very glad we came.'

'Yes, my love. It was a very good thing,' Mariah replied. 'It is a pity you didn't get to know Mr Harvey a little better while we were there, Kitty. He is such a nice man.'

'I know, but it was deliberate on my part,' Kitty said. 'I don't want to hurt him, Mariah, because I don't have feelings him. Perhaps one day I will love again, but it isn't now and it isn't Mr Harvey.'

'I dare say you did the right thing – but I am not sure he will give up, my love.'

'I will tell him that he can be my friend but nothing else – is that fair, Mariah?'

'Yes, dear Kitty. Very fair, but I can't help wishing that you did love him just a little bit. He would make a good husband for any woman.'

'Stop matchmaking,' Kitty said. 'Why do I need a husband when I have my dearest Mariah?'

27

Sally never caught sight of the men following her, but she knew they were there. Walking from her office to the shops or to an appointment, she often felt a slight prickling at the nape of her neck, but she never turned to look. Each morning, Sally took her children to school in the car. A few times, she'd noticed a vehicle pull out a discreet distance behind her. It was never the same one.

If American gangsters were following her, they would be followed in their turn. It made her feel a little foolish and seemed unreal. Surely it couldn't really be necessary, here in London in streets she'd walked safely all her life? Mick had gone a bit over the top in response to her anxiety, but she admitted privately she felt safer because of it. If Mick was looking out for her, she would be fine.

Sally continued to work, meet sales people, and entertain her friends. She was conscious that she was being more careful, locking doors and making certain that windows were all closed when she went out, especially those downstairs, though because she had a live-in housekeeper and her mother, stepfather and lots of friends were often in the house, she knew it was unlikely any attempt would be made to kidnap her from her home. It would come when she was out or with the children. Sally had curtailed their freedom a little. If they wanted to go to a friend's house, she made sure that she took them and picked them up afterwards, and quite often took someone else with her. There was safety in numbers. However, it was now June and nothing had happened. When she mentioned to Mick it might be safe for him to recall her shadows, he shook his head.

'No, Sally. I shan't do that, my darlin'. You haven't been told, but my friends have prevented two attempts to snatch your children as they played with others, and a car was pulled over and men forced out at gunpoint when they planned to grab you on your way home from Harpers. They were searched and they had weapons. They were taken away from them and the men were warned that any further attempts to harm you or the kids would be met with more than a beating. Since then, nothing more has been seen of them and I've been told they've left London. However, the vigil will continue for a bit longer, until I am satisfied that they have given up.'

'Oh, Mick. I never guessed or saw anything,' Sally exclaimed, looking at him in horror, and he laughed wryly.

'That was the objective, Sally. I wish I could be as certain that Ben was being protected as well, but my friends have less influence over there than here.'

Sally nodded and a small shiver went down her spine. She'd sent a telegram to Ben asking him to return but had received another in reply to say she must not worry. He had contacted the proper authorities and was being protected by them; they wanted to speak to him and he would be meeting with them quite soon. He'd sent his love and promised to come home when it was all settled.

It was towards the end of June that Sally received another letter.

My dearest Sally.

I wanted to tell you that I have sold all my aunt's shares. I offered them to other board members, but my offer was declined, so I dumped them on the market and they slumped to a new low. I was not popular with my colleagues for that decision, but they had their chance. I lost a lot of money, but, as you told me, family is more important. I feel I have let my aunt down, but there was nothing left to do. In all likelihood, the men who brought the company down, now own it, so I expect to see the shares soar before long. It doesn't matter to me.

I have been asked to remain in New York until a hearing can be convened and I can give my evidence before a judge so that a case can be brought against my cousin and others. As soon as that is done, I will secure the first passage home, my love. Tell the children Daddy will be home soon and we'll have a family holiday at the sea together.

I love you, Sally. I didn't know how much until I realised that I might have lost you. Forgive me. It won't happen again. When I am home, I am stopping put with those I love.

Take care my darling. See you soon.

Ben xx

Sally smiled in relief as she folded the letter and put it away in her desk. Thank goodness that was all over! Ben had come to his senses and their lives could go back to normal.

When the children came in for their tea after school, she told them that Daddy would be home in a few weeks and they would have a holiday at the seaside.

'Can we go to that lovely cottage by the beach we went to last year?' Jenny asked, her excitement bubbling over. 'It was so nice. We just walked out of the back door, across a lawn and there, down a few steps, was the beach. Hardly anyone came there and Lulu could run and play all day long.'

'So could you and Peter,' Sally said with a smile and bent to kiss them both. 'I will write and book it – for three weeks or a month if it is free. If not, we'll have to find another one just as nice.'

'That one is the bestest,' Jenny said with a pout. 'Why don't we buy it for our very own? We could go whenever we wanted then.'

'Yes, that is a very good idea,' Sally told her with a nod. 'I will ask the owner to let me know if there is a chance of buying it.'

'Oh, please buy it, Mummy,' Jenny begged. 'Peter wants you to, don't you?' She looked at her brother, who nodded in solemn agreement.

'Well, I promise I shall try,' Sally said. 'I have some money saved and I think it would be enough to buy us a lovely seaside home.'

Both children jumped up and down with excitement and Mrs Hills came in to see what it was all about. 'Mummy is going to buy us the cottage we stayed in last year at the beach,' Jenny declared, her face shining.

'I promised to try – if the owner will sell,' Sally warned. 'If not, we'll find one for ourselves – but that would be perfect for us.'

'You won't find many as nice as that one,' Mrs Hills said, smiling to see them all so excited. 'I enjoyed the two weeks I spent with you.'

'It isn't a big house like this one, but it is ideal for holidays.'

'It would do you and the children good to get away more,

ma'am,' Mrs Hills said with a motherly smile. 'Your mother would love it there too, with you and with her husband, too.'

Sally's eyes sparkled, because the excitement had made her start to tingle. 'I'm going to write that letter now and ask if we can have it this summer – and also ask if she has thought of selling it.'

Jenny squealed in delight and followed her mother to her desk. Sally wrote a brief letter, signed it, sealed it into an envelope and put a stamp on.

'I am going to meet a friend this evening so I shall post it on my way,' Mrs Hills said, smiling.

'Good,' Sally replied. 'And now, if two children haven't had their tea and washed before getting into bed in half an hour, there will be big trouble.'

Jenny and Peter dissolved into laughter and went away with Mrs Hills to have the tea she had prepared for them.

Sally picked up her briefcase. She would have a light supper of soup and sandwiches in a little while, but first she had some stock lists to check – and more importantly the sales figures. If Kitty was right, there was another small drop in every department, other than hats, bags, gloves, and jewellery. It seemed that Sally's own departments were holding their own, but even the ladies' clothes were down, though not as much as some of the others. True, the stock levels were higher in glass and silverware, because Fred had found those tea chests, but the actual sales were down. Because they had reordered when they didn't actually need to, they now had more of certain items than was sensible.

Perhaps she should have a sale next month? Sally pondered the idea. It would be a genuine reduction and not because something had been slightly damaged. She frowned at the thought. A sale in July? Normally, she only ran sales in January, except for ladies' fashions, which needed to be turned over constantly or become stale. What reason could she give and not make it obvious that Harpers needed to turn over some extra money? Sally thought for a while and then she smiled. She would tie it in with the pageant. She would take 25 per cent off and advertise that for each twenty-five pounds she raised, twenty-five shillings would go to a charity for old soldiers.

It was a brilliant idea. Sally felt a thrill of pleasure. She would not limit it to the silver and glassware department. For one week only, Harpers would give twenty-five shillings for every twenty-five pounds they took. And that would give the staff in the office something to do!

A look of mischief came into her eyes as she imagined Mr Stockbridge's disapproval. A big sale in the middle of summer and a charity giveaway! Unheard of! It would be fun and help a good cause, Sally thought. A great deal of work, but fun, too. It would create a buzz of excitement in the store – and who knew, it might catch on.

28

It was the afternoon – following Sally's announcement of her big mid-season sale – when Beth returned home, that an unsettling approach was made. She had just got in and put her kettle on when a knock sounded at her door. Opening it, she saw a young woman she'd never seen before standing there. The woman was smartly dressed but wore very heavy make-up, her hair blonde and fizzy.

'Yes, what can I do for you?' Beth asked. For some reason, she had a prickling sensation at her nape and did not invite the stranger into her home.

'Are you Beth Burrows?' the girl asked with a cockney twang.

'I am Mrs Burrows, yes,' Beth confirmed. 'May I know who you are and what you require?'

'Yer don't need ter know me name,' the woman replied. 'I come askin' if yer know what 'appened to 'er next door. She ain't bin seen since yer picked 'er up in yer car and drove orf. Me and some friends of mine are worried about 'er.'

'Has she disappeared?' Beth asked, appearing to be startled since she had decided that to play ignorant would be best should she be approached by anyone. 'I had no idea. I work most days and I hardly see her. How long has she been missing?'

'I told yer – since yer give 'er a lift in yer car.'

'But that is a while ago!' Beth cried in feigned shock. 'Have you been to the police? How do you know her? Elizabeth didn't have many friends.'

'Elizabeth!' the woman cried in scorn. 'Bleedin 'ell – 'er name was Betty Lou...'

'Indeed?' Beth drew herself up haughtily. 'I think you must be mistaken, young woman. The person I knew was a very quiet lady named Elizabeth. I hardly met her, because I was so busy, but I happened to see her in the street and she asked me to take her to see her doctor, so I did – and that is all I know. I am sure if she wished to contact you, she would. I dare say she has just gone to visit her mother or some such thing. I really do not know. Perhaps I should contact the police—'

A look of alarm entered the woman's eyes. 'Nah, you don't need to do that, Mrs Burrows. She's probably gorn to visit 'er mother like you say. I won't trouble you no more...'

'Perhaps you should contact the police...' Beth called after her, but she was walking away and did not look back.

Beth went inside and shut the door, making sure it was locked. She was shaking as she went through to the kitchen. Had she pulled it off? Had the woman believed her?

The kettle was boiling its head off. Beth made a cup of tea and sat down to think calmly. She'd wondered if those looking for Tel Woods would come to interrogate her, but they'd been careful; they had sent a woman who might have been one of Betty Lou's friends, but somehow Beth knew her mission hadn't been friendly. Had she managed to convince them – would they send the bully boys in next? What could Beth do to convince them?

She smiled as she realised she had already suggested it to her visitor. She must do as she would normally if it was brought to her attention that a neighbour was missing – contact the police. Tel would surely have changed his name once again. It would be quite safe to inform the police that her neighbour Mr Terence Forrester and his wife, Elizabeth, had been missing for weeks. She would apologise to them for bothering them and they would make a few useless enquiries and that would convince the gangsters that she knew nothing.

It was simple and she realised she ought to have done it sooner. Going through to the hall, she picked up the phone receiver and asked for the number of the local police station.

It took several minutes to make the report and she was asked to pop in and sign something when she could, which she agreed to. By the time she had finished on the telephone, Fred and the children were at the door, knocking to be let in.

Fred looked at her as she opened it. 'Something wrong, Beth? You usually leave the door open for us,' he said, an anxious look in his eyes.

'Oh, it is nothing really,' Beth said with a little laugh. 'Someone came looking for my neighbour. I hadn't realised, but they haven't been seen for a while. I gave her a lift to the doctor some weeks back and, apparently, she hasn't been seen since. I hadn't noticed—'

'And that made you feel uneasy so you locked your door?' Fred gave her a long look but said no more.

'I just reported it to the police. I hadn't taken any notice and that isn't like me.'

'No, it isn't,' Fred said. 'Still, better late than never.'

'Yes, that is what I thought, Dad.' Beth smiled. 'What do you want for tea, boys?'

'Scrambled egg on toast,' Tim replied promptly.

'Fried egg sandwich...' his elder brother said.

'All right. You can both have what you want. I will have scrambled egg with Tim – what about you, Dad?'

'Fried egg sandwich with tomato sauce,' Fred said with a broad grin. 'You spoil us, Beth. We're all hungry.'

'So am I,' Beth agreed. 'We've been very busy at work. Sally has come up with a brilliant idea to tie in with the pageant, but it is going to make a lot of work. I have been helping Kitty to make posters advertising it.'

Fred nodded and smiled. He had clearly accepted her story about the missing neighbours. She could only hope the gangsters would do so too.

* * *

The next day, Beth went to sign her statement at the police station. She was invited into a small room and given a cup of tea and then a sergeant came to talk to her.

'We have had a further report on the missing family, Mrs Burrows. We are trying to trace them, but it might interest you to know that Mrs Forrester never visited the doctor on the day she went missing.'

'No? How strange,' Beth said. 'It was where she asked to go. I understood the little boy had a cough.'

'Well, she must have changed her mind. Do you know if she had a family living outside London?'

Beth furrowed her brow in thought. 'She may have mentioned a mother, but I don't know her name or where she lived.'

'Ah, that is a pity. No one seems to know anything about the family at all.'

'They were very quiet,' Beth said, hesitated, then, 'I don't know – but did they go off owing money?'

'Not that we've heard of,' the sergeant said. He frowned. 'You didn't know them by another name, I suppose?'

'Another name?' Beth shook her head, her mouth suddenly dry. 'I don't understand – why do you ask?'

'Just checking,' he said. 'It's another line of enquiry.' He smiled at her. 'Thank you for coming in, Mrs Burrows. We will be in touch if we have any more questions.'

'Yes, of course,' Beth said. 'I barely met Elizabeth's husband, but I quite liked her. She was a nice lady. I do hope nothing has happened to her.'

'Yes, so do we,' the sergeant said and gave Beth an odd look. 'I shan't keep you any longer, Mrs Burrows. Thank you for getting in touch.'

Beth gave a little shiver as she emerged into the warm sunshine. For a moment there, she'd half thought he suspected her of some foul deed – but at least they appeared to accept her story. She could only hope that would be an end to it.

If Jack knew what she'd risked for the wife of a criminal he despised, he would be furious with her. She just prayed he never would.

29

The pageant took place on a blazingly hot Sunday in July. Sally Harper made time to be there as their float joined the others on its long parade through the streets of London's West End, past the shops that were supporting them and back again. She started their collection off with fifty pounds in notes.

'If our bucket got filled with notes we would collect a fortune,' Kitty said with a laugh, adding the five pounds she and Mariah had collected in florins and half-crowns for the purpose. 'Thank you for your generosity.'

'It is the least I could do after all your hard work,' Sally told them. 'I'd love to walk with you and help collect from the crowds, but I have a luncheon party for some of the fundraisers and people who have made a large contribution to the charity we're helping, and then the children have been invited to tea at some friends this afternoon.'

'I am looking forward to it and so is Ruby,' Kitty told her. 'Jenny from accounts and Miss Jones from glassware are helping, too, and half a dozen others have given up their Sunday afternoon to help count what we collect afterwards.'

'Yes, I know – and then you are all being taken to tea at Lyons Corner House by Mr Stockbridge.' Sally laughed as she saw Kitty's surprise. 'I thought you all deserved a treat for the hard work everyone has put in – and it all looks beautiful. It was such a good idea of yours, Kitty.'

Kitty blushed in pleasure. The event had been taken over by others, because something of that size needed an army of helpers, but it had been her idea in the first place and it was nice that Sally Harper remembered that.

Kitty smiled and waved as she took her leave of some of the other people who had turned out for the start of the event, then looked at Ruby. Like Kitty, she hadn't been asked to be on the float dressed as a nurse or Suffragette but was one of the many helpers who would walk beside the float as it made its slow progress.

'Ready, Ruby?' she asked. 'I think we are about to move off now.'

There were thirty or forty floats in all, every one of them dressed in bright colours with a myriad of themes: a circus with performers, a builder restoring London after the Blitz, a cricket match, a football match, a mermaid in a scanty costume and a host of others that Kitty hadn't had time to see, though one was from a florist and covered in hearts of beautiful blooms and she'd loved the smell that wafted all the way back down the line.

'It is so exciting,' Ruby said, her pretty face alight. 'I've helped work on our float, but I never realised how many we'd end up with or how clever and funny some of them would be. Did you see the one with someone dressed as Charlie Chaplin and a polar bear?'

'No!' Kitty looked at her in amazement. 'What on earth does Charlie Chaplin have to do with a polar bear?'

'I have no idea, but they are giving free mint sweets away to children as they pass, so perhaps it has something to do with those sweets. You know the ones I mean... they feel very cool when you suck them. I think Fox's make them.'

Kitty wasn't sure which sweets she meant, but they were beginning to move off now, the float ahead of them having travelled far enough for Harpers' float to start without catching up to the one just in front. Everyone was supposed to travel at the same speed so that the walkers with buckets could keep up without getting out of breath, people had time to see and be seen and interact with the crowd. Already, Kitty could hear the first band starting to play and, faintly from somewhere at the front, cheering as the crowds showed their appreciation for the first floats.

She started jingling her bucket. She'd taken Sally Harper's contribution out and given it to Mr Stockbridge to keep safely. He'd nodded his approval and added five shillings to the bucket.

Kitty gasped when she saw the streets ahead of her. People were lining the pavement on either side, waving flags, and now she could hear the cheering mingling with the music from the first marching band, while at the rear of the column another was just starting to play. An entirely different tune, as it happened, which made Kitty smile, because everyone was supposed to play the same. It didn't matter. Kitty realised that the voices of the huge crowd that had gathered to watch them pass was drowning out the bands anyway.

Ruby darted past her to collect some pennies from a small girl and thank her. 'I never thought all these people would turn out for us,' she said to Kitty.

Kitty smiled and nodded. 'Anyone would think it was a royal procession,' she said. 'It's wonderful to see everyone looking so happy. It is just true British spirit.'

Ruby nodded. 'I expect it is the lovely weather and folk making the most of any reason to have fun.'

'Yes, I expect so,' Kitty said. 'I'm glad they have, though, because so many people have put hours of hard work into this and it is for a good cause – well, several good causes, really.' Harpers was donating what they collected to charities for soldiers wounded in the war, of whom there were still many in homes up and down the country. Other people were collecting for children, the homeless and animals, as well.

Ruby nodded happily, darting off again to collect some more pennies from two little boys. Kitty stayed one side of the float, but Ruby was all over the place.

'I am determined to fill my bucket,' she told Kitty.

'If you do, there are spares on the float. We are supposed to change them so they don't get too heavy to carry. If you fill yours, it will make your arms ache.'

Ruby just laughed and carried on, flitting from one side to the other. She was missing a lot of contributors, but Kitty picked up the ones she missed. She changed her bucket when it got heavy, even though it wasn't more than half full. It was so much easier with an empty bucket and people kept wanting to fill it for her.

Eventually, even Ruby had to slow down and admit defeat. She changed her bucket, giving Kitty a rueful grin. 'I never thought it could get so heavy...'

'We still have a way to go,' Kitty told her. 'You will be worn out when you get there. I'm glad we're being taken to tea. We shall need it!' She looked around her. The sea of faces just went on and on and the sun was very hot. She was offered a glass of water from the float and sipped it gratefully, returning it when she'd finished. Some floats had given their walkers paper cups which had been discarded in the road, but Harpers girls had been given tumblers from the canteen.

* * *

By the time the floats did the full circuit and returned to their starting point, all the walkers were exhausted. The heat had taken its toll and some had given up long before the end, others coming to take their place, but Kitty and Ruby had stayed the course.

Everyone was elated. It had been such fun and buckets had been half filled and emptied time and again. There was a huge oak chest that had formed part of the float's décor and it was filled with notes and coins. It had to be lifted off the float by a rope and pulley because it was so heavy. Kitty thought they might have done better to leave it in buckets but then discovered that they'd run out of buckets because they were nearly all filled to the brim.

'We collected so much money,' Ruby exclaimed excitedly as she saw it all being carried inside the hall where the counting was going on. 'However will they carry it all to the bank?'

'I have no idea,' Kitty replied. 'If I'd realised, I would have given notes, but I wanted my bucket to jingle for a start. People have been so generous.'

'Most of my collection was pennies and halfpennies,' Ruby said. 'There were so many people and most of them gave us something.'

'Yes. I am not sure if all the floats got the same response but ours did well – and that's because it represented something that really means a lot to many folk.'

'Well, the counters will take over now,' Ruby said as she saw the girls and young men lined up at tables to count the money. They had piles of little thick blue paper coin bags which took about five pounds in pennies and khaki paper bags that held five pounds in silver. It would all be sorted into bags of different denominations and then taken to the bank so that ten of the khaki bags would equal fifty pounds and the teller didn't need to count it, just weigh it on his scales. 'I would rather do our job than theirs.'

'Oh, definitely,' Kitty agreed, then nudged her. 'Mr Stockbridge is beckoning us. He is taking us Harper girls to tea at Lyons Corner House.'

'I know.' Ruby linked arms with her. 'Isn't it lovely? We are so lucky to work for Mrs Harper. She thinks of such lovely things for us.'

'Well, we deserve it,' Kitty said, smiling at her. 'I'm starving. I hope they've got some of those lovely little individual cauliflower cakes. I love those.'

Ruby looked puzzled and Kitty laughed.

'They have green marzipan wrapped round them and white icing on the top so they look like tiny cauliflowers. Haven't you ever had one?'

'No – but I like marzipan so I'd like to try.'

Ruby giggled as she and Kitty went to join Mr Stockbridge, who was gathering all his chicks about him and checking his list like a mother hen.

It was as they all trooped into the popular café that Ruby caught sight of a taxi passing by. She had no idea why she looked at it, except it slowed down to let the girls cross the road and, as Ruby glanced at the passenger inside, her heart caught.

It was Captain Saunders. Her Captain Saunders! She gasped and her face went as white as a sheet.

'What is wrong?' Kitty asked, seeing how pale she looked. 'Ruby – are you ill?'

'No...' Ruby breathed deeply. The taxi had passed, taking its passenger with it. 'I thought I saw – but I couldn't have done. He died...'

'Oh, dear, you must have had a touch too much sun,' Kitty said, taking her arm and guiding her into the cool of the restaurant. 'Sit down, Ruby. They will bring our tea in a few minutes. They are always so quick here. You'll feel better when you have had something to eat and a nice cup of tea.'

'Yes...' Ruby closed her eyes and then opened them again. 'Yes, it must have been a bit too much sun. It can play tricks on the mind, so they say.' She smiled at Kitty.

'Good, you are feeling better already. It is nice and cool in here,' Kitty said. 'After we've had tea, I am going to call a taxi and take you home.'

'No, don't be silly. I shall be fine.'

'Mariah would never forgive me if I let you go alone,' Kitty said and touched her hand. 'She thinks you are a lovely girl and suggested I should ask you to come and live with us. She says we have plenty of room and she doesn't like to think of you in that boarding house.'

'Live with you?' Ruby stared at her, her conviction that she had seen Captain Saunders forgotten for a moment as she stared in disbelief. 'Mariah thinks I should live with you and her? She hardly knows me.'

'Mariah either likes someone or she doesn't – and she believes I should have more friends – go out more often...'

'That is so kind...' Ruby's eyes were moist. 'Are you sure?'

'Yes, if you like the idea,' Kitty replied. 'She suggested that I speak to you this afternoon – but we've been far too busy.'

'Oh, that is so lovely of you both,' Ruby said, her eyes wide with wonder. 'I have been biding my time until I was ready to move, but— Oh, yes, I would love that. Yes, please, Kitty.' It was the kind of arrangement she'd often thought she would like, and Mrs Flowers was so grumpy at times.

Kitty smiled. 'Good. Mariah will be pleased. As I said she likes you and she says it is as easy to cook for three as two – and we share the expenses, so it won't cost you as much as you pay now.'

'I'll help with the chores, too,' Ruby said eagerly. 'I've thought how nice it must be for you having your own home. I can't believe you want me to share.'

'It means we can be company for each other. Mariah likes the theatre,' Kitty told her. 'I don't often go with her. I prefer the cinema but we sometimes go with each other and you could come too if you wish... or you and I could see a film. Mariah isn't as keen on the cinema as a live show.'

'I love both, but I seldom have anyone to go with. Shirley invites me now and then, but she is courting now.'

'Is she?' Kitty nodded and smiled. 'She will get married soon then. Fortunately, Sally Harper keeps her staff on if they marry. Not every employer will. It's because married ladies have babies and want a lot of time off work.'

'Sally is willing to keep a job for six months before giving it to another member of staff. She says if the girl doesn't feel able to return by then she probably won't, but if she has someone to look after the child and returns within that time, there is no reason to take her job from her. I expect it is because she has children herself that she understands.'

'She is thoughtful and kind,' Ruby said. 'I don't think I would want to return to work if I had a husband and child – but of course not all husbands can provide a living for their wife and child.'

'Yes, just so,' Kitty agreed, then looked up as their tea arrived. 'Oh, look, there are two cauliflower cakes as well as fruit cake and a scone – and cucumber sandwiches. Delicious. I am very hungry.'

'Me too,' Ruby said. She sipped the tea Kitty poured for her and started with her sandwiches. As she ate, she was remembering the face she'd glimpsed inside that taxi. He had looked just like Captain Robert Saunders – and, what's more, he'd looked startled as though he'd seen and known her, too!

Yet surely it couldn't be the man she'd been grieving for these past months? How could it be? Why would a solicitor lie to her? And there was her legacy. None of that could have happened if Captain Saunders was still alive. No, she was mistaken. She had to be...

30

It was at the beginning of August that Beth received a visit from a plain-clothes police officer accompanied by a constable. They knocked at her door and asked if they could come in, showing her their credentials. She felt a shiver of unease at her nape but controlled it as she led the way into her neat kitchen.

'Forgive me for not taking you into the front room, Inspector Henderson, but I have some cakes in the oven and I would rather they didn't burn.'

The inspector gave her a puzzled look but nodded. 'I am sorry to disturb you, Mrs Burrows. It is about that report of a missing person you made earlier this summer.'

'Oh, have you found Elizabeth? I do hope she is all right,' Beth asked and her anxiety was real, because she would hate to hear that her one-time neighbour was in trouble or, worse still, had been murdered.

'No, we haven't found her or her husband,' Inspector Henderson replied with a frown. 'In normal circumstances, I would suspect foul play – but in this case I believe it to be a case of the suspects deliberately covering their tracks so as to disappear. So if you were concerned for Mrs Woods' whereabouts, you may set your mind at rest.'

'I'm not sure what you mean,' Beth replied, uneasy because he'd used Tel's real surname. 'I was and am concerned for a lady I liked, though I hardly knew her, of course, but she was very pleasant.'

'Well, that is as maybe,' he said, fixing her with a stern look. 'What was an attempted murder has become murder, Mrs Burrows. Mr Woods – or Forrester as he calls himself these days – severely wounded a member of a rival gang; that man has now died of his wounds, so Mr Woods is wanted for murder, amongst other crimes...'

'Oh dear, that is terrible,' Beth said. 'I am very sorry to hear it – but I do not see what this has to do with Elizabeth Forrester.'

'Her name, as I believe you know, was Betty Lou. He took her from the streets when she was little more than a child. For a while, she worked with his other girls, most of them rescued from wretched lives and given a home to use for their "business", but then he took her away and made her his woman – or perhaps his wife. We don't know for certain whether he married her...'

'Oh, the poor girl,' Beth cried in genuine shock. 'What she must have suffered!' It was no wonder she had been reluctant to go anywhere without her husband, Beth thought. 'I had no idea. I only knew her as Elizabeth Forrester.'

'I am almost inclined to believe you, Mrs Burrows, except that I know you are very friendly with Tel Woods' mother, Bella Woods.' He glared at her. 'Don't take us for fools, Mrs Burrows.'

'Yes, Bella is my friend,' Beth admitted it openly. 'I met her through a girl who works for Harpers who used to live near her. I saw how badly she suffered with her legs so I took her to the doctors. I buy fruit from Bella's son, Jerry. He used to have a barrow near the Underground but now he has a little shop. It's inconvenient for me to shop there so he brings me a box of fruit once a week – and I visit his mother regularly to help her with her hospital visits.' She met the inspector's gaze proudly. 'I fail to see what this has to do with a criminal. I never met Tel Woods. Bella will not have him in her house. If Mr Forrester is the same man – and I have only your word for it – then I had no knowledge of it. If he committed a murder and other terrible crimes, I know nothing of them.' Again, her words had the ring of truth, for she had never met Tel as himself, only as the respectable Mr Forrester. Yes, he had asked for her help and she had given it, but she'd given it for Betty Lou, who was an innocent young woman life had treated unfairly. 'Is it a crime to give a young woman and baby a lift, Inspector Henderson, for it is the only thing I am guilty of?'

'I am well aware of that,' he said. 'However, it is a criminal offence to withhold knowledge of the whereabouts of a man wanted for murder.'

'Yes, certainly it is,' Beth said fearlessly. 'If I had any idea, I would tell you, Inspector. I do not agree with murder or criminal activities. Helping a young woman in trouble is one thing, but I can assure you, I would not withhold knowledge of a murderer's whereabouts if I knew it.'

He gave her a long hard look. 'Very well, I believe that much is true. You are either a fool or a rather clever young woman, Mrs Burrows. I must give you the benefit of the doubt because there is no proof – but please believe me when I say that if I find out you are hiding something from me, you will be sorry.'

'Threats, Inspector?' Beth arched her brow. 'I do not think I've done anything to deserve that...'

He shot her a look of dislike. 'We shan't trouble you again – unless further evidence comes to light.'

'Then I am sure we shall not meet again,' Beth said and smiled.

He gave her a sharp nod and went out, followed by the constable, who winked at her as he left. Beth wondered what that was for but thought perhaps he knew Jerry Woods – one of his network of friendly Londoners who passed on information about small things, like when a club was likely to be raided, perhaps.

She closed the door after them, trembling all over as she realised that she could have been in serious trouble. She had helped Betty Lou join Tel but that was the end of it. She had no idea where they had gone – and even the van he was driving was likely stolen and would be abandoned, leaving no trace of where he'd chosen to begin his new life.

It didn't feel good to know that she'd helped a murderer. Yet he hadn't been then, because the victim had still been alive – and, according to Tel, he had attacked him in self-defence. The police must know that, of course, but they wanted to arrest him for a crime that his fancy lawyers couldn't get him out of or that carried more than a couple of years' penalty. So they weren't being strictly honest either.

Smelling burning, Beth gave a cry of alarm and rushed to take her tray of cakes from the oven. They were black and ruined. She looked at them in annoyance and then took them outside to the dustbin. Even the birds wouldn't eat those!

Returning to the kitchen, Beth caught sight of the clock. Fred would be here with the boys any minute. She just about had time to whip up another batch of honey and almond buns if she was quick. She needed to put the inspector's little visit out of her mind and forget about it. Tel had done a good job of disappearing, so hopefully both the criminal element and the police would give up the search as a bad job and she could stop worrying about it.

She had just removed her batch of perfectly baked cakes when Fred and the boys came trooping in a little later. The boys clamoured to be allowed a bun, but they were too hot and they had to wait a few minutes before they could eat them without burning their tongues.

'Everything all right?' Fred asked her as she made tea and then started to slice bread for their cheese and tomato sandwiches. 'You seem a bit quiet?'

'Oh, no, I am fine,' Beth said, giving him a brilliant smile. 'It was just that I went upstairs to sort some laundry and when I came down my cakes had burned so I had to start again.' She was becoming a practised liar and she didn't much like that – but she would stop now, because she hated lying to Fred.

'Ah, I thought I could smell a faint trace of burning,' Fred said and laughed. 'As long as you are all right, Beth. You know I am here for you if you needed anything – anything at all.'

'Bless you, Fred. I know that,' Beth said, darting at him and giving him a quick hug. 'I promise you I am all right, nothing to worry about. Just a case of a little mistake that won't be repeated.'

31

Mariah asked her friend Arnie to help Ruby move her things into their third bedroom. Since all she had was her clothes and a few books and small trinkets, he was able to do so in one journey. However, she was still glad he was there. Mrs Flowers stood glowering at her as if she had committed some crime, coming to check that she hadn't taken anything from her room. None of the cheap ornaments held any appeal for Ruby, so everything was left in place, not that it pleased her disgruntled landlady.

'So you're off then,' she sniffed in disgust, arms akimbo. 'The ingratitude of some leaves me speechless. I took you in with no references – an orphan brat from the streets with hardly a penny to your name... Now you've come into money, you throw my kindness in my face.'

'That isn't quite true,' Ruby said with dignity. 'I had a reference from Sister Mary Rose – and I paid you my first month's rent in advance.'

'That's right, show your real nature now that you've gone up in the world. Just watch that your rich friends don't drop you as easily as they've taken you up.'

'My friends are working folk just like me,' Ruby said. 'I work in the same office as Kitty – and Mariah is a lovely person. It will be like having my own family.' She felt a spurt of anger. 'And if you hadn't read my letters, you wouldn't know I'd come into money, because I haven't told you!'

'The cheek of you, minx!' Mrs Flowers simmered. 'Off she goes with no thought for me or how I'll fill my room—'

At this, Arnie had had enough. He turned towards Mrs Flowers, his good-natured face stern as he said, 'This is a boarding house, missus. People come and go – Ruby has paid her way and she gave you notice, which she didn't have to, so watch your tongue.'

Mrs Flowers opened her mouth to retaliate but, seeing his look, subsided.

Ruby turned to look at her as they left. 'I shouldn't worry too much, Mrs Flowers. Shirley says that Jenny from accounts might take the room. They are best friends, so it will suit them both.'

Mrs Flowers opened and shut her mouth but no words came out. As the door closed behind them, Arnie grinned. 'What an old battleaxe,' he said. 'If I'd been you, I'd have been out of there the day after I moved in...'

'She is a decent cook and her rooms are clean,' Ruby said. 'To be honest, I just let her spite go over my head. You get so you don't listen after a while.' She descended into giggles. 'Did you see her gape when I told her Jenny might move in? She looked like a fish out of water gasping for air.'

Arnie chuckled. 'You'll do,' he said. 'You'll do for my Mariah. That's what she would have found funny too...'

'I love your Mariah,' Ruby said, looking at him with interest. 'When are you going to marry her?'

'When she's ready,' Arnie said. 'I've been ready these past ten years, but first she wouldn't leave her brother and father, then she had to look after Miss Kitty.'

Ruby's eyes sparkled. 'She says it is because she doesn't get on with your mum but I don't believe her.'

'Well, she would say that, wouldn't she?' Arnie said with a nod. 'Truth is, Ma thinks the world of her.' He grinned at her. 'Now you're going to live with Kitty, mayhap she'll decide it's time. See what you can do to persuade her, lass. I'd like to be wed afore I'm too old to carry my bride over the threshold.'

'You've got a while to go yet,' Ruby said with a little laugh and he gave a roar of laughter as he opened his van door for her to get in before stowing her things in the back.

'Aye, I have that – but I live in hope.'

'I won't push Mariah out of her home,' Ruby said. 'But I will do all I can to help so that if she feels able to leave us, she will take that step and marry you.'

'Bless you, you can't do more. Mariah will make up her mind when she is ready. I know Miss Kitty tells her she should wed me while she is young enough to have a child.' He shut the door of the van and went round to the front, bending to insert the starting handle.

'Do you want children very much?' Ruby asked, looking at him as he started the van with the handle and jumped into the driving seat.

'I wouldn't mind a son to take over from me,' Arnie admitted. 'But it's Mariah I truly want. I just want to wake up and find her next to me in the morning and feel her warmth beside me all night.'

'Then tell her that,' Ruby suggested. 'I am not certain, Arnie. I might be wrong, but I think Mariah feels she is too old to have a child now. I know women older than her have them – but a first one at her age might be a little dangerous for her. She might not want to risk it but probably thinks you'd want a family.'

Arnie braked and turned to look at Ruby, astonishment on his face. 'Ma said something similar to me the other day. You see, Mariah's mother died after giving birth to Larry – not immediately, but it weakened her, and the doctor said it was having another child when she was nearly forty. Mariah is thirty-eight.'

Ruby nodded. 'She told me about her mother and I saw something in her face then.' She smiled as he restarted the car. 'I am glad I told you.'

'So am I, Miss Ruby,' Arnie said. 'I'll be making certain she knows I'm not bothered about children. I've got a nephew – my sister's eldest. He can come into the business with me when he is old enough.' He nodded and smiled. 'Mariah means the world to me. No child could ever take her place and I'll tell her that...' He started to whistle.

'I'm glad. Perhaps she will marry you then...'

Arnie stopped whistling and looked at her. 'If she does, I'll owe you a debt I can never repay, Miss Ruby. What can I do for you?'

'Nothing apart from what you did today,' Ruby replied. 'I was so glad you were with me, Arnie. I think she might have had a real go at me if I'd been on my own.'

'It was my pleasure to help you,' he said. 'One day you will need something and then I'll be only too pleased to help.'

* * *

Ruby settled into her room quickly and then went down to help Mariah get their tea ready. 'You go and sit in the parlour with Kitty,' Mariah said, smiling at her. 'I'm used to doing the cooking.'

'Won't you let me help – teach me, please?' Ruby said, smiling at her. 'You get things ready so beautifully, and I've never had a mother or sister to show me how things should be done. I probably shan't ever marry, but if I did, I'd like to know how to cook. I'm not sure I could even boil an egg...'

'Now that's a daft thing to say,' Mariah chuckled but was clearly pleased with Ruby's interest. 'Kitty always leaves most of the cooking to me, because she knows I like it – but she is better at other things. Mending and making neat beds and polishing furniture until you can see your face in it. We both like cleaning silver and brass, because Father had such lovely bits and pieces so we share that task, but Kitty does a lot of the housework and I do the cooking.'

'I can help you a bit, even if I only prepare the vegetables,' Ruby said. 'Another time, I can help Kitty with other jobs and I will keep my own room neat and tidy.'

'That's a good girl,' Mariah said with a nod of approval. 'This evening, I am cooking a pie I made earlier, but the potatoes need peeling and the cabbage has to be chopped into pieces so we can press it down in the saucepan. Then, when it is cooked, we let butter melt into it and add a little salt and pepper; it is delicious.'

'How did you make the pie – what sort is it?' Ruby asked, genuinely interested.

'It is my own shortcrust pastry. I will show you how to make that on Sunday morning. The filling is minced chicken and diced carrots and onions. I use the meat left over from the weekend roast, then I put it through my mincer so it comes out looking a bit like sausage meat. Then I put the onions and diced carrots into the mixture and stir it together. I line a pie dish with pastry and then put in layers of my mixture, adding a few extra vegetables in-between. Then I make up a gravy using chicken stock and a little flour, salt and pepper. I cook that on the range until it is lovely and thin, then pour it over my minced chicken, place a lid of pastry on top and then put it in the middle of the oven to cook – like this...'

She placed the pie dish in the oven and smiled as Ruby showed her the saucepan filled with potatoes that she had peeled and cut in halves.

'Yes, that is right. They will cook through quicker and we'll mash them with butter, but if I was making a stew, I'd leave them whole and pop them in the pan half an hour before it was ready. Now do the cabbage, slice it into chunks to cook and we will chop it with butter when it is ready; it will be very tasty like that with a pinch of salt and pepper. It is not an expensive meal,' Mariah told her, 'because we had a chicken dinner, and we also had some cold chicken in sandwiches, so this is the back meat and the legs. All the breast was eaten previously, but when you taste it, you won't know what was used because it has a lovely flavour from its gravy.'

'It sounds simple the way you describe it,' Ruby said. 'I thought cooking was so difficult, but you make it easy.'

'Cooking is easy,' Mariah assured her. 'You just have to learn how long to cook things and what to do, then it is simple.'

Ruby laughed. 'I shall believe you. I can't wait to taste it and to learn how to make pastry.'

'Now that is an art,' Mariah said with a touch of pride, 'but I can teach you to make it so it melts in your mouth.'

'What are you two talking about?' Kitty asked, coming in at that moment.

'Mariah is going to teach me to cook,' Ruby said. 'She makes it sound so simple.'

'It isn't,' Kitty replied with a smile. 'She has given up on me. I can bake cakes but pastry is beyond me. The last treacle tart I made could sink a battleship it was so heavy.'

'Your trouble is you're in too much hurry,' Mariah scolded. 'You have to treat pastry with respect, a firm but light hand.'

'That is why you do the cooking, dearest Mariah,' Kitty teased and smiled. 'Something smells delicious anyway. I'm starving.'

* * *

Ruby settled in immediately. It was as if she'd always lived with her friends. She got up early and helped to get breakfast ready, then she and Kitty left for work. When they came home in the evening, Ruby helped serve the meal, which was normally already cooking, but then washed up, telling Mariah and Kitty to sit down. She kept her own room clean and tidy and at the weekend helped Mariah prepare their meals, learning to cook the simple dishes they all loved. She took a turn at the ironing and did a little bit of dusting, but between the three of them, there wasn't much to do. It all worked beautifully and Ruby was conscious of being happier that she'd ever been.

She still thought about Captain Saunders, but, although she looked at the faces of the passers-by when she was out and about, she never caught a glimpse of anyone who looked like him, and she began to think she must have imagined it. Kitty was right; she'd had a touch of the sun.

Mariah had taken to going out more often with Arnie. He usually called for her one evening a week and took her to a concert or the cinema. They often asked if Ruby and Kitty would like to go, but they always refused.

'I'm all right with my book,' Ruby said one evening. 'I am going to that film with Shirley and Jenny on Thursday.'

'I don't want to see it,' Kitty said. 'I might like that musical that's coming on next week at the Odeon. We could all go to that one...?' It was agreed that they would.

Kitty was invited to a party at Sally Harper's house another week, and Mariah kept Ruby company. They talked and Mariah gave Ruby another cooking lesson and the evening passed pleasantly.

* * *

One evening in early September when Kitty and Ruby came home, they found Arnie in the kitchen and Mariah just about to put her coat on.

'Arnie's mum isn't well,' Mariah explained. 'I've got sausages for your supper and there's plenty of vegetables and I've made a treacle tart for afters. You just have to put it in the oven, Ruby. I'm sorry, my loves, but Arnie can't cope. I've packed a little bag and I may be gone a few days, but I know Ruby can look after you, Kitty.' She threw them an apologetic look. 'I will come back as soon as Arnie's mum can spare me.'

'You mustn't worry about us, dearest,' Kitty assured her. 'We shall miss you, but we'll manage. I promise.'

'I know you will,' Mariah said. 'If Ruby hadn't been here, I couldn't have left you, but I know you will be fine...'

'I'll take good care of her,' Arnie said. He grinned at Ruby as he picked up Mariah's case and ushered her out.

'Well...' Kitty looked at Ruby in surprise. 'I never thought Mariah would ever give in, but do you know – I think she might marry him at last.'

'Will you mind if she does?' Ruby looked at her anxiously.

'I shall be delighted for her,' Kitty said and put an apron on. 'Come on, let's get supper ready. I fancy some chips for a change. What about you?'

'Yes. I'd love chips,' Ruby said. 'I think Arnie really loves her. He wants to marry her so much.'

'I know – but I thought she never would.' Kitty looked thoughtful. 'I've noticed a change in her lately and she has been going out with him more often. Do you know anything about that?'

'Not really,' Ruby said. 'I think Arnie worked it out for himself. Let's hope they get together soon – if you think it's what she really wants?'

'Yes, I am sure she does, but she would never commit. Something must have changed her mind.'

'I expect she will tell you if she decides she will marry him,' Ruby said, because it wasn't her place to tell Kitty what she'd discussed with Arnie. 'I hope it won't make you unhappy if she does.'

'No, not at all,' Kitty assured her again. 'I shall still see her often. Mariah will continue to open her little shop sometimes and she will visit us often – I expect we would be invited round for lunch on a Sunday. I will miss her being here all the time – but I'll still have you.'

'Yes, I'm not going anywhere,' Ruby replied but felt a little guilty. Had she interfered when she ought not?

'Are you going to see Marianne this weekend?' Kitty asked as Ruby started to cook the chips she had sliced while they talked.

'No, not this week; I saw her last weekend. If Rupert asks me, I'll go to his mother's for tea, but I'm not going to any more of those evening parties. I didn't like the one he took me to.'

'He isn't a special boyfriend then?' Kitty asked.

'No – just a friend. He likes to pretend I am more to his family, but his sister knows the truth. He is a bit of a naughty boy really and it is a shame, because his mother and uncle are lovely people.'

Kitty nodded. 'I didn't think you loved him. There was someone special, wasn't there?'

'Yes – but he didn't feel the same. He was just kind to me – and then he died, but he left me a lot of money – an independence really.'

'That was nice of him,' Kitty said. 'Perhaps he liked you more than you thought, Ruby, but he felt he couldn't commit to marriage – perhaps because he was ill.'

'Yes,' Ruby agreed. 'It might have been that. I could have been so happy with him. I would far rather have him, even as just a friend, than his money.'

'Yes, I know just how you feel,' Kitty agreed. 'Larry left everything he owned to me – but I just wanted to be his wife. I loved him very much. Mariah hopes I shall marry again, but at the moment I don't feel that I shall. It is only a few years and in time I might change my mind, but not yet.'

Ruby nodded in sympathy. It was a small bond between them. They had both loved and lost. She looked at Kitty curiously. 'Mariah says there is a very nice man who keeps coming to ask after you?'

'Mr Harvey.' Kitty smiled and shook her head. 'He is nice and he is kind – but I don't love him.'

'Then don't marry him,' Ruby said with conviction. 'Wait until your heart tells you that a man is special again – even if it never happens, it is better to wait than marry someone who doesn't match up.'

'Yes, I shall,' Kitty agreed. 'Besides, I am quite happy with my life as it is. Those chips look wonderful, Ruby. Do you think these sausages are done?'

Ruby pricked them with a fork. 'Yes, they are fine. Come on, let's eat. I fancy some pickled onions with these – we didn't do any veg.'

'Doesn't matter for once,' Kitty said laughing. 'Pickles will go down a treat.'

32

It was raining when Ben Harper left the building where he'd been detained for the past three hours, answering questions about his reasons for selling all his shares in the prestigious store, thus causing their price to crash overnight. It was the second grilling he'd endured and he was heartily sick of it. He'd written to Sally, explaining why he'd been so long delayed. Ben had hired a lawyer to help him and yet still they were refusing to accept his word. How ridiculous that they seemed to believe that he was one of a cartel of businessmen trying to manipulate the American stock exchange! In vain, he'd explained that his discovery of the fraud taking place at the store had disgusted him, making him wish to be done with it. He had been cautioned and warned not to leave New York until they had made further enquiries.

Frustrated and angry, Ben stood staring at the New York skyline outlined against a darkening sky. Because of the torrents of rain, rare in this city at this time of year, it had grown dark much earlier than usual. He shivered, cursing the water trickling down his neck as he wore only a light suit, shirt and tie. No thought of an overcoat had been in his mind as he'd gone to his meeting earlier that day, nor did he carry an umbrella.

'Damnation!' he muttered loudly, causing a passer-by to startle. He shook his head and apologised. How he wished he'd never made that promise to his aunt, nor got involved in the dirty business that was ruining a once prosperous business. Yet he had, and, being the man he was, he had been swept up in the excitement of it all. Sally had been right all along. She usually was and he knew he should have listened to her, but he'd been gripped by a kind of fever. It had gone now and he was desperate to be back in London with his family, but the authorities had forbidden him to leave until their investigations were over. Meanwhile, he had to kick his heels here. His relations with his cousin were dire and he knew that he was being followed.

Glancing over his shoulder, Ben was about to hail a yellow cab when it happened. He saw an elderly woman fall to the ground in the middle of the busy road. Without a thought for himself, Ben dashed out, narrowly avoiding the cab, and was hooted at by the driver. He bent down and looked at the old woman. She opened her eyes then and Ben saw she wasn't elderly at all and there was triumph in her face.

His life seemed to flash before his eyes in the instant before the speeding car struck. 'Sally,' he murmured. 'Oh, Sally my love. I am so sorry—'

* * *

Sally received another brief letter from Ben. He had been detained for a short time by the American Government authorities, partly because of the evidence he had lodged with their department, and, partly, he said, because the dumping of all his aunt's shares had led to a huge fall in the company's value, which had not yet recovered.

> *They want to know why I did it, though I have already explained. It seems I am not the only one who has been selling shares recently and there is a feeling of unease over here amongst financiers and some large shareholders. Apparently, some experts feel that the market has become overloaded with wheeler-dealers and some chicanery is going on, which could lead to panic on the market.*
>
> *I believe I have explained my reasons, though I'm not sure they quite believed me. I feel guilty, Sally, as if I ought to buy the shares back, but I really do not want anything to do with the people who are taking the company over. Whether or not they will take any notice of my evidence or just brush it under the carpet, I have no idea. I wish I could have come home sooner, but they confiscated my passport and have not yet returned it. I am thoroughly sickened by the whole business. I have been made to feel as if I were the criminal and I suspect the real culprits will get off scot-free, which disgusts me. At the moment, I can't wait to get home to you and don't feel I shall ever wish to come here again.*
>
> *Enough of my complaints! My heart longs to be with you all and I pray you are well and happy. I shall be with you as soon as I can, God willing. I love you, Sally. Always remember that and tell the children how much I love them.*
>
> *Your own Ben xxx*

Sally looked at her letter for several minutes before putting it away. She didn't know why, but she had a ominous feeling of foreboding. No, that was ridiculous! She was letting her imagination run wild. Yet she had the most dreadful feeling that this would be her last letter from Ben and that she would never see him again.

'No! No, don't be stupid! You can't think things like that...'

Agitated, Sally jumped to her feet, and gave a wail of despair. Her eyes felt gritty with tears and her throat was tight. She pressed her fist against her mouth as she felt the scream build inside her and fought to suppress it. Then the door opened and Mrs Hills entered the sitting room.

'Whatever is the matter, Mrs Harper?' she asked after taking one look at Sally's face. 'Have you had bad news?'

Sally shook her head, staring at her, unable to catch her breath. 'No – I don't know...' she gasped. 'I just had the most terrible premonition – I think something bad has happened to Ben...' The letter had fluttered from her hand to the floor. Mrs Hills darted forward to pick it up, reading it quickly.

'He says he is coming home as soon as he can...' she said, looking puzzled. 'What is it, Sally? Please tell me.'

Sally stared at her, coldness flooding her body as she knew quite certainly that he was gone. 'Ben has been killed,' she said. 'Since this letter was sent – he is dead.' She flopped back in her chair, feeling the world spin around her as the pain in her chest intensified until she thought she would die of it.

'But... I don't understand.' Mrs Hills struggled to make sense of what she was hearing and witnessing. 'What makes you think Mr Harper has met with an accident?'

'It wasn't an accident,' Sally said and didn't know where the words came from. 'He was killed by the men he exposed as criminals.'

'You can't be sure of that...' Mrs Hills shook her head. 'Has anyone rung to tell you or...?' She was clearly perplexed, not able to believe what Sally was saying. 'You're ill. You've been working too hard...'

Sally closed her eyes as the tears trickled down her cheeks. 'No,' she whispered. 'I don't know why I am certain Ben was killed – I just feel it in here.' She placed both hands over her heart, which felt as if it were breaking in two.

At that moment, the front doorbell rang.

Mrs Hills hesitated. 'Should I answer that? You are obviously ill...'

'Please answer it,' Sally said. 'It is probably a friend.'

She lay her head back against the chair, feeling numb all over. Inside, the pain was raging, but she was only dimly aware of it. She heard voices in the hall and closed her eyes. Mick was here. He had come to tell her the news she already knew.

'Sally, my love...' Mick's voice throbbed with emotion. His eyes met hers across the room and he read her agony. 'You know, don't you? Of course you would. When you love someone as much as you loved Ben, you know...' He came to her and knelt at her side, taking her hands in his. 'I know it doesn't help, but I'm so sorry, my dearest friend. I wish with all my heart it wasn't true, but it is... Ben was killed a week ago. I got a telegram this morning...'

Sally gasped for breath, a great sobbing cry bursting from her as Mick reached out and took her in his arms, holding her as she cried out her anger and pain. It was some time before she calmed and Mick let her ease back from him. He gave her a large white handkerchief and helped wipe her face and then she blew her nose.

'Tell me,' she said in a voice of agony. 'Did he suffer, Mick? How did it happen?'

'He was knocked down by a speeding car,' Mick said and saw

the surprise, doubt and horror in her face. 'He went to help an old woman who had fallen in the road and a car drove into him – quite deliberately. Yes, he was killed by mobsters, Sally, but it will never be proved. It has been recorded as an accident, a hit-and-run by a drunk driver – presently untraced.'

'Oh, Ben, it's just what you would do.' Sally nodded, her throat tight with tears and now there was bitterness in her voice. 'Someone knew exactly what he would do. His cousin must have been involved! He and his gangster friends. Damn them!' Her grief was tempered by anger. 'They will never be brought to justice for his murder – and no doubt they will get away with their fraud, just as Ben suspected.'

'Yes, I think that is about the sum of it,' Mick replied. 'I could ask for enquiries to be made by my friends. We might manage to trace the driver and punish him…'

'While the real culprits, the ones who ordered it, remain unpunished?' Sally shook her head. 'I see no point in it, Mick. Ben has gone now and it won't bring him back.' She shook her head. 'I knew he mustn't go back to America, but he wouldn't have listened even if I had been able to tell him…'

Mick nodded. 'Ben believed what he was doing was right, Sally. He would always have done his duty by his aunt's shareholders, because he was that sort of man.'

'I know…' Sally lifted her head and looked at him. 'How do I go on without him, Mick? What am I supposed to do with my life now?'

'You will go on living just as you always have,' Mick told her, fixing her with a stern look. 'You know your duty, Sally Harper. You don't need me to tell you. You have two children, your mother, and a business to run – and that is going to take all your energy and strength in the years to come. If I am right and the

American economy is in trouble, you will have your work cut out to bring Harpers through the slump that is coming.'

Sally sat up straighter and looked at him. 'Ben's last letter says the same thing, or almost – but you knew, didn't you? You've known it was coming for months; that is why you sold your shares at the top of the market.'

'I had a gut feeling,' Mick agreed. 'You and I are alike in many ways, Sally – you knew about Ben and I've felt the slump coming. I'd give every penny I have to bring Ben home safe to you, Sally – but he was told to cut and run for his life by my friends and he refused...'

Sally gulped and then lifted her head. 'I'm going to need help,' she said. 'Will you help me, Mick? There will be big decisions that I can't make alone.'

'You didn't need to ask,' Mick said with a soft smile. 'You'll never be alone. I shall always be close enough to do whatever you need me to do. Just lift the phone and I'll come. Whatever you need, Sally. I am always your friend.'

'Yes, I know,' she replied. 'Bringing Ben's body home – will you do all that for me?'

'I have already set it in motion,' Mick said. 'I've been advised it would be best to have him cremated and bring the ashes home – but you can bury them here and have a church service.'

Sally swallowed hard. 'Yes, I understand. Do whatever you feel right, Mick. Once Ben is home, I will arrange a church service and burial.' Her eyes stung with fresh tears as Mrs Hills came cautiously into the room. She blinked hard. 'I know – the children will need fetching from school in another hour. Will you do it, please?'

'Of course. Do you want me to say anything to them, Mrs Harper?'

'No, please just fetch them as normal. I will find a way to

break it to them when I am ready. Perhaps not yet... Jenny has a concert coming up and Peter has an important football match. I will tell them before the funeral, when I feel a little less like screaming and weeping.'

'I am so sorry, Mrs Harper. I didn't believe you until Mr O'Sullivan said... But now I have thought about it, I know folk do sometimes get feelings, especially when they are very close.'

'It's all right,' Sally said. 'Would you telephone my mother for me, please, Mrs Hills? It would make it easier if you told her – and Beth. Beth will tell everyone at Harpers, because I shan't go in for a few days.'

'Yes, of course,' Mrs Hills replied, giving her a sympathetic look as she left the room.

'What can I do for you, Sally?' Mick asked, looking at her in concern.

'Nothing more for the moment,' Sally said and attempted a smile, though it didn't reach her eyes. 'Just be here for me when I need you, Mick. I know my duty and I can be strong – but not all the time.' She shook her head, holding back a new wave of tears. 'I am going to my room now for a while. I want to be in full control when the children come home...'

'I could tell them for you?'

'No. Thank you for the offer, but I must do it myself. Perhaps you could take them somewhere this weekend? They like being with you and I think there is a football match they both want to see. Ben used to take them – and I'm not sure I can face it.'

'Of course I will,' Mick said. He hesitated, then, 'You are stronger than you think, Sally Harper, but I shall always be here when you need a shoulder – as will your mum and Mrs Hills too.'

'I have good friends,' Sally agreed. 'I can rely on Harpers' staff to carry on and both Kitty and Beth will step up to help me, I know.'

'Do you want me to go or stay?' Mick asked. 'I'll stay here and read my paper – or come back when you need me.'

'You go home,' Sally said. 'Come back tomorrow, please. I am going to need your advice on so many things, my dearest friend – but for now I have to be alone.'

Sally went out of the room and up the stairs.

Mick hesitated and then left by the front door. A short distance down the road, he stopped and spoke to a vagrant for a moment, tossing him a coin, and then walked on. Sally's minders would continue their work for a while yet. Mick thought the men who had been shadowing her for weeks would probably give up now that Ben had been dealt with. Sally could do nothing but those powerful men across the pond might need convincing that she didn't have any evidence to use against them, so Mick would keep his watchdogs in place for a while.

* * *

Sally gave way to her grief and cried for a full half an hour. Then she got up, washed her face and put new make-up on. She had just changed into a fresh dress when she heard the sound of Mrs Hills speaking to the children – and another voice. Yes, that was her mother... She must go down and greet them.

Aware that her eyes and nose must look red despite the make-up, Sally put on a smile as her children came rushing to her for hugs and kisses. Peter had scored a goal during the football game his class had played and was as proud as punch. Jenny had gained a perfect ten in her arithmetic test, so fortunately they were both full of their own achievements and didn't notice their mother's puffy face.

'Granny took us for ice creams because we did well,' Peter said, his face glowing from the fresh air. 'I had chocolate and vanilla with hundreds and thousands on top and Jenny had strawberry with cream and a real strawberry...'

'A real strawberry,' Sally said. 'Gosh, that was a treat. Real strawberries are hard to find at this time of year.'

'The woman said they came all the way from France on a ship,' Peter said. 'Was she telling the truth, Mum?'

'Yes, I think she probably was,' Sally said. 'I think it must make them very expensive.'

'Strawberries don't taste the same out of season,' Sally's mother said and Sally nodded her agreement. 'These were probably grown in a hot greenhouse, though I doubt they sent them all the way from France.'

'Perhaps not,' Sally said, aware that her mother was making small talk to cover Sally's distress. 'Well, my loves, I think you should go and have your tea with Mrs Hills while I talk to Granny.'

'Sally, my love,' her mother said when the children had gone safely into the kitchen. 'I don't know what to say to you. I could hardly believe it when Mrs Hills told me... I just want to say that we are here for you whenever you need us.' She shook her head in stunned disbelief. 'You must be in unbearable pain – it was such a shock.' She held Sally tightly as a shudder of grief ran through her. 'Saying we are sorry doesn't help I know – but, believe me, I feel your pain. I was very fond of Ben and your father liked him a lot.'

Sally nodded, holding her grief inside. She wanted to wail and rant and tear her hair out as anger and pain ravaged inside her, but she knew she could not give way to her grief. She held her mother's hands, drawing her down to the settee beside her. It was true that her stepfather had told Sally many times how much he liked Ben and her mother loved him; they would be feeling their own pain. Everyone was going to miss him. He was Sally's rock, her driving force, and without him she just felt empty – useless. Yet she had her children to think of and Harpers. She had to stay strong for them, even though her world had fallen apart.

Unable to speak, Sally nodded, silent tears running down her cheeks.

'Is there anything we can do, love?' her mother asked, looking at her anxiously. 'Would you like me to tell the children for you?'

'No!' Sally found her voice then. 'No, I will do it, Mum. I don't know how or when, but I have to do it myself.'

Her mother nodded her understanding. 'It is probably best. I know it will be very hard, Sally, but I wouldn't leave it too long if I were you. Jenny is a bright girl and she listens when you don't realise... She won't forgive you if she hears a whisper from someone else...'

'No one would tell her.' Sally accepted a handkerchief and wiped her face. 'Not without my permission.'

'These things get around,' her mother said, looking sad. 'It only needs one of the mothers at her school to hear about it and then a child will say something – and that can hurt, especially if Jenny didn't know.'

'Yes, I suppose it could happen that way.' Sally looked struck and gave a shiver of anguish. 'I suppose it may get into the papers. Ben was a prominent businessman.' She swallowed hard, grief and bewilderment in her eyes. 'What am I going to do without him, Mum? How can I do it all – the business, friends, mostly importantly the children? How can I make up for the father they adored? I'm just one woman...' Sally gave a little sigh of despair. 'I'm not sure I can do it...'

'The children come first, Sally,' her mother told her. 'Your father and I will do all we can to help. We can fetch them from school and attend the school meetings and sports days, concerts, all that sort of thing – but they need their mother, too. You have to be there. If something has to give, then it has to be Harpers – and your charity work.'

Sally nodded. Listening to her mother helped her to think rationally. 'It is what I've been training Kitty for,' she said after a moment's thought. 'I was planning to step back in another couple of years, but she will have to take on more of the decisions now. I may need to promote another member of staff to be her assistant.' She nodded, her panic receding a little as she realised so much of it was already in place. 'I know Beth is doing as much as she can manage, but...' She shook her head. 'The problem isn't Harpers... it's me. I feel so empty inside and alone —' Sally smothered a sob. 'I love him so much and I need him.' She gave her mother a look of desperate appeal. 'What is the point of it all without him?'

'I do understand, my love.' Sally's mother took her hand. 'You've never asked me much about your real father and I haven't told you... We were very much in love. Jon was young, only nineteen. His father wanted him to marry well and he didn't approve of me. So he sent Jon to work in a manufacturing business up North. He said it was to teach him discipline and that when he had seen the light he could come home.' She sighed and looked sad. 'The night before he was sent away, we made love. It was just the once, but that was all it took. Jon promised to come home as soon as he'd earned enough to marry me. He said if he did well, we might live up North and have nothing to do with his family. Like a fool, I didn't tell him when I discovered I was having you...' Sally's mother closed her eyes. 'He fell in love with a beautiful girl – the daughter of the manufacturer and rich... and they married. I was left alone and pregnant and, when I couldn't get work, I had no choice but to let you be taken in by the nuns.'

Sally stared at her. 'You told me my father died...'

'He did die a few years later,' her mother said. 'By then I had put my memories of him to a far corner of my mind. I was deserted, my heart broken. I wondered whether it was worth the effort of going on living... but after you were born, I had you and I loved you. I couldn't keep you when it became too difficult, but I vowed I would go back and get you when I could afford to look after you and I did – but they had hidden you away and wouldn't tell me where. It took me years and years to find you, but I never gave up – and you mustn't give up either, Sally.'

'Oh, Mum,' Sally said, fresh tears springing to her eyes. 'You make me feel ashamed. I had years of wonderful married life – and I have so much to be thankful for; you had nothing...'

'Nothing but memories,' her mother said with a wistful smile. She laughed. 'I saw Jon once years later. He came into a restaurant where I was working. He didn't know me, but I knew him, even though he was as fat as a pig.'

'Mum!' Sally remonstrated with a half-laugh.

'Well, he was, and nasty with it, Sally. Something was wrong with his soup and he caused such a fuss.' She grimaced. 'You wouldn't have wanted to know him – and he wouldn't have acknowledged you. Perhaps he would now you are the wealthy Mrs Harper – but all he would be interested in was what he might get out of knowing you.'

'That sounds bitter, Mum.' Sally looked at her hard.

'Yes, well, that's why I don't talk about him,' her mother said. 'Men like that are best forgotten. He used me and forgot me when something better came along.'

'Oh, Mum...' Sally clung to her hand. 'I'm not sure I can be as brave as you were.'

'I had no choice,' her mother said, giving her hand a squeeze. 'Nor have you, Sally Harper. You just have to grab life and hold on to it no matter what.'

Sally nodded, smiling through her tears. 'Yes, I know and I will – but it hurts.'

33

Beth burst into tears when Sally's mother rang her a little later that afternoon. 'I can't believe it,' she exclaimed. 'I know Sally has been worried about him for a while – but a car accident?'

'Yes, so it seems. Sally is devastated. She would like you to break the news at Harpers. Can she leave that to you and Kitty, Beth? She doesn't feel up to coming in for a while, so she will be relying on you both to see things carry on as best they may – at least until she is able to make decisions for the future.'

'Sally won't think of selling Harpers?' Beth asked, shocked. 'I know it is a huge burden for her but...'

'Oh, no, I am sure she has no thought of selling, but there may have to be changes. Sally will decide what she wants to do when she is feeling a little less numb.'

'Yes, of course. We are all shocked. I know Jack will be... Give Sally my love and tell her that I am ready to help as much as I can.'

'Sally knows that, Beth, but you are already doing as much as you can. Sally will have to find some extra senior staff, but she can't think of that for now.'

'No, of course not...' Beth hesitated. 'I should like to see her, but I don't want to intrude...'

'I think she is too upset at the moment but perhaps tomorrow?'

'Yes. I will come after I have been to Harpers. I am sure to have lots of messages for her from everyone.'

'Yes. It will be a huge shock and the staff will wonder what is going to happen to Harpers. Reassure them that their jobs are safe, Beth. Sally is going to need more senior-level staff, but she has no intention of selling – not at this time anyway.'

'Yes, I understand,' Beth replied. She was thoughtful as she replaced the receiver. Sally's mother didn't seem at all sure that Harpers would not be sold at some future date. Jack would be left wondering what would happen to the restaurant too – but she wouldn't think negatively! Harpers and the restaurant could come later. Sally must be hurting so much! Beth wished she could go straight round there and comfort her, but she'd been asked to wait until the next day and so she would.

She frowned as she thought about her task of letting the staff know. Ruby could type a memo for all the heads of departments, but somehow that didn't seem right to Beth. She would make a tour of the departments herself and inform the supervisors.

They ought to have the alterations department make up black armbands. The staff would want to show their respect for Ben Harper. He had been a popular employer. Ought they to have something in their windows to mark the tragic passing of Harpers' owner? Beth decided to speak to Mr Marco first. He and Ben had been great friends over many years and he would know what was appropriate.

Hearing the click of her front door, she turned in relief as she saw her father-in-law and sons enter. They had been to a circus as a treat for Tim's birthday and were very excited. Fred entered the kitchen, took one look at Beth's face, and sent the boys up to bed.

'Don't forget to wash your hands and face,' he told them. 'Your mother will bring you a hot cocoa and a biscuit if we hear no noise after ten minutes...'

'I want to tell Mum all about the circus.'

'When I bring the drinks up, Tim. Do as Grandpa tells you, there's a good boy.'

Tim subsided and they went out, chattering excitedly.

'What is wrong, Beth love?' Fred asked.

'Ben Harper has been knocked down and killed by a car in America,' Beth told him. 'Sally's mother rang me. Naturally, Sally is devastated... and she asked if I would break the news at Harpers.'

'Ben Harper killed in an accident?' Fred was stunned. He sat down in the nearest chair. 'That is terrible, Beth. Sally must be out of her mind with grief. I remember when they first got together – if ever two people were in love it was them. I am so sorry.' He frowned. 'If you want to go and see her, I can stay with the boys...'

'Her mother says leave it until tomorrow,' Beth said. 'I shall have lots of messages for her after I break the news...'

'Yes, of course. I know you will do everything you can to help her, Beth. She will need her friends now. I can do whatever she needs – take the children out if she likes. The circus is on the Heath for another few days.'

'Yes, I will tell her,' Beth said, sniffing hard and reaching for her handkerchief. 'I can't believe it, Dad. She was so worried about him; they had a quarrel and she thought they might be heading for a break-up – and then he told her he was sorry and he was coming home. Now he's gone and he can't come home...'

'Death is so final,' Fred said sombrely. 'I can hardly believe it

– a strong man like Ben Harper, killed because he didn't look where he was going...'

'Accidents happen,' Beth said. 'Sally won't know how to tell the children – Jenny is such a Daddy's girl. She will take it hard... so will Peter, but he is very loving towards Sally.'

'They will both take it hard in their own ways,' Fred agreed. 'It is a terrible thing for a child to lose a father. Hard enough for Sally, but she is still young.'

'Oh, Dad, don't say she might marry again. I don't think Sally would ever think of it...'

'Stranger things have happened,' he said. 'But what I was trying to say was you only ever have one father – a stepfather doesn't replace him. I think older men in a child's life can help, but you can't replace a father.'

'Or a mother, not really,' Beth agreed. 'I know some stepmothers are very kind and loving to their stepchildren – but it can't be the same, can it?'

'Not in Jenny's case,' Fred said, looking thoughtful. 'I think anyone who tried would get the cold shoulder. She is a young lady with very decided opinions.'

'You mean Ben spoiled her?' Beth asked with a raised eyebrow. 'I know he did. Sally hinted at it a few times. She had difficulty in making Jenny do what she was told, because she used to claim her daddy would let her have the ice cream or the new dress or whatever she wanted.'

Fred frowned again. 'It isn't going to be easy for Sally, telling her that Daddy won't be there to indulge her any more.'

* * *

'That is impossible!' Mr Marco cried when Beth gave him the news. 'I cannot believe it to be true – Ben would never step out in front of a moving car. He was far too aware of all he had to live for...'

'I don't know the details yet,' Beth told him. 'I have only learned from Sally's mother that he was killed by a car. I haven't heard what actually happened.'

Mr Marco furrowed his brow. 'Something is not right,' he said. 'I wonder— but I should not speculate. You wanted to know what would be appropriate for the windows? Let me ponder for a while. I think perhaps an empty window apart from a backdrop of a grey curtain and a formal notice of the death. We want something tasteful to show respect – so we shall not show off any goods. No just the grey curtains – silk, I think, artistically draped and a large noticeboard. Our girls always wear black for work, as you do, Mrs Burrows, but the men have grey suits, so they must have black ties and armbands.' He was silent for a moment. 'Should we be closed for a day? You must ask Mrs Harper what she wishes in this respect – perhaps this Saturday? That gives me time to dress the window and prepare the notice, but the closure must be her decision.'

'I shall ask her this afternoon,' Beth told him. 'Please go ahead with the window. That sounds respectful to me. I will see what she thinks about closing for a day – or longer.'

Mr Marco nodded. His message for Sally would be the first of many. Beth went up to the office. Kitty and Ruby were both working. Ruby looked up from her typing.

'Miss Wilson has Mr Stockbridge with her,' Ruby said. 'Shall you go in or wait until they have finished?'

'I need to speak to them both – and you should come, too, Ruby.'

'Have I done something wrong?' Ruby looked alarmed.

'No. It is worse than that, I am afraid.'

Beth knocked at the office door and entered. Kitty and Mr

Stockbridge had been having a meeting about staff and were comparing lists, but they both stopped and stood up as they saw Beth's face.

'What is wrong?' Kitty cried. 'Is Sally unwell?'

'She may be for a while,' Beth replied. 'But it isn't Sally – it is Mr Harper. He has been knocked down by a car and killed in America...'

'No!' Mr Stockbridge turned pale and sat down on the nearest chair with a bump, obviously shaken. 'That is terrible! How could such a thing happen to a man like that?'

'Poor Sally!' Kitty said and swayed, sitting down in her own chair, her face a pasty white. 'Oh, how awful for her. I know how it feels to lose someone to an accident like that... She must want to die. I know I did for months... I was only able to carry on because I had Mariah and she needed me, but I wished I could die, too.'

Ruby was sobbing noisily behind Beth. Mr Stockbridge frowned and hushed her. 'This is a severe blow for Mrs Harper – and for the store. Mr Harper was its beating heart...'

'I can't agree,' Beth said. 'Mrs Harper is the driving force at Harpers and always has been since the war – but she must be too devastated to even think about the store for a while. So she is relying on all of us to do our jobs, to step up and shoulder more responsibility until she is able to come back and get things going again.'

'I am sure we will all do our duty,' Mr Stockbridge said heavily. 'But a store like Harpers needs more, Mrs Burrows – it needs someone to drive it forward, to nurse it and nurture it so that it grows.'

'Yes, I know,' Beth agreed. 'That is why we all have to put in one hundred and one per cent. Whatever needs doing, we must see it gets done – until Mrs Harper can return and take the reins again.'

'That is all very well,' Mr Stockbridge said, a grumble in his voice. 'But someone has to take decisions. I can do that as far as staffing is concerned – but there is a level above which I cannot go—'

'I can and will,' Kitty spoke decisively. 'Mrs Harper has been leaving more decisions regarding the stock to me lately and I can take that step forward.'

'I'll help,' Ruby said. 'I know I can't make decisions, but I'll stay late to type up anything you need, Kitty.'

'And I will keep you advised on the various departments – whether they are up to scratch in display and stock presentation,' Beth said.

'We will manage for as long as it takes,' Kitty said firmly. 'Please tell Mrs Harper that I will oversee the stock and see to the various departments until she feels able to come in.'

'I will tell her, Kitty,' Beth replied. 'And now I have to make a tour of the departments and let all the supervisors know so they can tell their counter staff. I think that is nicer than sending a memo. And Mr Marco is arranging a window to show respect. He has asked whether we should close for a day or longer. I will ask Sally when I see her later.'

'Yes, that is a good idea,' Kitty agreed. 'Both the Harpers are popular and the staff are bound to be upset by the news. I think several of the girls will cry.' She took out her handkerchief and blew her nose hard. Her eyes looked red and the tears were not far away.

Ruby had stop crying but was blowing her nose and wiping her cheeks. Beth left them to start her tour of the store. Mr Stockbridge followed her out.

'Have you heard anything more concerning the accident? It

seems very odd that Mr Harper should be knocked down and killed – I mean, he wasn't the kind of man who just rushed across the road without looking.'

'It does seem unbelievable,' Beth said. 'But then, accidents are like that, aren't they? One moment everything is fine and then...' She shook her head. 'I don't want to believe it. I keep thinking it is a bad dream and I'll wake up and it will go away...'

'And what does Mr Burrows think about it – is the restaurant in jeopardy?'

'Jack doesn't think so,' Beth replied. 'He was naturally very upset last night, but he thinks Sally will simply continue as before once she gets over her shock and the worst of her grief.'

'Yes, well, one must hope so,' Mr Stockbridge said but sounded and looked doubtful.

It was clear to Beth that he didn't believe Harpers could continue as it had been without Ben Harper at the head. Beth knew that Sally was perfectly capable of it – but would she want it? To carry a business like Harpers alone was a huge burden for a woman with a family to care for. No matter how hard she worked and how much she delegated, her family life would probably suffer.

Yet Beth knew that Sally loved Harpers and believed in her heart that it would probably be her salvation. The future would be lonely for Sally without Ben. Her work was fulfilling and if she let it could probably take over her life giving her little time to grieve for her loss – but did she want that? Beth believed that Sally's mother thought she should relegate Harpers – leave it to others to run or sell it rather than neglect her children. Only Sally Harper could make that decision when she was ready.

34

'Oh, Beth, I am so glad to see you,' Sally exclaimed as Mrs Hills brought her into the sitting room.

'Sally, my love!' Beth opened her arms and they embraced, both of them hugging fiercely. The years of their friendship, the hardship, pain, laughter and hope were all there as they bonded as only best friends can. 'I wanted to come last night, but I thought it might be too soon?'

'No. I needed you and I shall need you very much in the next few weeks,' Sally said, blinking hard to hold back her tears. 'I can't stop crying, but I must or the children will know something is wrong.'

'Are they in school?' Beth asked, looking round.

'No. Mum and Trevor have taken them out for the day. They are buying Jenny some new clothes and Peter wants football boots, then a trip to a tea shop and then the circus. They should be tired by the time they get home and tomorrow I must find the courage to tell them.'

'Yes. You mustn't leave it. Because Jenny will pick it up somehow.'

'I know. I will tell them tomorrow. I just needed a day to get myself together. I couldn't sleep a wink last night and I came down at two o'clock and made myself a brandy and hot water—' Sally choked back a sob. 'It was Ben's favourite brand...' Sally shook her head. 'Everywhere I look, he's there, Beth. His clothes in the wardrobe, his slippers by the bed – his cigarette box I bought for him last Christmas...'

'Oh God, it must be awful,' Beth said. 'My heart aches for you, Sally. It really does – but you have to keep strong—'

'For the children, I know...' Sally blinked hard. 'Mum says they must come first.'

'Yes, of course the children are important and you may have to spend less time at Harpers – but remember all the people who are relying on you there, Sally. I know someone else can keep things ticking over and they will for a time – but you are the beating heart of Harpers. You always have been. Ben recognised your talent for buying and... Oh, it is so much more than just buying the right stock. You made Harpers the successful business it is today with your drive and your care for others. Ben was a good businessman and had an eye to expansion, but you are the one who knows the names of all her staff, from the errand boys to the managers. It is you who remembers to ask the new salesgirl how she is getting on and if she is happy in her job; it is you who remembers that Mr Brown suffers from a bad chest in the winter and his wife has terrible chilblains...'

Sally stared at her for a few minutes in silence, and then she broke down and sobbed as Beth held her close. 'Oh, Beth,' she gasped when the storm of weeping had abated. 'Is that how you truly see me?'

'Yes, I do – and so do most of your staff. Mr Stockbridge might think Harpers needs a man at the helm, but he was devoted to Ben. Everyone else adores you and they all sent good wishes and wanted to tell you how sorry they are and how hard they are going to work to make sure that Harpers doesn't suffer until you can return.'

'Oh, Beth,' Sally said when she could breathe again. 'I've been in such turmoil, wondering if I can hold on to Ben's dream for the children, wondering how I can manage but...' She sat back and looked at her friend. 'I was considering taking advice about selling.'

'Now is not the time to make decisions, Sally. Think carefully before you do anything, love. Sell Harpers and half your life is gone,' Beth told her firmly. 'Yes, I know you love Jenny and Peter, and you must make time for them – but they will grow up and they won't need you all the time. Harpers will always need you. Delegate. Employ an assistant for Kitty, but don't give up, Sally. You would hate your life within six months...'

Sally nodded, meeting Beth's compelling gaze. 'You know me so well. I suppose we've been through so much together. Yes, I've been torn, because Mum thinks I should consider letting Harpers go – I would have more than enough money – but it is the children's inheritance. Surely, I should guard it and protect it for them – it may grow and become even more successful over the years...'

'Exactly. Harpers isn't a gold watch or a diamond, it is a living, breathing thing and it needs its heart – and that's you, Sally Harper.' Beth's gaze held hers and Sally relaxed, recognising the truth.

'Yes.' Sally smiled, her head coming up, her shoulders squaring as she accepted the bittersweet burden Beth had placed on her. 'Ben said something similar to me not long ago, though not in the same words. I do have to go on for the children, but also for Harpers. So many people depend on it for their living...'

'Without you, it would change. It could prosper with another owner, but it wouldn't be *your* Harpers.'

'Yes, I do see,' Sally said. 'Thank you, Beth. I feel stronger now, more able to face the future.' She closed her eyes for a moment and drew a deep breath. 'I think Harpers should close for three days next week – Tuesday to Thursday. Not Monday because that is half-day for many of the staff. We must have something in the window.'

'Mr Marco has that in hand,' Beth told her. 'He was most upset, as you may imagine, but spoke of showing respect, so you know he will do something tasteful and fitting.' She hesitated, then, 'Perhaps a book where staff and customers, anyone, could write messages and tell you how they feel? We could have it on a little table inside the door where people would see it.'

'What a lovely idea,' Sally said and took Beth's hand, squeezing it. 'I am arranging a church service in three weeks' time. Mick is trying to arrange for Ben's ashes to be sent home; they may not arrive in time for the service, but the internment will be private – family and close friends. The church service will be for Harpers' staff and anyone Ben knew in an official way or through business. I will advertise it in *The Times* and allow those who wish to show their respects to come – the internment will be by invitation only.'

'I think that is a good idea. Will you close Harpers for a while that day?'

'Yes. I shall have the service from ten thirty in the morning to twelve thirty and the shop will close during those hours. Anyone who wishes to attend may; others may prefer to stay at their posts and wait for the reopening at twelve thirty.'

Sally nodded, picking up her pad and pen. 'I shall have a room at Claridge's for the reception. It was Ben's favourite hotel and I believe a lot of people will want to pay their respects – he was well thought of and liked.'

'Yes, he was, and with good reason,' Beth replied gravely. 'Ben did a lot for this country during the war.'

'He did...' Sally gave a little shiver. 'If only his aunt hadn't asked him to investigate a loss of profits in the New York store...'

Beth looked puzzled. 'I don't understand – unless you mean that he would not have been over there...'

Sally raised her head and looked at her. 'Mick has friends over there – and we had Ben watched because we suspected there might be foul play. Big money was involved, Beth, and Ben stirred up a hornets' nest—'

Beth was horrified. 'You don't mean? You can't—'

'We can't prove it and we may never know the truth, but Mick and I both believe that driver drove straight into Ben as he attempted to help an old woman lying in the road.'

'Murder— No!' Beth gasped in dismay. 'Oh, Sally. That is shocking. Surely it can't be true?'

'Two attempts were recently made to snatch the children from the school playground – and there was one foiled attempt that Mick thinks was meant to involve me in a car accident.'

Beth felt as if all the breath had been knocked out of her. 'Sally, that is frightening...'

'Yes, it was,' Sally agreed, then gave a strangled cry. 'Last night I wished they had managed to kill me, too...'

'Sally! No! You must never ever think that,' Beth cried.

'I know. It is self-indulgent and stupid,' Sally said. 'Why would I want to cause more pain to my family? Don't worry, Beth. I shan't do anything foolish. Ben would never forgive me if I deserted his children when they need me most.'

'Nor would I,' Beth said. 'I love you, Sally Harper. So do a lot more people, so don't you ever think you are alone, because you are not.'

Sally sniffed hard but her tears were done. Beth's straight talking had sorted her tangled thoughts. She knew what she had to do with the rest of her life, and she would do it, just as she always had.

* * *

Sally told her children that Saturday morning, they were tired from the day they'd spent shopping and still full of their visit to the circus.

'Come here, Jenny, Peter,' she said as they were brought into the sitting room after having their breakfast in the kitchen. 'Sit with me on the sofa, one each side, and give me your hands. I've got something I have to tell you and it isn't nice or easy...'

'Have we been naughty, Mummy?' Peter asked, his eyes wide and scared.

'No, my darlings, you haven't done anything wrong. You are both good children and I am proud of you...'

Peter clung to her hand. Jenny sat up straight beside Sally but withdrew her hand, refusing to give it to Sally. 'What have you done?' she asked, accusation in her face. 'Are you going to say you are too busy to come to my school concert?'

'No. It is nothing like that,' Sally said. 'I shall come to hear you sing, Jenny – but this is something very sad I have to tell you...'

'It is about Daddy, isn't it?' Jenny gave her a hostile stare. 'I heard Granny whisper something to Grandad, but I didn't catch what she said... Daddy isn't coming home for Christmas, is he?'

Sally drew a deep breath. 'No, he won't be coming home for Christmas, Jenny...' She held Peter's hand tightly and made a grasp for Jenny's. 'He can't come home, because he had an accident and—'

Jenny wrenched her hand from Sally's and jumped to her feet. 'You promised he was coming soon! You promised... It is all your fault! You don't want him to come because you quarrelled. I heard you before he went away...'

'We did have a little quarrel,' Sally admitted. 'But I do want him to come – he just can't, because he had an accident.'

Peter tugged at her hand and she looked at him; his face was white, his eyes big and scared. 'Is Daddy dead – like my rabbit the cat got and killed? Daddy said that was an accident...'

Sally's heart felt as if it were being torn apart once more. She wanted to deny it all, but she had to tell them the truth. 'Daddy was knocked down and killed by a speeding car,' she said, her throat tight with pain. 'He is in heaven now with the angels – he told you that was where your rabbit went, didn't he?'

Peter nodded solemnly. He stared at her in silence but didn't cry, though she could see the pain and grief in his eyes and her fingers curled about his protectively.

'No! It is a lie!' Jenny screamed, her face white with fear and horror. 'You made it up to punish me for loving Daddy best. You are horrid and cruel and I hate you...'

'Jenny! I wouldn't do that...' Sally reached for her, but Jenny kicked out at her and then turned and rushed from the room, crying and screaming her anger and pain.

'She didn't mean it, Mummy. Jenny gets upset and says things she doesn't mean,' Peter said and climbed onto Sally's lap. 'Don't cry, Mummy. I love you. I will look after you. Daddy told me that if anything happened to him, I was to look after you and Jenny – and I will. I promise.'

'Oh, Peter,' Sally said, putting her arms around him and cradling him to her as the silent tears slipped down her cheeks.

'I love you so much and I know Daddy is watching from heaven. He will be so proud of you.' She stroked his hair. 'When did Daddy say that to you, my love?'

'The night before he went away again. He came to my room and I was awake. He kissed me and told me he loved me – and then he said if ever he didn't come home, because he couldn't, I was to take care of you for him…'

'Oh, Peter,' Sally said, her face pressed against his hair as she breathed in his little boy scent. 'Oh, Ben… Ben…'

So Ben had realised the risks he was taking. Sally closed her eyes. She'd wanted to warn him, but he'd known – and he'd tried to cut loose and get back to them, but he'd done his duty first and the men he was up against wouldn't forgive that…

Sally held her son for a long time as the pain swirled inside her. She knew she had to go on and she would, but she would never cease to regret all the time lost to them. Nor would she forget all the happiness and love she'd known with Ben.

Why couldn't you just walk away, Ben? She asked the question in her head. *What did it matter if those shareholders were being cheated?* Yet it had mattered to Ben. He was an honourable man and he'd done what he knew to be right, even though it had cost him his life.

35

Ruby was as shocked as everyone else at Harpers. She hadn't known Mr Harper at all really, but he was the owner of the store and Sally Harper's husband, the father of her children. Ruby adored her employer, as did many of the girls at Harpers, and her heart ached for her. How could she bear the loss of a man who meant so much in her world? It was unbearable.

Over the weekend, Ruby's thoughts were with Sally Harper and they cast a cloud over both her and Kitty's lives. It also made Ruby think about her own life and the love she might have had if only Captain Saunders had lived. Kitty thought he must have cared for her deeply to have left her such a legacy and it made Ruby's heart ache to think of what she had lost. She decided that she wanted to visit his grave, and if she was refused entrance to the Saunders' family crypt, she would visit the church and place flowers on the altar. Perhaps someone could tell her where he'd lived and she might go and look at his home, perhaps lay her flowers there. Yes, she decided, she would do that as soon as she could get time off from work.

On Monday morning, Ruby learned that Harpers was to close for three days, from Tuesday to Thursday, as a mark of respect for the tragic death of Ben Harper. Since Monday was her half-day, Ruby decided it gave her plenty of time to do what she needed to do and then she wouldn't have to ask for some of her holiday, because she was determined to work as hard as she could to help Kitty and Mrs Harper.

She confided in Kitty and her friend thought it a good idea. 'Yes, you should go, Ruby. Harpers will be closed and we shall be needed when it reopens – so take the time now and do what you have to do. You have been grieving and wanting to visit his grave and if you can't do that, a visit to the church should help. At least it will be where the service was held – and you might talk to the vicar. He could probably tell you things you want to know about Captain Saunders and how he died.'

Ruby told Kitty how grateful she was for her advice and encouragement.

* * *

Ruby packed a small bag that afternoon and went to the railway station to discover the times of the trains. All she had to go on was the solicitor's address, but he must live somewhere close by – and she could go to his office and ask where the church Captain Saunders was buried from was situated. No one could object to her visiting the church, even if the family crypt was private.

Ruby felt happier once her decision was made and slept well that night. In the morning, she was up early and caught a bus to Paddington Station. Her train was due on time and she was able to buy her ticket – a two-day return – and some magazines. She would find a small hotel and stay overnight and be back in time to get ready for work on Friday.

It was, Ruby reflected, the first real holiday of her life, even though only for a couple of days. She had never stayed in a hotel, always just staying at home when she had time off work. Her only pleasure trip had been a visit to Southend with some girls who worked in the factory when she had a job in the canteen. It hadn't been much fun as the wind had been cold and none of the other girls had really wanted Ruby along; she'd just been asked because it was a staff outing.

To catch a train to Truro in Cornwall was an adventure and Ruby was both nervous and excited. Her purpose in visiting was sad, but Kitty was right, Ruby needed to make this journey, because otherwise Captain Saunders' death would haunt her. She had to visit the places he'd known and pay her respects – say thank you for what he had done for her and tell him she loved him.

As she settled into her seat and the train started off on its long journey, a kind of calm came over Ruby. She was doing the right thing. That glimpse of someone in a taxi that looked like Captain Saunders had unsettled her mind. Once she'd seen where he was interred and the church, perhaps his home – and, if she could manage it, talked to the vicar, then she would feel better about things and the stupid hope that he might still be alive would vanish into the mist of forgotten dreams.

* * *

Ruby hadn't brought any food with her, so she was pleasantly surprised when someone announced that meals were being served in the dining car. She could never have afforded such a luxury on her wages, but she had drawn thirty pounds from her bank account to cover the cost of her trip. She had no idea how much it would cost for taxi or bus fares from Truro to wherever she needed to go. It was quite possible that she might have to take another long train or bus journey so she'd drawn as much as she dared carry in her purse, which was tucked inside her jacket pocket, beneath her overcoat.

The meal was a revelation to her, because it was just like going to a high-class restaurant, the tables set with fine white cloths, sparkling glasses and cutlery. Ruby couldn't imagine how they could cook on a train that seemed to her to be travelling quite fast, let alone serve wine. However, the waiters all seemed able to cope and her meal of roast chicken, potatoes and green beans and carrots was perfectly cooked and presented, as was the glass of lemonade she asked for instead of wine. It had a slice of lemon and ice and clinked as she sipped it.

Ruby suppressed a desire to giggle. Despite the shadows that had made life seem so sad of late, this was an experience she might never have again and she could not help enjoying herself. Anyone would think she was a great lady! The waiters were so polite and assiduous in seeing that she had everything she needed. It was a wonderful service and a real treat for a girl from an orphanage.

So she tucked into her meal and had the apple pie and custard afterwards, followed by a cup of fragrant coffee and a mint chocolate. Sheer luxury!

After her meal, Ruby went back to her seat and began to read her magazine. It was a long journey, perhaps another hour until she reached her first change of trains, but the meal had made the time go faster. Her heart raced. It might be too late to see the solicitor today, but she could find a small hotel, then go exploring in the town. It was her holiday and something she might not repeat for a long time, though now that she had her legacy, she would be able to take a holiday now and then... but perhaps to somewhere a little nearer home.

* * *

Ruby stood uncertainly on the platform at Truro and looked about her. It was nearly dusk and she felt a bit lost and disorientated. Uncertain of what to do, she thought for a moment and then approached a young porter.

'Excuse me,' she said. 'I wonder if you could help me?'

'I'll try, miss,' he said and touched his cap. 'Do you need something fetching from the guard's van?'

'No. I just have this small bag,' Ruby said. 'I'm a stranger here and I need directions to a small hotel. Something clean and not too expensive – if you know of such a place?'

His face lit up, his grin reaching from ear to ear as he nodded eagerly. 'You've come to the right person, miss. My sister runs a lovely little boarding house. It ain't posh or fancy, but it is clean; the food is good, and her prices are much less than the hotels.'

'Oh, thank you,' Ruby said, her relief showing as she laughed. 'That sounds wonderful – can you tell me where to find it?'

'I'll do better than that, miss,' he said. 'Give me your case and I'll carry it for you. My sister's place is just round the corner and I'm off duty now. I'll take you there.'

Ruby thanked him, hardly believing her luck. It looked as if everything was falling into place for her. She smiled as her young benefactor set off at a good pace, hurrying to keep up with him as he strode confidently through the gathering dusk.

'Staying long then?' he asked.

'No, just a couple of nights. I will be returning to London on Wednesday – or I expect to. I've just come to... visit someone...'

'London is a big city,' her chatty escort remarked. 'I shouldn't want to go there myself – dark and dirty, that's what I've heard.'

'Oh, no, London is beautiful,' Ruby replied. 'There are wonderful buildings and parks – but some of it is depressing. It is true that there are slums, some of the houses unfit to live in.'

'That's what I heard,' he said nodding wisely. 'Better off here, that's what Mum says and Bessie says the same. Bessie is my sister. You'll like her, miss. She will look after you.'

He stopped outside what looked like a big house and opened the door. A bell rang as he did so and Ruby followed him into a small reception area. She was in what must once have been a large and splendid home but was now furnished in a mediocre way that would never suit such a staircase and the beautiful high ceilings. A rich family must once have lived here, Ruby decided, but her thoughts flew as a woman came bustling into the hall. She was red-cheeked and on the plump side with a pretty face, a soft mouth and bright eyes.

'Well then, Jacob, who is this then?' she asked, looking at Ruby curiously.

'It's a lady off the train looking for a room for two nights,' Jacob replied with a cheeky grin. 'Don't say I don't bring you customers – that's two this week...'

Bessie nodded, her interest plain as she looked at Ruby. 'Never been to Truro before then?'

'No. I've never been outside of London much. I asked your brother if he could recommend somewhere—'

'And he brought you here. Well, you're lucky. I do have a nice big room free. It is thirty shillings for two nights, breakfast and evening meal included...'

Ruby hesitated, because that sounded an awful lot to her. She had paid Mrs Flowers much less, but then she'd paid by the week and this was a sort of hotel, she supposed. Bessie looked clean, as did her house, and it was convenient, close to the station for when she went back to London.

'Thank you,' she said. 'That will be fine, Mrs...'

'Ransome, but you can call me Bessie, if you like. Most of my visitors do. I like to look after them – give them tips on where to go and what to see while they are here. They want to know about the cinemas and places of interest, also where the best place to have a nice lunch is...' Bessie looked at Ruby expectantly.

'Yes. Well, I might ask if you know where a solicitor's offices are,' Ruby said. 'I had thought I might explore a bit, but it took longer than I imagined to get here and I shan't see much in the dark.'

'No. I can give you a nice dinner, Miss...? But you won't do much exploring this evening – unless you fancy a visit to the cinema?' Bessie noticed her brother still standing there, waiting. 'Off home with you then, Jacob.'

'Oh, just a moment.' Ruby fished in her pocket for half a crown and gave it to him. He gave her another big grin and went off whistling.

'Far too much,' Bessie remarked. 'He gets two bob off me every time he brings me a new customer.'

'He was helpful and he carried my case.' Ruby laughed quietly to herself as she realised Jacob had a nice little sideline going.

Bessie led the way upstairs, chatting non-stop as she went. She told Ruby about places of interest and advised her that if she needed to catch a bus anywhere she should look in her guide, which would give her the number and where she should buy a ticket if it wasn't available on the bus.

'Most of my visitors come to go touring,' she said. 'Even at this time of year. The weather can be beautiful and mild and there's a lot of lovely scenery to be enjoyed here, Miss— you didn't give me your name. I'll need it for my register.'

'It is Ruby Rush, and I'll pay you in advance if you like.'

Bessie looked at her and then shook her head. 'I know who I can trust, Miss Rush, and I don't think you'll be running off without paying your bill. Now, here is your room – I hope it is to your liking?'

She opened a door with a flourish and Ruby entered, looking round her with pleasure. It was the largest bedroom she'd ever been in and nicely furnished with chintzes and a pretty bedspread to match the curtains.

'This is lovely,' she said. 'Thank you. I shall enjoy staying here.'

'That is what we like to hear,' Bessie nodded approvingly. 'Well, I'll leave you to unpack. Dinner is at seven, but you are welcome to use the lounge or the bar downstairs. You can sit and read. We have lots of newspapers and magazines – and you can have a drink in the bar if you wish.'

'I wouldn't mind a pot of tea in the lounge,' Ruby said and Bessie beamed at her.

'It's an extra, but my prices are all on that list by the bed.' She nodded her satisfaction and went off, leaving Ruby to sit on the bed and look about her.

It all seemed a bit like a dream to Ruby. She had enjoyed her day so far and everything had gone perfectly, as if it had been meant. Her bed even felt comfortable and it was very clean and fresh; the whole room smelled of lavender polish.

She picked up the leaflets beside the bed, glancing through them with interest. There were quite a lot of things going on, shows and cinema trips, also events that had been put on, perhaps to attract tourists or for the amusement of local folk. Once she had visited the solicitor to find out the direction of the church she wanted to find, Ruby would enjoy exploring. She might even take a bus to one of the beach resorts nearby. She had another two days before she needed to be back at work, but it would probably only take a day to see all that she had come to see...

36

Kitty missed Ruby that evening. Mariah had popped round to see her on Sunday to say how sorry she was to learn of Mr Harper's death, but she couldn't leave Arnie's mother, because she was confined to bed and needed constant care.

'I feel dreadful leaving you two to manage alone, especially now you'll have so much more to do,' Mariah had said, looking upset. 'But Arnie's mum needs me – and he doesn't know how to look after her, though he does all he can, bless him.'

Kitty had assured her that she was managing fine, and she was – but the house seemed empty with both Mariah and Ruby gone. She had brought a load of work home from the office, thinking she would get ahead with it, but on Tuesday morning she felt in need of some fresh air and decided to go out for a few hours.

It felt so strange not having her work to go to. Kitty wondered if she should call on Sally Harper to express her sympathies but decided that it was far too soon. What Sally needed now was quiet time, space to reflect and talk to her family. Kitty didn't envy her the task of telling her children.

Jenny was highly strung and very much her father's girl; she would take it hard. It was more difficult to gauge how Peter would react; he was a thoughtful, quiet child who might brood inwardly. No, Kitty didn't think that would be easy for Sally at all.

She found herself walking in the direction of Harpers store. It was as if she was drawn there, even though she knew it was closed. She stood looking in the window Mr Marco had so tastefully arranged. The curtains were draped, dark grey velvet at the back with paler grey silk folding across in delicate swathes and then a noticeboard edged in black with the sad announcement – nothing else. It was beautiful and it brought a tear to Kitty's eyes.

She wasn't the only one to stand staring at the windows and she found herself listening to the comments of those who paused their busy day to stop and stare.

'That is so sad...'

'Yes. He did a lot for this country during the war, you know...'

'An American, wasn't he?'

'Yes, but his wife is a London girl. She must be devastated...'

'I wonder what will happen to the store now. I hope it doesn't close...'

'Why aren't they open?' An irritated voice broke the pattern of soft sympathetic tones and Kitty looked at the woman who was staring at the closed notice in frustration. 'I particularly wanted to buy a present for my daughter today.' She gave an exasperated sigh. 'Oh well, it is their loss. I'll go to Selfridges!' She stomped off, leaving Kitty frowning.

'What a selfish woman,' a quiet, cultured voice spoke from beside Kitty. She turned her head to look and saw a man in a smart pinstriped suit. He was wearing a bowler hat, which he tipped to her when he saw she had turned in response to his remark. 'I think it is rather splendid that Mrs Harper has chosen to close the store out of respect for Ben. He certainly deserves it...'

Kitty's brow arched a little as she met his gaze. 'You knew Mr Harper?' she asked.

'Yes, I knew him,' the man replied and offered her his hand. 'I am Stephen Arnold and Ben was a personal friend. We met during the war – he helped us out with a delivery of badly needed ammunition and other supplies, drove one of the trucks out himself.' He smiled at her. 'I think you work here, don't you? I believe I saw you coming from Mrs Harper's office just around last Christmastime, when I called to see Ben about a reunion for some of the officers and men who were wounded...'

'I'm Kitty – Kitty Wilson,' Kitty replied, taking the hand he offered. His fingers closed around hers in a cool, firm clasp and his eyes lit up as he smiled. 'Yes, I work with Mrs Harper as her assistant.'

'Ah, that's it,' he said, nodding as if something had clicked in his memory. 'I thought I remembered. Ben told me that Sally had taken on a young woman as her assistant. He was very pleased; said you were shaping up well, and would be a big help to Sally in the future.' A shadow passed across his face. 'I am afraid she is going to need your help a lot more now.'

'Yes, I think so,' Kitty agreed. 'It was such a terrible shock. All the staff were upset over it. I think Mrs Harper did right closing the store, because a lot of the girls were crying at their counters and it is best if we all have time to conquer our emotions.'

'Yes, of course. Ben said Sally knew the name of every member of staff. No doubt they were all feeling distressed for her as well as the death of their employer.'

'Mr Harper was well liked by everyone,' Kitty agreed. 'I think I can safely say that most of the girls adore Sally Harper. They all look up to her and respect her, because she is so fair and generous – and when other stores let many of their girls go at the end of the war, Sally kept hers. She gave the men their jobs back, but the girls stayed on.'

'Yes, I can quite see why they would,' he agreed. 'I don't know her as well as I knew Ben – we've met many times, of course, at parties and functions, but it was really Ben I knew.' He sighed deeply. Then, as Kitty nodded and would have moved on, he touched her arm. 'Please don't think me pushy or forward – but I'm feeling a bit down over this...' He indicated the window. 'Would you be kind enough to give me your company over lunch?'

Kitty was surprised, but, seeing the genuine sadness in his rather nice grey eyes, she didn't feel that he was being inappropriate. 'Well... Yes, I will, Mr Arnold. I know it is most irregular to accept an invitation from someone I have only just met but...' Kitty smiled sadly. 'I am feeling lost and sad, too. I tried to get ahead with work but needed to come out and found myself standing here.'

His smile lit up his face, his eyes warm and friendly. 'How kind of you to take pity on me, Miss Wilson. I was going to Claridge's – one of Ben's favourite haunts when he met friends. We will raise a glass of wine to him – gone but never forgotten.' He offered her his arm. 'Shall we walk? It will give us a little time to introduce ourselves properly. I was Captain Arnold during the war, which was when I met Ben, of course. I don't use it now – except at reunions. I work for the Ministry of Food now – visiting farms, and I have a farm myself, which my brother manages for me.' He looked at her, eyebrows arched. 'I believe it is your turn next?'

Kitty laughed. He was gentle, kind and amusing. She found herself drawn to him and discovered that she liked being in his company. 'Well, there isn't that much to say really. I work for

Sally Harper, a job I really enjoy – but I live with my friend Mariah Norton...' Kitty's smile faded. 'I was engaged to Mariah's brother, Larry, but he was killed in an accident on the docks before we could marry.'

'That was terrible for you,' Mr Arnold said, genuine sympathy in his face. 'That is something one never quite forgets, I'm afraid.' He nodded. 'It is there in your eyes, Miss Wilson. We hold our first love close to our hearts, as is right and proper.'

'You?' Kitty asked, gazing into his face.

He inclined his head. 'She was a nurse overseas during the war – came out to be near me – but she caught a fever from one of the men and died...'

'I am so sorry,' Kitty said and pressed his arm. 'How awful for you both.'

'Yes, it was.' He gave her his gentle smile. 'As you, I have suffered loss. It tempers us, Miss Wilson. Makes us stronger in the end. We never forget, but we go on and we learn to live and find happiness again.'

'Yes, we do,' Kitty said and her heart gave a little lift as if some of the shadows had gone. She was enjoying herself, finding pleasure and comfort in the company of a stranger – a man she met by chance and might never meet again.

* * *

Stephen, as he'd insisted Kitty call him, had treated them to a wonderful lunch of lobster bisque with soft rolls, roast beef and all the trimmings, and a sherry trifle for afters, followed by a coffee. He'd offered brandy as a liqueur, but Kitty had refused.

'I've had a glass of wine and I really should work this afternoon.' She smiled at him. 'But I do thank you for a lovely meal – and for your company. You have made me feel so much better.'

'May I return the compliment,' he said and touched her hand lightly. 'I must say that I have seldom enjoyed a lunch more – but, like you, I must go back to work. You will allow me to send you home in a taxi?'

'Thank you, yes, why not?' Kitty laughed. 'This has been the strangest morning, Mr Arnold – but a very pleasant and unexpected one.'

'Quite extraordinary,' he agreed, eyes sparkling with amusement. 'Once again I thank you, Miss Wilson.'

After paying the bill, he accompanied her out to the taxi rank that always formed near the hotel and summoned one for her, paying the driver despite her protests that she could pay.

He stood back and looked at her. 'Perhaps we shall meet again one day, Kitty. I do hope so...'

Kitty laughed and blushed, but didn't answer. He held up his hand as the taxi drew away from the kerb, watching it go.

'Where to, miss?' the driver said. 'The gent just said to take yer wherever you wanted to go?'

Kitty gave him her address, realising that Mr Arnold hadn't asked her where she lived or pushed to accompany her home. He had behaved as a perfect gentleman. It was such a pleasant morning but had no strings attached. He hadn't even asked her if they could meet again – just said that they might meet and that he hoped so.

Kitty found herself intrigued. She would have expected him to ask for another meeting if he wished... but perhaps it was best left like this; they both had lost loves and perhaps this one meeting was all there could be for them – like ships passing in the ocean.

Shaking her head, Kitty got out of the taxi and let herself into her home. She smiled as she put the kettle on to make herself a pot of tea. Her feeling of loneliness had quite gone and she was singing a little song to herself as she settled down at the kitchen table with her tray of tea and her paperwork.

She certainly didn't need anything to eat after that lunch but she could drink a cup of tea as she worked. What a lovely, unexpected treat the morning had turned out to be. Kitty still felt a deep sympathy for Sally Harper and was determined to do all she could to help her through her grief and distress, but something had shifted in her own world. She wasn't sure what it was, but she felt somehow lighter and she realised that she had somehow found herself; she was content just to be her, Kitty Wilson.

She went upstairs to her bedroom. Beside her bed was a picture of Larry in his best suit. It had been taken at a friend's wedding and was the only photograph Mariah had possessed of her brother – and she'd given it to Kitty. Smiling, Kitty picked it up and kissed it.

'I love you, my dearest Larry,' she said, touching his face. 'I always shall – but it has stopped hurting as much.'

The pain had become muted, softer, more a sweet remembrance now of the gentle, kind man who had been so good to her and won her heart by his care and love for her.

Kitty set the frame back where it belonged and then returned to the kitchen. She had work to do. The more she got done now while Harpers was closed, the less would pile up for Sally when she felt like returning to her desk.

Kitty picked up her pen and wondered how Ruby was getting on in her quest to find Captain Saunders' resting place. Would she be able to visit his grave – and would she too find peace at last?

37

Ruby looked at the imposing front of the lawyers' offices, hesitating before she dared enter. Now she was here she wondered whether she ought to have come, remembering that the solicitor had advised her not to in order to protect Captain Saunders' family's privacy. Yet surely a request to at least visit the church where the service had been held was not too much to ask?

She took a deep breath and went inside, impressed by the rich colours of the Persian carpets laid over a wood block floor. A large desk was the focal point of the reception area and a young woman sat beside it, her head bent over something she was reading. She looked up as a bell rang and saw Ruby, her smile seeming to welcome.

Ruby walked towards her. 'I've come to see Mr Philip Rowley,' she announced breathlessly, her heart hammering.

'Yes – what time was your appointment?' the girl asked, looking at her book. 'Your name is...?'

'Ruby Rush,' Ruby said. 'I don't have an appointment... I just want to ask—'

'I'm sorry. Mr Rowley is booked solid all day,' the girl told her, the smile of welcome fading. 'He never sees anyone without an appointment.'

'Oh, but— I've come all the way from London especially to ask him something. I won't take more than two minutes. I just want to know where Captain Saunders was buried so I can visit the church...'

The girl looked at her oddly for a moment, then, 'Miss Ruby Rush...?' She hesitated, clearly confused. 'Please sit down, Miss Rush. I won't be a moment.'

Ruby sat as the girl disappeared through a door behind her desk, clearly flustered. Ruby's heart was fluttering and her mouth felt dry. She wondered if she should go quickly before the girl came back but she didn't move. It was only a moment or two before the girl returned.

'Mr Rowley says he can spare you two minutes,' she said and looked at Ruby strangely. 'Please come through.'

Ruby followed her into a larger office, which was well furnished with carpets, a big desk and beautiful mahogany bookcases. A man got up and came towards her, offering her his hand. He was short and plump with gold-rimmed glasses and he looked nervous. 'Miss Rush – I am sorry, but I am very busy. You should have made an appointment...'

'I had an unexpected holiday and I very much want to see the church where the service was held for Captain Saunders,' Ruby said. 'I know his family do not wish me to see inside the family crypt – but, surely, I may see the church and just sit there to mourn him? Please, Mr Rowley. I do so want to say goodbye to him. I loved him, you see. I can't just take what he so kindly gave me and forget... He means— he meant too much to me.' Tears sprang to her eyes and slipped down her cheeks as she pleaded. 'Just the church...'

The solicitor looked uncertain, but she could see he was moved by her tears. He hesitated, then, 'Well, I don't suppose it would hurt if you were to see the church, Miss Rush – if that would content you?'

'Oh, yes, please,' Ruby said. 'I should feel so much happier.'

'Well, his family church is in the small hamlet of Little Stoneham and lies just a few miles from here. You can catch a bus at the stop in the main street – number fifty-five...' He glanced at his watch. 'There should be one leaving in half an hour.'

'Oh, thank you. I shall go straight away.' Ruby beamed at him. 'It is so good of you. I can't tell you how happy this makes me.'

Mr Rowley looked distinctly uncomfortable. 'I am sorry, Miss Rush. Had I realised how deep your feelings were for Captain Saunders...' He shook his head. 'I can only apologise.'

Ruby smiled, thanked him again and left his office feeling a surge of relief. At last, she could say goodbye to the man she had loved in a way that she felt might bring her peace of mind.

Walking quickly away from the solicitor's office, she turned into the main street and looked for the bus stop. Fortunately, it had a shelter and a seat and she was able to sit down and wait for her bus out of the cool breeze, though never had half an hour passed so slowly. At last it drew up at the stop. Ruby paid her fare and asked the conductor if he would tell her when they reached the village and if the bus could stop as near to the church as was possible.

He laughed and nodded to her. 'There's only one stop, miss, and the church is plain to see. Not much there apart from the village shop, some houses and Stoneham Manor, a few miles down the road.'

'What is Stoneham Manor?' Ruby asked. 'Is it a stately home open to the public?'

The conductor chuckled. 'Well, some think it ought to be – but it belongs to the Saunders family now. They are the wealthiest family in the district – bought the manor a couple of hundred years ago when Lord Stoneham came to ruin, so they say.'

Ruby felt a tingle at the nape of her neck. Captain Saunders' home was close by. After she had seen the church, she could ask someone where the house was and walk to see it. She smiled happily as she watched the countryside go by. Everywhere looked so pretty, the trees glorious in their autumn shades, still holding to their leaves even though it was almost the end of October.

It was just a short drive and Ruby could see the church and the one small street with its cluster of houses as she got off the bus, thanking the conductor. She stood for a moment looking about her. There was a house not far from the church, which she thought might be the vicarage, a few other small houses and the main street, but it was mostly farmland as far as the eye could see. As she walked towards the church, she saw a sign pointing to Stoneham Manor and her heart danced for sheer pleasure. She wouldn't even have to ask the way...

The church was beautiful, perhaps Norman, Ruby thought. The Saxon churches were usually smaller and rounder, where this one had lovely proportions with a long nave and an impressive steeple. There were gravestones in the churchyard, but Ruby didn't look at them, because her Captain was buried in a family crypt. She couldn't see anything in the churchyard that might be a crypt, but perhaps it was in the foundations of the church, beneath the nave – or at his family home. Ruby didn't know much about such things.

She entered the church. It was empty, but someone had been there recently and vases of fresh flowers stood on little tables at the side of the nave. The benches were obviously old and had been there many centuries, the seats worn smooth, the backs carved with mythical figures. Someone had made cushions for kneelers and the church was obviously one that had a living benefactor for it was beautifully kept.

She noticed a plaque on the wall, saying that one Lord Stoneham had given a new altar to the church in 1745, and another said a Mr Thomas Saunders had restored the roof and steeple in 1898.

Ruby sat in the front pew. She thought it might be where the Saunders family had come to listen to service for years and years and she closed her eyes, letting the warmth of the autumn sun play on her face as it cast patterns on the stone floor, lighting up the jewel-like colours of the stained glass.

She prayed for Captain Saunders to have peace and, in her heart, she told him how much she had loved him. 'I shall never, never forget you,' she said and the tears slipped down her cheeks.

Hearing the door open behind her, Ruby wiped the tears from her cheeks and stood up. She turned, her neck prickling suddenly as she saw someone coming towards her and her heart suddenly began to race wildly.

'Ruby... Oh, Ruby,' he said in the voice she remembered so well. 'Forgive me. I couldn't believe it when Rowley rang me and told me you were coming here – and what you said to him. I didn't know... Please believe me, I didn't know. I am so—'

Ruby didn't hear his last words because she had swooned. She fainted because the man who had spoken was Robert Saunders. Her Captain Saunders. The man she loved and had come here to mourn...

* * *

When Ruby came to herself, she was being carried into a small sitting room. Her head was still spinning and she felt disorientated, unsure of what was going on. Something very strange had happened.

'She needs water, Captain Saunders,' a woman's voice sounded anxious. 'And perhaps some smelling salts...'

'Brandy would probably be better,' he replied. 'She has had an awful shock. If you would fetch it for us, Mrs Hartley, please – and just give us a few moments. I think she is coming round.'

'As you wish, Captain Saunders.'

The mist cleared and Ruby found herself looking up into Robert's face. A face she had never expected to see again in this life.

'Robert?' she said in wonder, because surely she was in one of her daydreams. 'Is it really you – are you alive? Or am I dreaming?'

'I am alive, Ruby, my dearest girl,' he replied. 'I am so sorry. I would never have put you through all this had I known you had strong feelings for me. I thought you just a kind girl who would help anyone...'

Ruby pushed herself up to a sitting position. For a moment, she was overjoyed that he was alive and she clutched his hands, touching him in wonder because she couldn't believe it. 'But how...?' she asked and then she felt a cold tingle down her spine as his words got through to her. She let go of his hands and sat up straighter. 'I don't understand. Your solicitor allowed me to believe you were dead – even today he didn't tell me the truth. I was told you were dead and given a legacy. How could he have made such a terrible mistake? How could he give me such pain and not tell me as soon as he knew you were alive?' Ruby stared at him in bewilderment.

'That is it, Ruby,' Robert said and she saw shame and regret in his eyes. 'Rowley did what I asked him to do. He didn't approve; he argued against it, but I told him that it had to be that way...'

'You asked him to lie to me – to tell me you were dead when you were still alive?' Ruby searched his face and saw the truth there. She felt a sharp pain in her heart, a small cry of anguish escaping her lips. 'Why did you do that? I thought you must care for me but...' Her anguish was turning to anger now. 'All the pain and grief I have suffered because I thought you were dead and I could never see you again, never be your wife...' The suspicion crystallised in her mind and now her anger was white hot. 'That is it – I'm not good enough to be your wife so you lied to me to make me think— How dare you! Why did you do all that just to give me some money? Well, I don't want it... You can have it all back...' Ruby sprang to her feet and would have run away, but her swirling head betrayed her and she fell back into his arms as he caught and held her.

'No, please don't think that, my darling,' he begged in a voice choked with emotion. 'It was the exact opposite – I could never be good enough for *you*. With my mood swings and my nightmares... and other things...' He tipped her chin towards him and then he was kissing her with a sweetness that would have made Ruby swoon again, except that he was holding her tight in his arms and she couldn't move. 'I loved you so much for your kindness, the way you broke through the madness that held me that night – and I wanted to tell you, but then my father was dying and I had to return home...' He looked down at her fiercely. 'I thought never to love again and it frightened me. My wife died in childbed and it sent me nearly crazy. I went off to fight in the war and believed I should die – but I didn't...' His gaze mesmerised her. 'I am only half a man, Ruby. I love you, but my injuries mean that I can't give you a child, and although I am better than I was, the nightmares still happen. Tell me truthfully – would you have wanted to marry a man like that?'

Ruby took a great gulping breath, then, 'Yes, I would with all my heart – but I am so angry with you, Robert. I am not sure I can forgive you—'

A little cough announced the return of Mrs Hartley with a small glass of brandy and a tea tray set for two. 'I baked this morning,' she said. 'The seed cake is fresh, as are the buns. I think you might feel better if you ate something, miss.' She set down the tray and looked from one to the other. 'Well, what a sorry pair you look,' she said and then smiled at Ruby. 'He has been very unhappy, miss. I don't know why, but perhaps you do – and he is really the kindest and best of men, so whatever he has done to upset you, I think it is your Christian duty to forgive him if you can.' She then beamed at both of them and went off.

Robert looked at her ruefully. 'She will be planning our wedding now. I have known Hilary since she came here as a new bride...'

Ruby picked up a piece of seed cake and began to eat it. Her thoughts were in turmoil, her head still woozy, but it was her heart that wouldn't behave.

Robert sat down next to her and watched her face as she ate the cake. 'It's very good,' she told him. 'You should try a piece. I'm going to have a cup of tea – I think you might like the brandy. I hate it...'

Robert picked the small glass up and downed the lot in one go, his eyes never leaving her face. 'Ruby, do you believe that I love you – that I just wanted to make sure you were all right for money? I never meant to hurt you. I knew you were kind and that I had fallen in love with you. It began the day we met at the bathroom door and you were in such a hurry but didn't ask if you could go first, but I insisted you did and you looked so shyly at me. I liked you for your shyness and your smile whenever we met in the hall, and then you helped me that night and you showed no fear when I attacked you. I think it was then I knew I loved you, but I didn't know you loved me – and I got cold feet once I was home and the weeks passed. I thought you would have forgotten me – and I am not good enough for you...'

'Don't be so stupid,' Ruby said and took another sip of her tea. She was a practical girl and calmer now and she wasn't going to throw away a lifetime of happiness, even if she was cross. 'I ought to be furious with you, Robert. I am furious! However, I am also very, very happy that you are alive...' Tears started to her eyes, but she warded him off as he would have taken her into his arms. 'I love you very much – but I'm not sure I can trust you after what you did. Are you sure you want to marry me?'

'I have never been more sure of anything in my life,' Robert said. 'If you can find it in your heart to forgive me, Ruby, I shall spend the rest of my life making it up to you, my dearest girl.'

'Then... you'll have to wait a few months,' Ruby told him. 'Mr Harper was killed in a car accident just recently and Mrs Harper needs the staff she knows around her. I have promised to work hard – and I shall stay until we can find a new girl and get her used to the routine. I think next May might give us enough time, and in the meantime, you can come up to London and court me.' Ruby was smiling now, her eyes alight with mischief as the happiness surged through her. 'If I am worth having, I am worth a little courting, don't you think?'

'Oh, Ruby,' Robert replied and he was laughing now. 'You are so much the girl for me. I knew there was something special between us, but I fell into doubt and did a foolish and cruel thing.'

'Yes, you did,' Ruby agreed. 'But I love you, so I have decided to for—'

She got no further for she was crushed in his arms.

At the other side of the slightly open parlour door, where she had been listening, Mrs Hartley smiled in contentment. Well, that had worked out all right. She'd known their dear Robert was breaking his heart over something, but they'd had no idea it was a girl. Now at last it seemed there would be a new mistress up at the Manor – and a bright, pretty thing with a lot of go in her by the look of it. They would soon see things put right once Miss Ruby was mistress of her new home.

38

'Well,' Kitty said, looking at her in astonishment after Ruby poured out her story. 'This is a day of surprises – Mariah came this morning and told me that, although Arnie's mum is getting better, she will always need a bit of care – and she has finally agreed to wed him.'

'Oh, I am so glad for her,' Ruby cried. 'I'm so happy, Kitty. I know Robert did things that hurt me – but it was all for my sake, because he loves me and thought I was young and lovely and deserved better. I can hardly keep still. I'm just bursting with love and happiness.'

'I can see you are,' Kitty said, smiling at her. 'I don't approve of what he did – but if he didn't know you loved him, he was just trying to look after you, Ruby.'

'Yes, I know. I am so lucky,' Ruby said, then her smile faded. 'When I get married next year, it will mean you'll be on your own, Kitty...'

'Please don't worry about that,' Kitty begged. 'I don't mind being alone – and I can find someone to share if I want.'

'Yes, lots of the girls would be happy to share the expenses with you,' Ruby agreed. She gave Kitty a hug. 'I just wish you could find someone, too, love.'

'Perhaps I will one day,' Kitty said. 'At the moment, I am happy in my work – and Sally Harper needs me. She needs all her staff just now.'

'That's why I won't marry until next summer, to give her time to find a new secretary – one better than me.' Ruby giggled. 'That shouldn't be too hard.'

'We shan't find a more loyal girl than you,' Kitty said and kissed her. 'I am delighted you are happy... Oh, that reminds me, your friend Marianne visited the shop and asked for you. I spoke to her and she said your final fitting for the bridesmaid dress is this weekend. Her wedding is the week after...' Kitty hesitated, then, 'She said something else... her brother has gone off abroad somewhere with his friends and his uncle has threatened to disown him.' She frowned. 'I was worried in case you would be upset – but now I know you never cared for him, did you?'

'Oh no, he was just using me anyway,' Ruby agreed. 'He introduced me to his sister and that was nice – but she will be going away after the wedding so that is all finished. She was more of an acquaintance really.'

'You don't need either of them,' Kitty said. 'You have real friends now, Ruby – and a man who loves you.'

Ruby smiled and did a little twirl of delight. 'He is coming up on Sunday and he wants to meet you and Mariah. I shall have my fitting on Saturday and then I'll be here with you. Robert will take us all somewhere for lunch... if you'd like that?'

'I think that would be nice. Mariah may be too busy, but she will be so pleased you've found happiness, Ruby. We both love you.'

'And I love you, too, and I'll never forget you or lose touch – even when we're in the country.'

39

It was the 24 October 1929. Sally stared at the headlines in the evening paper in shock and horror. The stock market on Wall Street in America had crashed, shares falling to an all-time low. She was about to reach for her telephone when Mrs Hills announced that she had a visitor and Mick walked into the room.

'You've seen the papers?' he asked, looking worried. 'I've had several telegrams from friends today and they've seen a fortune wiped out just like that – businessmen bankrupted overnight...'

'Oh, Mick, it is terrible,' Sally cried. 'Did you have any shares at all?'

'No. As you know, I sold them all months ago. I never expected it would be this bad, but a few of my friends have been unloading their shares recently...' He hesitated, then frowned. 'I've been told that the authorities are holding on to some money from shareholders they believe dumped their shares a while back in order to destabilise the market – and I understand that Ben's money for the shares he sold will not be paid until they are satisfied that it wasn't done deliberately on his part. I've instructed a lawyer to do what he can – but you may never get what is owed.'

'I don't care, Mick. I wish his aunt had never left him anything.'

'Yes, I understand that,' Mick agreed, sympathy in his eyes. 'You're still feeling raw, Sally – but you may need all your savings...'

'What do you mean?' She stared at him, not immediately understanding.

'The stock market here will follow Wall Street within days,' he said. 'I know Harpers wasn't floated on the stock exchange and you can thank your lucky stars for that, Sally. However, it will very likely cause the economy to fall into depression and that will have a knock-on effect on every business in the country, including Harpers.'

Sally gasped as she understood fully what the crash on Wall Street would mean for not just America but Britain and other countries, too. 'That is terrible, Mick. I'd noticed a slight downturn in trade over the past months – but this will be much worse.'

'I doubt you've ever seen the like,' Mick told her gravely. 'Even during the war, America was strong and prosperous, and so we benefited from them in many ways, even though we suffered deprivation of many kinds – but that anchor has gone. America itself will be in depression and that must affect us all because so much trade goes through them... and well, just everyone relies on a strong dollar.'

'It's going to be bad,' Sally said. 'I see what you mean now, Mick – that money from those shares would have come in handy, even though it was only a few thousand dollars.'

'I don't wish to pry, but do you have much in the way of savings?'

'We always have a float at Harpers but...' Sally shook her head. 'No, Ben doesn't have much put by – in fact, we owe the bank ten thousand pounds.' She bit her lip. 'I just bought a small seaside cottage to have holidays with the children next year. I paid three thousand pounds for it – that could have paid a slice of our debt to the bank.' She shook her head. 'I don't suppose I could resell it at the moment.'

'Don't try. You will just lose money,' Mick said. 'We will try to get your money for those shares – but if you run into problems, come to me, Sally. I have money sitting in the bank doing nothing.'

'Yes, you were wiser than most of us,' Sally said ruefully. 'Thank you for the offer, Mick, and I promise that I shall ask if I need help. I'll see how badly trade is affected and...' Sally shook her head, refusing to be gloomy. 'Perhaps the American stock market will recover...'

'We must pray it does for so many people's sakes,' Mick agreed. He smiled at her. 'Well, that's business over – how are you doing in yourself, Sally? It's early days yet, I know.'

Sally blinked hard, refusing to cry again. All her tears had gone and she felt empty inside. Even the crisis in America hadn't really touched her, though she knew times could become very hard for everyone, Harpers included.

'The service for Ben is next Sunday,' she told him. 'I think I shall feel better once that is over. I have decided that once we've had the church blessing, I shall return to Harpers to work the following Monday. Especially with the news from America. We shall have our work cut out to steady the ship, Mick – and I am going to need all the help I can get...'

Mick reached out to take her hands in his. 'You know I am

always there for you, Sally. Whatever you want, whatever you need, you only have to say. My time and my money are at your disposal...'

'Oh, Mick...' The tears she had refused to shed started to her eyes. 'You are such a good friend. I need all my friends and family right now – but you really are the best of friends, my dear Mick.'

'I am your friend,' he confirmed, but as Sally looked into his eyes, she knew that he wanted to be much more. She dropped her gaze, because much as she loved and appreciated Mick as her friend – for the time being at least – he could only be a friend. She did not think now that she could ever marry again, but life moved on and Sally knew she must move with it. Harpers needed a beating heart to make it run successfully, and the challenges ahead would take all the strength and time she had to overcome.

'Jenny is still refusing to speak to me, even though I've tried to comfort her many times, but she is taking it so hard,' she told Mick with a rueful look. 'Peter is struggling too. Could you let him know he has a friend in you, Mick? He is such a good boy – and Jenny can't help her tantrums. She loves me, but she loved her daddy more and she can't forgive me because I told her he was coming home and now he isn't...'

'That isn't your fault,' Mick said softly. 'Don't worry, Sally me darlin'; she will come round in time – and Peter will grow all the better for wanting to protect his mother. I'll be here on Saturday mornin' and I'll take them both to a football match – just as Ben used to.'

'Afterwards, you must come back for lunch,' Sally said. 'I will take Jenny shopping after lunch and you might take Peter to the pictures. It will take their minds off the church service the next day.'

'Are you taking them to that?' Mick asked and Sally nodded.

'They are old enough to understand and I think it may help them,' she said and smiled sadly. 'I am hoping it will help me.'

Mick touched her hand once more. 'I'll pray for you, Sally. I'll pray for us all – because we are going to need it these next months and years.'

* * *

It had been a long day, but at last everyone had gone and Sally was alone in her sitting room, her children asleep upstairs. The church of St Saviours, Hampstead, had been packed out. Sally had invited 150 guests, including her staff at Harpers, but she thought even more had turned up, many of them men – old soldiers that Ben had helped in some way. She'd known he supported various missions and charities, but the personal stories the men had told her had brought tears to her eyes. Sally had invited everyone to return for the buffet meal at Claridge's.

Sally had ordered a buffet for 150 at Claridge's and because she'd ordered lavishly there was plenty of food to go round. There was such a mix of people: the girls and men of Harpers, businessmen, old soldiers, friends, politicians. Ben had been well liked and well respected and Sally couldn't remember all the offers of help she'd been given from people she either didn't know or had met only once or twice.

After the reception, Sally had brought the children home, where she'd been joined by Mick, Beth, her mother and stepfather, her dear friends, Maggie, who had come up from the country and had wept buckets all the way through the reception, and Rachel who had travelled down from the north, where she'd been overseeing some new stock at Jenni's shop, and Fred. No one – except the children – had wanted anything to eat, despite

Mrs Hills having baked lots of treats, they only wanted a cup of tea.

They had all offered comfort and love, but by the time they finally left, Sally's head had started to ache. She slipped off her shoes and sat with her head back against the sofa, feeling her tiredness wash over. It had all gone splendidly and she'd smiled, talking and responding with gentle dignity, refusing to cry even when the vicar said wonderful things about Ben. Now, she was alone and the tears came, sliding down her cheeks, because, oh, she did miss Ben so much.

Sally knew she could keep busy all day. She could run Harpers efficiently; she could entertain friends and look after her children and all things she had to – but it was so unutterably lonely when she shut the curtains at night and knew that Ben would never again sit beside her on the sofa or take her in his arms and make love to her. They'd had a good love-life and Sally would miss that as well as all the funny little everyday things that you hardly noticed until they were no longer there.

She closed her eyes for a moment. It was the same for all widows. And she just had to get on with it, but it damned well hurt...

Sally became aware that the sitting room door was being pushed slowly open and her heart missed a beat.

'Who is it?' she asked, and then a small dark nose came round the door and Lulu rushed towards her, wagging her tail. She jumped on the settee, covering Sally's face with kisses and pushing up as close as she could to her, as if she sensed Sally's loneliness. 'Oh, Lulu,' Sally sniffed and hugged her. Normally, Lulu would have jumped down, but she burrowed deeper into Sally. 'Do you miss him, too?'

Sally caressed the dog's fur, feeling comforted and not quite as alone.

A moment later, the door was cautiously pushed open again and Peter looked round.

'Can I come in, Mum?' he asked. 'I was feeling lonely...'

'Of course you can, darling,' Sally said and held out a hand to him. He ran to her, squeezing up close to her and laying his head against her arm, looking up at her.

'You're sad, Mummy,' he said. 'Don't be sad. Daddy wants us all to be happy. I shall look after you, I promise.'

'Thank you, my darling, I know you will.' Sally looked down at him and saw Ben's eyes looking back at her. Her heart caught with love. How could she think that Ben had gone when there he was in his son? Sally felt a great surge of joy as she realised that she still had Ben – or a part of him. 'You are just like your daddy and he would be so proud of you. You know how much I love you, darling—'

'Mum...' A wail of distress came from the doorway and Sally saw that Jenny was standing there in her nightgown, bare feet, and had been crying. 'Mum, I am sorry for what I said to you. I don't hate you. I love you. I just miss Daddy—'

'Of course you do, my love. We all do,' Sally said and smiled at her. She held out her free hand and Jenny flew across the room, squeezing up against her as Sally hugged both her children to her and realised how incredibly lucky she was to have them – and so much more. Sally Harper had an awful lot in her life, so much more than many others in her position.

Smiling through her tears as she held the children close, Lulu snuggled firmly on her lap, Sally nodded. Yes, she would always miss Ben and wish he was still with her but she had so much. She would make sure that she added some kind of assistance for widows to her already overflowing charity list, because so many were not in her fortunate position. Sally was young, rich, and attractive. Life wasn't finished for her; it was merely the start of a new chapter...

* * *

MORE FROM ROSIE CLARKE

The latest book in another emotional, heartfelt saga series from Rosie Clarke, *A Family Fortune*, is available to order now here:
www.mybook.to/FamilyFortuneBackAd

ABOUT THE AUTHOR

Rosie Clarke is a #1 bestselling saga writer whose books include Welcome to Harpers Emporium and The Mulberry Lane series. She has written over 100 novels under different pseudonyms and is a RNA Award winner. She lives in Cambridgeshire.

Sign up to Rosie Clarke's mailing list for news, competitions and updates on future books.

Visit Rosie's website: www.lindasole.co.uk

Follow Rosie on social media here:

- facebook.com/Rosie-clarke-119457351778432
- x.com/AnneHerries
- bookbub.com/authors/rosie-clarke

ALSO BY ROSIE CLARKE

Welcome to Harpers Emporium Series

The Shop Girls of Harpers

Love and Marriage at Harpers

Rainy Days for the Harpers Girls

Harpers Heroes

Wartime Blues for the Harpers Girls

Victory Bells For The Harpers Girls

Changing Times at Harpers

Heartbreak at Harpers

Troubled Times at Harpers

The Mulberry Lane Series

A Reunion at Mulberry Lane

Stormy Days On Mulberry Lane

A New Dawn Over Mulberry Lane

Life and Love at Mulberry Lane

Last Orders at Mulberry Lane

Blackberry Farm Series

War Clouds Over Blackberry Farm

Heartache at Blackberry Farm

Love and Duty at Blackberry Farm

Family Matters at Blackberry Farm

The Trenwith Trilogy

Sarah's Choice

Louise's War

Rose's Fight

Dressmakers' Alley

Dangerous Times on Dressmakers' Alley

Dark Secrets on Dressmakers' Alley

The Family Feud Series

A Family at War

A Family Secret

A Family Fortune

Standalone Novels

Nellie's Heartbreak

A Mother's Shame

A Sister's Destiny

Sixpence Stories

Introducing Sixpence Stories!

Discover page-turning historical novels from your favourite authors, meet new friends and be transported back in time.

Join our book club Facebook group

https://bit.ly/SixpenceGroup

Sign up to our newsletter

https://bit.ly/SixpenceNews

Boldwood

Boldwood Books is an award-winning fiction publishing company seeking out the best stories from around the world.

Find out more at www.boldwoodbooks.com

Join our reader community for brilliant books, competitions and offers!

Follow us
@BoldwoodBooks
@TheBoldBookClub

Sign up to our weekly deals newsletter

https://bit.ly/BoldwoodBNewsletter

Printed in Great Britain
by Amazon